COLD HANDS, WARM HEARTS

Dillon stepped into the shadow of the barn and took one of Grace's hands in his. His other hand was still held behind his back as he frowned at her.

"Dammit, didn't Olivia give you a pair of gloves to wear?"

Grace nodded to the leather gloves on the straw beside her stool. "They were too big, and very hot, and they kept slipping and my hands were sweaty...."

Dillon gripped her wrist in his hand. His skin was so brown, so dark against her own pale arm, she couldn't help but stare. He didn't let her go as he pulled a crude bouquet from behind his back.

"What are those?"

Dillon looked almost embarrassed, and Grace wondered if he'd ever given a woman flowers before. It seemed terribly out of character.

"Bluebonnets," he said gruffly. "There's a field of them not too far from the house." With the iron grip he held on her wrist, Dillon pulled her toward him. "I picked them for you...because they're the color of your eyes."

Grace forgot about the burning pain in her hands as she looked up at Dillon's face. Suddenly she was aware of the unattractive and ill-fitting dress she wore, another of Olivia's daughter's castoffs, and of the fact that her hair was falling from a once neat bun to wisp around her face. And she forgot all that and everything else when Dillon lowered his lips to hers and kissed her.

Other *Leisure* and *Love Spell* books by
Linda Winstead:
CHASE THE LIGHTNING
GUARDIAN ANGEL
WEST WIND
IN ENEMY HANDS

Love Spell books by Linda Winstead writing as
Linda Jones:
SOMEONE'S BEEN SLEEPING IN MY BED
DESPERADO'S GOLD
BIG BAD WOLF

LINDA WINSTEAD

NO ANGEL'S GRACE

LEISURE BOOKS  NEW YORK CITY

For three very special Heart of Dixie friends: JoAnn Westfall, Tammy Godsey, and Gayla Hiss.

A LEISURE BOOK®

April 1997

Published by

Dorchester Publishing Co., Inc.
276 Fifth Avenue
New York, NY 10001

Printed in the United States of America.

No Angel's Grace

Chapter One

New Orleans, 1872

"I still don't know why I had to tag along." Billy leaned back on the rough wooden bench and stretched out his long legs. The heels of his working boots snapped against the walkway as he brought them down with all the force of his massive weight.

"I told you." Dillon Becket paced nervously in front of his friend and employee, his own boots clicking with each step. "Kids like you. They sure as hell don't like me, and it's going to be a long trip from here to the Double B." Dillon turned his eyes to the older man. "What the hell am I going to do with a little girl?"

Dillon looked to Billy's pale blue eyes for answers. Any answers. But the gray-haired man continued to grin as he stretched long, muscular arms over his head. Billy's smiles came easily and often, and those smiles deepened the wrinkles that lined his pleasant face. "Well," he drawled, "Whatever you do, don't look at her like that. You're likely to scare the poor little thing right into the Mississippi."

They'd been in New Orleans almost a week, awaiting the arrival of the steamer from England. The timing couldn't have been any worse. Dillon was aware, every minute that passed, that he should be on the cattle drive. Its success was crucial to the survival of the Double B, and he had been forced to trust the herd to a hired trail boss. It went against his every instinct to trust such an important task to another man, but he'd had no choice. Colonel Cavanaugh's urgent request had brought Dillon to New Orleans for the repayment of an old debt. It was a request he couldn't refuse, no matter how much he wanted to do just that.

Billy stood to look toward the water. Though he was well over fifty he had the strength and build of a younger man, and he was nearly as broad as he was tall. Dillon couldn't remember a time when Billy hadn't been there. His father's employee, his father's friend. As much a part of the Double B as Dillon was. And never so much as in the past six months.

"That must be it," Billy said with a growl.

Dillon turned and watched the approaching ship with rapidly mounting anxiety. Christ. A kid. What the hell was he going to do with a kid? Surely the child would not travel alone. Maybe there would be a governess or a nanny on board, and maybe, just maybe, the woman could be persuaded to make the trip to Texas and to stay for a while. Hell, he couldn't afford to pay another salary, not now.

They watched silently as thé ship docked and the passengers began to disembark.

"How old is she?" Billy asked, not for the first time since they'd left Texas. He was never satisfied with the answer.

"She was a baby when Colonel Cavanaugh joined the Confederate Army and sent her to live with relatives in England. An aunt. That was eleven years ago, so I'd guess she's maybe . . . twelve or thirteen."

"He shoulda sent you a picture or somethin'," Billy grumbled as he studied the passengers who began to crowd the dock. There was only one child among them . . . a ragged-looking little boy who clutched at his mother's skirts as he tried to find his land legs again.

"I expect he intended to be among the living when I arrived," Dillon snapped. "Christ, Billy, how am I supposed to know what was in the man's mind? I hadn't seen him in . . ." Dillon's breath was damn near stolen away, and he forgot exactly what it was he had been about to say.

"Damn." He swore under his breath, and from the corner of his eye saw Billy's head turn to follow his gaze. A woman had stepped from the ship and was making her way cautiously down the gangplank.

She had black hair only partially covered by a close-fitting bonnet, and an emerald green feather danced in the wind above her head. Her matching green gown clung to her torso and flowed about her legs, and even though her skin was covered by a high collar and long, wide sleeves, Dillon thought she was the most enticing woman he had ever seen. She walked as though she were a queen, and when her feet were firmly on the ground, Dillon realized that his were not the only eyes that had been following the lovely lady.

She searched the crowd, standing on her toes and peering over and around heads as she looked for a familiar face. When her eyes lit on Dillon they lingered for just a moment. Dillon tipped his hat in a gentlemanly manner as he returned that gaze.

She raised her finely shaped eyebrows slightly and gave Dillon a cold look that was apparently meant to put him in his place. Somehow she was belittling and chastising him with that icy glare that touched him for such a short time.

The baggage was carried off the ship by sailors who cursed loudly and ignored the passengers who were searching for their bags and trunks. The sailors' brash voices, their colorful curses, were almost indecipherable, their accent was so heavy. The accent was not one of refinement, but was as harsh as their words.

Dillon watched and waited, and still there was no sign of the little girl.

"Maybe it's the wrong boat," Billy offered as Dillon continued to search for the Cavanaugh girl.

Dillon shook his head. "It's the right one. Hell, I hope nothing happened to her on the crossing."

The dock gradually cleared as the passengers collected their baggage and departed, all of them apparently glad to have solid ground beneath their feet after the long voyage. They smiled and laughed and left in groups small and large.

The coldly enchanting woman who had caught Dillon's eye waited alone, surrounded by a mountain of luggage. He couldn't keep his eyes off of her, though she was doing a fine job of completely ignoring him and every other man in the vicinity—her nose in the air, a distant gaze in her eyes.

Dillon took a few steps toward the ship and the lady. As much as he disliked the idea of boarding the ship—just the thought of the swaying deck made him queasy—he needed to speak to the captain. Perhaps the Cavanaugh girl had missed the ship. Perhaps it was the wrong ship after all. That would muck up his plans for certain. He had three tickets to Galveston, and that ship was sailing the following afternoon.

He stopped close to the dark-haired woman in the green dress. Damn, but she was gorgeous. He looked for a flaw, but found none. Her skin was milky pale and he saw not a mole, not a freckle. And her hair, up close, looked like black silk.

"Ma'am." Dillon removed his hat and held it against his chest. "Do you need any assistance?" She didn't look worried, all alone there amid her trunks, but he knew she had to be. Who was supposed to collect her? And what fool would leave a woman like this one unattended?

She gave him the same look she had earlier, a condescending glare obviously meant to put him off. Standing this close to her, he could see that her eyes were the color of bluebonnets.

"No, thank you," she said primly. "My father will be along shortly."

"I do hate to see a young lady—"

She sighed—a deep and unnecessarily loud lament—cutting off his offer of help. "If you don't leave me alone, I shall be forced to call a constable."

Dillon jammed his hat back on his head. "A constable? Honey, I don't know where you're from, but in Texas we consider it a crime to leave such a pretty girl stranded. I'd be happy to—"

She lifted her hands from her sides, holding her palms toward him and displaying long, slender fingers. Her bluebonnet eyes took in his hat, his buckskin jacket, his heavy denim trousers, and, finally, his boots.

"Excuse me, sir, but I don't intend to stand here and carry on a conversation with a . . . a Westerner who's so obviously out of place. Are you lost? Perhaps it is you who needs assistance."

"Look," Dillon began. He'd just been trying to be helpful, and maybe he'd been thinking of delaying his necessary venture onto the ship. This woman was irritating the hell out of him, with that patronizing air and her clearly disgusted perusal. A few moments ago he had envied the man who would collect the beautiful lady. Now he pitied him. He had plenty of problems of his own, but at least they didn't involve her. "Sorry to have bothered you." He tipped his hat and turned toward the ship.

Someone of authority, a dignified man in a formal uniform, was disembarking, and that meant that perhaps Dillon wouldn't have to venture onto the ship after all. The man left the ship with an air of authority, and smiled broadly at someone over Dillon's shoulder.

"Miss Cavanaugh," he boomed. "Your father has not arrived yet to meet you? I'd be more than happy to arrange transportation for you."

Dillon turned around very slowly. There was only one passenger remaining on the dock. Only one. Impossible. The lady in the green silk dress smiled at the officer, but it was a smile as empty of emotion as her eyes.

"How very kind you are, Captain Harper." Her eyes flickered to Dillon and back to the captain.

"It probably would not be wise for me to linger here."

Dillon stared at her as the captain passed him and presented himself to the lady in green. Not possible. With denial planted firmly in his brain, Dillon walked toward her.

"Miss Cavanaugh." Dillon's words were soft as he stood near the woman and Captain Harper.

"Captain, this man has been harassing me," she snapped, refusing to look at Dillon.

The captain turned to challenge Dillon, but hesitated when Billy appeared at his side, his massive arms crossed over his chest, a scowl on his usually passive face.

"Miss Grace Cavanaugh?" Dillon asked, something cold gripping at his chest. *Say no,* he prayed. *Please say no.*

She lifted her chin, and her eyes met his with a flash of blue fire. "Yes," she said, the biting edge in her voice as defiant as her eyes. And then she sighed, and an odd acceptance stole over her face.

"Your father was Colonel Hudson Cavanaugh?"

The color drained from her face. "Was?"

Dillon realized his mistake immediately. Somehow she'd never received the news her father's lawyer had sent.

"I'm sorry, Miss Cavanaugh. Your father passed away over a month ago." Dillon took his hat from his head again and clutched it in front of his heart. He had expected her to know. He had expected her to be a child. "He . . . he asked me to look after you."

Color spread across her cheeks, and she stammered as she battled to maintain her composure. "I . . . I don't . . . I don't believe you. My father wouldn't have . . ." The color drained from her face again as it apparently occurred to her that this was exactly what her father would have done.

"I'm so sorry, Miss Cavanaugh," the captain offered, and then he backed away, leaving the three of them alone.

Dillon introduced himself and Billy, not certain if Grace heard him or not. Her eyes were glazed, and she remained pale . . . as white as the untouched snow atop a mountain peak. Her hands were clutched almost demurely, and Dillon was certain that he saw a slight tremble there. He reached out to comfort her, to lay his hand on her arm, and that was when the color flew back into her face.

"Don't touch me, Becket."

At least she remembered his name.

Grace looked the two of them over, suspicion replacing the shock that had clouded her eyes. "What proof do I have that you're telling the truth?"

Dillon drew a letter from his pocket. "This is the message the colonel sent to me just before he died. He asked me to take care of you. I've spent some time with his attorney this week. We can go by his office, if you like."

Yes, Dillon had a few questions of his own for the attorney. Why hadn't he said anything about Colonel Cavanaugh's daughter being a grown woman? Dillon went over every conversation in his head, and he could recall no reference at all that had been made concerning Grace Cavanaugh's age. In the brief conversations he'd had with the lawyer, she'd been referred to as the colonel's daughter. And that was all.

Grace took the letter from his hand and read

it slowly. She read it once, and then again. Finally she appeared to be satisfied.

"So he knew he was dying when he finally asked me to come home." It was a statement, not a question, and no response was required or even looked for. Dillon could see her mind at work as she gathered her wits and faced the man before her. No tears. No wails of regret. Just steely acceptance.

"It was quite noble of you to agree to my father's request, but it's not necessary. I'm twenty-two years old, and have no need for a guardian. If you would be so kind as to escort me to the house, and perhaps to introduce me to Father's solicitor . . ."

Dillon's pained look stopped her before he even opened his mouth. When he did finally speak, he had her full and undivided attention. "Miss Cavanaugh, the house has been sold, and unless you have some funds of your own . . ." His words died slowly and painfully.

"Are you telling me that . . . that my father . . . that there's no . . . that I'm . . ."

Dillon could think of no other way to say it but straight out. "Your father was in hock up to his eyeballs when he died. The house and everything in it were sold to pay his debts. There's nothing left. I'm sorry."

She had no idea how very sorry he was.

Grace closed her eyes, and Dillon watched as she pulled herself together. "What do we do now, Becket?" she asked sharply, her eyes flying open.

"I have a ranch in Texas. We set sail tomorrow afternoon for Galveston. When we get back to the Double B we'll think this through."

Dillon placed his hat back on his head and impatiently thumbed it so it sat far back. A husband, he thought to himself as he looked her over. It was, of course, much too early to broach the subject with Grace. She had just learned of her father's death and her precarious financial situation. But that was what they would have to do. Find her a suitable husband.

"A ranch," she repeated in a dead voice. "In Texas. I have read about Texas." She sounded decidedly less than enthusiastic about the prospect of going there.

"Are all these trunks yours?" Dillon asked, as distressed at the prospect of traveling with such a mountain of luggage as Grace seemed to be at the idea of venturing into Texas.

Grace looked around her, at the trunks of all shapes and sizes, and she picked up a small carpetbag that had been resting at her feet, clasping the handle with both hands. "Of course."

Dillon groaned, but Billy smiled and stepped closer to Grace, and he gave her his most winning smile. "Don't worry none, Miss Grace. You'll like the Double B. You can go riding all you want, and Olivia will sure be happy to keep you company."

Grace gave Billy a glare as cold as the one she had given Dillon earlier, and that almost made Dillon smile himself. Billy wasn't accustomed to such a reaction to his Texas charm.

"I've never ridden a horse in my life, and I have no idea, nor do I have any desire to know, who Olivia is."

Billy seemed unruffled by her response.

"But don't concern yourself," she continued. "I won't be in Texas for very long."

These had been, surely, the longest twenty-four hours of his life.

Dillon closed his eyes and leaned his head back against the hard wooden seat. It was comfortable enough. And perhaps if Grace believed him to be asleep she would leave him alone. He'd never known a woman who could complain more—more often or more loudly. She'd argued with the attorney, complained about the small hotel where they'd spent the night in New Orleans. Hell, she'd had her own room, and it had been relatively clean. She'd complained across the water to Galveston, even as he battled down the nausea that had assaulted him with just as much vengeance as Grace Cavanaugh had.

She'd practically seethed when they'd had to wait for the train. It hadn't satisfied her at all when he'd explained to her that the train was always late.

And now . . . Maybe he could pretend to sleep for a couple of days.

"Becket." Grace tapped him lightly on the knee, and he opened one eye slowly. She was sitting across from him, her knees close to his, and she was leaning forward slightly as she peered into his face. He sat up and pushed his hat back on his head.

"What is it, Grace?" he asked tiredly.

"Is this the best you could do? Don't they have private cars, or at the very least individual compartments? This is . . . it's . . ." Grace looked surreptitiously around the crowded car. "It's quite disgusting."

Dillon pressed two fingers to the bridge of a nose that was straight and sharp as the blade of a knife. "Even if this rail car did have private compartments, or if there were private cars available, I couldn't afford it." He hated to admit that to anyone, and he especially hated to admit it to

Grace, but it was the truth.

What had Colonel Cavanaugh done to him? Again this morning Grace had donned a new and obviously expensive outfit, complete with matching hat and fan. She'd emerged from her cabin wearing a blue outfit that damn near matched her eyes. And pretty . . . hell, pretty wasn't nearly a good enough word for the way the woman looked. She would be perfect—if she could manage to keep her mouth closed for any length of time.

She looked thoroughly disgusted at the moment, as she leaned back and away from him. "I thought you were some sort of cattle baron."

"Just a rancher, Grace," Dillon said, tilting his hat forward so that it covered his eyes. Damned if he would tell her his troubles. Spoiled brat, with her expensive clothes and her cute little nose up in the air and her damn bluebonnet eyes.

Grace relaxed, letting go of the coiled tension within her, when she decided Dillon was asleep. For a while she would have to be on guard against him. Of course, he had been a perfect gentleman so far. He hadn't touched her since their meeting on the dock, when she'd told him not to. It had been a purely instinctive reaction to his hand on her arm, even though she'd realized he was only trying to comfort her.

Still, he was a man, and he looked at her so strangely sometimes. No. Not strangely. It was less sophisticated, perhaps, but that look was all too familiar. He looked at her the same way nearly every man she'd met had since she'd turned seventeen. As if she were standing before him stark naked.

Fortunately he seemed to have no patience

with difficult women. He wouldn't give her any trouble at all.

She tilted her head so she could see beneath the hat that shielded most of his face. He was rather good-looking, in a different sort of way. His hair was a tad too long and it was dark, though not nearly as dark as hers. When the sun hit his chestnut hair a bit of red was revealed. It curled a little, too, there where it touched his collar.

He was handsome enough, but his face was hard and he hadn't smiled once since she'd met him. Maybe he was afraid that granite face would crack.

What had he done to make her father hate him enough to foist her upon him? Obviously Dillon Becket was not happy at the prospect of having her around. Not that that was a new predicament for Grace. Her father had resented her presence from the time of her birth until the day he'd died. And still she wondered how he could do this to her.

He'd ignored her all her life, and now this. Penniless and left in the care of a less-than-reputable cowpoke who had no money to speak of. He had managed to have the last laugh, her father, even after all these years. Had he really hated her so much?

Grace knew that she should feel a deeper sadness at her father's death, but she couldn't manufacture emotion where there was none. Eleven years had passed since he'd sent her to England, and she'd rarely heard from him in all that time. She had known, from the very day he'd sent her away, that it was a relief for him to be rid of the baby who had caused his beloved wife's death.

A heavy burden for an eleven-year-old who'd

managed for years to adore her father in spite of his cold indifference.

Billy was seated beside Dillon, and he stretched his long legs out so that his boots rested beneath her seat. He gave her a warm smile, and in spite of herself she returned it.

"Are you comfortable, Miss Grace?"

Grace started to tell him that she was already tired of the rocking train, and that the smoke that was drifting through the open windows was most likely ruining her suit, and that a man on the opposite side of the aisle and two seats back had been leering at her since they'd left the station. But she didn't. She'd save those comments for Becket.

"I'm fine, Billy." She leaned forward and spoke in a soft voice. "Was Becket teasing me when he said we'd be spending the night on the train?" She tried to keep the distress from her voice, but failed.

"Nope," Billy answered as if the prospect didn't bother him at all. "Enjoy the ride while you can. Once we get off the rail we'll have near a week gettin' to the ranch."

"How?" Grace decided, as the question left her mouth, that she didn't really want to know. Already she'd been tossed by storms at sea, jostled by this blasted rail, and now . . .

"Carriage. Dillon borrowed a carriage from a friend and we left it at a livery in San Antone. He figured it might be quicker than waitin' for a stage, and easier for you than travelin' on horseback."

"Thank goodness for that, at least." Grace turned away from Billy to stare at the scenery that sped past. Green. From what she'd heard of Texas she hadn't expected it to be so green.

"Did you know my father, Billy?" she asked without turning to face him.

"Nope. Dillon served with him during the war, he tells me. Said he was a fine man, and that he cared for you very much." The last words were spoken very softly, and Grace did turn to look at the burly man then.

She started to tell Billy that Dillon must not have known her father well at all, if he believed that. But one look at Billy's kind face told her his words were meant to comfort her.

How could she explain that his kindness showed more caring than she'd ever known from her father?

"Thank you," she whispered.

Perhaps she should try to be civil to Billy, and even to Becket. How difficult could it be?

"A bath," Grace repeated, snapping at Dillon as he watched her through narrowed eyes. "You do know what that is, don't you? Do people bathe in Texas?"

He could suddenly see Grace seated in a tub, bubbles all over her skin, a bare leg in the air, her dark hair falling around her shoulders instead of tightly restrained as it was now. He closed his eyes to rid himself of the image. She was his responsibility. Colonel Cavanaugh had not trusted Grace into his care so he could daydream about her naked and wet and covered with soapsuds.

"What's wrong with you?" Grace snapped.

"I have a headache," Dillon said, keeping his eyes closed. Damned if that wasn't the truth.

Grace was uncommonly quiet, and Dillon finally opened one eye slightly. She was studying him with a frown on her face.

"I'm sorry," she said softly. "It's probably this blasted rail. I've never been so badly jostled in all my life."

Dillon knew the ride was rather comfortable, compared to what was to follow. Grace Cavanaugh didn't know what jostled was until she'd traveled across the plains in a speeding stagecoach. His headache suddenly got worse, sharper. It was a lot easier to stay mad at Grace when she was harping at him over one thing or another. She looked so delicate at the moment, so . . . so female.

"When will I get a bath, Becket?" She leaned forward and asked her question in a low voice.

"Maybe the hotel will be able to provide a tub and a little hot water."

Grace smiled. He really wished she wouldn't do that. Her eyes lit up, and her face looked absolutely rosy.

"An inn?" she asked. "When we get to San Antonio?"

Dillon shook his head. "We'll get in tomorrow before noon. We can get in a few hours of travel before we stop, and there's a hotel in Clanton where we can spend the night."

Grace's smile was supremely content. "I'll have a bath, and I'll have supper in my room, and I'm likely to sleep until noon."

It was clear that the prospect delighted her, but Dillon knew he had to set her straight. "I don't know what sort of hotel you're accustomed to, but out here they can be a bit . . . rustic."

He was surprised that she continued to smile with an almost dreamy expression on her face as she ignored him. She had no idea what she was in for.

A fellow passenger made a move for the seat

next to Grace. There was room for two on the bench, but so far Grace had had the seat to herself, while he and Billy shared the bench facing her. The railway car was not full, so there were several empty seats.

"Howdy-do," the man said as he plopped down beside Grace. He was dressed in the dark pants and coat and white collar of a city dude, but his speech was purely Texan. "Name's Lancy. Lancy Carter. You folks look mighty familiar, and I just figured I'd mosey on over and say howdy."

Grace scooted away from the man. She grabbed her carpetbag from the bench and set it on the floor so she'd have more room to remove herself from the stranger. But he followed her, edging even closer. His arm pressed against hers, and she all but recoiled, leaning away from the man as well as she could.

Dillon leaned forward, closing the space between himself and the bothersome man. The intruder, Carter, smelled of whiskey and cheap cigars, and for some reason he was scaring Grace half to death. Carter had scared away the smile Dillon had thought he hated. Right now he was missing it.

"I don't know you," Dillon said in a low, menacing voice. "I've never seen you before, and I don't care to get acquainted."

Carter was oblivious to the implied threat, and he turned to Grace. "What about you, pretty lady? I've been watching you since we pulled out of Galveston. I hope you don't mind me saying this, but I have been admiring you." Carter laid his hand on Grace's knee, and her face went absolutely white.

"That's it!" Dillon shouted, jumping from his seat and grabbing the offensive man by the shirt-front. A paper collar came loose and stuck out at a comical angle as Dillon hoisted the man to his feet. "You stupid idiot. If you can't take a hint I'll just have to help you back to your seat." He dragged Carter across the aisle and unceremoniously dumped the man onto his own bench. Carter blinked rapidly and stared up at Dillon, his eyes widening as Dillon moved his face closer to the seated man.

"If you look at, attempt to speak to, or even think about laying your hands on that lady again, I'll castrate you." He ignored the man's white face and the trembling hands that moved to cover the threatened part of his anatomy. "You see," Dillon continued calmly, "I'm a cattle rancher, and I know how. As a matter of fact, it wouldn't take any time at all." Dillon pulled a knife from his boot and began to explain to the man, in low tones, exactly how the procedure was performed.

After Dillon finally left the shaking man and returned to his traveling companions, he sat next to Grace and stretched his legs across the space, resting his boots on the seat where he had been sitting before Carter's interruption.

He took a deep breath and ignored Billy's amused and questioning stare. Hell, he didn't need the old man to tell him that he had overreacted.

But Grace had looked so terrified when Carter had leaned against her and put his hand on her knee. Truth of the matter was, Dillon hadn't been able to help himself. Something inside him had just snapped.

"Are you all right?" He studied Grace carefully, finding her still pale and shaken. What was she afraid of?

Grace nodded silently, and Dillon waited for

her to order him off of her seat and back to his own . . . but she didn't. Instead she thanked him in a voice so quiet he almost didn't hear her, and then she turned her face away from him to gaze at the slowly changing landscape.

He wanted to tell her that everything would be all right. She had the look of a woman who needed to be reassured, but there was still a distance there, a gulf he didn't think he could breach.

But his confident and strident and demanding Grace looked suddenly like the lost little girl he had expected to find in New Orleans.

Chapter Two

The landscape they rolled past was lit with the brilliance of a full, silvery moon, though the inside of the railway car was in broken and shadowed shades of gray. A lantern burned at one end of the car, keeping the passengers from being lost in complete inky darkness. Grace had already decided that she would no doubt prefer the total black of night to the eerie shadows that filled the car.

Billy and Dillon were both asleep, as were most of the passengers. The railway car was filled with the rumblings of low snores and deep, even breathing, and an occasional murmur from a dreamer that could be heard above the roar of the wheels against the tracks. A few children were able to stretch out on their own benches, but the adults all slept sitting up.

Billy snored, but it was low and steady . . . almost comforting. His gray head was resting against the back of his seat, and his hat rested at his side.

Dillon, on the other hand, made not a sound. He slept like the dead, with his hat lowered to cover most of his face and his feet still stretched across to the other seat. Though she was reluctant to admit it, even to herself, Grace was grateful that Dillon Becket had remained beside her, shielding her from the aisle and from the obnoxious Carter.

Carter had not even looked her way since Dillon had returned him to his seat, and that was a relief. Why did some men think it was acceptable to lay their hands on any and every woman they met? While Carter wasn't as zealous as many of the presumptuous so-called gentlemen she could remember, his touch was still disturbing. More disturbing than she cared to admit.

Grace had serious doubts about getting any sleep herself. How could anyone expect her to sleep fully dressed, sitting upright, speeding along in a train that seemed likely to jump the tracks at any moment? The noise alone was enough to wake the dead.

She removed the small, fashionable bonnet from her head and placed it atop the carpetbag at her feet. Her head ached, and she removed the pins that held her hair snugly at the nape. As her hair fell about her shoulders, she massaged the back of her neck and felt the tension fly from her neck and shoulders.

Why had her father asked Dillon Becket to be her guardian? That question had been in her mind since she'd read the letter her father had sent the rancher, but she'd been hesitant to voice it. Why not the lawyer? Or one of Hudson Cavanaugh's business associates? There were no relatives to turn to, and perhaps as there was no money her father hadn't felt that he could turn to any one of the lawyers or businessmen he'd dealt with over the years.

But why Dillon Becket? She looked at his cheek and his chin—all that she could see of him under the hat he wore. His arms were positioned over his chest in an almost defiant manner, and his ankles were crossed atop the opposite seat. There was a definite air of control about the man. Even as he slept.

He seemed much too young to be one of her father's friends. Surely he wasn't much over thirty. Their chosen lifestyles were very different, also. Hudson Cavanaugh had always been such a dedicated businessman, and by the age of thirty had developed the hint of a paunch that would turn into a distended belly before too many years had passed. From what Grace could remember, her father had always been pale and soft.

Dillon Becket wasn't pale or soft. His skin was so browned by the sun it looked tough, and there were tiny lines around his eyes that she assumed would deepen if he were ever to smile.

And he was anything but soft. From his sharp nose to his rigid jaw to the leanness of his body, he was hard all over.

Grace closed her eyes and leaned her head back. She expected no sleep to come, but if she could only relax . . . if she could only chase the thoughts that haunted her from her mind. Why had her father sent for her? He could have left her in England to fend for herself, but he had chosen to drop her in Becket's lap. Why had Becket agreed? It was clear that he was less than happy about the situation. Why hadn't Hudson Cavanaugh sent for her sooner? Years sooner?

Her stay in England had been expensive, and her father had sent money whenever she'd requested it. He'd never hinted at the precarious financial situation she now knew had plagued him.

And all she'd ever really wanted was for him to ask her to come home. To love her the way a father was supposed to love his daughter. To forgive her for being born and causing her mother's death.

But he never had.

Grace sighed. She should have cried. For her father, for the absence of his love, for herself. She was truly alone now. She'd been alone for years, but there had always been the belief in the back of her mind that one day she and her father would be reunited and everything would be the way it was supposed to be. She should have cried, but there were no tears left. She'd used them up long ago.

In spite of it all, her eyes closed. The rocking of the train, the exhaustion that ravaged her body, the deep, even snoring all around her . . . it all combined to lull her into a deep and dreamless sleep.

Dillon woke because something was tickling his nose. He brought a hand up to brush away whatever it was . . . and found that impossible. There was too much of it, and it was everywhere.

There was a soft warmth against him that told him he wasn't sleeping alone, and he sighed contentedly and pulled the body next to his closer. Her head was in the crook of his shoulder, and his arm held her tight. It was her luxurious hair that was tickling his nose, and Dillon buried his face in that hair. It smelled good and clean and—

His eyes flew open when he remembered exactly where he was and who the woman sleeping against him was. The sun was just rising, a glorious ball of orange that bathed the car with warm light. And it was Grace's hair in his face, Grace's body snuggled against his.

Dillon thumbed his hat back off his face and lifted his head slightly so that his nose was no longer buried in Grace's hair. That black silk was spread across his chest, and apparently his movements disturbed her, because she moaned low in her throat and adjusted herself slightly, dropping one hand onto his lap.

A low chuckle reminded him that he and Grace were not alone, and he lifted his eyes to meet Billy's.

"Mornin', boss," Billy whispered gruffly, a wide smile plastered on his wrinkled face. "Sleep well?"

"What's so damn funny?" Dillon whispered, still reluctant to release Grace. At least while she was sleeping she couldn't complain or hound him with her endless questions.

Billy shrugged his shoulders. "Nothin', boss. I just been sittin' here watchin' Miss Grace sleep." He cocked his head to one side and peered at her face, a face that was half hidden by a curtain of black hair. "She shore is purty, ain't she?"

Dillon grunted in what might have been construed as an agreement. Grace was more than pretty. She was perfect.

"What do you suppose Miss Abigail is gonna think about Miss Grace? Ain't exactly the little girl she's expectin'." Billy looked as though the prospect pleased him more than it should.

But Dillon groaned. He'd been so busy dealing with his own surprise that he hadn't had time to think about Abigail. Hell, she'd be madder than a skinned rattler.

Billy leaned forward slightly and lowered his voice even further. "You two shorely do make a purty picture, all snuggled up there nice and cozy." He ignored the scowl Dillon directed at him. "And I was just thinkin' how nice it's gonna be to have such a purty lady around the Double B."

"Nice?" Dillon raised his eyebrows in disbelief as he whispered his response. "Nice, hell. I doubt she can do one damn useful thing. All a woman like her does is complain and throw parties and expect to be waited on hand and foot." He glanced down at Grace, and all he could see was the top of her head. "I'm gonna have to find her a husband, Billy." That statement made him frown. "It won't be easy,'cause she's sure to be picky as hell. He'll have to have money."

Billy frowned as Dillon turned his thoughts to the prospects for Grace. "Sounds kinda familiar," he growled.

Grace shifted, and her hand rested over the bulge in Dillon's denims. If she felt it stirring she gave no notice, but merely turned her face up so that Dillon could watch as she licked her lips and pressed her cheek against his chest.

"Jesus Christ," he muttered. His face grew warm as he moved Grace's hand back to his thigh. He couldn't take much more of this. As if she knew, even in her dreams, that she was bedeviling him, Grace returned her hand to his crotch and lifted her face as she returned her head to his shoulder. The buttons at her neck had come undone, and exposed a slender white throat. A vein throbbed slowly, enticing, entrancing. . . .

"Wake up, Grace," Dillon said hoarsely. Maybe he was her guardian, but he was only human.

"Let her sleep," Billy whispered, his wide grin back in place. "She's exhausted, poor little girl."

"Grace," Dillon repeated a little louder as he repositioned her hand. "Wake up, honey."

Grace's hand moved again, this time to rest between his thighs, and she sighed contentedly . . . warm and safe and lost in deep sleep.

"Hellfire," Dillon muttered as Grace's warm breath brushed his throat. He took a deep breath and forcibly set her away from him, jarring her rudely awake. She shook her head, sending that long, dark hair about her shoulders and down her back. She blinked hard, three times, and looked directly into Dillon's face. Those bluebonnet eyes were wide and still touched with sleep.

"Oh, I did fall asleep after all, didn't I?" It was evident that Grace didn't remember sleeping nestled against his chest, or tormenting him with her slender hand. She took a deep breath, and Dillon took no comfort from the fact that she appeared well rested and calm.

She gave him a small smile. "It doesn't look like you slept very well, Becket."

With a snort he turned away from her, took the hat from his head, and—to spare himself any further embarrassment—dropped in onto his lap.

Apparently they were to spend as little time as possible in San Antonio.

Becket was in a particularly foul mood, and he had been that way all day. He scowled on an irritatingly regular basis, and muttered constantly. A dark, stubbly beard shadowed his face, and it did nothing to soften his tough exterior. It seemed that even Billy was giving him a wide berth.

Grace realized that she was the root of his problems, the reason for his bad temper. She knew that because every time he looked at her he narrowed his steel gray eyes, and his mouth hardened. It was no wonder that he hated her. She had been foisted upon him and he obviously liked the idea as little as she did. It occurred to Grace that her father, who to her recollection had smiled as infrequently as Becket, must have had a sense of humor after all.

At the moment Becket was cursing under his breath as he attempted to tie her luggage to the top of the carriage. It was, Grace conceded, a fairly nice conveyance, with room for two on the driver's seat and as many as four in the coach. It was painted a shiny black, and was embellished with a fashionable gold stripe.

The flat top was perfect for transporting luggage, but perhaps not quite as much as she had brought along.

"Do you really need all of this?" Dillon asked for the tenth time, leaning over to look down at Grace. She stood below him, her pale face turned up to him, her carpetbag handle clutched in both hands.

"Of course I do," she said in a sensible voice. "Everything I own is in those trunks."

Dillon tried to remind himself that what she said was true. That she had just lost her father and learned that he had left her penniless. But hellfire, nobody traveled with so much baggage. "Why don't we leave a few of these trunks behind and have them delivered later by stagecoach?"

"No!" Grace's horror was evident in her voice. "They could be damaged or stolen."

Dillon grumbled, but he returned to his attempts to secure every trunk on the roof of the carriage. She was right. The baggage handlers could be mighty rough. But that wasn't why he agreed. He agreed because he couldn't stand to look down at her anymore. She hadn't had an opportunity to change clothes or bathe or dress her hair in front of a mirror, and yet she showed none of the signs of neglect he knew he and Billy displayed. Even as she stood there with her hair pulled straight back in what would have been a much too severe style for any other woman, even as she looked up at him, wearing that slightly rumpled blue suit that matched her eyes, he remembered how he had awakened that morning: with Grace's head against his chest and her hand in his lap.

It didn't matter how attractive she was, or how attracted he was to her. His plans were set. If the cattle drive didn't bring in enough money to pay off the loan his father had taken out six months earlier, Dillon knew he would have to marry Abigail and use her dowry to pay off the loan. Billy said that was cruel and heartless, but Dillon knew that was the way things were done. Marriages had long been a kind of business. It united warring families. Joined large tracts of land.

He had to save the Double B.

Besides, under the covers one woman was much like another. And Grace Cavanaugh wasn't his type in any case. She was whiny and demanding, and too soft for life on a ranch. He couldn't picture her tending the garden or rustling up enough supper for twenty or thirty men, or feeding the chickens or milking a cow. She was only good for preying on a man's mind and spending his money.

"Becket," Grace called, looking up from where she stood just outside the open carriage door. He ignored her, fastening down the final length of rope. "Becket!" she called more sharply, and he finally glanced down at her.

"What now?" he asked in a voice that betrayed his lack of patience.

Grace shaded her eyes against the sun as she looked up at Becket. Sweat dripped from his face and stained his blue shirt. His hat had been pushed back, and tendrils of sweat-dampened chestnut hair framed his face.

"You forgot one," she said softly.

Becket wiped his face with the pass of one already damp sleeve. "I did what?"

"You forgot one," she said a little more loudly, and then she stepped aside so that he could see the small trunk her skirts had been shielding.

The expression on his face said more than the stream of obscenities that came from his mouth. Her own face remained calm as she continued to look up at him. In fact, she was suppressing a smile.

Billy joined her, a parcel of supplies for their trip in his hands. "I think I got everythin', boss. Enough jerky and hardtack to get us home if we don't find nothin' else. Coffee and some extra matches . . ."

"Toss me that trunk, Billy," Becket ordered.

Billy ignored Becket's sharp tone and dark scowl, and handed up the small trunk. With his usual broad smile he turned to Grace. "How 'bout that carpetbag? You want it up top, too?"

Grace unconsciously pulled the bag closer to her. She didn't really know these men. What would they do if they knew what she carried in her bag?

"No, thank you," she said firmly. "I'll keep this one with me."

Becket jumped down from the top of the carriage. "Let's get something straight, Grace," he began harshly. "This is not going to be an easy trip. Billy and I will take turns driving, and we'll likely do some traveling at night when the roads are good and the moon is bright."

He placed his face close to hers and seemed to try to stare her down, even though she had said not a word. "We will sleep in the carriage or on the ground, and I don't want to hear a word of complaint. I need to make good time and get back to the Double B. Tonight we'll rest up in Clanton. There's an overnight stop there, and we can clean up a bit and get a good night's sleep."

Grace was still trying to figure out why that last statement seemed to make him so angry, when he crossed his arms defiantly across his chest and growled at her. "And after that I don't want to hear another word about private compartments or bubble baths."

Grace lifted her eyebrows slightly. "I don't recall that I ever mentioned a bubble bath. I only requested an opportunity to bathe as any civilized human being would feel the need to do. Perhaps that's a foreign concept to you, Becket." It was clear that she was growing angrier with every word she spoke.

Dillon watched the wariness steal over her eyes, and his lips hardened. It was true, he conceded silently, that the bubble bath had been his own fantasy.

He took a deep breath and tried to calm himself. The bubble bath picture was back in his mind, as clear and sharp as if it were real. "I'm just trying to prepare you for what's ahead,

Grace. It won't be an easy trip."

"Thank you for the warning, Becket," Grace said insincerely, ignoring his offer of assistance and taking Billy's hand as the older man helped her into the carriage. For Billy she had a warm smile, Dillon noticed as he watched her step gracefully into Abigail's carriage.

If he weren't an honorable man he would leave her in San Antonio to shift for herself. Damned if she wasn't a passel of trouble. Hell, she could find her own husband, or get a job as a . . . As a what? A governess to some rich man's kid? Perhaps a tutor, if she was well educated. A schoolmarm? That thought almost made him smile. Almost. He had a sudden vision of Grace teaching a pack of unruly kids while she pranced around in her silk gowns and jaunty hats.

But he was an honorable man, and he owed Colonel Cavanaugh his life. Literally. This was the favor the man had asked in return, to see his daughter cared for. Dillon would honor that request, and find her a suitable husband. It wasn't a task he looked forward to, but if she cooperated it shouldn't be too difficult. Who wouldn't want a wife who looked like Grace?

"You, Dillon Becket," he breathed softly as he climbed into the driver's seat to join Billy, trying to convince himself that a woman like Grace Cavanaugh held no appeal for him. Billy gave him a wicked and knowing smile, pale blue eyes twinkling in a leathery face.

"Shut up," Dillon said in a low voice.

"I didn't say nothin'," Billy said innocently.

Dillon allowed Billy to take the reins, and he leaned back and closed his eyes. His life was going to hell in a handbasket and it looked, at the moment, as if Grace Cavanaugh was leading the way.

Beside him, Billy started to hum a bright song that definitely didn't match Dillon's mood.

Clanton was a poor excuse for a town, but there was a two-story building that served as hotel, saloon, gambling hall, and restaurant. There was a livery next door, and a general store that Dillon always avoided. The supplies were of poor quality and always overpriced.

Grace's disappointment, as she alighted in front of the overnight stop, was clear in her eyes, but she said nothing. Dillon gave her a look that warned her not to. Her obvious reservations were not relieved upon their entrance to the building. It was late in the day, nearly dark, and the large room was filled with diners and gamblers and drinkers who lined the bar.

They'd not been standing in the doorway but a moment before every eye in the place was on them. Or rather, on Grace. Though her dress was modest, it was a fact that many folks in these parts, and in much of the West, thought that only whores wore silk. The fact that Grace was stunningly beautiful would only fuel the fantasies of every man in the room.

Disappointment was etched on Grace's face as she surveyed the smoky room. She edged closer to Dillon, just a little. "Becket, they're looking at me as though I were the last pastry on the baker's shelf," she said in a low voice.

Dillon left her in Billy's able care, and located the owner of the place. The first thing he did was arrange for Grace's bath. If she had the bath maybe she'd stop talking about it. Hell, maybe he'd quit daydreaming about it.

He and Billy escorted Grace up the stairs, Billy in front and Dillon behind. He knew without turning around that they were being watched. That Grace was being watched.

"You'll need another dress," Dillon said to the back of her head. "Something not so fancy. You got a plain calico in one of those trunks?"

Grace turned her head and glanced over her shoulder with the bearing and haughty air of a queen. "Good heavens, no," she said softly.

Dillon grumbled under his breath. "Have you got anything out there that doesn't make you look like a high-priced whore?"

Grace came to an abrupt halt there at the top of the stairs. "I beg your pardon?" she asked icily. "Would you care to repeat that, Becket?"

Dillon frowned at the back of her head. She hadn't even turned around to look at him. "Not particularly."

"The small green trunk with the brown bands," she said almost sweetly, resuming her step.

Dillon followed her, allowing himself a small sigh of relief. He hadn't meant to say it, and he sure as hell hadn't meant for Grace to hear it. Lucky for him Grace seemed not to have taken the question the wrong way. She certainly wouldn't hold his little slip of the tongue against him.

Grace closed her eyes and lowered herself even deeper into the warm water. The room was little more than a closet, and Becket had complained about the price of a fresh tub of hot water. But she was having her bath, and she was enjoying it.

The small green trunk rested against one wall of the tiny room, and Grace smiled as she stared at it and contemplated her plans for the evening. Revenge wasn't a word she liked to use, but it didn't seem fair for Becket to insult her and get off without learning a lesson.

A high-priced whore. She'd been tempted to slap his face then and there, but she had learned, over the years, that there were more subtle ways to get a man's attention.

She'd done her best to behave courteously since leaving the train in San Antonio; she really had. Becket had been testing her temper for days, and she'd decided just that morning to try a different approach. She'd held her tongue, as best she could, but it hadn't been easy. The man could irritate her with a single glance, a single word.

And this time he'd gone too far. Grace dipped her head back into the water, rinsing out all the soap. It felt so good to wash the grime and sweat off of her body. She'd never felt so unclean in all her life, and according to Billy the days on the trail ahead of them would be even worse. How was that possible?

When she dried herself with the questionably clean towel that had been provided for her, Grace removed the red dress from her trunk. She held it up and studied it closely, rubbing her fingers against the rich material. It was wrinkled, but there was nothing she could do about that. She hadn't worn this particular dress in five years, since she'd been seventeen. That had been quite a memorable night.

Grace slipped her arms into the cool red silk, allowing the dress to drop over her head and fall into place. She'd filled out in the past five years, and the gown fit more snugly through the hips and across her breasts than she remembered.

When she looked down she saw an indecent

amount of her own flesh, and for a fleeting moment she wondered if this was such a good idea.

She towel-dried her hair and let it hang loose, parting it down the middle and tossing the heavy strands so that they fell straight down her back. There was not a hint of curl in those black locks. There never had been.

She tied the sash at her waist and smoothed the clinging silk over her hips. Doubts nagged at her briefly, and she made herself remember. High-priced whore?

Her hand was on the door handle when she remembered that Billy had been left guarding the door.

"Billy?" she called sweetly through the closed door.

"You 'bout done, Miss Grace?"

"Yes," she answered. Poor Billy. He'd be shocked, but there was nothing to be done for that. "Why don't you go on downstairs and order us some supper. I'm starving." There was no response for a moment, and Grace added, "I'll be right down."

She grabbed the carpetbag and opened it, delving inside for the ornately carved box that held her most treasured possessions. She removed the lid and looked down at the array of gold and gems, the tangle of jewelry she had collected over the past five years. Her eyes fell to the piece she was searching for, a ruby pendant, and she grasped the chain between pale, slender fingers.

"All right, Miss Grace," Billy finally answered. "But don't you take too long."

Grace smiled as she placed the pendant around her neck. The chain was icy against her flesh, and the ruby rested between her breasts, cold and hard.

"I'll be right there, Billy. I promise." She stuffed the carpetbag and its contents into the green trunk and closed the lid, locking it securely. With cold fingers she tucked the key into the sash at her waist, and fondled the ruby that rested close to her heart.

Chapter Three

Dillon leaned back in the wobbly chair and fastened his eyes on the stairs. He didn't much like the idea of leaving Grace unattended in this place, even for a few minutes. Billy sat in the chair directly opposite Dillon's, and he was already bending over his bowl of stew, a hunk of corn bread clutched in one hand as he balanced on his own less than sturdy chair. There didn't seem to be a place to sit in the entire room that didn't rock on at least one short leg.

The three bowls of stew steamed invitingly, but Dillon waited. This was certainly not the sort of place Grace was accustomed to, but there was nothing to be done about that. There were a couple of other women in the room, but they seemed to belong there. There was the proprietor's wife—a stout woman in a dirty gray dress. A thin, tired-looking woman—the wife of a fellow traveler who was headed for San Antonio. Most of the patrons were men, drifters who slurped down their stew in large, noisy gulps, and tossed back cheap whiskey as they leaned against the bar. The bar was nothing more than an unsteady plank laid over a couple of barrels. There wasn't anything in the room that didn't look like a stiff breeze would knock it over.

Most of the patrons surveyed the room with suspicious eyes, and most every man in the room—himself and Billy included—was armed. Cigar smoke hung over the room like a low cloud, and even Dillon's undiscriminating nose detected the sour odor of unwashed bodies.

It was definitely not a place for a lady like Grace.

The door opened, and Dillon turned his head to watch an entire family rush into the room. They were dust covered and wide eyed, a middle-aged woman herding four little girls into a smoky corner while her husband sought out the owner of the bustling establishment.

And that was why he didn't see her at first. The room was suddenly quiet. The only sound was the gurgle of Billy choking on his stew. Several of the men in the smoky room stared with their mouths hanging open. Others leered openly as Grace descended the staircase without an outward sign that she was causing a commotion. A low murmur began to build, replacing the momentary silence.

Grace smiled at him as she walked slowly toward his table, her hips swaying underneath the clinging red material, wisps of still-drying hair framing her face and falling in a black waterfall down her back. Wide sleeves that came to a point over her hands danced with every step she took.

The damn dress was cut so low he could see

the rounded globes of her breasts, and it fit so tight that as she calmly took her seat he could see the nub of her nipples pressing against the fabric. A delicate gold chain encircled her neck, and a teardrop-shaped ruby rested between her breasts.

"What in the name of the devil do you think you're wearing?" His voice was hoarse and gravelly, and so low it wouldn't travel beyond their table. He didn't know whether he should be furious with her or lean back and enjoy the view. Then he remembered that she was Colonel Cavanaugh's daughter, and his responsibility. And she was sitting in a room full of leering men.

"What's the matter, Becket?" Grace asked sweetly, leaning forward to take a piece of corn bread and giving him a generous view. "Don't you like it? You certainly didn't care for the way I dressed before." She met his hard glare with a fire and determination that told him she had not easily dismissed his earlier comment. "I thought you might find this more appropriate for the evening."

The newly arrived family rushed past them, the man herding his family up the stairs, the woman doing her best to shield her daughters' eyes.

Dillon rose to his feet slowly, and whipped his buckskin jacket off the back of his chair. "Put this on, Grace," he said in a low voice, holding the jacket out to her.

"No, thank you." Grace looked up at him and smiled, and Dillon had a clear view down the front of her dress. From what he could see—which was damn near everything—her perfection didn't include only her face. Her breasts were white, and the skin looked so soft he had to clench his fists around the jacket to keep from reaching out and touching them, just to see if they felt as silky as they looked.

Dillon leaned close to her, bending forward and stopping when his face was so near to hers he could feel her breath on his lips. He looked down, taking in every inch of skin that was exposed by the low-cut gown, letting his eyes rest on those hard nipples. If she was going to show, he was damn well going to look.

"Put it on, Grace, or I'll put it on for you," he threatened. "Don't think I won't."

"I'll make a scene," Grace whispered.

Dillon raised his eyes to meet hers again. "You'll make a scene? Honey, this isn't New Orleans, or England, or wherever the hell you've been spending the past eleven years. This is Texas. If I were to shoot you, that might be considered making a scene. If I were to toss you up on this table and give you exactly what you're asking for by wearing that dress, I reckon that might be called making a scene. But if I yank you up by the hair, and you take to yellin' and screamin' while I dress you in front of these people . . . hell, honey, that ain't a scene. That's exactly what you deserve, and ain't nobody gonna lift a hand to stop me."

He saw it, sensed it really, the moment she lost her nerve. It had come when he'd threatened to toss her up on the table. Maybe she thought he'd really do that. Maybe she believed him to be capable of anything.

The only outward sign of her defeat was a slight softening of her eyes. And she licked her lips as if they'd suddenly gone dry. Damn, but he wished she wouldn't do that.

"Now that you mention it," Grace said as she

rose languidly to her feet, "I am a bit chilly." She offered an arm to Dillon, and he slipped the soft buckskin over her red silk. He crossed behind her and repeated the gesture, then freed her hair from under the collar—hair as black as a moonless night on the trail, and shiny as moonlight on the water.

Dillon returned to his own seat as Grace turned up the sleeves of his jacket and began to eat her stew, taking dainty bites. He still had a generous view of her neck and upper chest through the vee in his jacket, but her breasts were covered, and it seemed that the other men in the room had turned their attention to other matters.

Billy was shaking his head and staring into his nearly empty bowl.

Dillon could hardly eat as he watched Grace. The prospect of finding her a husband was looking dimmer and dimmer. At first glance she was perfect, but if she pulled a stunt like this in Plummerton he'd never be able to marry her off. And half the time when she opened her mouth she was complaining. If only he could show her off from a distance, or drug her. Just a little bit. Just enough so that she would sit there quietly for a while. After she was married, well, it would be too late for her poor husband to bring her back.

With a shake of her head, Grace looked him full in the face. "Well, you look pleased with yourself, Becket. If I didn't know better I'd think you were on the verge of a smile."

Dillon didn't answer her, but met her gaze as she stared at him, unflinching, with those startling bluebonnet eyes.

"I'm not wearing this jacket because you told me to, Becket," Grace said in a low, warning voice. "I'm wearing it because I felt a chill in the room."

She looked like a defiant child, all bundled up in a coat that was far too large for her, her eyes wide and bright as she challenged him.

"I didn't intend to insult you," Dillon said in a low voice, doing his best to apologize.

Grace leaned forward, and the jacket gaped open. This time Dillon didn't mind, because no one could see but him. "You said I dressed like a high-priced whore," she hissed.

"That's not what I meant."

"Did he really say that?" Billy asked, and Grace turned to the gray-haired man.

"Yes, he most certainly did."

Billy looked most relieved, now that he had an explanation for Grace's strange behavior.

"You've twisted my words around, Grace. That's not exactly what I—"

Grace ignored him and kept her attention on Billy, who watched her with great sympathy on his face. "Does the man think I have no feelings? Perhaps my reaction was a bit extreme, but I was very upset."

Billy patted Grace's slender hand with his own hairy paw. "You poor little thing. Are you feelin' all right now? Dillon probably didn't mean nothin' by what he said. He just ain't got no manners at all."

Dillon sat back and watched as his best friend and his new burden discussed his lack of breeding and his poor manners as if he weren't even in the room. Grace was loving it. Billy was coddling her, comforting her . . . his old ranch hand relishing his new role as Grace's friend and protector.

Dillon pretended to ignore their conversation,

cleaning the dirt out from under his fingernails and leaning back casually in his unsteady chair.

When Grace excused herself and asked to be escorted to her room, Billy jumped to his feet and offered to accompany her. He got no argument from Dillon. Billy might be years past his prime, but he was strong, and big enough to make any man think twice about getting in his way. Grace would be safe with Billy at her side.

Grace rushed down the stairs, her feet barely touching one step before they were flying to the next. Billy was right behind her, his tread much heavier on the steps than her own. Again he asked her what was wrong.

She saw Becket across the room, seated at a table with four other men. Glasses of whiskey sat on the round table, as well as discarded playing cards and a pile of silver and gold. They were all smoking foul-smelling cigars, even Becket. He was so intent on the cards in his hand that he didn't even see her cross the room.

"Becket?" she whispered, clutching his buckskin jacket to her body with suddenly cold hands. "Dillon?"

He glanced over his shoulder, nothing but irritation in his eyes. "What do you want, Grace?"

"May I speak to you . . . privately?" She didn't want to air her fears in front of all these men. They were looking at her boldly, probably remembering what she wore beneath the buckskin jacket.

Becket waved a dismissive hand in the air. "We just got started. Say what you have to say, honey. I'm kinda busy right now."

Grace leaned forward, holding the buckskin close to her chest so that it didn't gape open.

"There's just one room. With four beds. And there are already people in those beds. The lady said I was to . . . to sleep in one of them. With those other women."

Becket looked over his shoulder to her. "There are two rooms. One for men. One for women. I'm sorry if it makes you uncomfortable, but I can't do anything about it." He turned away from her, dismissing her fears. Dismissing her.

Uncomfortable? She wasn't uncomfortable; she was terrified. She couldn't possibly climb into bed with a stranger. A filthy bed, at that. And she had seen several large bugs scuttling across the floor as she'd surveyed the room.

"Where are you going to sleep?" she whispered. "In the other room upstairs?"

Becket turned back to her, his already tested patience evidently gone. "Why? Are you planning on joining me?" He didn't even bother to lower his voice, and every man at the table was listening raptly.

She could feel the blood drain from her face, and she drew away from him sharply. "I can't sleep in that room, Becket."

He returned his attention to his cards. "Just close your eyes and snuggle up to one of those women the way you snuggled up to me last night."

One man guffawed, but a glare from Billy cut the man's hilarity short.

"I did no such thing," Grace said indignantly. "I'd sooner snuggle up with a snake."

Becket nonchalantly pitched a coin into the center of the table. "That can be arranged, Grace."

She reached over Becket's shoulder and snatched the cards from his hand. With a snap of her wrist she sent his cards sailing through the air. He turned to her as she grabbed up the closest glass of whiskey and poured it over his head. The golden liquid trickled over his chestnut hair, down his harshly rigid face, down his neck, and under his collar. He even managed to catch a drop or two with his tongue.

"Do I have your attention now?" Grace seethed.

"I'd say that you do," Becket answered in a deceptively calm voice.

"I can't possibly sleep in that room. It's filthy and bug infested, and I will not sleep with a stranger." She tried to keep the emotion from her voice, but she couldn't keep that tiny tremble from creeping into her last words. She only hoped that Dillon Becket had not noticed.

"What do you suggest?" Becket stood and faced her, clenching his hands at his sides. Grace stared at his hard face, the harsh angles, the tiny lines at the corners of his eyes. She could see every hair of the stubbly beard that covered his cheeks. There was heat radiating off of his body that wrapped around her like a living thing.

She should have been terrified.

"I don't know." Her voice was much calmer now.

Billy leaned forward. He had been close behind her the whole time, and he looked at Becket with censure. "I can rig her up a bed in the carriage. It'll be cramped, but she won't have to share it with nobody, and it's cleaner than this place."

Becket finally swiped a hand across his face, removing the last signs of the whiskey from his shadowed cheeks. "It won't be safe," he said sharply.

Grace opened her mouth to protest, but Billy cut her off. "I'll keep watch," he promised.

Becket raised disbelieving eyebrows. "All night?"

"I'm an old man. I don't sleep none too well, anyway," Billy said gruffly. He ignored Becket and laid a hand on her shoulder. "You wait right here while I see to your trunk, and then we'll head on out to the carriage. Does that sound all right to you, Miss Grace?"

She nodded, never taking her eyes from Becket's face. "If you don't mind." Her fear was slowly vanishing, and she felt a rising disappointment that Becket hadn't taken her worry more seriously. Somehow she had expected him to look after her. But he didn't care. He was no better than her father.

There was just enough moonlight to illuminate Billy well as he sat with his back against the carriage wheel, a rifle in his lap as he kept a close watch over Grace. Dillon approached with a purposely lazy gait, his hands in his pockets.

He should have climbed the stairs and gotten a decent night's sleep without wasting another moment of thought on Grace Cavanaugh . . . but that wasn't going to happen.

"How's it going?" he whispered.

Billy shrugged his broad shoulders, but he wasn't relaxed as he usually was. "It's been quiet. Miss Grace fell asleep right away, and ain't nobody been out here." Billy made it clear by the tone of his voice that he was still peeved with his employer. "How'd you do, boss?"

"Pretty good," Dillon whispered as he glanced into the carriage window. "I won fifty bucks."

Billy didn't say a word, but Dillon heard a faint

harumph under the big man's breath. He looked down at a silver head. "Every little bit helps."

He returned his gaze to the woman in the carriage. She was curled up on the narrow seat, her face half covered as she buried her nose into the buckskin jacket she still wore over her tantalizing red dress. A bit of moonlight lit her face, and she looked amazingly peaceful for a woman who had, a few hours earlier, tossed his cards about the room and doused him with his own whiskey. He shook his head. He'd always heard that looks could be deceiving, and Grace was certainly proving the point. She looked like an angel, sleeping so peacefully, but he knew she was not.

"She is right purty, ain't she?" Billy asked from directly behind Dillon. Dillon started, just a little. He hadn't even heard the big man rise to his feet.

"No," Dillon said testily. "She isn't *right purty*. She's beautiful. The most beautiful woman I've ever seen."

Billy smiled, that generous smile that seemed to come so easily to him. "You make that sound like a bad thing, boss."

"She's gonna be a passel of trouble, Billy." Dillon took another glance at the sleeping angel who was no angel, then turned away and lowered himself to the ground. He leaned the back of his head against the carriage door. "Like tonight. Why the hell couldn't she just . . ."

Billy's censuring expression and a *tsk* that was loud in the still night stopped Dillon's question.

"What?" he snapped.

Billy sat beside Dillon and spoke in a low voice. "I always thought you were purty smart, but I'm beginnin' to have my doubts, boss."

Dillon sighed and waited for Billy to continue. The old man wouldn't need any prompting to explain his less than flattering observation; that was certain.

"Didn't you think she acted kinda strange when that fella on the train put his hand on her knee?" Billy turned a questioning face to Dillon. "And I tell you, when I took her hand to help her into the carriage this afternoon, why, her whole body stiffened up. I could feel it, in her hand and her arm, and I could even see the cords in her neck tense up."

"She's a very proper lady, Billy," Dillon said in a wry voice. That was one of the problems. A very proper lady like Grace Cavanaugh didn't belong in Texas, in a common trailside hotel, or on a ranch like the Double B.

Billy was shaking his head thoughtfully. "I reckon I know that. It's more than that, though."

"So what are you tryin' to say, Billy?"

Billy leaned closer and lowered his voice even more, until it was a hoarse whisper. "I'm thinkin' she don't like to be touched."

Dillon snorted. "Didn't you see her this morning? She was all over me, and her hand was right on my—"

"I know," Billy interrupted. "But she was sleepin', so it don't count."

Dillon lifted his head and turned to the hand who had worked for his father for years, and was now his most trusted employee. "You're not getting any ideas about Grace, are you, Billy? She's young enough to be your own daughter!"

Billy's voice was low, but there was a menacing quality in the tone that was usually so nonthreatening. "Dang right. Elizabeth would be about her age, if she'd lived. Don't be thinkin' I'm lookin' at Miss Grace in an improper way, boss. She needs a friend, that's all, someone to look after her."

Billy had two grown sons who'd gone their own way years earlier, but his only daughter, Elizabeth, had died shortly after her birth. Counting back, Dillon realized that Elizabeth would have been just Grace's age.

"Sorry," he mumbled.

"Besides"—Billy leaned into Dillon's face and again lowered his voice to that hoarse whisper—"I think she likes you."

That statement elicited another snort from Dillon. "If she likes me, I'd hate to see how she treats the folks she doesn't like."

"You didn't let me finish," Billy said. "If Miss Grace don't like to be touched, the very idea of climbing into a bed with one of those strange women must have been just awful. And this place ain't none too clean, especially for a lady like Miss Grace."

Dillon leaned his head back against the carriage door. Billy had a point, damn his hide. He asked himself again what he was going to do with a lady like Grace on a working ranch. She didn't fit in, and she never would. Abigail was a gentle lady herself, but she'd lived in Texas all her life. And besides, she was . . . necessary.

In spite of his reluctance to share his reservations with Billy, he found himself doing just that. He had to talk to somebody, he reasoned with what little reason he had left, and Billy was a good listener.

"She doesn't belong here, Billy. She's stubborn and disagreeable, and she's got no stamina or patience. I'll bet there's not one sensible dress in all of those trunks." He pointed a finger to the sky and the mountain of baggage on top of the carriage. "Every time she opens her mouth she complains. And what kind of woman pulls a stunt like the one she pulled tonight?"

"Which time?" Billy asked with more than a hint of humor in his voice.

Dillon turned a scowling face to the man. "Does it matter?"

Billy made himself more comfortable against the wheel, shifting his large body and resettling the rifle in his lap. "Well, you shouldn'ta called her a high-priced whore."

"I didn't—"

Billy lifted a hand to still Dillon's protests. "And you shoulda listened to her when she came down to talk to you about the room."

"I had a full house." The excuse sounded lame as it came out of his mouth.

"I was standin' just outside the door when she come outta that room like the devil was on her tail, and she didn't stop to talk to me. She didn't tell me what was wrong. She went down them stairs in a flash and went lookin' for you, boss."

Dillon felt the first flashes of guilt, and willed them away. He didn't have time for this nonsense. "She'd better not come to depend on me to listen to all her complaints. I ain't got the time or the patience for it. What does she think I am? Her—"

"Guardian?" Billy finished for him.

Dillon closed his eyes. He cursed Colonel Cavanaugh's soul, and then retracted it quickly. The man had saved his life, after all. "I'm going to have to find her a husband, Billy, and fast."

Billy grunted in obvious disgust. "Why don't you sell her to the highest bidder. She's right good-lookin', and oughta bring in a pretty penny. Maybe even enough to pay off the loan. Maybe even enough so you won't have to marry Miss Abigail." The old man's voice was gruff.

It had been clear to Dillon for some time now how Billy felt about his plan to marry Abigail if the cattle drive didn't bring in enough money to pay off the loan. Billy was the only one Dillon had confided in, and he'd been regretting letting even Billy in on his plan.

He and Abigail were already a couple, of sorts, in Plummerton. Abigail had been trying to get him to the altar for five years, and it looked as if she might finally succeed. Theirs was a comfortable relationship, and he could be assured that Abigail would never appear in public in a red dress that was slashed damn near to her navel. Of course, she would never appear in private in anything so daring, either, he imagined. She was a right prim and proper lady, but not quite so delicate as Grace. Abigail would make a good wife.

The only problem was, every time Dillon thought about actually marrying her he broke out in a cold sweat.

They both heard Grace stir in the confines of the carriage and rose to their feet together. One look told Dillon that she hadn't moved much. She had repositioned herself a little, and had pulled the collar of his buckskin jacket closer to her face. She looked amazingly contented, given her cramped position and the stunts she had pulled just that night, and Dillon had a sudden urge to climb into the carriage with her. To hold her the way he'd held her on board the train. He fought back a sudden lump in his throat.

"She's stubborn, and disagreeable, and nothing but trouble for me, Billy."

"Yeah," Billy said in an easy drawl. "I like her, too, boss."

Grace woke slowly, as she usually did, but there was something strangely comforting about rising this morning. She buried her nose into the softness that brushed her face. It smelled of Dillon Becket, and she liked that. It made her feel contented and warm and—

She rose swiftly, sitting up on the carriage seat and pushing the buckskin away from her face. Dillon Becket! She had no intention of allowing herself to feel anything for the man. Certainly nothing as comforting as she'd felt upon waking. The remnants of a dream, she decided, had made her feel momentarily safe. That was all it could be.

"Good morning."

Her head snapped up, and she saw the offensive man leaning against the carriage and peering into the window, looking at her as if he knew something she didn't.

"Good morning, Becket," she snapped, brushing the hair away from her face with a swift swipe of her hand.

"I'm glad you're awake," he said calmly. "It seems we'll need to unload another trunk so you can choose a more . . . suitable traveling outfit." He chose his words carefully, maintaining his emotionless expression. "Problem is, there are so many trunks I don't know where to begin."

Grace gathered the buckskin jacket close around her, and stepped from the carriage. There was nothing to be done for it. Dillon Becket offered her his hand, and she took it. He was watching her too closely, as if he were gauging her reaction as their palms met. She held on to his hand for no longer than necessary, then turned to look up at the top of the conveyance.

"That trunk there," she said, pointing to a large piece of baggage near the edge.

Becket climbed atop and loosened the ropes, then handed the trunk to Billy. Grace opened the trunk and pulled out the dress that was on top, a plain yellow muslin gown. She held it up and turned a stoic face to Dillon.

"Will this do, Becket?" she snapped. "Is this suitable enough for you?"

Dillon felt a rush of contentment as he looked at the dress. It was plain, to be sure, and had a high neck and long sleeves. He wondered if yellow would do to Grace what it did to Abigail. Turn her skin all sallow and sickly looking. He certainly hoped so.

"Perfect," he said as she lowered the dress. "Get changed as quick as you can. We've got to get on the road."

Grace marched back to the roadside stop with her head held high, Dillon's too-large buckskin jacket wrapped around her, and red silk flowing around her legs. Billy was right behind her, a faithful watchdog. Dillon knew he wouldn't have to worry about Grace with Billy beside her.

Not that he had any intention of worrying about her.

When they emerged, what seemed like a long time later, he had already returned the large trunk to the roof, and was ready to pull out. He watched Grace approach the carriage with a neatly folded red dress in one hand, and his buckskin jacket held away from her body with the other. As if she'd really rather not be touching it.

"Thank you," she said, returning the coat to

him with a wrinkling of her nose that showed her distaste for the object of clothing. "It is quite warm."

Dillon didn't say anything. The dress that had been plain in her hands was striking on her body. It fit her perfectly, from the swell of her breasts to that tiny waist, over her hips, draping softly and covering all but the tips of her dainty white boots.

And, damn it, her face wasn't sallow against the yellow muslin. It was warm and rosy, and her lips seemed even darker, more tempting. And how many women could wear their hair like that and get away with it? It was pulled back severely, with no curls to soften her face. Still, she was the most beautiful—

"What's the matter, Becket?" she asked crisply. "Are you ill? You look absolutely green."

He ignored her as best he could. "Help her into the carriage, Billy," he ordered. He didn't even want to take her hand at the moment.

It was going to be a very long trip home.

Chapter Four

They traveled quickly for the first three days of their journey, and Grace saw Becket infrequently. She remained in the carriage day and night, leaving her sanctuary only for the necessary stops. Becket seemed driven to reach his home as quickly as possible, and resented halting their tedious journey for even a short time.

Becket and Billy shared the driving duties. When Becket was guiding the horses, Billy sometimes joined her, though she was certain the driver's seat was more comfortable and a bit cooler than the confining coach. The air inside the conveyance was stifling, overly warm and stale, and she thought once or twice about asking Becket if she could ride up front with him. But she didn't. She was certain that he would refuse, in any case.

Her confinement gave her time to think. Too much time to think, actually. After a couple of days it occurred to her that she had actively avoided contemplating her life for the past five years. She'd simply flitted from one place to another with little or no thought to where she might find herself next.

A far-off rumble of thunder interrupted her speculation, and reminded her of where she'd landed this time. She never would have thought to find herself in Texas.

Grace had never been particularly philosophical about her life, but she wasn't a mindless fool. She had learned to be on her guard at all times, and there was no one in the world she trusted completely, no person she would think of telling her secrets to.

The first night on the trail, she had slept fitfully. The carriage was simply pulled to the side of the road for a few quiet hours, and Grace couldn't allow herself to relax. Every noise she heard was an imagined Indian, or a wild beast.

She'd tried to sleep, but it was useless. It was impossible to get comfortable, and her mind was spinning as she speculated on the possible dangers that surrounded her. After what had to be several long hours, she'd practically jumped from her seat, startled by a faraway and indistinct sound. A howl. Or was it a scream? In the complete dark of early morning, she had been able to feel her own pounding heartbeat.

And then she'd leaned her head out of the carriage window. Billy had been sleeping on the ground not five feet from the carriage. He was snoring, facing the sky as he slept on the hard ground with nothing but a thin blanket between his back and the dirt.

Without making a sound, she'd scooted across the seat and peered out of the opposite window. Dillon Becket slept as peacefully as Billy, but without the older man's slack-jawed snore. Grace had a feeling—no, she knew—that if she so much as sneezed they would both be there.

She felt surprisingly safe, there between the two men she barely knew, and she hadn't had any trouble sleeping since that night.

Another rumble of thunder, closer this time, drew her to the window again as they rolled down the road. They were on a smooth stretch of road for once, and she wasn't at all jarred as they sped over the dusty trail. Dark clouds, a wall of gray, were bearing down on them at an astounding speed. The wind picked up, and reddish brown dust clouds danced across the horizon, hiding whatever awaited down the road and across the flatlands.

The carriage slowed and left the road as the winds picked up again. How could even this seemingly sturdy coach weather a storm? They would all surely be flung about in that dark cloud that was descending on them.

She leaned her head out of the window. Billy was talking to the horses and tethering the reins to the sturdiest-looking tree in the area. It appeared awfully scrawny to Grace. Much too fragile to weather the storm that was coming. Becket set the brake and brought out a large tarp to cover the baggage on the roof.

It took both men to secure the tarp, and before they'd finished large raindrops had begun to fall. The wind did indeed shake the carriage, and Grace grabbed at the seat with both hands.

Billy joined her first, giving her a reassuring smile as he settled himself on the seat across from her. "Looks like a gully-washer's comin'."

Grace had no idea what a gully-washer was, but she got the general idea and agreed. If nothing else, Billy's great weight should help to stabilize the coach, she reasoned.

Becket flung himself into the coach and plopped down beside her. He shuttered the windows, taking away all the light but a few slices of gray that filtered through.

Grace scooted across the seat so she was sitting at the very corner, as far away from Dillon Becket as was physically possible. As her eyes adjusted to the dark, she saw that he was looking at her, staring very impolitely, to be exact.

"You don't have to be afraid, Grace," he finally said as he settled himself into the opposite corner. He didn't want to get any closer to her than she did to him, evidently. "The storm will pass over pretty quick. The worst of it, anyway."

"I'm not afraid of storms, Becket," Grace answered in a firm voice.

Becket was silent, but he didn't take his eyes from her. Even in the dimly lit carriage, she could see the tension in his face, in the set of his jaw, in his eyes. It was as if he were on the verge of explosion all the time, as if his exterior calm were all an act.

"You know," he said in a low voice as Grace continued to stare at him, "I really don't care what you call me. Becket's fine, if that makes you happy. But do you have to say it as if you're spittin' out a bit of rancid beef at the same time?"

Billy chuckled, and Grace was reminded of the older man's presence. She wasn't alone with Dillon Becket, and she had nothing to fear from the man.

"It certainly was not my intention to insult you, Becket." She said his name more softly, without the harshness she knew was normally there.

"That's better." He seemed satisfied, and

leaned back to close his eyes. A gust of wind rocked the carriage, and he didn't even stir.

Grace soon decided that she was the only one concerned about the storm around them. The carriage was pelted with torrential rain, and still Becket didn't move a muscle.

Before long Billy was taking advantage of the unplanned stop by taking a nap, sprawling across the seat and snoring softly. How could they be so calm? She cringed with every strong gust of wind that rocked the coach, and jumped with the cracks of thunder overhead.

She jumped again when she looked at Becket and found he was watching her. He hadn't moved at all. He'd just opened his eyes.

"It'll all be over soon," he assured her.

All she could do was nod.

Billy's soft snoring continued uninterrupted, a surprising comfort to Grace. She waited for Becket to close his eyes once again, but he continued to stare at her, even after she silently accepted his assurance.

"There's something I've been wanting to ask you," she began hesitantly. The crack of thunder that sounded was farther away, proving to her that the storm was, indeed, moving away from them, and the carriage had survived.

"Go right ahead," Becket prompted when she faltered.

"Why?" Grace sat with her back ramrod straight, her hands folded primly in her lap. There was little enough light in the coach, but she knew she had Dillon Becket's undivided attention. "Why you? My father never mentioned you in his letters." She didn't think it was necessary to tell him that her father's letters had been few and far between.

"I owed your father a debt," Becket answered in a low voice. Grace was not surprised. He seemed to be the kind of man who took his obligations seriously.

"Money?" Grace prompted. "He loaned you money for your ranch, and this is how he asked to be repaid?"

"No," Becket said shortly. "Not that kind of a debt."

She waited for an explanation to follow, but Becket was silent. The storm abated rather quickly, though fat raindrops continued to pelt the carriage. They echoed on the tarp and struck the shuttered window on Becket's side of the coach. The only sound other than the steady rainfall was Billy's soft snoring.

"Would you tell me?" she asked softly. "I'd . . . I'd like to know."

Night had fallen, and the inside of the coach was completely dark. Grace wished, for once, that she could see Becket's face. Maybe she would be able to tell what was going through his mind.

"He saved my life," Becket said, just when Grace had decided that he wasn't going to answer. "During the war."

There was a moment of silence as Grace absorbed the information. She'd never thought of her father as the heroic type. "That . . . that doesn't sound like my father."

"We were running from the Yanks," Becket said hoarsely. "Doesn't sound very noble, but that's the truth. It was sixty-two, and I hadn't been in the army very long. It . . . it wasn't what I expected." He was quiet again, and Grace began to believe that he would say no more . . . and then he continued.

"Evidently I took a bullet in the back. I don't remember. Last thing I recall is running across this little creek. But I'm told I was shot and fell, face first, into the water. They said Colonel Cavanaugh turned around and came back for me. Picked me up out of the water and carried me to safety."

"That's remarkable," Grace whispered. Her father? He had never seemed, to her, a man for whom self-sacrifice was an option, and she couldn't picture him as the heroic type. But he was if he had truly saved Dillon Becket's life. "Was it very painful, getting shot?"

She thought she might have heard a small laugh escape his lips, but that was impossible. "Hurt like hell, but I knew I would survive. And I did. Of course, every eighteen-year-old thinks he's invincible."

Grace leaned forward just a little. She could have reached out and touched his leg, but she kept her hands to herself. "You were eighteen? That would make you twenty-eight now?"

"Yep."

"You look older," Grace said before she thought better of it. "I mean . . . I thought . . . just a little older." Would he be terribly insulted?

"It's the light," Becket said, saving her from rambling on and trying to explain herself.

Grace smiled. She could barely see her own hand in front of her face, but for a moment she imagined that Dillon Becket was smiling, too.

"So my father saved your life, and ten years later he asks you to repay him by taking care of me?"

"Yep."

She felt a weight in her chest, unexpected and inexplicable. Her father had forced her upon a man who she was certain, if she understood Dillon Becket at all, couldn't possibly refuse. "It's very gallant of you, Becket, to take me on."

"I'm not a gallant man, honey, but I do pay my debts." His voice seemed a bit gruffer than it should have been, and Grace knew, at that moment, that she was as unwanted here as she'd been all her life.

"I won't be a burden to you, Becket," she said, and her voice was suddenly cold, distant. "It will just take a little time to sort through the situation."

He didn't respond. Didn't tell her that she wasn't a burden, or that everything would work itself out. He was ominously quiet for several minutes, as the softened rain beat against the coach.

"Go to sleep, Grace," he said gruffly. "Tomorrow's going to be a long day."

The moment Grace fell asleep, he knew it. Her breathing slowed, became deep and even, and the dark form beside him relaxed. Within minutes she was pressed against him, her head on his shoulder.

He could have returned her to her corner, probably with enough ease that she wouldn't awake, but he didn't. He rather liked the softness and warmth of her body against his.

This was the baby. Grace's observation about her father had been astute. Turning back to save his life had been out of character for Colonel Cavanaugh, but Dillon couldn't deny that the old man had done it. After all, once he'd healed and returned to his unit, Cavanaugh had taken a special interest in him. Perhaps even the colonel had been puzzled by whatever force had driven him to risk his life for a green private.

That was the reason Dillon had heard about the baby. The baby who had come and taken Colonel Cavanaugh's beloved wife's life. The baby who was in England with Cavanaugh's elderly aunt. The colonel had spoken about his wife's death with such heartbreak that Dillon had never questioned the fact that the baby was indeed a baby.

But Grace had been eleven years old when Colonel Cavanaugh had sent her to England. Eleven years old. Not a baby, but nearly a young lady.

What had her childhood been like? What kind of father is a man who thinks of his child as a baby eleven years after her birth? Dillon couldn't recall a single time the colonel had referred to his daughter as Grace, or *my little girl*, or anything other than *the baby*.

Billy said Grace didn't like to be touched, and Dillon had to agree. He'd purposely taken her hand on that morning in Clanton, and he'd felt what Billy had noticed. Grace stiffened almost imperceptibly and released his hand as soon as her feet touched the ground.

But when she slept she came to him. Searching for the touch she'd been denied all her life, and had come to fear? Maybe she didn't fear it at all, but craved it. Maybe that was why she gravitated to him when she slept.

Dillon leaned back and shifted Grace so that her head was against his chest. She murmured in her sleep, and pressed her face against his cotton shirt.

If Billy hadn't been snoring just a couple of feet away, and if Grace wasn't Colonel Cavanaugh's *baby* . . . if the path Dillon had set for himself had had any leeway in it at all . . . if she didn't say his name as if she were spitting out something gamy . . . he would teach her what it was like to be touched in all the right places. He had an unshakable feeling that Grace would fit him properly. Perfectly, in fact.

But he couldn't afford an entanglement of that sort. Not with a woman like Grace. If he bedded her she would expect him to marry her, and he couldn't do that. Not even, he told himself, if he had any such inclination. Which he most certainly did not.

So he scowled and placed a restraining hand at her back, simply to keep her from slipping to the floor—he told himself—and he closed his eyes. And he knew, with bitter certainty, that he would dream of bubble baths and bluebonnet eyes.

The rain had ruined the trail, leaving a morass of mud where a perfectly good road had been the day before. Becket swore at the mud as if it would make a difference, and waded in the sticky stuff until he was covered to his knees with splashed muck.

Grace surveyed the scene from the open carriage door. She'd been mortified to wake against Dillon Becket's chest, and to find Billy watching the two of them with a satisfied expression on his still-sleepy face. Fortunately Becket seemed as determined to ignore the awkward situation as she was.

And now, mortified again, she had to relieve herself. There was no way off the conveyance but through the mud, and she didn't want to ask either Billy or Becket for assistance.

Becket glanced up and stared at her as if he'd only just noticed her there. Then he slopped toward her angrily. He looked positively frightful this morning, as though he hadn't slept at all, or if he had, as if his dreams had been horrid. She didn't dare ask him.

He stopped directly in front of her, and without a word lifted her from the carriage, flung her indelicately over his shoulder, and carried her to the other side of the road. There the ground was rocky, with scrubby patches of grass that kept it from becoming the mess the road had become. Grace looked away from Becket and the muddy road. There were a couple of rather large bushes not too far away, and that was all that was available, as far as cover was concerned.

Becket turned back to the carriage, ignoring her predicament, and Grace made her way to the only semblance of privacy she could see.

When she emerged from behind the bushes, she screamed. Dillon Becket was tossing her trunks to the side of the road. He looked none too pleased as he dumped one piece of her baggage after another into the mud, where they landed with a sickening splat.

Becket lifted his head when she screamed, turning a tired and determined face to her.

"What do you think you're doing?" She didn't even think about where her path would take her as she stepped onto the muddy road. She sank down in mud to her ankles, as she looked up at her guardian.

"Sorry, honey," he said in a voice that held no remorse. "This is all making the carriage too heavy to make it down the trail. It's gotta go." He tossed another, smaller trunk to the ground.

"Everything I own is in those trunks!"

"If there's anything valuable in these things, get it out now," Becket instructed without a hint of concern. "If we pull out onto the road with this weight on top we'll be up to the hub in no time."

Grace glanced down at the mess she was standing in, at the mud her hem touched. She was nearly up to the hub herself. "Can't I keep just two or three trunks?"

Becket ran his fingers through tousled hair, pushing it straight back. It made his face look more severe, sharper. "Two," he snapped. "You may choose two trunks from what's left up here." He looked down at the trunks by the side of the road. He obviously had no desire to drag the muddy trunks back atop the carriage.

"That Saratoga trunk," Grace said, pointing beyond Becket. "And the small tan one with the red strap. And the other tan bag with the blue strap," she added quickly. "Please."

Dillon quickly and unceremoniously unloaded all but the three selected bags. He tried not to look at Grace's face as she forlornly watched each piece drop to the ground. He told himself again and again that there was nothing to be done for it. No woman needed so many clothes anyway. Not even Grace Cavanaugh.

But she looked so somber as she watched her belongings collect beside the road. He wished he could tell her that he would replace everything. But he could replace nothing. The yellow dress she wore, the dress that was brushing the mud as she tried futilely to lift the skirt just enough out of the sludge that surrounded her, was evidently the simplest gown she owned. And it was clearly an expensive, well-made piece of clothing. Finer than anything he could give her.

"You're ruining your dress," he said gruffly. "And your white boots. Damn white boots," he muttered under his breath.

Grace glanced down at the hem of her gown briefly, and when she lifted her face to him again her frown deepened. "Well, I had planned to burn it upon arrival at your ranch. Surely after five days of wear it won't be fit to save. But now . . ." She looked wistfully at the pile of bags and trunks at the edge of the road. "I suppose I will have to find a way to salvage it."

She picked her way to the coach, graceful even as she battled the muck and stepped inside, unassisted.

Progress was slowed considerably due to the condition of the road. The carriage lurched on a regular basis as the wheels hit pockets of muddy water, and Grace had to hold on to the seat to keep from being thrown to the floor. The sun did come out, though, and warmed the coach considerably. The bright sun did nothing to improve Dillon Becket's mood, apparently. She heard him cursing at the horse and the road and, she assumed, at her.

It was not quite midday when she heard that swearing increase, and this time Billy chimed in. His curses were much milder in nature—a couple of *drats* and a *darn*—but they were delivered every bit as intensely as Becket's vile obscenities. That alone was enough to make Grace look out the window.

At first count she estimated half a dozen riders were bearing down on them, appearing with no warning from behind a large outcrop at the side of the trail. One rider gave a bone-chilling yell as he pointed his rifle at the driver's seat of the carriage. A pistol was fired into the air as the vehicle was pulled to an abrupt halt, tossing Grace onto the floor.

"Good morning, *señor*."

Grace pulled herself off the floor and peeked out the window. A single rider approached the carriage while his companions sat their horses a short distance away, their rifles and pistols trained on Becket and Billy. "If you would please dismount?" He waved a slender hand and smiled incongruously.

He was, Grace decided, the leader of the group. He was taller than the others. Mexicans, she decided as she eyed the group without being seen. They all had black hair and dark skin, and several of them wore colorful serapes. But not the leader. He was dressed all in black, and almost formally. His flat-brimmed hat was trimmed with a band of silver conchos, and he sported a thin mustache rather than the bushy abominations his companions preferred.

Billy remained in the driver's seat while Becket jumped to the ground. Without a word of instruction from the leader, one of the Mexicans took Becket's pistol from its holster, and though Grace couldn't see Billy, she assumed another of the bandits was disarming him as well.

She moved away from the window, and slid her carpetbag as far under the seat as it would go.

"Your valuables, *señor*," the leader instructed in a calm voice.

Grace remained on the floor, slinking lower inch by inch. Maybe they wouldn't bother her. Maybe they would take Becket's money and then let them go.

There was not much chance of that, she reasoned, but she remained still and quiet, hoping they would overlook her. Becket was arguing, blast him! Didn't he know that these bandits would shoot him if he didn't shut his contentious mouth? She took a deep breath and released it slowly, readying herself for the confrontation that was surely to come.

The door of the carriage was thrown open, and a short, squat Mexican with sweat-dampened hair and grimy fingers grabbed Grace's wrist and yanked her through the carriage door. Before she knew what was happening, she found herself face-to-face with the leader, her wrist still gripped by the unsavory bandit.

She kept her head down, but cut her eyes to the side. Billy was still on the driver's seat, and the man who had taken Becket's pistol held that weapon to Billy's head. At least they seemed calm, these thieves. Perhaps if she could remain calm, no one would be harmed.

Becket was standing a few feet away from her, his fists clenched at his sides. He was flanked on either side by grinning bandits, and one of them had a rifle pointed nonchalantly at Becket's side.

"Ah," the leader said as he lifted Grace's face gently, firm fingers on her chin. He smiled wickedly, revealing straight, white teeth. "A treasure more valuable than all your gold, *señor*."

Becket didn't move, but he glared at the bandit who still held her wrist. "Get your hands off of her."

The heavy air was filled with the almost musical ring of more than one hammer being cocked.

But the leader stopped the violent intentions of his companions by dropping the hand that had touched Grace's chin, and waving his fellow thief away. "You may release her, Paco."

As soon as Paco had released his grip on Grace's wrist, the leader took Grace's hand and bent over it, as courtly as any prince.

"You are brighter than the sunshine, *señorita*," he said as he lifted his face to grin at her, his black eyes twinkling. Amazingly Grace felt no fear. Even this man could be handled, as all men could. He was, although a thief with a villainous band of men behind him, much more akin to the nobility she was accustomed to than Dillon Becket was or ever would be.

"You are a . . . a highwayman?" Grace asked in a small, breathy voice. The handsome bandit continued to hold her hand, but his touch was light, unlike the grasping sweatiness of the swarthy Paco.

"Sí," he agreed, obviously pleased to be called a highwayman rather than a bandit or a thief. "And these are my men." He waved a hand to indicate the less-than-reputable-looking band of compatriots that surrounded him, but he never took his eyes off of her.

One of those men climbed atop the carriage and opened one of Grace's trunks, rifling through it with his dirty hands. Grace watched the man with mounting dismay, and then turned to the bandit who still held her hand.

"You're not going to take my clothes and things, are you?" There was an almost pitiful quality to her voice as she looked up at the dark bandit with her eyes purposely wide and innocent.

"Is there nothing of value in those trunks?" he asked.

Grace shook her head. "No. Just my clothes. I did have several trunks, but Becket here tossed most of them on the side of the road." She cocked her head and looked at the ground. "What's in those trunks is all I have left in the world."

The leader ordered the bandit from the carriage top with a sharp command delivered in Spanish. Becket finally stepped forward, ignoring the thieves who held their weapons pointed at his back.

"You can let go of her," he snapped. "I've given you all my money, and she doesn't have anything you want, so—"

"I disagree," the bandit leader said, turning to face Becket for half a second, then returning his dark eyes to her. "Come with me, *querida*. I will dress you in silk and lavish you with gold and jewels. Leave this *gringo*, and ride with me."

Grace couldn't breathe. Surely he wouldn't . . . but of course he could, if he wished. If this man decided to throw her over his horse and ride away with her there would be nothing she could do. Dillon Becket would probably be happy to be rid of her. Billy might try to stop the bandit, and might get himself killed in the process.

In spite of it all, Grace maintained a cool facade, and actually smiled at the bandit. It was up to her to end this.

"That's very kind of you, and most flattering." Out of the corner of her eye she saw Becket step forward. One of the bandits who had been right behind him the whole time wrapped a strong arm around Becket's neck and yanked him backward with a sharp jerk.

"But I couldn't possibly go with you. For one thing, I can't ride a horse." She tried to sound apologetic, but just a little. "And my father, who recently passed away, has given me into the care of this man. I must respect my father's last wish."

"This Becket is not your husband?"

"Good heavens, no," Grace assured him, a touch of horror in her voice.

The bandit didn't look horribly disappointed. "My sympathies, *señorita*, on the loss of your father. Although I must say I question his judgment in leaving you in the hands of such a man as this."

Grace had to bite her tongue to keep from agreeing with the thief.

He leaned closer, and spoke so softly that only the two of them could hear his words. "I would know your name, beautiful one, so that when I am lonely, and I close my eyes and see your face, I can whisper that name." His voice was silky, and soothing in an odd way. Grace had learned to dismiss sweet words that meant nothing.

"Grace Cavanaugh," she whispered back, not certain if it was wise to answer his question truthfully or not. But the bandit was a hypnotic man, smooth and handsome, with those marvelous flashing black eyes. And what could it hurt? She'd surely never see him again.

Her eyes dropped away from his and fell on the wide silver bracelet at his wrist. It was studded with turquoise, and caught the sun on its bright surface.

"What a beautiful bracelet," she muttered. "I've never seen anything quite like it."

The bandit grinned widely, and released Grace's hand at last. He removed the bracelet and slipped in onto her own wrist. "A gift, my beautiful Grace. Perhaps you will not forget Renzo so quickly now."

Grace curtsied slightly. "You're a most generous highwayman, Renzo."

She ignored Becket, who was apparently about to choke as he tried to pull away from the bandit who held him.

Renzo ordered Becket's pistol and Billy's rifle

left several yards from the carriage. He let them know that the only reason he did this was so that Grace would be properly protected for the remainder of the trip.

The bandits disappeared as quickly as they had appeared, rounding the big rock formation and vanishing in a heartbeat.

Becket collected the weapons, and then he turned to Grace. "What in the name of the devil did you think you were doing?"

She glared at him, all innocent eyes, as serene as she could manage to appear. All in all she was quite collected. "Whatever do you mean, Becket?"

He leaned close to her, placing his nose almost on hers, but she didn't back away. She refused to back away from Dillon Becket.

"You were flirting with that damn bandit."

Grace raised a hand to her chest in what she hoped would appear to be mortification. "I most certainly was not. How dare you accuse me of such a thing."

Unfortunately the wrist she raised sported a silver bracelet studded with turquoise.

Billy jumped to the ground and expertly placed himself between the two of them, practically shoving Becket back. "Let's go, before they decide they want the horses and these weapons and Miss Grace's trunks. We should count ourselves lucky that nobody was hurt."

"I agree," Grace said calmly, turning to the older man with a nod.

Becket scoffed and turned away while Billy assisted her into the carriage. "Lucky my ass," he growled. "I'm ninety dollars poorer. Of course, Grace got herself a little trinket out of the ordeal."

Grace settled against the seat and took a deep breath. Becket was probably wishing that she had been abducted by the Mexicans. That would have solved his problem nicely. Her heartbeat slowed, gradually, to a normal rhythm. In spite of his compliments and courtly manners, she had a feeling Renzo was a great deal different from the men she was accustomed to dealing with. He would not have been put off again and again. He might appear to be the perfect gentleman, but she sensed that beneath that charming smile there slept a man who didn't take no for an answer.

Like Dillon Becket. The difference was that Becket didn't try to hide behind civilities. What he showed the world was who he really was. That honesty scared her, as it would scare anyone who'd lived a life of deceit. She had learned to recognize and deal with men who played the same games she did. Almost always her judgment was flawless. Almost always.

She waited until the carriage was well down the road before she pulled her carpetbag from under the seat. She lifted the bag and placed it on her lap, and opened it to remove her ornately carved box.

She raised the lid with something akin to reverence. If the bandits had had any idea what she had hidden in the coach, it wouldn't have mattered how taken Renzo was with her. Gold and gems sparkled. The ruby Nancy's father had given Grace, the first piece in her collection. The diamond-and-ruby-studded serpent that Mikhail had given her. The Russian had been so sure of himself. So blasted confident.

Sapphires and emeralds, garnets and pearls. The contents of the box were all that she possessed that was worth anything at all.

And each piece represented a man who had tried to win her—and had lost. She removed the silver bracelet and dropped it atop the other jewels. She stared for a moment at the jumble of gems, transfixed by the sunlight sparkling on gold and silver.

Grace laid a slender hand over the pile of jewelry, and let her fingers delve among the stones and precious metals. In spite of the warm touch of the sun, the sparkling contents of the box were surprisingly cold.

Chapter Five

After their unpleasant overnight stop in Clanton, Grace had wondered what Plummerton would be like. She was relieved to find that it appeared a bit more civilized. It was awfully small, though. She could see nearly the entire town from the main street. Still, there were several two- and three-story buildings, and what looked to be a decent hotel. It surely had more than two rooms for sleeping.

Becket's mood had not improved since their run-in with Renzo, the charming bandit who had taken Becket's money and flirted so outrageously with her. Her reluctant guardian was, if possible, even more sullen than before, and avoided her so completely she couldn't pretend that it was accidental.

They didn't stop in the small town of Plummerton, but passed straight through. The Double B was just a couple of hours away, she knew.

Billy, at least, hadn't been snubbing her. He had told her all about Plummerton and the people there, though he seemed to be holding something back. Billy was such a naturally open person that he didn't lie very well. Even if it was only a lie of omission.

Actually it was less than an hour later when Grace saw the ranch through the carriage window, and she was pleasantly surprised. The two-story white house was hopelessly, marvelously out of place, a veritable mansion sitting there surrounded by fields as flat and devoid of civilization as one could imagine. Rougher-looking buildings, more of what Grace had expected, sat in the near distance. There was a barn and a long narrow building. Both were well constructed, but almost primitive in appearance.

But the house itself was lovely. It looked freshly painted, and there were lots of windows, all open to allow the faint breeze to ruffle curtains and cool the house. Maybe having Dillon Becket as a guardian wouldn't be so terribly awful, after all. Grace knew she could make herself comfortable in such a house as this.

They pulled to a stop just outside the front door. A wide front porch wrapped around the house, and well-tended rosebushes added color to the white porch and railing. Surely it wasn't Becket who saw to such niceties.

She was admiring the view when he appeared at her window, partially blocking the picture before her.

"What a lovely home, Becket," she said with a smile. She would have to make peace with the man if she was to stay here, though at the moment he didn't look as if that were possible. "I had no idea."

His eyes widened, and he raised his eyebrows. "This isn't my house. This is the Wilkinson ranch. Jesus, Grace. I hope you're not expecting the Double B to look like this place."

"I was just surprised to find such a house out here in the wastelands, that's all." Her smile faded. "Why have we stopped?"

"I borrowed this rig from . . . Wilkinson. We should have been back a couple of days ago, and it's not much out of our way. Just thought I'd let them know we're back." Becket was looking at her so strangely, Grace wished she had a hand mirror close by. Was her hair sticking straight up? Was there a bit of the quick lunch they'd shared plastered to her face?

"Wait here," Dillon ordered gruffly, emphasizing his point with a shake of a long brown finger as if she were a naughty puppy. "I'll be right back." He spun away from her and marched up the steps. A man—a butler way out here?—admitted him quickly, and closed the door so that Grace was once again watching a lifeless house.

"Purty fancy, ain't it?" Billy appeared beside her, out of nowhere. He'd approached so quietly Grace jumped when he spoke.

"Yes, it is." She couldn't help but smile at the older man. If not for him, the trip from New Orleans to the Double B would have been unbearable. "Who lives here?"

She could have sworn Billy was about to blush. The color rose in his cheeks, just slightly. "Well, old man Wilkinson, though I don't reckon he's back from the cattle drive yet. His boys, Wade and Kirby. I seem to recall that the old man was takin' Kirby with him this year, and leavin' Wade behind to see to the ranch." Billy nodded his head slightly, giving that statement much too much thought.

"Is that all?" Grace prompted.

"Well, there's . . . uh . . . Miss Abigail."

Grace leaned closer to the man, poking her face out the window. "What is it, Billy?" she asked, lowering her voice. "What are you not telling me?"

"It's nothin'." He looked away from her, pretending to study the ranch that lay beyond the house.

"Billy?" Grace's voice turned cajoling, and she watched as the older man's face turned red.

"Well, it's just that Dillon and Miss Abigail . . . I mean . . . I thought maybe you . . . you seem to like the boss well enough, and he hasn't said . . . but this is . . . I mean to say . . ."

"You're making no sense at all," Grace said slowly and calmly. "Are you trying to tell me that this Miss Abigail and Becket are friends?"

Billy nodded.

"Very good friends?" Grace asked silkily.

Billy nodded again.

"Well, I don't see why that's anything to blush and stammer about. It's really none of my concern who Becket's lady friends are." She leaned forward and placed her chin in her hands, trying to appear as nonchalant as possible. "It's just rather amazing to me that he has any lady friends at all. Your Dillon Becket is rather lacking in charm."

"You're not upset?" Billy asked, as if he had expected her to burst into tears at the news that Dillon Becket had a love interest.

"Not at all," Grace declared. Most convincingly, she thought. "Why on earth should I be upset? I don't plan on being in Texas for very long, you know."

Billy really did look surprised at that calmly delivered statement. "Where you goin'?"

"I don't know yet. But I don't intend to stay on a . . . on a cattle ranch in the middle of nowhere for the rest of my life. I'm an educated woman, Billy. I speak five languages, am quite good at mathematics, and have studied philosophy since the age of thirteen." Grace stopped suddenly. She sounded, even to her own ears, as if she were trying to convince herself, and not just Billy, that she didn't belong here.

"So Becket's love life, or lack thereof, is of no particular interest to me." She had calmed herself, determined not to show Billy that she was consumed with wonder. What did this Abigail Wilkinson look like? Was she some shoot-'em-up cowgirl in britches and a wide-brimmed hat, with a pistol strapped to her thigh? That would be a fitting partner for Dillon Becket.

Billy seemed to be relieved, though Grace wasn't certain that he completely believed her. He nodded, but said nothing, and he wasn't able to meet her eyes. He was busy studying the house, and then the fields beyond. For a while he studied the dirt at his feet, or else his dusty boots. It was impossible to tell what held his interest so fully.

They both jumped when Becket came bursting through the front door, a scowl on his face.

"We're spending the night," he barked.

Grace raised her eyebrows and stared him full in the face. Whatever the reason, he wasn't particularly happy about staying.

"How marvelous," Grace said cordially. "I can't wait to meet all the Wilkinsons." She kept her eyes on Becket's face, trying to judge his reaction. His jaw twitched, and his eyes glinted like gunmetal. Apparently his Abigail had him on a short leash.

"Well, Grace"—he opened the carriage door and offered her a hand—"you'll meet the Wilkinsons. A couple of them, anyway. And you'll meet most of the people from this part of Texas. There's going to be a party tonight. It's meant to welcome us home."

"Is one of the Wilkinsons clairvoyant?" Grace asked as she laid her hand in Becket's. "How did they know we'd be arriving today?"

"They didn't," Becket snapped. "I was in New Orleans longer than I expected. We should have been back several days ago. This fandango's been in the works for a while, I suppose."

Grace removed her hand from his as soon as her feet were firmly on the ground. It had not escaped her attention that Becket had not once mentioned Abigail Wilkinson's name to her.

"I can hardly wait to meet all your friends, Becket," Grace said sweetly. She looked up into his stony face and smiled. "Just imagine! A party on my very first day here! I expect it will be a great deal of fun."

Becket glared at her, and Grace almost backed away. Almost. A muscle in his cheek twitched, and a little of her good mood vanished. He really did dislike her.

"Don't worry, Becket," she assured him as she turned her back to his censuring face. "I give you my word, I'll be on my best behavior."

She heard a grunt behind her as Becket fell into step to the rear. Whether it was a grunt of approval or a grunt of disbelief, she couldn't say.

* * *

Dillon squirmed in the borrowed suit. He and Kirby were about the same size, but apparently the younger Wilkinson's neck was a bit smaller. He wished, and not for the first time that day, that they had gotten stuck in the mud on the road. He'd prefer to be there, up to the hub still, than at one of Abigail's parties.

With Grace.

The time to tell Abigail that Grace Cavanaugh was not a little girl, but a grown woman, had come and gone. The words he'd rehearsed in his mind had seemed inadequate as he'd faced Abigail. He had intended to tell her the truth, had in fact steeled himself to do just that.

All he could hope for now was that he could manage to get by with a curtly delivered *I thought I told you,* or a surprised *I didn't even think to tell you.* Which one? The bluff? Or the offhand comment that it really didn't matter? Neither one seemed quite right.

If Grace had been a plain woman, or even an ordinary one, he wouldn't have been so tongue-tied. Abigail was, if not yet officially his intended, the woman he was most likely to end up married to. What would she think about Grace living at the Double B? Hellfire, he knew damn well what she would think.

"What's the matter, boss?" Billy asked, and Dillon realized that he had stopped in the middle of the stairway.

"Nothing," Dillon snapped, resuming his plodding steps upward. "What the hell are you doing here?"

"I want to see Miss Grace all gussied up nice before I head out to the bunkhouse with the Wilkinson hands. I'll bet she's plumb gorgeous."

Dillon ignored Billy's statement, and stopped

outside the room Abigail's maid had said was Grace's. He stared at the door for a moment, putting off the inevitable.

Grace had spent the entire afternoon getting ready for the damn party, as had Abigail. What was it with women? All he'd had to do was clean up right quick, shave, and put on some borrowed clothes. Took him about twenty minutes.

Gathering his nerve, Dillon banged on the door.

"Just a minute." Grace answered his knock in a soft voice, and he felt as if his gut were in his throat.

When she opened the door he knew it was true. But it wasn't just his gut, it was his heart as well, and he couldn't speak.

Grace was wearing an ice blue satin gown that had a low, square neckline. It wasn't indecent, not like the red dress, but it was . . . extraordinary. Something sparkled at her throat, and he lifted his eyes slowly from her chest to her face.

Her skin looked as fragile as a rose petal, all soft and glowing. Her silky hair was piled atop her head in a style much less severe than usual. A single strand, falling artlessly, curled softly and just touched her shoulder, and her bluebonnet eyes sparkled.

He'd never seen anything more beautiful. Had never even imagined that a woman could look like this. She looked more angel than woman, with that very small smile turning up the corners of a perfectly shaped rose-colored mouth.

Dillon reached out, took the doorknob in his hand, and pulled the door shut. He couldn't possibly take her downstairs and introduce her to Abigail.

"What's the matter, boss?" Billy asked. He had

forgotten that the older man stood behind him, wanting only a glimpse of a *gussied-up* Grace Cavanaugh.

Dillon opened the door and stepped aside, allowing Billy a brief peek inside Grace's room, and then he pulled it shut again, keeping his hand on the doorknob.

Billy nodded his head in silent agreement.

Grace tried to open the door, but Dillon held it firmly shut as he tried to think. He just needed a few more days—another way to break the news to Abigail. He allowed the door to open just an inch or two.

"You're not going to the party, Grace," he said coldly.

"I most certainly am," she said confidently through the crack in the door. "I've spent hours getting ready, and I certainly do not intend to spend the evening up here while you—"

"Give me the dress," Dillon interrupted. He was answered with complete silence.

He pushed into the room with a deep sigh. "Billy, take her trunk." He blocked Grace's path to the door while Billy sheepishly did as he was told.

"Billy, don't you dare," Grace begged, but her eyes remained on Dillon, and remained defiantly angry.

"He works for me," Dillon said softly.

Billy stood by the door while Dillon searched the room. He took Grace's filthy yellow dress as well as the trunk, leaving nothing but her small carpetbag. He even looked inside that, and was satisfied that no clothing was concealed there.

"You can't be serious, Becket," Grace snapped.

Billy removed her trunk from the room, leaving Dillon alone with Grace. Her eyes flashed at him, and he really couldn't blame her for being angry. But neither could he allow her to meet Abigail looking like this. There was no way he could explain his actions to her, either.

"I'm going into the hall," Dillon said calmly. "I want you to take off that dress and hand it to me."

"You're insane," she whispered.

"Not yet, but I'm gettin' there."

"I will not—"

"If you don't give me the dress, I'll take it off of you myself," he threatened.

Grace opened her mouth to protest, but was silent as she apparently recognized the determination in his eyes. Her mouth snapped shut in enraged surrender, but her eyes . . . her eyes were like blue fire. There was no surrender in those eyes.

Dillon retreated to the hallway and leaned stiffly against the wall. He didn't have long to wait before the door opened, just a few inches, and the ice blue satin was thrust through the opening.

"I hope you're happy, Becket," she said coldly.

Dillon ran his fingers over the heavy satin in his hands as Grace slammed the door to her room shut.

"As happy as I'm likely to get," he muttered under his breath. "Billy will be right here," he said to the door. "In case you get any ideas about coming downstairs in your drawers."

He was answered with complete silence.

Grace paced in the elegant bedroom, her arms hugged to her body. How dare he! How dare he strip her and leave her with nothing more than her underthings! So he was afraid she would embarrass him in front of his friends.

"I didn't want to go anyway," she muttered to herself. "Any friends of Becket's can't possibly be worth the time and effort it would no doubt take to penetrate their thick skulls. I can just imagine the scintillating conversation I'll be missing. All about cows and manure and such."

"Miss Grace?" Billy's voice was muffled though the thick door. "Are you all right?"

Until he'd spoken Grace hadn't realized that her voice had been continually rising as she talked to herself. She glared at the door, but refused to answer. Traitor. She'd begun to believe that Billy was her friend. What a silly notion.

"Miss Grace?" There was alarm in his voice.

"Don't worry, Billy," she answered him sharply. "I'm just fine, and I'm still here. The drop from the window is a bit much for me, even if I were likely to attempt escape by that route wearing nothing but my unmentionables."

Billy was silent, and Grace felt a smidgen of satisfaction. She'd embarrassed him again, no doubt. No more than he deserved.

She threw herself on the bed face first, burying her nose in the sapphire blue coverlet that felt cool against her too-warm face. Blast him! Blast all men, especially Dillon Becket. He was so smug, so sure of himself. How dare he take away her clothes and keep her prisoner in this room? She yanked at the covers and wrapped them around her shoulders, cocooning herself against Dillon Becket and the rest of the world. He would be sorry. Somehow . . . some way . . . if it was the last thing she ever did . . .

Grace looked down at the sheets she was sitting on. White as newly fallen snow, soft and satiny to her touch. A mischievous smile crept across her face and stole away the uncertainty that plagued her.

With a spark of life in her heart again, Grace pulled the silk sheets from the bed and quickly wrapped one around her body. One look in the cheval glass showed her that the line of her drawers was much too evident, and the chemise bunched unattractively under the thin silk. She dropped the sheet and stripped to the skin.

So Dillon Becket was ashamed of her, just as her father had always been. She had never been good enough, or smart enough, and even when she'd begun to mature and turn into what some people called a little beauty, it had been all wrong. Even at ten years old she'd looked too much like her mother to suit her still-grieving father.

Once again she wrapped the white silk around her body, more carefully this time. After a few sloppy attempts she managed to drape one end of the silk over her left shoulder, leaving the right shoulder bare. She rummaged through the jewelry she had discarded on the dresser, and opened the carved box. The piece she wanted was sitting on top of a jumble of jewels. With a smile Grace took the serpent pin Mikhail had given her and pinned it at her breast, securing the sheet in place.

Grace studied her reflection in the tall mirror. And frowned. She looked like a woman wrapped up in a sheet. With a critical eye she took down her hair and brushed it until it hung straight down her back. That was a little better.

She ran her fingers through the jewelry that sparkled on the dresser. A short choker of diamonds and rubies, a perfect complement to the pin she wore, was fastened at her throat. She slipped on one bracelet and then another, and then another. It didn't matter that the styles and the gems didn't match. Grace wore pearls and emeralds and topazes on one wrist, rubies and sapphires and garnets on the other. When she moved she clanged merrily, like a pocket full of silver.

She turned to the mirror again. Better. She pinched her cheeks and bit her lips, making the color rise in her pale face, and then she glanced down at the remaining gems on the dresser, and lifted the final piece.

A garnet choker was laid atop her head and pinned into place. The gems circled her head, and tiny lengths of worked gold that were placed between the garnets dropped against her hair and her forehead.

The sheet dragged against the floor, and Grace lifted the hem of her makeshift gown. At least Becket hadn't taken her slippers, though she would have gone downstairs in her bare feet, if necessary.

"Billy?" she called tentatively at the closed door. "Are you still there?"

There was a short pause before Billy answered. "Yes, Miss Grace. I'm right here."

"I'm sorry I was so rude to you earlier," she said pitifully. "But I was disappointed."

"You don't need to apologize to me, Miss Grace," he said gruffly. "I'm just sorry . . . well, the boss don't mean to be a jackass, most of the time."

"So it just comes naturally to him?" Grace smiled, pleased with herself already.

"I reckon."

She leaned toward the closed door, placing her

nose almost in the crack. "Billy, could I ask you to do me a favor?"

"I can't bring you no clothes," he said quickly. "The boss made me promise."

"It's not that. I'm . . . I'm rather hungry. Do you think you could manage to sneak me up a little something to eat? And some water, perhaps? I hate to be a bother."

On the other side of the door, Billy sighed heavily. "Of course, Miss Grace," he said, evidently relieved that her request was so simple.

There was a single heavy footstep moving away from the door. "And Billy?" she called hesitantly. "Just slide it inside the door. I'm suddenly very tired. Arguing with Becket is quite exhausting, I've discovered. I might even take a short nap before I eat."

Billy agreed, and Grace listened with her ear pressed against the door as the heavy man strode down the hallway and descended the stairs. It took only a moment to arrange the fat pillows under the blue coverlet, so that if Billy did glance toward the bed when he slid her requested food into the room he would believe she was sleeping there.

She glanced toward the bed, one hand on the doorknob. It did look as though someone slept there, she thought with a small smile. And then she opened the door and stepped into the carpeted hallway.

Grace slipped noiselessly down the stairs, listening to the sounds of the party as they drifted toward her. People laughing and talking. The clink of glasses against silver trays.

She stood in the doorway, to the side where no one could see her, until she spotted Becket. He was conversing with a simpering blonde, most likely Abigail Wilkinson. His back was to her, and she kept her eyes on that back as she slipped into the room and headed in the opposite direction. Away from Dillon Becket.

There were at least thirty people in the airy room, she judged, mingling in small groups and drinking from fine crystal. It didn't take long for her to get herself noticed.

A very tall, very blond man approached her with what she instantly recognized as a lecherous grin and an interested sparkle in his narrowed brown eyes.

"Ma'am." His drawl was definitely Texan, slow and lazy and casual. Honey brown eyes peered strongly, intimately into her own. "I don't believe we've met. It's rude of me to introduce myself, I know, but your beauty has taken my breath away, and I couldn't wait for someone to introduce us properly." He grinned, and Grace returned his smile. A charmer. She knew how to handle a man like this one.

"Kind sir." She mimicked the accent Mikhail had spoken with, the accent of a Russian who spoke English with little difficulty. "I . . . I very much appreciate your kindness. I know no one here, but for my master."

His eyebrows raised slightly at this, but he said nothing about her *master*. "My name is Wade. Wade Wilkinson." Grace extended her hand and he took it, kissing her knuckles softly, gallantly. "And if you will tell me your name," he said in a low voice, lifting his eyes to her again, "you will know two people here tonight."

Grace bit her lower lip. This man was Abigail Wilkinson's brother, and this was his house. "My new name is Grace. Everyone must call me Grace now." Her accent was pronounced, but not too heavy.

Wade Wilkinson continued to hold her hand, and to look at her with that amused twinkle in his eyes. He was quite handsome, she had to admit, in a colorless sort of way. His sun-bronzed face was nicely shaped, his hair and eyes earthy, his mouth a bit too wide.

"My real name," she continued unshaken, "is Nadezhda Borisovna Khachaturyan, but that is much too difficult for my master's tongue. You see, after he von me—"

"After he *won* you?"

Grace nodded, and then dropped her head so she was looking at the floor. She sighed very deeply and wished silently that Wade Wilkinson would release her hand. "Yes." She breathed the word. "Lost on a turn of the cards. A sad state to find oneself in after . . . well, life was so different before . . . before my father died." She continued to stare at the rug beneath her feet, afraid to look into Wilkinson's face lest she smile.

"What happened, darlin'?"

It was all the prodding Grace needed to continue. "My family vas a part of the Russian aristocracy. Ve lived in a palace near St. Petersburg, and I vas to marry a prince. Prince Mikhail." She lifted her eyes to the man who towered over her. "But my father died, and my brother Vladimir took me from my home. He . . . he had taken up with the *narodniki*, the radical students who rouse the peasants to violence. Vladimir sold me, and I left my country on a very big sheep."

"A sheep?"

Grace stared unflinchingly and unsmilingly into the man's face. "Yes, Mr. Vilkinson, a sheep. The captain of the sheep took me to New Orleans to be sold, but he lost me in a game of chance to my new master. He has been most kind," she said humbly.

Wade Wilkinson continued to smile at her. "Well, this is most interesting. Abigail's parties are usually as dull as ditch water. Just exactly who is your . . . master?"

Grace turned her head slightly, catching a glimpse of Becket's back. "Master Dillon." She pointed surreptitiously to the other side of the room. "Please do not tell him I am here." A hint of desperation entered her voice. "I beg of you, sir. I vas told to remain upstairs, but ven I heard the people talking, the people laughing"—she sighed wistfully—"I had to come down, just for a moment."

"Why would he make you stay upstairs?" At last Wade's grin faded.

"He is ashamed of me. Ashamed of my terrible accent. He says to me, 'Grace, ven vill you learn to speak correctly. You are embarrassment to me, Grace.'

"I am ashamed. He thinks I am a most inadequate concubine."

Wade's eyes nearly popped out of his head, and Grace noticed with pleasure that she was attracting a small crowd. "Concubine?" the rancher asked in a harsh whisper.

"Yes." Grace cocked her head to one side. "Do not all Texans have concubines?"

Another man whispered into Wade's ear, and Wade pointed to Becket, who was still lost in conversation with his pasty blonde.

"Dillon Becket?" The second man's eyes widened.

A young girl, surely no more than eighteen years old, stepped forward, her eyes wide with wonder. "Did I hear you say that you're from Russia? And you were going to marry a prince?"

"Once that vas true." Grace turned to the girl and kept her face as solemn as she could. It was proving to be more and more difficult. "But no more. I find myself reduced to this. I vas educated to marry a prince, and now I have been reduced to chattel." Her voice was low and sad. "But I must learn to accept my fate. At least Master Dillon doesn't beat me quite so much as my last master, the horrible captain of the sheep."

Wade leaned closer to her, staking his claim in a primal sort of way. "Darlin', if Dillon ever lays a hand on you, you just let me know. We don't beat our women here in Texas."

"Tank you, Mr. Vilkinson," Grace managed to whisper.

"Call me Wade."

"Vade," she said shyly.

Everything was going beautifully, and then Grace heard a familiar voice bellowing her name.

Chapter Six

Dillon spared little attention for the slowly growing crowd on the opposite side of the room. Abigail was flirting with him as shamelessly as Grace had flirted with that damn bandit, smiling and laughing, batting her lashes, and he was enjoying it. It was nice to spend an evening with a woman who was pleasant, and mild mannered, and sweet. Abigail made him forget, for a few moments, about the woman who was sitting upstairs, unclothed and under guard.

At least, he tried to convince himself that he had forgotten about Grace.

But finally it seemed that every person in the room, but for Abigail and himself, was gathered together—a cluster of craning necks and close-pressed bodies—and his concentration was disturbed.

"What's going on over there?"

Abigail fluttered her eyelashes and whipped

open her lace fan. "Shall we find out?" She laid her hand on his offered arm, and they walked together toward the mob.

Several party guests in the pressing crowd glanced over their shoulders, and when they saw Dillon approaching with Abigail they moved aside, parting and making a pathway to the center of the mob.

As a blue-clad female body moved away Dillon saw a woman's back, and he knew it was Grace. Whether it was the hair or her shape, a shape that was all too clear in whatever the hell she was wearing, he didn't know. But she lifted her arms in the air in a perfectly synchronized motion, palms upward, and lamplight sparkled off the multitude of bracelets at her wrist.

He hadn't planned to bellow her name, but couldn't have stopped himself if he'd wanted to. Her name flew from his lips in a shout that shook the rafters and quieted the room. Even Abigail was shocked into silence, and she released his arm and stepped away.

Grace turned to face him, her movements deliberate and sensual, a slightly victorious smile appearing briefly on her face. It was a smile meant for him alone, just before she dropped to the floor in a fluid motion.

She placed herself at his feet, an offering of white silk and glimmering jewels, of pale skin and shimmering black hair.

"I am so sorry, Master Dillon," Grace said to the floor, her strange accent muffled. "I am vicked voman to disobey your command."

"What the hell are you doing down here?" he yelled, still stunned by her appearance. "And why are you talking like that?"

"Like vat, Master Dillon?" she asked innocently.

"Stop that, dammit," he demanded, grabbing her arm and pulling her to her feet.

"Do not beat me, Master Dillon," she pleaded most convincingly. "I vill do better. I vill practice my English every day."

Wade stepped forward chivalrously. "It doesn't seem fair to punish the girl for her accent. I personally find it charming. And you must admit she speaks English a whole hell of a lot better than any of us speak Russian."

Several guests agreed, and Dillon could only shake his head in wonder. "Russian?"

"No." Grace turned a sorrowful face to the crowd. "I am in Russia no longer. I must learn to speak proper English."

Abigail stepped forward, her lips a thin line, her eyes no longer sparkling and flirtatious. "Dillon? This is Grace?" Her voice was a harsh whisper. "I thought you said . . . I expected . . . and you said she was tired from the trip."

Wade grinned wickedly and leaned forward just slightly. He was enjoying himself too damn much. "She's his concubine," he said in a low, but not very low, voice.

"What?" Dillon bellowed.

Abigail began to fan herself furiously. "Dillon, can you please explain this?"

Grace's eyes were wide and innocent. "Is not right word, concubine, Master Dillon? Slave? Mistress?"

"Shut up, Grace," Dillon warned.

Wade placed himself protectively at Grace's side.

"Damned indecent of you, Dillon. Berating the girl for her accent and banishing her to her room." Wade gazed down at Grace, and it was clear that he was captivated. "Darlin', we don't have slaves in Texas. You can go anywhere you want to, and Dillon Becket can't stop you."

Dillon took a single step backward and crossed his arms over his chest, pushing his anger aside. "Yes," he said calmly. "You can go anywhere you want, Grace. Anytime." He let his eyes rest on her slender throat and a bare shoulder.

She stared at the floor, and after a moment she lifted her face to look into his eyes. For a second, perhaps, there was no artifice there, no devilish glee. "But I have nowhere to go," she whispered.

Quickly a false smile stole over her face. "So now I am going to live in Texas, on a very big ranch. Vith cows and horses and Indians."

Abigail studied Grace from head to foot, her eyes widening as she realized, about the same time Dillon did, that his ward was dressed in a sheet.

"What is that you're wearing?" Abigail asked softly.

Grace turned her full attention to Abigail, and Dillon definitely did not like the fire he saw in those bluebonnet eyes. "It is a simple costume," Grace said serenely. "All that my Master Dillon vill allow me to vear. He has taken all my clothes from me," she revealed in a voice that was only slightly lowered. "I had some suitable English costumes, but my master has taken them all avay."

Grace turned those burning eyes to Dillon. "Is that not correct, master?" It was a challenge. She was telling the truth, in a way, at least as far as her clothing was concerned.

He could have argued, but decided against it. "I reckon that's about right," he drawled.

Grace returned her attention to Abigail, studying her hostess's gown with apparent avid interest. "You are vearing a most interesting costume yourself. Vy do American vomen vish to make their derrieres appear so very . . . so very . . ." She cocked her head to one side and craned her neck to get a better look at Abigail's bustle. She gestured with her hands, bracelets rattling as she held her hands far apart. "Vide?" she finally finished.

"Grace." Dillon faced her with his arms crossed and a deepening frown on his face. "Go to your room."

Grace bowed deeply at the waist, her palms together at her breasts. The gold and jewels across her forehead danced against her pale skin. "As you command, Master Dillon. I vill be vaiting for you." Her voice was soft, but not so soft that every pair of straining ears in the room couldn't hear.

"Let her stay, Dillon," Wade chimed in, his interest in Grace clear on his face. Dillon wanted to smash his grinning lips. "She's a charming girl. No need to keep her all to yourself."

"I am not—" Dillon began.

Grace turned to her rapt admirers. It was clear whose side they were on as they glared at Dillon. "No," Grace said sweetly. "I must obey my master. It has been most pleasurable to meet you all. Perhaps some of you vill come to see me after I am settled at my master's ranch, if he vill allow it, and I vill try not to embarrass him vith my poor English. I need much practice."

She turned and bowed once more to Dillon, as he maintained his stiff stance and held his tongue. He knew, deep down, that if his control broke he was going to kill her.

"I vill see you in a short vile, Master Dillon," she whispered loudly.

Every eye in the room was on her back as she left the room, walking slowly and seductively to the door. Once there she lifted the sheet from around her feet and fairly ran toward the stairs.

Billy looked from Grace to the closed door and back again. "Miss Grace, I thought . . . I thought you was asleep."

Grace threw open the door and turned to the silver-haired man who had almost become a friend to her.

"Whatever you do, Billy," she said breathlessly, "don't allow Becket to enter this room."

"Why, the boss ain't gonna—" Billy stopped short when Becket appeared at the top of the stairs, and Grace slammed the heavy door shut.

But there was no lock, no bolt, and she didn't think that even Billy could keep her safe from Dillon Becket now.

By the time the door crashed open, Grace had removed herself to the far corner of the room, and she had armed herself with the only weapon she could find—a porcelain vase filled with water and freshly cut white roses.

"Stay right where you are, Becket," she said firmly.

Against Billy's protests, Becket closed the door. Grace could actually feel her heart sinking. He was going to kill her. She could read that intent in his eyes.

She held the vase in position, ready to heave it toward his head, if necessary.

"I should beat you to within an inch of your life, Grace Cavanaugh," he said much too calmly.

"You wouldn't dare," Grace said with more courage than she felt.

Becket didn't move away from the door. He just stood there and stared at her, those gray eyes narrowed and speculative. When he finally did move, all he did was loosen his knotted tie and unfasten the top button of his white linen shirt.

Grace let her arms fall just a little. Becket didn't look as if he intended to rush at her. At least not right away.

And then, amazingly, he smiled. It was a brief and extremely small smile, but it was there just the same.

"Russian, huh?"

"You shouldn't have taken my gown and tried to force me to stay in my room. I'm not a child, you know!"

"No, Grace," Becket said in a low voice, that hint of a smile reappearing on his face. "You're not a child."

He paced back and forth in front of the closed door, and the smile faded. Becket remained silent, and Grace finally relaxed enough to return the vase to the bedside table.

Becket stopped pacing and looked at her. "Concubine, you said?"

Grace could feel the color drain from her face, and knew she stood before him with her face as white as the sheet she wore. "It was a joke, Becket," she said bravely.

He stared directly at her and raised an eyebrow. "A joke? Is that what it was?"

Whatever the reason, his anger had faded, and he appeared to be amused with her. "That's too bad," he drawled lazily. "I'd begun to think that a concubine might be just what I need. And I really would prefer to be called Master Dillon, if you please. I like the sound of that."

Grace clasped her hands at her waist, searching desperately for a way to change the subject. She definitely didn't like the smug expression on Dillon Becket's face.

"Tell me, Becket." She spat his name, trying to make him angry again. "Weren't you planning to introduce me to your lady friend? Abigail, I believe her name is."

It worked. His face was solemn once again, his eyes like granite and his jaw clenched as he tugged at his already loosened collar.

"You would have met Abigail soon enough." His eyes traveled slowly over her body. She could almost feel his eyes on her breasts and her hips as he swept his gaze over her.

"When I do introduce you—properly—you can explain why it was you saw fit to attend one of her parties dressed in a sheet."

He looked at the bed, at the rumpled coverlet and the fat pillow form beneath. It had fooled Billy, but as Becket raised his eyebrows, Grace had a feeling she would never fool him so easily.

Becket looked up and took a single step toward her, and Grace's response was to lay a hand on the vase at her side. He stopped, and for a few seconds neither of them moved. Grace found that she was holding her breath . . . waiting . . . waiting . . .

Finally Becket turned away from her. "Get a good night's sleep, Grace," he barked. "Tomorrow morning we go home."

The Double B was evidently a smaller place than the Wilkinson ranch, and the ranch house itself was much plainer. It was in need of paint, and not nearly so grand in design as Abigail's house.

But there was something inviting about it. The two-story house was rustic but warm. Someone cared for the place.

There were blooming flowers climbing the railing that encircled the porch, and lace curtains in the windows. None of that was Dillon Becket's doing, she was certain.

He was in a frightfully calm mood, for a man who always seemed as if he were about to explode. He had remained so even as they'd left the hospitality of the Wilkinson ranch to Abigail's repeated and almost desperate insistence that Grace stay there.

She had heard the muted whispers. "Not proper," a frowning Abigail had insisted. "No trouble at all," the insipid blonde had practically hissed.

Grace wished that Wade hadn't been there. He'd evidently been let in on the joke, and grinned from ear to ear, standing on the porch and watching as she sat in the carriage and waited for Becket to conclude his business. Her little escapade suddenly seemed foolish. She tried to avoid Wade's brazen stare, but found that was impossible. Every time she glanced out the window she found him watching her. By the time they'd left, Wade Wilkinson had resembled a mindless, grinning fool.

Grace's door swung open, and Becket was there to help her take her first step onto Double B soil. He offered his hand with that infuriating look on his face. Amused, but not smiling. Content, but still near the bursting point. There was a look in those gray eyes that she didn't like at all.

A woman practically burst through the front door, her wide hips and bosom heaving as she walked quickly across the porch and down the steps.

"Where is she?" the gray-haired woman asked, excitement in her voice and on her pleasant face. "Where is that little girl?"

The woman was nearly face-to-face with Becket and with Grace, trying to peek over their shoulders and into the carriage. One corner of Becket's mouth turned up. Not a smile, Grace conceded, but the beginnings of one just the same.

"Olivia Grant, I'd like you to meet Grace Cavanaugh." He nodded to Grace, and the woman's smile faded momentarily. Then she gave Grace a motherly hug. Grace stiffened in the woman's arms, feeling smothered, and she pulled away as soon as she could.

"Well, I'll bet you were quite a surprise for Dillon," Olivia said, hazel eyes sparkling. Grace had to look down at the woman, who didn't stand quite a full five feet tall. "We all thought—"

"I'm starving, Olivia," Becket interrupted. "What have you got in the kitchen?"

He did his best to change the subject, but it was much too late. Grace had figured it out as soon as Olivia had asked about the *little girl*.

Grace looked over her shoulder and up to Dillon Becket. He was silent, and peered down at her with an almost sheepish expression on his face.

"So I was not quite what you expected, Becket?"

He shook his head.

"I'm sorry," Grace said, meaning it. "I should

have thought of that. My father . . . he . . ." she faltered.

"He always called you *the baby*," Becket offered by way of an explanation.

Grace forced a smile she didn't feel as she tried to make light of it. "I know. If my mother hadn't named me before she died, I don't suppose I would even have a name. To be honest, I'm surprised that he spoke of me at all. I was rather a disappointment to him."

The look that crossed Becket's face could have been pity or anger, but it vanished quickly, leaving him with that mask of control well in place. "Then he wasn't as smart a man as I gave him credit for being."

Grace pulled her eyes away from him and turned to the house. She didn't want his pity. She'd accepted her father's indifference, and even his hatred, long ago. Or so she tried to convince herself. "Nice house, Becket." She smiled at Olivia Grant. "I suppose you're the one responsible for the flowers and the more civilized amenities?"

Olivia nodded and took Grace's arm, leading her toward the porch. "That's the truth. As well as the cooking and the gardening, the chickens and the housekeeping. These boys are enough to drive a woman to drink." She gave Becket a sharp glance over her shoulder, but there was love there, too. "And it certainly will be nice to have a little female company around here."

Olivia chattered as she escorted Grace up the stairs and across the porch, leaving Becket and Billy to deal with what remained of Grace's baggage and to see to the horses and Abigail's carriage.

At the doorway Grace paused and glanced

back at the carriage. Dillon Becket was watching her with hooded eyes and the beginnings of a smile on his face.

Dillon watched Grace enter the house. His house. The door swung shut, shielding her from view.

He wasn't sure exactly when the decision had been made. Maybe it had been a gradual thing. Something that had started the moment he'd seen her, before he'd known that she was Colonel Cavanaugh's daughter. Maybe it had begun with his first glimpse into those bluebonnet eyes.

He wasn't certain when it had started, but he did know the exact moment the realization had struck him. She'd been standing in the corner of the Wilkinsons' guest bedroom, wrapped in a sheet and holding a vase as though she had every intention of hurling it at his head. There had been quite a lot of determination in those eyes, and a little bit of fear there, too. He didn't want Grace to be afraid of him.

His life had been damn dull before he'd met Grace, and the future had never promised to be much better. She was hardheaded and ornery and had a tendency to pull the damnedest stunts when she didn't get her way. She was spoiled and uppity and didn't like to be touched.

But when she slept she gravitated to him, and she rested in his arms as if she were searching for protection, for warmth. There was something in those eyes . . . something she held back . . . something he wanted to touch.

Whatever the reason, he was seriously questioning his intent to find her a husband. He didn't know how he was going to accomplish it, but he intended to keep her.

* * *

Olivia led the way up a narrow staircase, and Grace followed directly behind her. The interior of Becket's house was plain, but washed with light from several windows, and it had a comfortable feel. The furniture she'd seen thus far had been utilitarian, well worn but also well cared for. There were no fancy lamps, no mirrors on the walls. The rooms were almost devoid of color, dominated by oiled wood.

Warm. Every room in the house was meant to be lived in. Every piece of furniture she'd seen was meant to be used. There were no delicate chairs Billy would have to avoid, no tables with spindly legs.

"This will be your room, dear," Olivia said, pushing open the first door on the left as they reached the second floor.

It was, like the rest of the house, plain. A room meant for sleeping, and changing clothes, and perhaps finding a moment of quiet at the end of the day. There was no cheval glass, no vase of roses, no delicate figurines.

There was a large bed neatly made with a multicolored quilt, and a huge dresser that would certainly hold all Grace owned, and more. There was a hard-backed chair by the open window, and a fresh breeze cooled the room.

"It's lovely," Grace said sincerely. "I do hope I'm not taking someone else's room."

Olivia shook her head, and her smile faded. "No. This was Jimmy's room. He's passed on."

Grace's eyes widened, and she stared at the big, empty bed.

"Oh, no," Olivia said quickly when she noted Grace's reaction. "Not here. Jimmy passed on years ago . . . in the war, actually. He was Dillon's older brother."

Grace looked down at the woman who was trying so hard to make her comfortable in Becket's home. "What about the rest of the family?"

"There's just Dillon now," Olivia said in a low voice. She laid a hand on Grace's arm, and patted it comfortingly. "His mother passed on in sixty-seven, and his pa died four months ago. There was another brother, but . . ." Her voice broke, and Grace found herself comforting the older woman, patting her hand, drawing her a little closer.

"I'm sorry. I didn't mean to stir up bad memories for you."

Her heart broke for Becket, too. He was alone, just as she was. The only difference was that he'd had a family for a while and lost them. She'd never had a family at all. Which was worse?

It didn't matter. Alone was alone. And Becket had Billy, and Olivia . . . and Abigail.

Olivia shook off her melancholy and brightened noticeably as she looked up at Grace.

"We're so happy to have you here, child," she said, and she smiled as if she really meant it.

"Thank you, Mrs. Grant."

Olivia laughed and took Grace's hand in her own, patting it softly. "It's Olivia, dear."

"Olivia," Grace said softly, and she felt, for a moment, close to tears. Somehow she felt as if she'd known this woman all her life. Could trust her. Could share with her even her deepest secrets.

What she really wanted was to ask Olivia about Dillon Becket. Had he always been so hard? Had there been a time when he'd laughed with ease?

But she didn't, and Olivia finished the tour of the house without mentioning again the ill-fated Beckets.

Chapter Seven

Perhaps this wouldn't be such a bad place to stay for just a little while, Grace conceded as she ran a cloth over the back of the sofa that sat in the middle of the Becket parlor. She certainly had no intention of staying in the dust-covered and crude country for the rest of her life, but there was a certain peace here that she felt she needed.

Peace and quiet while she gathered her wits and decided what to do next.

She felt that peace strongly, here in the parlor Olivia had set her to dusting. It was a room obviously rarely used, and still she could sense the family Dillon Becket had once had here.

His mother must have chosen the furniture. The sofa was covered with a floral fabric, and the legs were finely carved. It was the only piece of furniture in the entire house that could be called frivolous. There were figurines on the two small tables in the room—a peasant man and an old woman, facing one another across the parlor.

And there were pictures. Just a few. The one that drew her eye again and again was a family portrait, the pose formal and the faces solemn.

It pictured an unsmiling couple and three somber boys. The mother was standing behind the seated father, Dillon Becket's father, with her hand on his shoulder. She was flanked on either side by strapping boys who appeared to be perhaps thirteen and fifteen. They looked a lot like Becket, like Dillon, with their sharp noses and dark hair that curled just a little.

And there was Becket, seated next to his father. He was the youngest, maybe ten or eleven years old when the picture was made, and already she could see that defiant spark in his eyes. He looked like his father. All three of the boys did. None of them had inherited their mother's fair hair or sweet mouth. They were all harshly handsome, hardened like their father even as children.

Grace reached out a finger and touched the little Dillon's face. He was the only one, now, and she understood how Olivia could cry for them, even after all this time.

She heard the front door open, and the dust rag flew to the picture. It wouldn't do for her to be caught studying Becket's picture so closely.

"Anybody home?" the cheerful voice called loudly, and Grace sighed. She wasn't exactly disappointed that it wasn't Dillon Becket entering the house in the middle of the day, but she didn't exactly relish the thought of facing that grinning fool Wade Wilkinson, either.

Grace looked down at the calico dress Olivia had insisted she wear. It was worn and plain, and just a little too large for her.

When she lifted her eyes, Wade Wilkinson was standing in the doorway, a wide grin on his face.

"Howdy, princess," he said lightly.

Grace could feel the heat rising in her face.

"Now, don't be going all shy on me, darlin'," Wade said as he stepped into the parlor, his dusty hat in his hand. "Well, now, I take that back. You sure are extra pretty when you blush like that. Puts roses in your cheeks."

Grace took a deep breath, calming herself as she placed the dust rag on the back of the sofa. "Have you come to see Becket? I'll see if I can find him for you."

At that moment she would have given anything to have Dillon Becket in the room. She didn't like Wade Wilkinson. Not at all.

"No," he said as he walked toward her. "I don't want to see Dillon. I came to see you, princess."

"That's very kind," Grace said nervously, "but—"

"No kindness intended," Wade said in a low voice. "I just wanted to see if you were as pretty as I remembered. And you are. Though I must admit, I liked you better wrapped in a sheet than wearing that old calico. But darlin', nobody makes calico look as good as you do."

He took another step toward her, and Grace took a step back. "It was very silly of me to react so outrageously to Becket's suggestion that I stay in my room. I dread to think what everyone must think of me."

Wade's grin widened. "Don't worry, darlin'. It was a hoot. The whole town was laughing about it yesterday."

"Truly?"

Wade nodded his head. "Truly, darlin'. You've got spunk. I like that in my women."

Grace took another step back, and found she'd backed herself into a corner. What did Wade mean when he said *his women*?

He took another long stride, and she was trapped. Wade was too tall and too broad to try to go around, and he leaned one long arm against the wall beside her head.

"Abby told me what happened," he said, his face much too close to hers. "About your pa, and Dillon being your guardian and all. I thought maybe you"—he leaned closer, and Grace realized with mounting horror that he intended to kiss her—"and I could be friends."

He was lowering his face toward hers, and Grace moved her head back until it met the wall. She could smell him, she could feel his heat, and she wanted him to get away from her. But this was all happening too fast, and she couldn't make a sound.

Wade stopped when his lips were almost touching hers. He looked into her eyes . . . too deeply, too intimately. "Don't be scared, darlin'," he whispered. "I won't hurt you. I just want a little kiss."

Suddenly Wade was gone, his face jerked away from hers without warning. She looked up, and there was Becket, dragging the bigger man toward the hallway. Becket had Wade by the collar, and was practically choking his intended's brother as he pulled him out of the room.

Wade recovered, though, and jumped to his feet, jerking out of Becket's grasp. "What the hell?" he shouted hoarsely as he spun to face Becket.

"Out," Becket said simply, his voice low and calm.

Wade tugged at his collar and planted his feet

wide apart. "Not just yet." He turned his back on Becket, and faced her with a hint of a smile on his face. "I've come to ask if I can court Miss Grace."

"No," Becket said sharply.

Wade didn't move at all, not even to turn his head away from her. "I wasn't asking you, Dillon; I was asking Grace."

Grace didn't have a chance to answer before Becket answered for her. "No. I'm her guardian, and I'm the one you ask for permission to court her."

Wade sighed heavily and spun around to face Becket. Grace tried to catch her guardian's eye over the taller man's shoulder, but all of his attention was on Wade.

"All right," Wade drawled. "I didn't know you were going to be so damned persnickety about this." He squared his shoulders. "Mr. Becket, might I have the honor of courting your ward, the lovely Miss Grace Cavanaugh?" Sarcasm dripped from his words, words too sweet and easy.

Becket's eyes finally lit on her, briefly, and then his attention was back on Wade. "No," he said sharply and finally.

"Well, damn, Dillon," Wadc said, slapping his hat against his leg. "Why the hell not?"

There was a moment of silence, and finally Becket looked at Grace. His expression hadn't changed at all. It was hard, intractable, and Grace couldn't help but wonder what hc was thinking as he stared at her so intently.

"Grace? Would you like Wade to call on you again?"

She realized that she was shaking her head, quick, small hitches that were much too telling, but she stopped before Wade turned back around to face her. "It's too soon after my father's death," she said breathlessly, wishing that she could sound as assured as Dillon Becket always did.

"There you go," Becket drawled.

Wade left without his trademark smile on his face, with a curt good day to her and a scowl for Becket. Grace sat on the sofa and took a deep breath, her discomfort easing as she heard the front door slam and the racing hoofbeats that followed.

She hadn't even heard him reenter the room, but Becket was there, lowering himself to take the seat beside her. He was close, but didn't touch her.

He studied her for a moment before he spoke. "Wade didn't hurt you, did he?" There was a hint of alarm in his voice.

"No," Grace said softly, shaking her head. "I . . . I shouldn't have allowed him to upset me so."

How could she explain? *I had no warning.* There was no time to prepare for a confrontation with Wade Wilkinson. She had remembered, as he'd closed in on her, another time when a man had trapped her against a wall. But that had happened long ago, before she'd learned to watch her back. Before Dillon Becket had been there to rescue her.

She'd made a terrible mistake. For the first time in years she'd let her guard down, had allowed herself to relax. That was a horrible blunder.

Becket leaned back, removing his hat and dropping it onto the table beside the sofa. "Wade doesn't mean any harm. He's a bit rough around the edges. Thinks of himself as a real ladies' man, but he's really just a cowhand beneath those pretty words."

Grace was staring into her lap, at the dark blue flowers that danced against a paler blue cotton background. And then Becket's hand was beneath her chin, lifting her face upward so he could study her with those piercing gray eyes.

"You don't have to be afraid here, honey," he said in a low voice that was at once comforting. "I don't want to see you pale and shaking like this."

"I'm not—" Grace began.

He took a hand in his and lifted it. She could see it, the slight tremble that he had noticed.

Grace closed her fingers around his, trying to stop the tremors. His hands were warm and strong. "I'm sorry, Becket, really."

"Dillon," he whispered, leaning slightly forward, moving slowly but certainly toward her. He was going to kiss her.

She knew she could back away and he would stop. But she didn't want him to stop. She wanted to know what it felt like to be kissed by a man like Dillon Becket. There was no fear, as there had been when Wade had approached her, but her heart did beat a bit faster as his lips came close to hers.

Grace was still clasping his hand, and when his mouth was almost on hers his lips parted slightly. "Dillon," she whispered, and then she parted her lips as he had, more out of instinct than anything else. Her heart was going to come through her chest, and she couldn't breathe.

"Land sakes!" Olivia cried as she burst into the parlor.

Grace snapped her head back and away from Becket, and he jerked away from her as well.

"I was in the barn, and I saw one of the Wilkinson boys riding away from here like the devil himself was on his tail."

Olivia was wiping her hands on a towel, her eyes on that chore rather than on Grace and Dillon Becket. If she'd seen them and been shocked, she was hiding it well.

"It was Wade," Becket said calmly, his voice and his breathing normal. "He wants to court Grace."

"Oh!" Olivia's eyes lit up, and she smiled as she crossed the room. "How wonderful! Here only two days, and already you have a gentleman caller."

"I told him no." Becket stood and grabbed his hat, placing it on his head and tipping it back slightly.

"Whatever for?"

Becket strode from the room without a backward glance. "Grace can tell you."

She watched his retreating back, his chestnut hair curling just slightly over his collar, and . . . good heavens . . . she could see every muscle beneath that sweat-dampened shirt and those denim trousers.

"I'm not ready," she said in a small voice. "It's . . . it's too soon."

"Of course," Olivia said, taking Grace's hand. The same one Becket had held. "How thoughtless of me not to think of that."

Grace stood, allowing Olivia to continue to hold her hand. She'd been in this house two days, and already her defenses were crumbling. In a way it felt wonderful, and in another way it was terrifying.

Grace swung the bucket in her hand as she walked slowly toward the well. It hadn't taken long to discover that Olivia Grant never ceased moving, and she expected the same unflagging energy from everyone around her.

This afternoon Grace had found herself idle for a change. Nothing in her hands that needed to be filled, cleaned, mended, or peeled. The next moment Olivia had handed her the bucket.

She wouldn't complain. At least, not unless Becket made the mistake of asking her what she thought about her new home. She wasn't conscious of the smile that stole over her face until she was wearing a full-fledged grin. Becket. Yesterday he had very nearly kissed her, and she hadn't been frightened at all. Quite the contrary. She found his closeness to be exciting, exhilarating . . . and a little unsettling.

As unsettling as the bright sun that shone into her face. As unsettling as the fact that she found this place remarkably beautiful. The rustic buildings, the green hills, even the flat, dusty sections to the south. All beautiful. As beautiful as Dillon Becket himself. Dillon.

He didn't fit the picture of the ideal man she had always clung to. Cultured, pale, refined. Distant. He was none of those. He was dark and hard and full of controlled passion. Dillon Becket would have been as out of place in London as she was in Texas. More.

Because she had never really liked London. She had never been happy there.

Grace drew water from the well. It was more of an effort than she liked to admit, and she felt an unwelcome trickle of sweat down her back. What she wouldn't give for a bath! She had seen a small tub in Olivia's kitchen pantry, but she hadn't dared to ask about using it. Where would she bathe? Right there in the kitchen? Who would haul the water? She knew quite well who, and she wasn't certain that it would be worth the effort.

But she was tiring of those quick and inadequate attempts at cleaning herself with a washcloth and a basin of water in her room. She wanted to lower herself into a tub of water and close her eyes and sit for an hour.

The murmur of voices on the other side of the house disrupted her dream. One was strange. One was Dillon Becket's.

She glanced down at the disgustingly ugly brown dress she wore. It was old and faded and worn thin in places. It was also stained with sweat. She couldn't let Dillon see her like this.

Grace left the bucket there by the well and lifted the ugly brown skirt to run from the approaching voices. She rounded the corner and backed herself against the wall of the house.

"Is she here?" a strange voice asked anxiously.

"I reckon she's around here somewhere," Dillon drawled lazily.

Grace knew they were talking about her, and was doubly glad she'd run.

"I . . . ummm . . . I'd like to call on her, Dillon." The voice was hesitant, unsure, the voice of an anxious young man.

There were several seconds of strained silence before Dillon answered. "Grace is not receiving gentleman callers. She's still grieving for her father."

"Oh." It was a dejected response, almost mournful. "I'm sorry to hear that. Damn, she's the prettiest girl I ever saw. When do you think she might be . . . well . . . done with her grievin'?"

There was a hint of hope in that voice.

"I expect it will be quite some time," Dillon said emotionlessly.

There was a full minute of silence, and Grace peeked around the corner cautiously, curious as to what her would-be suitor looked like.

Dillon was leaning against the well, lighting a cigar as he squinted against the sun. Her caller had his back to her. He was the skinniest man she had ever seen, and was bow-legged to boot. He shifted back and forth nervously and wrung an abused hat in his hands.

"What?" he finally ventured. "You figure a month or more?"

Dillon lifted his head and Grace quickly snapped her head around so he wouldn't see her. "Maybe longer. I'll have to let you know."

She knew Dillon was not a patient man, and that was evident on his face at the moment.

"I just wanted to . . . I don't know . . . get a head start on the other men in Plummerton."

Dillon sighed, a long and loud sigh full of frustration. "Should I expect more callers for Grace?"

There was only silence, and Grace peeked around the corner again. Her would-be suitor was nodding his head up and down.

Dillon muttered under his breath.

Grace returned to her place, back against the wall, and a small smile crossed her face.

"Well, what do you expect, Dillon?" the man asked, his voice filled with his own frustration. "There's not that many comely women in these parts, and you've already got Abigail Wilkinson spoken for."

Grace's smile faded.

"You could do me a big favor, Clifford," Dillon said, ignoring the man's outburst.

"What's that?" Clifford asked suspiciously.

There was another long moment of silence, and Grace resisted the impulse to take another peek.

She heard another deep sigh before Dillon began to speak. "I've been a mite jittery lately. What with rustlers to worry about, and renegades. Did I tell you we ran into a band of Mexican bandits on our way from San Antone?"

There was a brief pause. Grace didn't look to see if Clifford was nodding or shaking his head.

"Well, we did," Dillon continued. "Yep, I've been real jittery lately. Why, I reckon if I saw a stranger riding up toward the house . . . I might just have to shoot first and ask questions later."

"I . . . I . . . I . . ." Clifford stammered. "I've known you all my life, Dillon," he said nervously. "I'm no stranger."

Grace heard a loud, *tsk*ing sound. Dillon, no doubt.

"That's true. And I like you, Clifford, I really do. Did I tell you that my eyes are gettin' real bad?"

Another moment of silence. Grace didn't have to peek to imagine Clifford shaking his head vigorously.

"Yep. I'd feel just awful if I shot you or anybody else arriving unexpectedly here at the Double B. Just awful."

"I . . . I 'spect you would," Clifford said lamely. "I . . . I'll see you a-around. Maybe in town sometime."

"Clifford?" Dillon called in a voice that was suddenly light.

"What?"

"Spread the word, would you? About my bad eyesight and rustlers and Grace not receiving any visitors."

"Sure, Dillon," Clifford called nervously. "I'll do just that."

Grace stood with her back against the wall for a few long moments. She heard heavy footsteps in the dirt, going back the way they'd come. One pair of boots or two? She couldn't be certain. It wouldn't hurt to stand in the shade for a moment or two longer, in any case.

The smile that had disappeared at the mention of Abigail Wilkinson's name stole back. There would be no more awkward visits from men like Wade Wilkinson and the frightened Clifford. Dillon had taken care of that. As he seemed to take care of everything.

"You can come out now," Dillon said tiredly.

Grace peeked around the corner and saw Dillon standing by the well and looking right at her. It was too late to retreat again.

"Good afternoon," she said formally.

Dillon dropped a half-finished cigar into the dirt and ground out the tip with his boot.

What should she say? *Thank you*? It seemed an odd response, but appropriate. Before she could say anything, Olivia burst through the kitchen door.

"Land sakes, where is that water?" she asked brightly. Grace stepped around the corner and Dillon turned away, walking steadily and with long strides toward the barn.

Grace went to the well, her eyes on Dillon's back the entire time, and picked up the half-filled bucket. "Sorry," she said as she turned toward Olivia. "I'm afraid I was being horribly lazy and hiding in the shade for a moment."

Olivia just laughed. "No harm in that, child," she said warmly. "There's nothing quite as decadent, or as wonderful, as a stolen moment in the shade on a warm day."

The broad woman held the kitchen door open for Grace.

"Wonderful, yes," Grace agreed. She sighed. "But not as wonderful as a real bath, with soap, and water to my ears, and a fat and fluffy towel. And scented oil. Rose. No, lilac, I think," she said dreamily.

Olivia chuckled and took the bucket from Grace. "Do you want a bath, dear?"

Grace pushed away a sweat-dampened tendril of hair from her face. "Terribly."

"Well," Olivia said confidently. "We'll just have to see what we can do."

He was riding back to the house with an energy he normally didn't feel at the end of a long day.

Grace was there.

At least he hadn't been bothered with any more gentleman callers for her in the past few days. Clifford had done his job well.

He reined in his stallion as soon as the house was in view. There wasn't another place in the world like this one. No place more beautiful. No place he belonged the way he belonged here, on the Double B. It was more than his legacy; it was his heart.

Grace could learn to love it here just as much as he did.

A breeze kicked up and cooled his face. It was too soon to tell if he'd be able to offer Grace a life here, but he could imagine it well. Grace in his bed, the Double B secure again.

And he wondered, as he approached the house, if a man was meant to have everything he wanted.

* * *

Grace was concentrating so hard on the task before her that she didn't even hear Dillon until he was right behind her.

"Olivia has put you to work again, I see," he said lazily.

All she could do was glance over her shoulder to him. He was covered with dust, and sweat trickled down his face and neck. She'd seen very little of him in the days since he'd almost kissed her in the parlor. It had been five days since that almost-kiss she couldn't forget.

She'd been at the Double B a week, and she probably hadn't seen Dillon a dozen times.

Lots of work to catch up on, he'd explained one evening as he devoured the meal Olivia had prepared.

Right now he was covered with dust, and she was covered with flour. She was attempting to work the sticky biscuit dough with her hands, but her arms were white to the elbow, and while the apron she wore had caught the worst of it, her calico dress was pretty well covered, too.

Her own clothes had been deemed, by Olivia, to be unsuitable for everyday wear. The older woman had presented Grace with several plain dresses, dresses that had belonged to Olivia's daughter before the young Alice had outgrown them, married, and moved to Dallas.

"Well." Grace sighed with disgust. "These are supposed to be biscuits, but I'm not convinced yet." She stopped talking suddenly, her heart in her throat. Dillon was right behind her, so close she could feel the heat radiating off of his body and his breath against her neck.

"Looks like the makings for biscuits to me," Dillon said softly.

Grace had piled her hair on top of her head

earlier in the day, trying to keep herself as cool as possible, and his mouth was there, close to her skin. And then he leaned down and rested his chin on her shoulder.

Her initial response was to jerk away from him, but she didn't. In fact she rather liked it . . . though it made her so nervous her heart started to beat much too fast.

"What's the matter, Becket? So tired you can't keep your own head up?"

"Yep."

Grace punched the dough, and a glob stuck to her hand.

"You need more flour," Dillon said softly.

Grace grabbed a handful of flour and tossed it onto the dough. A cloud of flour rose off the dough, covering her even more than she already was. But he was right. As she worked the flour in, with Dillon's chin resting on her shoulder, the glob before her turned into biscuit dough. At least, it resembled the dough she'd watched Olivia work in the past several days.

One arm snaked around her waist as she kneaded the dough, and Dillon pulled her toward him—just a little—so that her back was against his chest. Grace started to protest, but the words caught in her throat. He'd been in the sun all day, and it was as if his skin had soaked up the sun, and now he was giving that heat to her . . . a gift at the end of the day.

She started to ask him what he was doing, but she was afraid if she did he would move away. Grace had never liked to be held, had cringed when exuberant friends hugged her and grown cold when men took her hand and kissed it. But this was different. Just as the almost-kiss had been different . . . just as Dillon Becket was different from every man she'd ever known.

So she kneaded the dough and ignored the hand that was splayed across her stomach and the breath at her neck. She pressed the heels of her hands into the dough, just as Olivia had instructed her, and folded the dough again and again. Dillon barely moved, except to begin rocking the thumb of the hand at her midsection back and forth in a slow, steady motion. When Grace looked down she could see the movement of that hand, trapped between her apron and the rose-colored calico.

"So," Dillon drawled. "How do you like the Double B so far?"

Grace started slightly at his question, and kept her eyes on the biscuit dough. "Just fine. It's really very peaceful here, if a little hot."

"Wait till summer gets here. August can be a real killer."

Grace licked her dry lips and beat the biscuit dough viciously. "Olivia is very nice, and so is Billy." She tried to keep her voice even, but there was a slight tremble there.

"What about me, Grace? Am I . . . nice?"

Grace's heart had been beating fast, and now it beat so rapidly she couldn't get a good breath. Dillon's hand moved upward, just slightly, so that it rested under her breast, over her heart.

"I . . . I've barely seen you since I got here," Grace said, emphasizing her words with a swift blow to the dough. "But you've never struck me as being particularly nice."

He murmured, apparently in agreement, and just when Grace was prepared to turn around and gently push him away, he slanted his head and kissed her on the neck. It was a quick brush of his lips across the tender skin at her neck, there where it curved into her shoulder . . . and then he released her. By the time Grace had collected herself enough to turn her head, Dillon was already backing away.

But his eyes were still on her, and her heart still beat too fast.

Dillon washed up in the bunkhouse, and if he'd been able to carry a tune he would have been whistling or humming. All week he'd tried to avoid Grace, and he wondered how to proceed.

She'd wanted him to kiss her there in the parlor . . . but he'd wondered later if the direct approach might not scare her off. He had a feeling she would bolt if she felt threatened. Straight to the Wilkinson ranch, most likely. Abigail would be all too willing to take her in. Abigail and Wade. He'd thought about actually asking if he could court her, as Wade had, but that seemed to make about as much sense as the first option. He didn't have much patience with courting—chaperons and rules and such—and didn't figure that would last long. Even with Grace.

He had to find a way to make her comfortable with him. She was already settling in nicely at the Double B. Not once had he heard a complaint about the plain accommodations or the fact that she was expected to help Olivia. It surprised him a little that she'd taken to the Double B so quickly, but that wasn't enough. There had to be a way to make her take to *him*. Something between grabbing her up and kissing her and spending the next six months in a ritual dance.

When he'd come across her in the kitchen he'd known what to do. She'd looked so tempting there in that pink calico. The hair on top of her head had probably once been secured neatly, but a few strands had escaped and fell across her shoulder. She'd looked as irresistible to him as she had when she'd stepped from the steamer in New Orleans.

So he'd laid his chin on her shoulder, and then he'd wrapped his arm around her waist. He'd felt her heart race, as his own had, and had waited for her to pull away.

But she hadn't. Even when he'd kissed her neck—it had been too tempting not to—she hadn't pulled away.

Dillon whipped off the dusty shirt he'd been wearing and tossed it to the floor. He dipped a thin towel into a barrel of cold water and started to scrub his face, his neck, and his arms.

"What the heck is the matter with you?"

The question pulled Dillon to the present, and he turned to glare at Billy as the man entered the bunkhouse with the same intent he had. Billy had already removed his vest, and was unbuttoning his filthy shirt.

"Nothing." Dillon resumed scrubbing.

"Well," Billy said in obvious disbelief. "I haven't seen you grin like that since you was thirteen. As I recall, you was smokin' one of your daddy's cigars and thought you'd got away with it."

"And I would have, if not for your big mouth," Dillon reminded the older man.

"It wasn't the cigar I was worried about, mind you," Billy said as he joined Dillon at the barrel. "It was that bottle of whiskey in the other hand that concerned me."

Dillon didn't answer, but continued to clean himself as well as he could under the conditions.

Billy was silent as well as they prepared to go to Olivia's supper table. The rest of the hands would be in shortly. They had their own supper table, and their own cook. One who wasn't quite so demanding. Olivia always insisted that they come to the table clean.

Dillon couldn't remember how old he'd been when she'd stopped checking his hands as he took his chair. Too old. Some nights he expected her to take his hands and check under the fingernails for dirt, still.

Even if Olivia weren't so particular, he didn't want to sit down across from Grace covered with dirt and sweat. Not tonight.

"So," Billy said thoughtfully as they donned clean shirts and headed for the house. "What kinda trouble you gettin' yourself into this time?"

Chapter Eight

During the days that had passed since her arrival at the Double B, Grace had become accustomed to the inflexible schedule. Billy and Dillon were up before dawn and out of the house before Grace left her bedroom. Dillon's room was just down the hall from hers, and sometimes—carly in the morning or very late at night—Grace would hear his footsteps in the hallway outside her door.

When Grace found her way to the kitchen each morning, Olivia was always there, looking fresher than anyone had a right to so early in the morning. There were chores to be done, around the house and in the barn, and Olivia was easing Grace into a routine of her own.

But in the evenings the four of them had supper together. It was a ritual that had apparently existed even before her arrival. Olivia talked about her garden or whether or not the chickens were producing enough eggs, and Dillon and Billy talked about the ranch and what they'd done that day.

Grace listened silently each night, trying to absorb it all, trying to understand this place and these people. It was hard work, running a ranch, and Dillon didn't expect anyone to work any harder than he did. But neither did he expect them to work any less.

Grace took special care preparing herself for supper on this evening, shedding the flour-dusted calico and slipping into a blue-striped muslin dress trimmed with ribbons. It had a plain collar, so at the last minute Grace delved into her jewelry box and fastened a strand of pearls at her throat. A matching bracelet graced her wrist, and she took a moment to study her reflection in the mirror.

Did she have the nerve to face Dillon at the table? He always sat directly across from her, while Billy sat at the head of the table and Olivia sat at the foot, nearest the kitchen door. It had seemed, that first night, an odd arrangement, eating with the servants, but it hadn't taken her long to discover that Billy and Olivia were much more than ranch hand and housekeeper. They were the only family Dillon had.

They laughed and cared for one another like no family Grace had ever known. It was the way she had always imagined family life should be, though she'd seen again and again that such attachments were rare. Her own family had been almost nonexistent. A father who ignored her, and an elderly aunt who'd shipped her off to school as soon as it was possible. Grace hadn't shed a tear when word reached her at school that the old woman had died.

She did remember a moment of panic when she'd heard the news of her aunt's death, a wrenching clutch deep inside that had reminded her how truly alone she was in the world.

She felt less alone now than at any other time in her life.

"Grace made these biscuits herself," Olivia declared proudly, slathering butter on one. They were golden brown and appeared to be edible, at least. Grace waited almost anxiously for Olivia's reaction.

Olivia took a small bite and chewed it slowly, testing. "You might have overworked the dough a bit. You must treat any bread dough gently, or the finished product will be tough."

Dillon broke a biscuit in half and popped the entire piece, devoid of butter or honey, into his mouth. "Tastes great to me," he said before he had even swallowed.

Billy laughed, but drizzled honey onto his own biscuit before he took a big bite. Then he nodded his head in agreement.

Grace smiled slightly. She knew that Dillon and Billy would have said the same, even if the biscuits were all but inedible.

"I was a bit distracted while I was working the dough," she said, staring at her plate. "I'll be gentler next time."

She knew Dillon was looking at her, even though she didn't dare lift her eyes to make certain. How could she ever look him in the face again?

Olivia clasped her hands together, obviously excited as an idea occurred to her. "I know! Let's have a party and invite everyone to meet Grace."

Grace stared at her plate, and Billy was silent,

but Dillon answered after a long pause.

"Oh, Grace has met just about everybody in these parts already."

His voice was so calm, so nonchalant, that Grace lifted her eyes to look at him. He was staring right at her as Olivia asked, obviously peeved at being excluded, when this had happened.

Dillon told her, in great detail, what Grace had done at Abigail Wilkinson's party. Most of the story was new to Billy, too, since he had been at his guard post outside her bedroom door at the time, thinking she was asleep. Perhaps he'd heard rumors in the bunkhouse, but sensible Billy would certainly dismiss such stories as outrageous and impossible.

Before he was finished with his telling of the story, Olivia and Billy were laughing so hard they had tears in their eyes, and Dillon wore one of his rare grins. Grace's face was so warm, she knew she must be blushing beet red, but she said nothing.

Olivia wiped the tears from her face as Dillon finished the story. "But why did you tell her she couldn't go downstairs in the first place?"

"He was probably afraid I would embarrass him in front of his friends," Grace said, trying to add a sharp edge to her voice.

"That doesn't sound like Dillon," Olivia said, admonishment in her voice.

"That's not why," Billy added, turning his attention to his plate.

"It doesn't matter now," Dillon said shortly. "I need another biscuit."

But Grace would not allow the subject to be dropped. She'd wondered . . . and now she knew there was another answer. "Why, then?" She turned to Billy, casting a quick eye to Dillon. His grin had faded, and his good humor was quickly disappearing.

Billy glanced at Dillon first, apparently weighing his options. "It's like this." He looked at Olivia, practically ignoring the parties involved. "Grace looked too good."

"What do you mean, she looked too good?" Olivia asked, as puzzled as Grace was.

Billy shrugged his shoulders and continued to eat.

Dillon cursed under his breath, was rewarded with a biting glare from Olivia, and then he stared across the table at Grace.

"He's right. Pretty stupid, I guess." His gray eyes darkened as he continued to look at her. "Pretty selfish, actually. I wasn't prepared. . . . I didn't know what to do with you, Grace."

"For future reference, Becket," Grace said sweetly, "taking my clothes and locking me in a room is not a suitable action."

His face paled and then reddened a little at her words, but Grace paid that no mind. He hadn't locked her away because he'd been ashamed of her. He'd been . . . what? Afraid to present her to Abigail? At least that made some sense. Especially since Abigail no doubt had expected her to be a child, just as Dillon had.

Grace felt something ugly growing in her chest. It was heavy and uncomfortable and there wasn't a thing she could do about it. She was jealous of that pasty-faced Abigail Wilkinson.

In a short time Dillon Becket had become important to her. As her protector, as her friend. As a man she was drawn to without question. And now there was more. Something between them that he had unleashed that afternoon, with his hand on her belly and his lips on her neck.

* * *

Grace's arms ached and her hands were burning. She was working the butter churn just as Olivia had instructed, but it was taking forever.

She sat on a stool with the churn between her knees. How many times had she slapped butter onto a biscuit or a potato without wondering how it came to the table?

And eggs, too. There were three small red scratches on the back of her right hand where she'd been pecked by a protective hen.

The longer she worked, the angrier she became. All those years of study for nothing. What was she going to do? Speak Latin to the cows as she milked them? Ugh! Now there was another disgusting chore. Perhaps she could recite Shakespeare to the chickens as they attacked her, or curse the blasted things in French.

A trickle of sweat ran down her back, and Grace closed her eyes. What was she doing here?

When she opened her eyes he was standing there in the wide doorway, leaning against the raw wood as relaxed as you please with his hands behind his back.

"Becket," she spat. She'd barely seen him for the past three days, and Billy had made his excuses at the supper table.

"Grace," he answered in a more civil tongue than she had been able to manage. "I see Olivia is keeping you busy."

Grace stopped briefly, and then resumed her chore angrily. "Busy? I guess you could say that." She gave him a colorful accounting of the chores she had been assigned, and her descriptions had him smiling before she was done.

"It's not funny, Becket," she snapped.

"I asked Olivia if you'd been giving her any

trouble, and she assured me that you'd been as good as gold. I should've known you were saving your grievances for me."

"It's not Olivia's fault," Grace said, lowering her voice. "Heaven knows the woman works hard enough, herself. I want to help her, I really do, but . . . but . . ."

"Everybody pulls their own weight around here," Dillon said calmly. "You'll get used to it." He seemed so nonchalant about the whole thing that Grace was further incensed, and she stood up clumsily.

"I'll never get used to this. It's too blasted hot, and it's not even summertime yet. I fall into bed every night so exhausted I can barely keep my eyes open, and when I wake in the morning I can barely crawl from under the covers." She thrust her hands out in front of her, palms upward. "And look at this." She glanced down at her own red, raw palms.

Dillon stepped into the shadow of the barn and took one hand in his. His other hand was still held behind his back as he frowned at her.

"Dammit, didn't Olivia give you a pair of gloves to wear?"

Grace nodded toward the leather gloves on the straw beside her stool. "They were too big, and very hot, and they kept slipping and my hands were sweaty. . . ."

Dillon gripped her wrist in his hand. His skin was so brown, so dark against her own pale arm, she couldn't help but stare. He didn't let her go as he pulled a crude bouquet from behind his back.

"What are those?"

Dillon looked almost embarrassed, and Grace wondered if he'd ever given a woman flowers before. It seemed terribly out of character.

"Bluebonnets," he said gruffly. "There's a field of them not too far from the house." With the iron grip he had on her wrist, Dillon pulled her toward him. "I picked them for you because they're the color of your eyes."

Grace forgot about the burning pain in her hands as she looked up at Dillon's face. Suddenly she was aware of the unattractive and ill-fitting dress she wore, another of Olivia's daughter's cast-offs, and of the fact that her hair was falling from a once-neat bun to wisp around her face. And she forgot all that and everything else when Dillon lowered his lips to hers and kissed her.

Nothing could have prepared Grace for the feelings he brought to life within her. She could move away if she wished, but she didn't. The hand that held the bluebonnets was light at her back, and Dillon continued to hold her wrist. A step back and he would release her. She knew it without doubt.

She slipped her free hand around his waist, moving her body closer to his.

If he had crushed her to him she might have panicked, but his touch remained light as he continued to take her mouth. He parted her lips with his own, and teased her with the tip of his tongue against hers.

Grace was afraid her legs would give out from under her, she felt so strangely weak, and as if he knew Dillon increased the pressure at her back, supporting her as he continued to kiss her softly.

His mouth was as warm as the sun, and he tasted just as she had known he would. He tasted the way his buckskin jacket had smelled. Masculine, of sweat and tobacco and plain soap and . . . Dillon.

Dillon's lips left hers, and she uttered a little cry of protest. But he nuzzled her neck and Grace let her head fall back, baring her throat. She was on fire everywhere. She could feel her own heartbeat, and his. She could feel, so divinely, his chest against hers, and she tingled from the top of her head to her—

"Wait a minute." She pushed against his chest, and Dillon reluctantly pulled away from her. "What are you trying to do to me?"

She saw the slowly clearing haze in his eyes, and knew that he wanted her. The frightening revelation was that, for a moment, she had wanted him just as much.

A minute longer and she would have given him everything. Dillon stepped away from her and produced the bluebonnets once again. They were a little worse for the wear. A few blossoms had been crushed behind her back.

For a ragged bouquet of wildflowers she would have given him what men all over England had tried to buy with diamonds and rubies and gold. Herself. Her body and her heart. She could never give one without the other.

Were all men the same? Was there no difference between Dillon Becket and a lecherous old man who'd never had to lift a finger to earn his keep? Or the son of an earl, a spoiled man-child who'd always had his every wish fulfilled . . . until he'd met Grace? An expatriated Russian aristocrat who had charmed his way through England, and many of the women there as well?

Dillon turned from her without a word, but was back moments later with a jar of salve. He took her hands in his and rubbed the salve over her reddened palms, not once able to meet her eyes. It was soothing, the salve and Dillon's hands on hers, and when he finished he instructed her to sit with her back against an empty stall, while he finished churning the butter.

"I did this when I was a kid," he said when he finally spoke. "It was one of my favorite chores."

Grace was grateful to lean back against the stall door, salved palms upward, bluebonnets in her lap where Dillon had dropped them. "And why was that?"

Dillon shrugged his shoulders and looked right at her. She might be trying to deny what had just happened, but he wouldn't. Or couldn't. He had a half-grin on his face, and a strange light in his eyes.

"I like it here," he said in a low voice. "It's cool and it smells of hay and horses."

"That's an asset?"

"It's home. When I was away, during the war, those were the smells that made me the most homesick. Horse dung and hay." He said it with such comical self-derision that Grace laughed aloud. And then he smiled.

"Do you like it here, Grace?" Dillon asked softly. Several feet separated them, and he continued to churn as she watched him closely. It was the second time he'd asked her that question.

"Most of the time," she said truthfully. "It can be very beautiful. I can see why you love it here. It suits you quite well."

"Does it suit you?" He didn't wait for an answer. "I hope you like it here well enough to stay. It's not what you're accustomed to, I realize that." His face hardened, giving him that intractable look she had learned to expect from him.

"I've been giving the matter some thought,"

Grace said, trying to sound sensible. "I'm well qualified to teach. Certainly I could find a job as a schoolmistress, or a—What are you grinning at?" she asked sharply.

"You don't look like any teacher I ever had, Grace Cavanaugh."

"But I could—"

"I'd like you to stay," Dillon said abruptly. "You don't have to. Your father entrusted you to me, but you're a grown woman, and I won't force you to stay if it's not what you want. You could teach, if you had a mind to, or you could sell some of those geegaws you wear all the time and travel back East. But I'd like you to stay."

Grace took a deep breath, and for a moment she didn't think she would be able to let it out. He wanted her to stay.

"Why?"

"Well, Billy and Olivia have grown mighty fond of you." Dillon pulled his eyes away from her and stared down at the churn as he spoke.

"And I of them," Grace said softly.

"I'm getting right fond of looking at you over the supper table, myself," he said gruffly.

Grace lifted the bluebonnets in her sore, greasy hands. She'd never worked so hard in her life as she had since her arrival at the Double B. Her room was small, and her own clothing, what was left of it, was for the most part unserviceable. The heat was horrendous, and while Dillon found the odors of the barn appealing, she most certainly did not.

But Billy had been a friend to her almost since the moment she'd met him, and Olivia was like a warm aunt, or even the mother Grace had never known. And Dillon . . . the possibilities there were mind-boggling. He stirred her blood, and made her dream of a future she'd never considered for herself before. A marriage . . . for love, not money. Children, and a home. A real home.

"I'll stay," she said after a long pause. "For as long as you'll have me."

Dillon slept in the room that had always been his, even though he was now entitled to the big bedroom. In his mind that was his father's room, still.

The window was wide open, the cool spring air a comfort against his bare skin. He'd worked hard from before sunup till past dark, his only break coming in the barn with Grace, so he should have fallen asleep right away, as he usually did. But tonight he couldn't.

He'd moved too fast that afternoon. He'd known that as soon as Grace pushed him away. But before she'd put a stop to the kiss, she had held her body against his with anxious lips and a pounding heart. She'd been scared, just a little, and to tell the truth, so had he.

He could marry her. Maybe. If the cattle drive brought in enough cash to pay off the loan. If not . . . Dillon chose not to think about that. Marriage to Abigail seemed impossible now, but he knew it wasn't. If that was the only way to save the Double B, that was what he would do.

He gave up on the idea of sleep, and resigned himself to a sleepless night. He stared at the ceiling with his hands behind his head and contemplated his next step. Slow and easy, that was the key. Grace would have to be gentled, like a skittish mare. Not broken. Never broken.

She was innocent, with no idea where kisses like the one they'd shared in the barn could lead.

And Dillon was determined to keep his distance, as much as he could, until he was certain he would be able to marry her.

Grace deserved no less.

In a few weeks the trail boss he'd hired would be back with the money to pay off old man Plummer. If it was enough, then he could ask Grace to marry him. If it wasn't . . .

If it wasn't, then he had no choice. He'd marry Abigail, because without the Double B he had nothing. Nothing to call his own, and nothing to offer a woman like Grace.

It was a plan of sorts, and Dillon finally fell into a deep sleep.

He dreamed of silken black hair and creamy skin, of bubble baths and bluebonnet eyes, and when he woke to the faint streak of gray that promised morning's light he knew that keeping his distance from Grace for the next few weeks was going to be the hardest thing he'd ever done.

Chapter Nine

Impossibly, the days grew longer and hotter. Grace never would have thought it possible to wish for the London fog and drizzle, but she did. Here, when it did rain, the drops came fast and heavy, and in the end managed to leave the air more humid and unbearable than before.

And Dillon Becket was proving to be much more difficult than the Texas weather.

After he'd kissed her in the barn, Grace had expected that she would see more of him, but in fact she saw much less. It was almost as if he were avoiding her. She began to suspect that he regretted their heated embrace in the barn, as well as his request that she stay at the Double B. There was no other explanation for his actions.

On a normal day she saw Dillon only at supper, and then he was uncommunicative, eating quickly and excusing himself before anyone else was halfway finished.

But Grace knew that there was still something between them. Something powerful and almost tangible. All she had to do was get Dillon's attention again and make it impossible for him to ignore her.

She hadn't decided exactly how to go about that, until she saw him standing there. It was yet another unbearably hot afternoon, and she had stolen a moment of cool comfort in the barn, a few precious minutes of sitting in the hay with her back to the wall and her eyes closed. Of course, she could only steal away for a short time. There was too much work to be done to be hiding in the barn.

As she made her way toward the house she saw Dillon. He leaned tiredly against the bunkhouse and sipped at a dipper of water, and he was most definitely watching her out of the corner of his eye. She so rarely caught a glimpse of him during the day that this was an opportunity she couldn't let slip by.

One of the ranch hands, a tall, lanky man in dust-covered denim, was walking a horse around the corral, occasionally stopping to lay his hand on the animal's foreleg. Grace turned and headed straight for the corral and the cowboy.

"Good afternoon," she called when she was near enough for the man to hear her. He lifted his head, and she saw that he was older than she had first thought. His face was tough as leather, though he had the body of a younger man.

"Ma'am." The man removed his hat and led the horse to the fence. His brown hair was streaked with gray, and he'd gone almost completely white at the temples.

Grace had never met any of Dillon's ranch hands. They didn't often come to the house, and

Dillon had certainly never taken her to the bunkhouse at the end of the day. In fact, this was one of the rare times she saw anyone but Billy around the house during daylight hours. She had wondered, on occasion, if Dillon had warned his own hands away from her the way he'd warned off Clifford.

She introduced herself, smiling, wondering if Dillon was still watching her and then certain that he was. The cowboy very politely introduced himself simply as Hartley. First name or last—or both—Grace didn't know.

"Do you think you could teach me to ride, Hartley?" Grace asked when they had finished their introductions.

Hartley raised his bushy eyebrows just slightly, and leaned against the fence. "You've never ridden before?"

Grace shook her head. "It seems to me that if I am to stay here, I should learn."

The cowpoke nodded in agreement. Studying him up close, Grace decided that he was probably only a few years older than Dillon, but he had deep lines at the corners of his eyes and around his mouth, and the white in his hair aged him considerably.

"I'd have to get permission from the boss. I haven't been here all that long, and I wouldn't want to step out of line." He grinned at her, and the creases on his face deepened. This was not exactly a charming smile. It was, in fact, pompous and sleazy at the same time. "But I'd surely be happy to teach you how to ride. There's a lady-broke horse that'd be just right for you, Miss Grace."

Grace gave him her most dazzling smile, in spite of the fact that he was practically leering at her, and leaned casually against the fence. She could hardly hold Hartley's apparent interest against him, since she had been the one to initiate this conversation. Besides, it was working. Dillon was headed toward them at a slow but steady pace. Grace could see him out of the corner of her eye, but she didn't acknowledge his approach.

"What do you think?" Dillon snapped.

Hartley dropped down and massaged the foreleg of the horse he'd been walking. "Needs a little more work. She's not ready to be rode just yet."

"Grace." Dillon shoved his hands behind his back and stared at her intently. "What are you doing here?"

She turned her face to him and gave him a bright smile, as innocent as a child. "Hartley has been kind enough to agree to teach me to ride. Isn't that marvelous?"

"He has too much work to do."

"But I really should learn, don't you think?" Grace asked, staring up into stormy gray eyes. It had worked. Dillon was jealous.

Dillon squinted one eye at her, and for a moment Grace was certain that he knew exactly what she was doing. Somehow he understood her better than anyone else ever had.

"I'll teach you myself," he said gruffly, dismissing Hartley with a wave of his hand.

"When?"

"Tomorrow."

"In the morning?"

Dillon sighed, resigning himself to his fate. "Tomorrow afternoon, Grace. Before supper." With that he turned his back on her and stalked away.

* * *

Grace glanced down at Dillon, wondering if this had been such a good idea after all. She was too far off the ground, and the mare she sat was prancing around the corral. It was true that Dillon held the reins, but Grace didn't think that would do her any good at all if the mare decided to toss her novice rider.

"Relax," Dillon said again, giving her a stern look.

"I am relaxed," Grace said ungraciously.

She wore another of Alice's outgrown castoffs, a split skirt that allowed her to sit the sidesaddle properly. She'd secured her hair at the nape of her neck, wanting to keep it out of her way, but she'd been so jostled that several strands had escaped. She was certain she looked a mess. Perhaps this was not exactly the way to attract a man, after all.

"Aren't we finished for today?" she asked.

Dillon's face relaxed, and he almost smiled. "It's only been five minutes, Grace."

She didn't believe him. Surely it had been more than five minutes! "I'm afraid I'm going to fall."

"You won't fall."

"But what if—"

"I'll catch you."

Eventually she did relax, as Dillon led the mare around the corral. Every now and then he'd look up at her, apparently trying to judge her stamina and her feel for the mare.

It wasn't long at all before she felt quite comfortable on the mare, and pretty sure that the horse wouldn't throw her off.

The sun was low in the sky before Dillon declared them finished for the day, and he lifted his arms to Grace to help her from the saddle.

She placed her hands on his shoulders and slid from the saddle, falling slowly downward. He seemed completely unaffected by her touch. The shoulders beneath her hands were stiff; the hands at her waist were cold. How could he be so distant? Just being close to him like this made her heart beat fast, and she craved the feel of his lips on hers once again.

When her feet were on the ground it would have been simplest just to step away and dismiss this experiment as a failure.

But Grace didn't care much for failure. She slipped her hands from Dillon's shoulders and wrapped them around his waist. With her chin resting against his chest she looked up and watched the beat of his pulse at his throat.

"Thank you, Dillon," she whispered.

He sighed just once, and then he took her chin in his hand and lowered his lips to hers. This time Grace didn't have to be prompted to part her lips, and when his mouth claimed hers she flicked her tongue against his.

Dillon was fire, with the heat in his hands and his lips. He was burning her, pressing his body to hers, pulling her against him. There was something hard and hot pressing against her belly, something as hard and hot as the rest of Dillon Becket. He was no longer coolly unaffected.

It was Dillon who pulled away with a low curse. "Christ, Grace."

She stepped away from him and smiled up into his scowling face. "See you at supper."

Grace spent a little extra time preparing for the evening meal. She bathed as best she could in the privacy of her room, and donned one of her own gowns. It was a pale green–striped silk taffeta with a draped bodice, and came just off her white shoulders. It was undoubtedly far too fancy for supper at the Double B, but it would get Dillon's attention.

She'd never had to work so blasted hard to get a man to notice her.

After years of walking a fine line between attracting a man and keeping him at a distance, Grace found herself anxious at the prospect of confronting Dillon. She was making herself vulnerable, and that was something she had always avoided. For the first time in her life, her heart was at stake. She had everything to lose . . . and everything to gain.

She fastened the pearls at her throat, and slipped on the matching bracelet, steeling herself for the night . . . for the days and nights to come. If she had to fight for Dillon Becket, that was exactly what she would do.

Dillon glanced up and then quickly looked down at his plate again. She was doing this to him on purpose, he was certain. Calling him Dillon, instead of the harsher Becket. Kissing him like she had in the corral, and now showing off her figure and her bare shoulders like this . . . it was more than a man could take.

"Isn't that right, Dillon?"

"What?" He lifted his head and looked across the table to her.

"I said," Grace repeated, "that I'll be riding by myself in no time."

Dillon shook his head. "Not for a while. And I don't want you to ever"—he emphasized his point with a piece of fork-speared beef wagged in her direction—"ever, ride out of sight of the house by yourself."

Grace raised her eyebrows slightly and glared

at him, challenging him, perhaps, to a staring contest. He looked down at his plate again. "Why is that?"

"It's not safe," Dillon said to his plate. "We don't see much in the way of Indians anymore, but there's still a few renegades around. And rustlers. And bandits like your friend Renzo," he added with disgust.

"Oh," Grace said in a small voice, and Dillon was forced to look up.

"Don't worry. Billy or I will ride with you when you're ready," he tried to reassure her. She looked a little afraid, but as he watched her face that expression changed, and she was his confident, assured Grace once again.

"Well, if you're too busy maybe that nice Hartley can escort me."

Dillon said nothing, but he shook his head slightly. She was doing this on purpose, he was certain.

"Of course," she said sweetly, "I'd really rather that you ride with me."

He decided to change the subject. "You sure are dressed up fancy tonight. Special occasion?"

It was Grace's turn to stare at her food as she shrugged those pale shoulders. "No. I just felt like wearing my own clothes for a change." She lifted her eyes to him. "Don't you like it?"

Dillon cracked a small smile. She was flirting with him. His obstinate, bullheaded, impulsive Grace was flirting with him. He liked it, but he didn't know exactly how much he could take.

"It's a little fancy for the Double B," he said kindly, studying the soft, draping material over her breasts, the white, tempting skin of her shoulders and neck. "But I do like it."

Grace smiled at him, and the beef he put into

his mouth nearly stuck in his throat. Damn, she was beautiful, especially when she smiled like that.

His eyes fell on the pearls at her throat. He had to change the subject. Again. How was he supposed to do the honorable thing and bide his time when she looked at him like that?

"For a man who had financial troubles, your pa sure did buy you a lot of geegaws."

Grace laid a slender hand over the pearls. "These are not *geegaws*, Becket. And I didn't get them from my father. My father never gave me anything, though he did send money whenever I asked, and paid the headmistress off when she threatened to send me home."

Dillon lifted his eyes to hers. He'd obviously touched a nerve with her. Her smile was gone, and that wary shield that had been so much a part of Grace when he'd first met her was back. And seemingly as strong as ever.

"So you bought those for yourself?"

Grace shook her head. "Of course not."

Dillon felt a curious sinking in his gut. "Your aunt?"

Grace shook her head again, but said nothing.

Dillon reached across the table and grabbed Grace's wrist. His hand was over the pearl bracelet. "Where did you get these?"

Grace sighed, but she didn't try to pull her hand away from him. "They were gifts. From a . . . a friend."

"A friend," Dillon said icily. "What was his name?"

"I would really rather not—"

"What was his name?" Dillon repeated, slowly and just a bit louder than the first time.

Grace's eyes flashed at him, daring him, before

she answered. "His name was Francois."

Dillon released her hand. "A goddamn Frenchman?"

Grace nodded.

"What for, Grace?"

Grace didn't look away from him, but she refused to answer his angry question.

"The necklace you wore at the Clanton stop . . ." Dillon paused, for a moment forgetting that Billy and Olivia watched him silently. "Another gift from Francois?"

"No. That was a gift from Sir Richard," Grace said coldly.

Dillon leaned back in his chair. He couldn't have resumed his meal or a normal conversation if his life had depended on it. "The pin that looks like a snake?"

"Mikhail."

"The emerald bracelet?"

Grace was staring at him with rapidly mounting anger evident in her eyes and the set of her mouth. "The earl of—"

She stopped speaking when Dillon shot to his feet and slapped his hand down on the table. His Grace. When had he begun to think of her as *his* Grace? The moment he had seen her? The night she had fallen asleep with her head against his shoulder? No wonder she had reacted so strongly when he'd asked her if she had any dresses that didn't make her look like a high-priced whore.

That's exactly what she was.

No decent woman would have accepted gifts like the ones she wore. They were expensive gifts for her favors. And he had been practically killing himself staying away from her until he was certain he could offer her marriage.

"Why are you looking at me like that?" Grace asked sharply.

"You didn't answer my question," he said evenly. "What did you do to earn all those fancy geegaws?"

He saw it in her face, the dawning realization of what he believed. What he knew. She was angry, and hurt, and a little scared.

"What did you do, Grace?" he repeated.

"Come on, boss. Take it easy."

Dillon turned to Billy. "This doesn't concern you, old man."

"What the hell did you do, Grace Cavanaugh?" he shouted across the table.

The look that stole over Grace's face as she stood wiped away the fear, and the hurt, and the anger. It was cold and calculating, pale and assured.

"What do you think, Becket?" she asked with an icy smile. "Come on, you're a big boy. Surely you can figure it out for yourself."

Dillon felt as if she'd kicked him in the chest. What had he expected her to say? Had he really expected her to deny it? He wouldn't have believed her if she had.

"I left school at seventeen, Becket. Five years ago. My father didn't want me." She caressed the pearls at her throat. "These men did."

There were unshed tears in her eyes, but she continued to stare at him. "I don't care what you think of me." She looked from one end of the table to the other, where Billy and Olivia sat silently. "I don't care what any of you think!"

With that she turned away haughtily and left Dillon with his rage.

* * *

Grace ran up the stairs, her hand clutching the pearls at her throat. How could she have been so stupid? How could she have believed that Dillon Becket was different from any other man?

She slammed the door to her room and threw herself onto the bed, and she let the tears fall. She cursed the tears as they fell, the tears she had refused to shed when she'd learned of her father's death. The tears she had refused to shed all those nights in England, sleeping in some friend's guest room, in a cold bed, wanting nothing more than to go home.

But she had no home. She hadn't had one then, and she didn't have one now.

The tears wouldn't stop. She muffled her sobs into the quilt, but the tears wouldn't stop.

There had been a moment, when she'd looked across the table into Dillon's angry face, when she'd wanted to tell him the truth. All of it. That none of those men had ever touched her heart the way he had. That she hadn't believed she *had* a heart until she'd met him. That all she'd ever given those men was a brief kiss or two, and a coy promise of what might be.

But he wouldn't have believed her.

It was late, and pitch black in her room before Grace's eyes finally dried. She had a pounding headache, and an empty ache where her heart was supposed to be.

It was all right, she assured herself. She'd never intended to stay in Texas. Not really.

Dillon watched Grace from the shadow of the barn, afraid to show himself. It had been more than a week since her revelation, and he hadn't spoken to her since. He'd been eating supper with the hands—beans and bacon and tough biscuits damn near every night. But he still watched Grace whenever he got the chance.

The anger that had consumed him was gone. Most of it, anyway. Grace was on her knees in Olivia's garden, pulling weeds with a vengeance. Her anger hadn't subsided at all. He'd been waiting. Waiting to see her smile just once before he could gather the courage to approach her, to talk to her again. But she looked as furious, still, as she had that night.

Of course, she had reason to be. He never lost control like that. Never jumped to conclusions and made accusations. Well, he couldn't say never. Not anymore.

It didn't matter what Grace had done before. That revelation had surprised him, as no one would ever describe Dillon Becket as a forgiving man. It simply didn't matter what had happened before they met.

She was here now, and he intended to see that she stayed. It couldn't have been easy for her, growing up away from home and without a family to love her. His own family was gone, but he had such wonderful memories of them. Grace didn't have even that.

There could be a whole new life for her here.

He was so engrossed in her it took him a moment to realize that he wasn't the only one watching. Two other men stood on the other side of the barn door. They would be clearly visible to Grace, were she to look up.

"Ever seen anything so damn tempting?" Dillon recognized the whispering voice as Hartley's. "Shit, I never figured watching a woman pull weeds would make my pecker hard, but dammit . . ."

"You better watch your mouth," Hartley's companion warned nervously. "If the boss was to hear you . . ."

"He ain't here," Hartley said bravely. "And I'll tell you something else: she likes me. I knew it that day she asked me to teach her to ride. Hell, I'll teach her to ride, all right. What do you think she'd do if I—" He stopped abruptly when Dillon's hand at the back of his shirt cut off his wind.

Dillon only glanced at the other hired hand, a tame kid who was particularly gentle with the horses. "Get out of here, Lonnie," Dillon said softly, and Lonnie was gone before the sentence was finished.

Hartley was choking, and Dillon loosened his grip slightly. "I could kill you," Dillon said in the man's ear. "It would be so quick you'd never make a sound. I could bury you in the south pasture and no one would ever find your sorry good-for-nothing carcass."

Hartley was still breathing raggedly, and his strong fingers clawed at Dillon's hands.

"You've got five minutes to get off this ranch," Dillon said menacingly. "If I ever see you again, you're dead."

Dillon released the cowhand, and Hartley spun to face him. "I didn't mean nothing," the man defended himself heatedly. "It was just talk. You can't bring a woman who looks like that one out here and expect us not to . . . to look."

"You've got just over four minutes. If I was you, I wouldn't waste any more time."

Hartley turned away from Dillon with a curse, and a couple of minutes later he was riding hell-bent away from the barn. Grace looked up from her chore briefly, then returned to her weeding.

* * *

If she'd heard him coming she would have run for the house. She had no desire to face Dillon Becket, not ever again. She'd reminded herself all week, whenever she'd felt her resolve weakening, that the man had accused her without even asking . . . well, he had asked, but she had seen the truth on his face. He'd already made up his mind. No respectable woman would take jewelry from a man, and therefore she was not a respectable woman.

And now he was before her, down on his haunches in the soft dirt. She glanced up briefly, was satisfied that he at least had the decency to look contrite, and then she returned to her work.

"What do you want, Becket?" she snapped.

"Still riled at me, I see," he said calmly.

Grace muttered under her breath. *Riled* was not the word.

Sweat was pouring down her back and her face. Her sleeves were rolled up, and the skin of her forearms glistened. Sweat! She'd never perspired like this in all of her life.

"I'm leaving," she said as she yanked up an offensive weed. "I want to go back to New Orleans."

Dillon was silent, and when she glanced up she saw that he was unusually pensive—for a rude cowboy who was as sweat covered as she was.

She grabbed another weed in her gloved hand, and Dillon's hand flew out to stop her. Grace yanked, dislodging his hand and pulling up the nasty weed.

"That's an onion," he said, taking the plant from her and gently placing it back in the soil. "Olivia loves her onions."

"When I get to New Orleans, I can assure you I will not be sitting in the sun pulling weeds, or churning butter, or milking cows."

"I don't suppose you will be," Dillon said calmly.

Grace resumed her chore, hoping that Dillon would take the hint and go away. But he didn't.

"If you really want to go," he said when he finally spoke, "I don't reckon I can stop you. But you don't have to leave."

Grace gave him a very unladylike snort of disgust. "Yes, I do." She glared at him, trying to put all of her hate and disgust into her eyes. "This is hell, Becket. My father so wanted to punish me for being born that he sent me to hell." She vented all of her frustration and anger. "Texas is hell and you're the devil himself."

Dillon shifted his weight from one leg to the other. He seemed to be reflecting on her statement before he answered.

"Well, I may be a devil, but you're no angel, Grace."

She threw a handful of dirt at him. She knew what he thought of her. Why had she ever believed that he was different from other men? Better?

Dillon ignored the dirt and reached out for her hand. Grace yanked it away from him and fell back, landing on her backside in the soft dirt. To her mortification, Dillon Becket was smiling at her.

"Come on." This time he offered his hand instead of taking hers. "You look like you need a break."

Grace looked up at him. Dillon, with a rare smile on his face, was rising slowly with his hand extended to her, palm upward. And she laid her hand in his and allowed him to pull her to her feet.

He pulled off her too-large gloves and dropped

them into the dirt, and then he took her hand again. They walked away from the house, and he continued to hold her hand. He held it so lightly she knew she could withdraw it if she wanted to, but she didn't.

A light breeze cooled Grace's sweat-covered face, and pushed back tendrils of black hair. She looked down at her borrowed dress. The skirt was covered with dirt, there at the knees where she'd been kneeling, and she knew there was dirt on her backside as well. The bodice of her calico dress was dampened with perspiration. They continued to walk, and walk, and walk, over hills that were little more than bumps in the ground, and over perfectly flat packed dirt.

Finally she snapped at him, "This is your idea of a break? A blasted walking tour of your ranch?"

"Almost there," he said as he turned her toward a small rise.

The sight before her as they crested the rise took her breath away. Bluebonnets. A field of them covered the ground and swayed in the whispering breeze.

Dillon sat on the ground and drew her down beside him. He stared out over the field of blue and squinted his eyes, deepening his crow's-feet. He kept her hand in his, and the pressure there gradually increased.

"I'm sorry, Grace," he said gruffly, and with the almost embarrassed tone of a man who never apologizes. "I flew off the handle, and I had no right." He thumbed his hat back and finally turned his head to look at her. "I don't blame you for wanting to leave, but I hope you won't."

"Dillon Becket," Grace said softly, her anger fading as she watched his face. He was a man obviously not accustomed to admitting his mistakes. "I should hate you."

"Do you?"

She shook her head. "No. I can't." She sighed.

Dillon grinned at her and tossed his hat to the ground. "I knew it." The sun glinted off his chestnut hair, gleaming red highlights kissed by the sun. He reached out and brushed the back of his hand across her cheek.

"Sometimes I just don't know what to think about you," Grace admitted. "You infuriate me one minute, and then . . ." How could she admit that she was falling in love with him? She couldn't.

"And then . . ." he prompted.

"And then you kiss me, or smile at me, and like a fool I forgive you anything."

In a heartbeat his face was close to hers, and then his lips were claiming hers. There was none of the tenderness she had come to expect from him, but a fierce and demanding possession that she welcomed. He held her tight, nestled her in his arms as he took her mouth.

He pressed her backward into the grass, and Grace wrapped her arms around his neck, pulling him to her. She wanted his weight against her, pressing against her, harder, hotter. . . .

Without warning, she pushed against him and shot up.

"What's wrong?" he asked, his voice low as he ran a finger over her cheek.

"I'm . . . I'm a mess," Grace admitted, and she felt the heat rise in her cheeks. "I'm sitting here wearing a filthy borrowed dress, and my hair is all tangled, and I'm covered with sweat. . . ."

"I like you covered with sweat," Dillon said huskily, and he leaned forward and kissed her throat, flicking his tongue slowly across the pulse there. "I like the way it tastes, and the way it feels." He ran a finger along the back of her neck, making her shiver.

"I've missed you," he whispered, burying his face against her throat, scattering small, wild kisses against her skin. He unfastened the buttons at her neck, exposing the hollow at the base of her throat and giving that one spot his undivided attention.

Grace felt as if she were melting, slowly, wondrously, beneath his touch. She wound her fingers through his hair and held him to her, until that was no longer enough. Her hands skimmed along his shoulders and his back, his strong arms and the hands that touched her.

His fingers didn't stop with the buttons at her throat. Slowly, never taking his lips from her skin, he unbuttoned her calico dress to the waist. His lips were caressing the swell of her breasts in a way Grace had never imagined. It was wrong, she knew, but she didn't want him to stop. Not ever.

He lifted his head from her chest, and a welcome breeze danced between them, cooling the skin where his warm lips had lingered. His lips found hers again, and Grace closed her eyes. This wasn't hell; this was heaven. It had to be. Dillon slipped his fingers inside her calico and cupped her breast, rubbing his thumb across the nipple until Grace moaned. She'd never felt anything like this. Had never known that it was possible for such feelings to rise within her.

All thoughts of protest were forgotten, and Dillon laid her back into the grass. He kissed the sweat from her skin, and laid his mouth over her nipple, the wet heat of his tongue penetrating the thin chemise she wore beneath the calico.

When he inhaled deeply, sucking her nipple into his mouth, it was all Grace could do not to cry aloud. There was an insistent tugging between her legs.

Grace took Dillon's head between her hands and pulled him to her. She had to feel his lips on hers again, couldn't live another moment without that sensation, and as he locked his lips to hers, pressing her into the grass, the throbbing between her legs increased until she couldn't stand it anymore, and a plea stuck in her throat. The little noise she heard was coming from her own mouth. *Please. Please.*

"Please stop," she whispered when he lifted his mouth from hers.

"I can't stop," Dillon whispered. A hand slipped beneath her skirt while he moved his mouth over her breasts. "I want you too much, I've wanted you for too long, and it's much too late to stop."

Panic welled within in her as his hand settled over her thigh. She could barely catch her breath with Dillon's weight on her chest, but her breathing came faster and heavier.

"I . . . I can't, Becket." She tried to snap at him, tried to force an icy disdain she didn't feel, but still she recognized the fear in her own voice.

He must have heard it, too, because his hands stilled, and he lifted his head to look into her eyes.

"You're serious," he said in a gruff voice. His own breath was coming hard and fast, but there was no fear in his eyes. Just frustration.

Grace took the opportunity to scoot up and straighten her skirt. She still throbbed for him, and in another moment she would have forgotten herself and . . .

"I'm sorry. I can't."

"Sorry?" Dillon pulled away from her, but stayed too close for her own comfort. She could still feel his heat and his anger. "Honey, you don't do this to a man and then ask him to stop."

"Do what?" Grace asked breathlessly.

Dillon grabbed her hand and thrust it downward, placing it between their bodies, and he pressed her palm against his swollen manhood. "This. You don't do this to a man and then say . . . Oh, hell, never mind." He released her hand and she yanked it away from him.

"I didn't mean to," she said in a small voice. "I didn't know."

Dillon grabbed her chin between his fingers and forced her to look at him. "Don't play the innocent with me, Grace Cavanaugh. I know better. Remember?"

Grace would have slapped him, but she was more stunned than angry. "You don't know anything," she said softly, and then she jumped to her feet and turned toward the house. She ran, buttoning her dress as she fled over the gentle slope.

She looked over her shoulder only once, to see if Dillon was following her, but all she saw was the faded green grass of the deserted rise and, in the distance, a flash of Dillon's bluebonnets.

Chapter Ten

Grace sat in one of a pair of rocking chairs that adorned the rustic front porch. She rocked slowly, trying to clear the mist from her mind.

She didn't belong here. She didn't belong anywhere. It had been a foolish fantasy to believe that she could live on the Double B with Dillon and Billy and Olivia, as if they were really her family. Grace knew she wasn't especially good in the kitchen, and she never would have finished churning that butter without Dillon's help, and she was hopelessly out of place among the animals. She'd almost fooled herself into believing that she could learn all that and more. But it was hopeless. As hopeless as Dillon Becket.

He had struck her from the beginning as being strong, certain of himself, in control. There was nothing that Dillon couldn't do. Nothing got under his skin. And she had thought him so unlike the other men she had known.

But now it seemed the only difference was his ability to make her want him, and that frightened her. She'd always been in control where men were concerned. Rigid control. A kiss on the cheek or on her hand. Perhaps a brief touching of the lips. That was all she'd allowed. Lips, cold and wet, lips that made Grace shiver in revulsion, were all she had known. She had learned to single out the men who were likely to pursue a woman they saw as a challenge. Men who loved the chase as much as the conquest.

She'd learned to promise with her eyes what her body and her soul refused to deliver, and she'd learned to recognize when the game was up and it was time to move on. From one schoolmate's home to another, to a holiday in Paris with one of those silly girls, and then back to the society she had learned to manipulate.

Only once had she stayed too long. Early on she'd made the mistake of playing the game with a man much too young. Margaret's brother, a good-looking hellion with a reputation as a ladies' man. Everything had gone perfectly, until one night when she found herself alone with Gifford. He had pressed her against the wall of his mother's parlor, and tried to take what she refused to give. She could still feel his hands, harsh and rough against her skin, and his wet lips on her face and her throat. She could still hear the ripping sound as he tore at her dress, and the panic that had very nearly stolen her sanity as he'd covered her mouth with one hand while he lifted her skirt with the other.

It had been his mother who interrupted Gifford, with a gasp and a shielding hand over her eyes. Naturally the woman had managed to convince herself that Grace was at fault. Grace remembered being as hurt by that as anything else.

She'd remembered that always, as she'd made her way from one home to another, hardening herself against the world.

And now she found herself in Texas with the one man whose lips were anything but revolting, the one man who made her lose control. Dillon Becket knew nothing of the rules of the hunt, or if he knew he ignored them.

He wanted her, like all the rest, though he never spoke of love or marriage. No doubt he saved those avowals of love for women like Abigail Wilkinson.

She didn't hear Billy until he was upon her, his boots clicking against the wooden porch. He lowered himself slowly into the other rocking chair and sighed, the sigh of a man who had been hard at work since sunrise. Soon the rocking of his chair matched her own.

"Mighty peaceful here at the end of the day," Billy said, his eyes on the setting sun. "The older I get the more I appreciate settling this body down and restin' my old bones."

Grace didn't say a word. She joined him in admiring the sunset, but any words she might have spoken were stuck in her throat. Billy and Olivia had all but ignored Dillon's accusations and her outburst over the dinner table. On the morning following that scene, Grace had expected to find herself ostracized, even by those she had come to think of as friends, but that hadn't happened. They let her know, with a smile or a tender touch of a hand, that they thought no less of her than they had before. That she was still welcome in their company.

"You hafta understand about Dillon," Billy said, staring toward the horizon and away from

Grace. "The last few years have been hard on the boy."

Grace snorted, a very unladylike sound escaping from her throat, and Billy smiled.

"He had two older brothers." Billy's smile faded. "Jimmy and Nolan. They both died during the war. Jimmy was killed at Gettysburg, and Nolan was sorely wounded there. He came home, but he didn't live three months. Dillon didn't know until he came home."

Grace had stopped rocking, and Billy stared at her across a still and sun-filled space.

"Opal, that was Dillon's mama, she was never the same after losing those boys. Now, Henry Becket was a hard man, and he tried to go on as if nothing had changed."

"Dillon's father?" Grace asked in a small voice, and Billy nodded slightly.

"Opal died five years back, and that was when Henry started to fall apart. All he could think about was this ranch. How to make it bigger and richer. For Dillon, I reckon, since the boy was all he had left." Billy stared at her, a judging look in his pale blue eyes. "Henry made some foolish mistakes. The most foolish of all was, he bought a bull. Cost him a fortune, but he wanted to improve the herd. Then the durn animal died on him, leaving Henry with one heck of a loan to pay off."

Grace said nothing as Billy took a deep breath and ran a beefy hand across the white stubble at his jaw. "Henry died not long after the bull, and the loan's comin' due in a couple of months. If Dillon can't pay it off, he'll lose the Double B."

"But . . . he can pay it off, can't he?" Grace asked in a small voice. She had learned, in a short time, how much the Double B meant to Dillon.

Billy shrugged his shoulders. "Depends. There'll be some money comin' in, in a few weeks. If it's enough . . ." He let the sentence hang.

"Why are you telling me this?" Grace asked, her frustration coming through in her sharp voice. She didn't want to feel any sympathy for Dillon Becket. She didn't want to feel anything at all.

Billy smiled again, one of those small smiles that came so easily to his lips. "I just thought you might want to understand why the boss sometimes acts like a jackass. He's got a lot on his mind, that's all. But he does like you. A lot, if I know him at all."

Grace shook her head and resumed her slow rocking. Like her? Of course he didn't like her. Dillon Becket wanted her, and he felt responsible for her, and that wasn't enough. Especially, she confessed silently, since she had fallen in love with the man.

"Well," Billy continued as she shook her head. "I like you, and Olivia likes you, and we both want you to stick around the place."

Grace snapped her head up to look at the older man. Had he heard or seen her with Dillon? How did he know she was thinking of leaving?

He chuckled. "You'd make a lousy poker player, Miss Grace. When I walked up onto this porch and saw that far-off look in your eyes, I knew you was thinkin' about leavin'. The Double B's bound to be real different from where you been livin', but you'll get used to it. If you'll give it a chance."

"I don't know if I can," Grace said truthfully. "But since I really don't have anywhere to go, and no money to speak of, I won't be leaving anytime soon."

Billy looked satisfied with that answer and leaned his head back, closing his eyes and settling his hands over his chest.

Grace wished that she could feel just a little of the contentment that was etched on Billy's face. Her mind was spinning, and her insides were churning, and all she could think of were Dillon's lips and hands, and what she'd thrown aside when she'd run from him.

Dillon paced back and forth in the small room. Tonight it wasn't the summer heat that was keeping him awake, but the knowledge that Grace was sleeping just two doors down the hall in Jimmy's old room. Maybe it would have been easier if Olivia or Billy slept upstairs, but Olivia had a room downstairs at the rear of the house, and Billy had his own small cabin behind the bunkhouse.

He'd damn near raped her that afternoon, had come too close to losing control. It had never happened before, and it sure as hell could never happen again.

It wouldn't have been so difficult if he hadn't been certain that Grace wanted him as badly as he wanted her. He'd felt it in the way she'd pressed her body against his, and he'd seen it in her eyes before the fear had stolen in and ruined it all.

He wouldn't have Grace afraid of him.

With a muffled curse he slipped on his pants, fastening two buttons and leaving the rest undone. He wasn't likely to run into anyone this late at night. Olivia had been asleep for hours, and Grace had taken to retiring early herself.

There was a bottle of whiskey in his father's study—his study, he corrected himself. That bottle hadn't been touched since Henry Becket's death.

Dillon had seen his father grow too accustomed to the comfort of the bottle, and was convinced it had contributed to his death. So he made a point of staying away from liquor. The only glass he'd given in to in the past year had ended up dumped on his head.

But for tonight, if the comfort of the bottle was the only comfort he was likely to get . . .

He stopped outside Grace's door. There was no lock on that door, he knew. He could step right in and slip into bed with her. That was exactly what he wanted to do, but he didn't dare.

He wasn't even to the bottom of the stairs before he realized that someone else was awake, as well. There was a soft light in the kitchen, shedding its faint tendrils into the hallway and the dining room. Just enough for Dillon to see where he was going.

Probably Olivia sneaking a midnight snack, cutting herself a slice of that cake she'd prepared for dessert. There was plenty left, since neither he nor Grace had had much of an appetite that evening. Christ, she hadn't even looked at him. She'd kept her eyes on her plate as she'd played with her food.

Dillon slipped quietly past the doorway. Olivia would never even know that she was not the only one awake.

And then he heard it, a gentle splash. Dillon stopped abruptly, certain that it was not Olivia who was bathing in the kitchen in the middle of the night. It was Grace, up to her ears in bubbles and naked as the day she was born.

He had to look. Hell, he had dreamed about it too much not to take a peek when the opportunity presented itself. He slunk quietly to the dining room, and to the kitchen door, staying in the shadows and moving across the floor on silent bare feet.

A single lamp sat on the floor beside the tub, casting a dreamlike circle of light all around Grace.

Her back was to him, and all he could see was a silky pile of black hair on top of her head and wet, soapy shoulders. He could hear her, the gentle splash of her hand as it dipped below the water. Damned if he couldn't hear the soap sliding across her skin.

Grace set the soap aside, there on the floor by the lamp, and began to rinse the lather from her body with handfuls of water. She raised a cupped hand to her shoulder and Dillon watched the water roll over her skin, rinsing away the soapy film and sheeting over her back.

How many nights had she done this? Slipped down the stairs and bathed in the kitchen while he tormented himself in his bedroom?

Grace took the neatly folded towel from the floor and stood slowly, revealing a perfect body. The water beaded and ran in rivulets down her body, dripping into the soapy water and onto the floor as she very gingerly stepped from the tub.

There was no other word for her body than perfect. It was pale and smooth and curved in all the right places. Her breasts were firm, and the nipples he had caressed that afternoon were dark against her alabaster skin. She pressed the towel to her face, and when she lowered it and began to dry her arms she stopped, her eyes on the doorway.

For a moment she didn't move, and Dillon wondered if she would scream or cower or cry. But she just watched him as he studied her, and when she lifted her hand to him, palm upward in an unmistakable invitation, he went to her.

Their eyes were locked as he took her in his arms, slowly, gingerly, as if she might break. There was passion and surrender in her bluebonnet eyes, and Dillon promised himself then and there that she would not regret that surrender.

He took her mouth with his, with tender passion that made him forget his doubts and his pledge to stay away from her. Her slick chest, still wet from her bath, pressed against his, skin to skin, heartbeat to heartbeat. Dillon's head was spinning, and he was drunk on the taste of Grace, the feel of her beneath his hands.

The towel hit the floor, landing silently at their feet. Grace wrapped her arms around his neck and grasped the back of his head, twining her fingers through his hair and pulling him closer. She parted her lips for him, thrusting her tongue inside his mouth, and her hips rocked forward as she pressed against his thighs.

Dillon lowered her to the floor, heedless of the water that had dripped from her body and pooled at their feet. He was about to burst. He'd waited so long for her, and to come across her just as she'd been in his dreams, only more beautiful, warmer, and real, was more than he could stand.

But he didn't want her to regret lifting her hand and asking him to come to her. He wanted to claim her as his own in a way that would make her lift that hand to him again and again. Every night.

He trailed his lips down her throat, and when

he took her nipple in his mouth Grace made a little noise deep in the back of her throat, a quick catch of her breath as she arched her back and lifted her breast to him. Her legs were spread beneath him, and he rested between her thighs with nothing more than a couple of near bursting buttons between him and the woman of his dreams.

He moved his mouth back to hers, and she kissed him hungrily. When he rested his fingers between her legs, touching her lightly, she arched against him and sucked his tongue deep into her mouth. She was ready for him, as ready as he was for her.

"Dillon." She whispered his name breathlessly and locked her hands behind his neck. "Dillon, wait."

He stilled. Wait? Was she kidding? Or was she just trying to kill him?

"Not . . ." she whispered, taking his face between her hands and gazing into his eyes, ". . . not on the floor of Olivia's kitchen." She gave him a small smile, and then bit her lower lip almost shyly.

Dillon groaned. "You ask a lot of a man, Grace," he said, but he stood, holding her body against him, and lifted her into his arms. She was so small, so light, as he carried her through the dining room and up the stairs, bending his head to kiss her throat and then her lips, unable to keep his mouth away from her skin.

They were near the top of the staircase when she spoke again. "There's something I have to tell you," she said in a small voice, breathless and hesitant. "About those other men . . ."

Dillon silenced her with a kiss, then lifted his lips slightly from hers. "It doesn't matter." And he didn't want to hear it, either.

"But I never—"

Dillon covered her mouth with his and pushed open the door to her room. It was closer to the stairway than his, and therefore the only choice.

He laid her on top of the bed and shed his trousers quickly. It was pitch black in the room, with no light other than the scant moonlight that broke through the window.

"But, Dillon," she protested weakly. "You should know."

"It can wait, can't it?" He asked as he lowered himself over her and took a nipple in his mouth. She ran her fingers through his hair and held him to her. Her breath was coming in short gasps, and her heartbeat was racing.

He slipped his fingers between her legs, and she cried out, a faint cry in the night. "Yes, Dil lon," she said weakly. "It can wait."

He couldn't stand it any longer, and he positioned himself between her thighs and pushed inside her. She was so small, so hot and tight, he had to enter her slowly. Her body adjusted to his, molded to his, and with an impatient thrust he found what she had been trying to tell him, but it was too late to stop.

He was inside her, above her, afraid that if he moved he would hurt her, afraid that if he didn't he would die right there.

Grace lifted her hips slightly, rocked against him, and that was all it took. He withdrew slowly, and then thrust to fill her, and again, stilling her cries with his mouth. And then the strong spasms rocked his body and drove away everything but the body beneath his.

She was breathing raggedly, whispery gasps in his ear. He could feel the tension in her body, in the arms that still circled his neck, in her lips as he kissed her.

"For God's sake, Grace," he whispered. "Why didn't you tell me?"

"I . . . I tried," she stammered. She sounded as though she were about to cry, and Dillon felt a wave of guilt. He'd never taken a virgin before, didn't know what to do, or what to say.

All he could do was comfort her, and show her that there was more to making love than the pain she had just experienced.

So he kissed her again with a hesitant tenderness. Some of the tension left her body, and he cupped her breast in one hand and ran his thumb over the dark nipple. It hardened to his touch, but Grace protested.

"I can't," she whispered. "Not again," even as he touched her there where he had fit so perfectly.

"I won't hurt you again, Grace," Dillon said, refusing to slow his tender assault on her body.

"But it did hurt," she argued weakly, her body betraying her with its reaction to his touch.

Dillon felt his own rising desire, and knew she wouldn't have long to wait. "I won't hurt you again, Grace," he repeated. "Trust me."

"I do," she said huskily. "I do trust you."

Dillon threw back the quilt that covered her bed and placed her between the sheets. He asked her to trust him, and she wasn't lying when she said she did. Dillon was the only man in the world she trusted, with the possible exception of Billy. But it was Dillon she would trust with her heart and her body. With her very life.

She still hurt a little, but that pain faded with every kiss Dillon gifted her with, with every touch of his surprisingly gentle hands.

She had known, when she'd seen him standing in the shadowed doorway, that this was going to happen. And she'd wanted it to. She'd wanted Dillon to hold her and stoke the fire he'd ignited within her.

His eyes were on her face as he moved to tower above her again, his weight on his forearms at her sides. She could feel him pressing into her moist center where she throbbed for him, and she slipped her hand between their bodies to guide him inside her.

The sensation of having him there took her breath away. He filled her completely, and made her anxious for . . . for what? For more. She lifted her hips as he slid in and out of her, driving her toward some elusive end. Something she had never even dreamed of.

It built within her, that driving need, and when it burst upon her, shattering her body and soul, she was certain that this was some kind of death . . . a beautiful death to be certain, but life as she'd known it ceased to exist.

Dillon whispered her name, and found his completion as she had, driving into her so hard and so far that she knew he was a part of her. That she would feel him within her even when he was no longer there. A warmth filled her. Love for Dillon, for what they had found.

She snuggled against Dillon as he rolled away from her, and he gathered her in his arms, kissing the top of her head and rubbing his hands over her arms.

She wondered if he would tell her that he loved her. Surely it would be best for him to say the words first. But they both remained silent, finding peace in one another's arms.

When Dillon finally spoke, his words were

truly unromantic. "I'm starving," he whispered as he nibbled her ear.

In response, Grace's stomach growled, and Dillon rubbed his hand over her belly. "You, too?"

"A little," she conceded.

Dillon stepped into his trousers and left her lying in the warm bed. The room was empty without him, hollow and lonely. But he was back in minutes, two huge slices of cake in one hand, the lamp she had left burning in the kitchen in the other. He nudged the door shut softly and set the lamp on the bedside table.

Grace could only smile up at him, at the supremely satisfied look on his face, at the hair on his chest . . . hair that narrowed and disappeared into the sloppily fastened trousers he wore.

"What are you looking at?" Dillon asked as he sat beside her on the bed. It creaked softly under his weight.

"Nothing," she said innocently.

"Well." Dillon broke off a piece of Olivia's white cake and popped it into her mouth. "It may be nothing right now, but give me a little while."

He fed her cake, and dutifully kissed away the crumbs he dropped on her chin, her chest, her breasts. "I'm glad I decided to keep you," Dillon whispered as he licked a dab of frosting from a hard nipple. She had decided that it was no accident that he tended to drop bits of cake there.

"Oh, are you?" Grace asked with a tender smile. "And when exactly did you make that decision?"

"When you threatened to throw a vase full of flowers at my head." He towered above her, his gray eyes misty with desire as he removed his trousers. Grace reached out to douse the lamp at her bedside, but Dillon stopped her, a gentle restraining hand over hers.

"I want to see you, Grace. I want to see your eyes, and the beating pulse at your throat, and my hands on your skin." His voice was husky, and Grace knew she couldn't deny him anything. Ever.

This time she watched his face as he entered her, watched the fire in his eyes and the slight tremble of his lips just before he kissed her. And only then did she know that she had claimed him, just as surely as he had claimed her.

Dillon was gone when Grace woke, but she could still smell him on the bed and on her skin. She was tender, maybe even sore, but she didn't regret anything that had happened.

She had a whole new life, away from the lying eyes of shallow men and the strict rules of English society. Texas was another world, and Dillon was not of the same cut as the men who had tried to buy her with rubies and gold.

Olivia looked at her strangely, and asked if she felt all right, when Grace apologized for sleeping late. The tub was gone. Billy had agreed to haul the heavy tub outside and dump the soapy water when he found it there in the morning. The water she had dripped onto the floor and then lain in with Dillon was gone. Dried without a trace. Grace felt a strange warmth steal over her. A warmth that came from deep inside her, where she kept a piece of Dillon.

She didn't even mind the thought of milking the cow, or feeding the ungrateful chickens, and she left the house with a smile on her face and a fullness in her heart.

And that was why she didn't hear the footsteps behind her, not until a black-clad arm encircled her waist and a gloved hand covered her mouth. She kicked at her attacker, but her efforts were futile. He merely clucked at her as he pulled her into the barn where no eyes from the house would see them.

"Shh, *señorita,*" a silky voice cooed into her ear. "Be still."

Grace recognized the voice and stopped struggling. A chill ran down her spine as she remembered the way the man had looked at her.

With a gentle black-gloved hand he turned her to face him, and the grip over her mouth eased. When she showed no indication of screaming for help, that hand dropped away. He smiled down at her, a completely nonthreatening grin that made Grace relax.

"Buenos días, querida," he whispered.

"Good morning, Renzo."

Chapter Eleven

He stepped away from her, but her back was to the barn and there was no escape but around or through Renzo. If it had been any one of Renzo's men she faced, Grace would have been screaming at the top of her lungs, but it was difficult to be afraid of a man who smiled so openly. Renzo's eyes twinkled like the eyes of a happily naughty child.

"How did you find me?" she asked uncertainly. "And what are you doing here?"

"You've been preying on my mind, Grace Cavanaugh. And you were most easy to find. A beauty such as yours cannot be hidden, and as I had your name, and your Becket's name . . ." He shrugged his shoulders. "It was a simple matter to locate you, *querida*."

A warning trickle traveled up her spine. Renzo was every bit as tall as Dillon, and he moved with an easy strength. If he decided to hoist her over his shoulder and carry her away, there would be little she could do to stop him.

He must have sensed her fear, because an almost tender light flickered in his black eyes, and he backed away from her one single step.

"Are you content here, *querida*? Or are you ready to come away with Renzo?"

It was an offer, Grace realized, and not a threat. "I . . . I'm happy here. You shouldn't have come. If Dillon were to see you . . ." She shook her head. "He was furious with you and your men. If he sees you he will probably shoot." Grace knew, as she warned Renzo, that she didn't want to see the charming bandit bleeding in the Double B dust.

Without warning, Renzo reached out and grabbed her arm. His touch was light, but she opened her mouth to scream and he clamped a hand over the lower half of her face, cutting her scream to a muffled cry. She knew then that she should've screamed when she had the chance.

Renzo half carried and half dragged her to the back of the barn. He was whispering for her to be still and quiet, but she barely heard him. What would Dillon think when he found her gone? Would he think she had run away from him and what had happened between them? Would he even bother to look for her?

They rounded the corner of the barn, and Renzo stopped suddenly. He held her tightly, one arm around her waist as he continued to muffle her protests with a gloved hand.

"Now will you be quiet?" he whispered.

Grace finally saw what was awaiting her, what Renzo had done, and she was still. The hand at her mouth loosened and slowly moved away, and Renzo released her.

Her trunks. All of them. They were covered with mud that was dried and hard. The trunks that had once had locks had been broken open and secured with a crisscross of heavy rope. But they were all there.

"A woman should not be deprived of her belongings," Renzo said as he stepped around to face her.

He was so obviously pleased with himself, so delighted with her stunned reaction, Grace found herself returning his smile. The bandit Renzo looked like a little boy who'd just gotten away with a mischievous prank.

"I would have carried these trunks to your door, but what you say is true. It would not do for your Becket to see me here. But"—Renzo took her hand and bent over it with a courtly bow, every bit as chivalrous and charming as the lords of London—"when I looked inside the trunks and saw the beautiful things there, the silk and the lace, the slippers and the stockings, I knew it would be a true crime for any woman other than you to wear them."

"This is very sweet of you, Renzo," Grace said as she eyed the baggage. She stepped around him and laid a hand on top of the largest Saratoga trunk. They were her things, but they seemed very unimportant at the moment. Silk dresses she could never wear. Lace fans that were all but useless against the Texas heat. But still, there were a few items among the frivolous that she could use.

"Thank you," she said sincerely. "Thank you so—" Grace spun around, and closed her mouth abruptly. He was gone. Gone without a word or even a cloud of dust to show that he had been there.

* * *

Once she'd finished helping Olivia in the kitchen, Grace ran up the stairs to ready herself for supper. Once or twice, during the long day, she'd wondered if Olivia could see that she was changed. Love had turned her into a silly girl, laughing at everything and finding beauty everywhere she looked. The incredibly blue skies, the thriving plants in Olivia's garden, Dillon's horses prancing in the corral. All beautiful.

It had meant crossing an ocean and forsaking everything she'd believed important: money, position, society. Dillon made her realize what was really important. What really mattered. She didn't care if she never left the Double B.

Her newly unpacked gowns were strewn around the room, over the bed and the single chair. Slippers, more than one woman could possibly need in a lifetime, it seemed, were scattered across the floor.

Maybe tonight Dillon would propose. The thought made her head swim. Happiness. She'd never been happy before, and she felt absolutely light-headed. It was as if a heavy burden had been lifted from her, and each and every step was lighter, easier.

She bathed as best she could with the basin of water in her room, and brushed her hair until it shone. She piled it on top of her head, but let loose tendrils frame her face and fall down her back. The gown she had chosen to wear—for Dillon—was a pale rose, simple and elegant. She couldn't imagine Dillon caring much for lace and frills, so she chose a gown that had none.

But it fit her perfectly, hugging her arms and her torso, flaring at the hips. The scooped neckline was modest, and for once Grace decided to leave the flesh there bare. Tonight she would wear no jewel that had been given to her by another man. No pendant or choker, no bracelet or ring. She would go to Dillon unadorned.

It occurred to her, as she fastened the last buttons at her cuff, that her father had finally given her a gift. He'd been free with his money, even to the last when, she now knew, his financial situation had been bad. Birthdays, Christmas, special occasions such as her graduation, had been commemorated coldly, with cash. *Buy yourself something,* he would write in his small, neat script.

But he had never chosen anything for her. Not one single gift. Until now. He had chosen Dillon for her, and for that she could forgive him anything.

Dillon watched Grace as she came toward him, down the stairs and across the room as elegant as any princess. He had to force himself to stay in his seat and not stand and go to her. To hell with food. He wanted *her*.

But Billy was seated beside him, and Olivia was bringing the last of the meal to the table. Surely they would be able to tell that something momentous had happened. He could see the truth in Grace's face—in her smile, in her eyes. Surely Billy and Olivia could see it, too.

"I hope you haven't been waiting for me," Grace said as she took the chair across from him. He could hardly stand to look at her, she was so radiantly beautiful. So he kept his eyes down, trying to look tired, which he was, and uninterested, which he wasn't.

"No," Olivia assured Grace as she took her seat

closest to the kitchen door. "You're right on time."

They fell into their usual, relaxed mealtime conversation, most of which Dillon didn't hear. He heaped his plate high, and then regretted it. How could he eat with this damn lump in his throat?

When he lifted his eyes just enough to see Grace's plate, he saw that she was moving her food around but eating very little. She didn't have any more of an appetite than he did.

What had he gotten himself into? He couldn't possibly have fallen in love with her. It was too soon, too fast, and besides, he didn't believe in love. He believed in lust, and he believed in commitment. He just didn't believe the two were compatible.

"That's a right purty dress, Miss Grace," Billy said, and Dillon lifted his eyes to look at her. He hadn't even noticed the gown she wore. He had been too busy either looking at her face or avoiding her completely. But he realized, now, that it was something new she wore.

"Yes," Olivia agreed. "That's such a pretty color on you. Is that one of the things you brought in this afternoon?"

Grace nodded her head. "Yes, it is, actually." There was hesitation in her voice.

Dillon frowned and set his fork aside. "What things?"

"Is that why them trunks are in the barn?" Billy asked before Grace could answer the question. "I thought I recognized them, but they're such a mess."

"That's why I didn't bring them into the house. They're ruined, I fear, but practically all the clothing is fine. A bit of mud seeped into one of the smaller trunks, but—"

"Your trunks?" Dillon asked sharply.

Grace nodded.

"The ones I left by the side of the road?"

She met his eyes then, and he saw there the same hesitation he had heard in her voice. "Yes. They were delivered this morning."

"Delivered by who?"

Grace set her own fork aside, and Dillon could see the determination building in her face. She was preparing to do battle, if necessary. "You don't want to know, Becket."

"Grace."

"All right. It was Renzo," Grace said quickly, practically spitting out the words.

Dillon shot to his feet, sending the chair he'd been sitting in flying backward. "The bandit?"

Grace looked infuriatingly calm and self-assured. "I told you that you didn't want to know."

Dillon grabbed his chair and righted it, then placed himself slowly and deliberately back into his place. He shoved the plate before him away and placed both hands on the table, leaning forward and looking into Grace's too-perfect face. "Tell," he ordered.

He listened to Grace's story without saying a word, proud of himself that he didn't interrupt even once. But when she told him that the bandit had asked her—again—to go away with him, Dillon ground his teeth together.

When she was finished he just stared at her for a moment. She was too damn calm about the whole incident. "From now on," he said in a low voice, his efforts at calming himself making his voice stilted, "you don't go anywhere without an escort."

"Don't be ridiculous. . . ." She stopped when her eyes met his, and she evidently recognized just how serious he was. "You can't expect me to stay in the house all day long, and I don't need an escort to the barn."

"You needed one this morning."

Grace smiled at him, and she placed her elbows on the table and her chin on her intertwined fingers. "If Renzo had intended to carry me off, he would have done so this morning. If I had intended to go with him, I would have done so this morning. But he didn't, and I didn't, so there's nothing to worry about, Becket."

He didn't have an answer for her, but what he belatedly recognized as fear clutched at his heart. He could have lost her just when he'd found her. If the damned bandit had carried her off he might never have seen Grace again. How could he protect a treasure like Grace? He couldn't. Not really. He didn't even have a right to claim her as his own. Not yet. Not until the profits from the cattle drive came in and he was assured that he would have something to offer her.

"Eat, you two," Olivia ordered, the unbending tone of a true matriarch in her voice. "You young people need to keep your strength up. I swear, I never saw you so finicky, Dillon." She leaned across the table and divulged her own secret. "There's pie for dessert."

Dillon pulled his eyes away from Grace, hard as that was. "Custard pie?" he asked, sniffing the air.

"Yep. And there's a little bit of cake left from last night, though not quite as much as I remembered."

Dillon had a sudden, clear vision of Grace with cake crumbs and dollops of sweet icing on her skin. He pulled his plate back toward him and began to eat. Olivia's normally delicious food had no taste, but that didn't stop him.

"That's right, Becket," Grace said innocently. "Clean your plate and you'll get dessert."

He looked up at her, trying to warn her with his eyes. But she was toying with her food again, looking down and avoiding his glare.

She tilted her head to one side and a strand of hair fell across one cheek. Her skin was still pale, but had more color than when he'd first seen her. The Texas sun? Or a flush he had put there himself?

Grace moved through the small room like a whirlwind, picking up discarded gowns and slippers, trying to make sense of the mess around her. She'd excused herself for the night, pleading exhaustion, as early as she dared. It was almost impossible to be in the same room with Dillon and behave normally, in any case.

Certainly he would come to her tonight. She told herself that, even though he'd seemed so distant. And he'd been so upset when she'd told him about Renzo's visit. Of course, that had been none of her doing, but Dillon seemed to think differently.

After she made some order of the room she surveyed herself in the small mirror that hung above the dresser. She swallowed hard, wondering if this was right. Would Dillon love it? Or hate it?

The nightgown she wore was so sheer she could see right through the material. Every curve, her dark nipples. The shocking nightdress was a pale lavender, and there were darker lavender ribbons at each shoulder.

It had been at the bottom of one trunk, and had appeared to be untouched. The clothing at the top had been manhandled, but she imagined Renzo and his band of thieves had been looking for something more valuable than the nightgown she'd never had the nerve to wear.

A nightgown bought with money her father had sent.

It had been one of her small rebellions. She and a couple of classmates had been shopping, and this had been what she'd bought. Angry at her father, feeling excluded from the circle of well-bred young ladies who tolerated her, she had bought the most outlandish, the most daring nightdress she could find. Even the dressmaker who ran the shop tried to talk Grace out of her purchase, suggesting more appropriate items. There had been a moment when Grace thought the lady would refuse to sell. The high price, and a little extra, changed the dressmaker's mind.

At the time Grace had imagined the girls whispering to their friends and sisters and maybe even their mothers about what that decadent and barbarian American girl had bought. And she had wondered what her father would think of his little girl buying a nightgown that clearly had no other purpose than seduction.

Once purchased, it had been stored in the bottom of a trunk, and Grace had forgotten about it. Until this morning.

She heard him climbing the stairs, his steps slow and uncertain. Would he come to her? Or would he pass by her door as if last night had never happened?

The heavy footsteps stopped outside her door, and the doorknob wiggled just a little, as if he'd placed his hand there but waited to turn it. And then he walked away, toward his own room, and Grace's heart sank.

She went to the window and looked across the ranch. The Double B was Dillon's place on this earth. And hers? Last night she'd been so certain, but now . . .

He could have smiled at her, just once, over the supper table. He could have cornered her at one time or another during the day for a small, tender kiss, a promise of what would come later. But he had ignored her, and scowled as always, and now . . . he had passed her by with such ease.

The door opened so quietly she didn't hear it. The first sound she heard was Dillon's rasping voice.

"What in the name of the devil are you wearing?"

Grace turned around slowly, suddenly shy about the diaphanous gown. "You changed your mind."

He lifted his eyebrows and closed the door behind him. "I did?"

"About coming here tonight." She wanted to sound strong, but her voice came out a hoarse whisper.

Dillon leaned against the door and watched her with clouded eyes. "You heard me?"

Grace nodded.

"You don't know what you're doing to me, Grace."

"I think I have a pretty good idea." She took a step toward him. "You're confused, and a little angry."

"I'm a lot angry," he said, but there was no anger in his voice.

Grace stopped in the middle of the room. Dillon would have to come the rest of the way . . . to her. "Why are you so angry?"

"Because I know I don't deserve what you gave me last night. Because I know other men will always want you, will always try to take you away from me. And I don't know if I can keep you."

Grace smiled. "You told me last night that you'd decided to keep me. You strike me as a man who gets what he wants, Dillon Becket."

He waited a moment to answer her, and he looked her up and down, taking in every inch of her body that was exposed through the sheer lavender nightdress. "Usually. Not always."

Grace lifted her hand, inviting him to come closer, to come to her, and he did.

Their lips met, softly at first and then hard. They spent the frustrated energy that had built during the long evening as they'd sat in the same room, and pretended . . . pretended that they didn't want just this. That energy burst forth and consumed them.

His lips were hot and moist, and tugged at her soul as he bent over her, searing her lips and her heart, making her burn for him.

Dillon grabbed a handful of the thin nightgown at her back and pulled her to him, crushing her against his chest, trailing his lips down her throat as he slid down her body. Grace moaned and grabbed a handful of dark hair at the back of his head. She was holding on . . . to Dillon, to a thin thread of control . . . holding on for dear life.

The heat of his tongue pressed the thin and silky material against her hardened nipple, and she felt the strong tugging between her legs. Hollow—that was how she felt. She gently pulled his head away from her breast and lifted his face to hers. She wanted those lips. She needed to tell him, before it was too late, before she got so caught up in the heat between them that she couldn't speak.

"Dillon," she whispered his name, her breath against his lips. One thumb was circling a nipple, and one hand rested at the small of her back, possessive and impatient.

"You never need to be angry," she whispered huskily. "No man has ever touched me but you." She felt the tears gathering in her eyes. Tears of joy at what she had found. "No man will ever touch me but you. If I could be magically transported to any place on this earth, I wouldn't go. This is the place I want to be. With you."

She led his hand from her breast to her shoulder, and together they untied the slender ribbon there. The material fell, exposing one breast to the warm night air. But Dillon didn't look down, and neither did she. Their eyes were locked, his gray eyes a softer shade than usual, a pale silver. His hand, still in hers, slid across her chest and rested on the other ribbon. When it was loosened, the nightgown slipped to the floor, pooling at her feet.

Dillon lifted her into his arms and carried her to the bed. He left her only for the moments it took to shed his own clothes, and then he was with her, burying his face against her hair and her shoulder. Whispering into her ear, telling her that she was beautiful, telling her how much he wanted her.

Dillon was warm, and with his touch he chased away the chill that had once surrounded her heart. He was hard, his muscles and his strong face and his granite eyes, and he needed the softness she could give him.

Most important, he was hers, and she knew as he came to her that she would never be alone again.

Chapter Twelve

Grace had come to love riding the gentle mare Dillon had chosen for her. He'd told her, with a twinkle in his eye, that the horse's name was Butter. It was true the fine animal was almost the color of butter, but she could feel the long-gone pain in her hands every time Dillon called the mare's name. And then she remembered that it had been Dillon who'd finished churning that day, and he'd actually put one of the younger hands to the chore since then.

Grace and Butter never traveled far from the house, and the pace was always leisurely. Once she was pronounced capable of leaving the corral, she was instructed never to ride alone. Dillon reminded her of that dictate on a regular basis.

It was Billy who usually accompanied her on her short rides. Dillon was always busy during the day, so dedicated to the ranch that she barely saw him between sunup and sundown. But at night he was hers, and that was enough.

The only cloud in her life was the fact that Dillon had not yet told her that he loved her. He hadn't said a word about marriage, either. Grace believed that it was true, that he did love her and wanted to marry her. But she longed to hear him say it, and to say the words herself.

She caught herself, now and again, actually mouthing the words during the day. *I love you, Dillon Becket.* But she was holding back, waiting for him to say it first.

If Billy or Olivia knew that there was anything between her and Dillon, they never gave any sign of it. Every morning Grace expected to greet harsh, disapproving eyes in the kitchen, but Olivia was always cheerful and bright. And Billy seemed never to change. He watched over her, and laughed with Dillon.

If Dillon had filled her heart, then it was just as true that Billy had filled an empty place inside her as well. He was the father she'd never had—warm and caring, funny and occasionally stern. He warned her about riding too fast or too far, and chastised her gently when she didn't clean her supper plate, declaring her much too skinny. She didn't mind his intrusions into her everyday life. It was what she had wanted and missed for years.

He had already told her that he would be unable to ride with her that afternoon. Dillon needed his help, and Grace had been instructed to stay close to the house. But she would miss her afternoon ride, and that was what prompted her to stray into the barn. She went to the stall where Butter was housed, and rubbed a creamy muzzle. The mare was bound to miss the exercise as much as she would, but there was nothing to be done for it.

"Afternoon, Miss Grace."

The sound of the unexpected voice made Grace jump, and she spun to face the intruder. She'd been so certain she was alone. But when she saw who it was her fear fled, and she smiled.

"Hartley. For goodness' sake, you scared me half to death. Why aren't you with the others?"

He hesitated, and she could almost see his mind at work as he searched for an answer. Evidently Hartley was not as bright as she'd first thought. He looked a bit . . . dim at the moment.

"I turned my ankle," he said in a low voice, "and the boss sent me back. I was looking for some of that salve he keeps in here."

Grace went directly to the cabinet where Dillon kept several different greasy salves, and studied the contents with a frown. "I don't know which—"

Hartley reached past her and grabbed a jar. He hefted it, testing its weight, and then replaced it. "You know, my ankle's a lot better. I don't reckon I need that salve after all."

Grace sidled around the ranch hand and made her way back to Butter. When she looked over her shoulder, Hartley grinned widely and shifted back and forth on booted feet.

"You goin' for a ride this afternoon?" he asked in an unnecessarily low voice. That gravelly voice suited his weathered face, Grace decided.

She shook her head. "No. I don't know my way around very well, and Dillon and Billy are both too busy to ride with me." Grace faced the stall and her mare. She really had become accustomed to her afternoon rides.

"It's such a pretty day." When he spoke Grace

realized that Hartley was right behind her. "Seems a shame . . . well, why don't I ride with you, Miss Grace?" he asked with a hint of surprise in his voice, as if he'd just thought of the idea. "My ankle's not as bad as I first thought, and we're working so far away from the house today I really don't have time to get back before the boss calls it quits for the day. It wouldn't be a problem at all."

"Thank you, but I really—"

Hartley opened the stall door and led Butter out; then he turned to Grace with a bright smile. "We won't go far. You'll be back long before suppertime, and I'm sure the boss won't mind."

The idea was tempting. She wanted to ride, and she wouldn't be alone. Dillon had told her to stick close to the house, but he hadn't known Hartley would be available to escort her. She almost declined again, and then Hartley patted Butter's neck. Such a beautiful animal. Certainly Dillon wouldn't mind. Not with one of his ranch hands along.

"All right," she said with a smile. "Let me go tell Olivia where I'll be."

"Well, I don't think so." Hartley reached out and grabbed her arm, wrapping long fingers around her wrist.

Grace's heart skipped a beat, and she looked down at the hairy hand that restrained her. Hartley leaned in, a bit too close for Grace's comfort. "If Olivia knows what you're plannin' to do, she might try to stop us. She's such a proper old woman."

The long fingers unfolded slowly, and Hartley backed away. Grace took a deep breath and relaxed. She was going to have to learn not to react so strongly to a casual touch. And she might as well start now.

"It'll be fun," Hartley whispered. "Just like kids sneakin' off when they should be doin' their chores."

Hartley saddled her mare and led Butter from the barn. His own horse was hitched behind the barn, and Hartley glanced toward the house twice as he helped Grace into the sidesaddle.

She looked toward the house just once. A short ride, he had said.

Hartley led the way, taking a southern path she'd never traveled before. After a short ride the landscape seemed to be more barren, not nearly as scenic as the land east of the house. But still, she was glad for the change, and glad for a chance to see more of Dillon's ranch. He and the hands were to the north this afternoon, she knew, and she wondered if that was why Hartley had chosen to head south.

Hartley brought his animal to a halt near a trickle of a stream, and dismounted with an easy grace. Without a word he lifted Grace from the sidesaddle, and Butter joined the other horse at the ribbon of water.

The sun was low in the sky, but it was still hot. A trickle of sweat ran down Grace's face. They'd traveled a lot farther than she'd intended, but Hartley seemed to know where he was going. Besides, she couldn't find her way back to the ranch without him. She'd been hopelessly lost five minutes after they left the barn.

"Time to head back?" she asked hopefully, sitting in the shade of a tall, flat rock and leaning against it. She was beginning to wish that she had stayed at the ranch. It was so hot, and if Dillon got back to the house before she did he would be worried. And she was such a mess. She had to have time to clean up before Dillon got home.

Hartley stood before her, his hands on his hips as he looked down. "I don't think so."

His easy smile was gone, and Grace felt a chill in spite of the heat. "But it will be late. . . ."

He dropped down in front of her, blocking any move that Grace might have made. She couldn't stand; she couldn't even lean forward without touching Hartley's hands or his knees.

"And to think, I would have been satisfied just to burn down his barn. But when I saw you standing there, like you was just waiting for me, I knew I could make him really sorry he crossed me."

Grace tried to stand up slowly, her back against the rock, but Hartley reached out and grabbed her wrists.

"I . . . I don't understand."

Hartley's grin was back, but it wasn't friendly. It was chilling. "He didn't tell you that he fired me, I reckon. Fired me because I made an innocent comment about you." He leaned a bit closer, and Grace found that she couldn't breathe. He was right in her face. "I tried to find a job, but nobody's hiring. Damned if I'll go hungry because of a self-righteous bastard like Dillon Becket."

Grace forced herself to take a deep breath, breathing in the stale odor that surrounded Hartley and threatened to choke her. She could handle men. It had been a while, but surely she hadn't lost her touch. "Why don't you just ask for your job back?" There was no fear in her voice, and she hoped Hartley couldn't see her fear in her face. "Dillon Becket does have a temper, and I'm sure he regrets his hasty decision in ending your employment at the Double B. I'll even put in a good word for you."

He laughed at her. Without loosening his grip on her wrist he threw back his head and laughed. "Darlin', it's too late for that. By the time the boss finds what's left of you, you won't be puttin' in a good word for nobody. Ever."

Grace looked into his eyes, and knew that he intended to kill her. She never should have left the ranch. She never should have ridden away with Hartley.

She yanked her hands away from her captor and slipped past him before he knew what was happening, gathering her skirt in her hands and running as fast as she could. North. At least, she was fairly certain it was north.

He hit her from behind, and Grace landed face first in the dirt. She couldn't breathe, with the man's weight pressing her into the ground. And he didn't move, but lay there on top of her for several long moments.

When he did move, he rolled Grace roughly onto her back and then yanked her to her feet. "Time's a wastin', darlin'," he said with a smile.

Grace lifted her head and screamed. She was so winded, what she had intended as an ear-piercing scream came out as little more than a whimper.

No one would have heard, anyway, she reasoned. Dillon was too far away. Grace tugged against the grip that imprisoned her.

"Be still, darlin'," Hartley said in a soft voice. He wasn't winded or anxious or agitated. He was frighteningly calm as he slapped her mare and sent Butter on her way home.

"What . . . why did you do that?" Grace whispered.

Hartley tossed her onto his saddle. "What do you figure the boss will think when that mare shows up with no Grace? He'll probably figure you fell off, or got took by Indians. I reckon by tomorrow morning he'll find you—or what's left of you—and I'll be waitin'. I'm pretty good at waitin', Grace."

He jumped up behind her, and Grace ended up facedown across Hartley's lap, her head hanging to one side. When she tried to lift her head, Hartley pushed her back down and slapped her bottom much as he had the mare's.

"And while he's mournin' over your body, I'll shoot him," Hartley said emotionlessly, turning the horse and taking off at a near gallop.

Dillon walked through the kitchen door and took a big, theatrical sniff of the fragrant stew that was bubbling on the stove. Olivia was bustling around the room, stirring the stew and checking the bread, stacking the plates and gathering together the silverware.

"I'm so hungry I could eat a horse," he said as he bent over the stew. He lifted the wooden spoon, but Olivia slapped his hand and he dropped it obediently.

"We might be having horse for dinner tomorrow night," Olivia snapped. "I had expected to have Grace's help this afternoon, and she rode off without a word. I'll just cook up that mare and—"

"What do you mean she rode off? By herself?" Dillon's playful mood had vanished. Grace didn't know her way around the ranch nearly well enough to set off on her own, and he had specifically told her not to.

"No. Not by herself. That . . . that . . . one of

the hands. I can't think of his name. He hasn't been here very long, and I haven't seen him around the place for a while." She screwed up her face. "Brown hair, going white. Wears it a bit long. Hart, is it?"

His blood turned cold. "Hartley?"

"That's it," Olivia said briskly. "They rode out of here hours ago, and I ain't seen hide nor hair of—" She stopped abruptly as she looked up into Dillon's face. "What's wrong?"

"I fired Hartley weeks ago," Dillon said as he fled the room with Olivia on his heels. As he strode across the room he checked the bullets in his Colt, although he knew it was fully loaded. He grabbed a rifle from the gun cabinet in his father's study—his study—and ran his hand over the barrel.

"I'm going to look for her. When Billy gets in . . ." Billy and the other men wouldn't be back for at least half an hour. He'd pushed ahead, driving his horse to the limit to reach Grace. "Tell him everything. And tell him to wait here. If I'm not back by morning, I want him to go to Plummerton and tell the sheriff what's happened."

Olivia stood by him as he resaddled his stallion. He'd already pushed the animal, and now he would have to ask for more. There was no other horse presently in the barn or the corral that had the stamina he might require.

Olivia had dogged his steps from the moment he'd told her about firing Hartley. She was wringing her hands and chewing her bottom lip.

"She will be all right, won't she, Dillon?" she asked for the fifth time as he mounted his stallion.

He looked ahead, and there was Butter, loping

toward the barn . . . riderless. His heart almost stopped.

Olivia repeated her question. But it wasn't a question at all. *She* will *be all right, won't she?* He looked down at the gray-haired woman. He wanted to reassure her, to convince her that everything would be fine. That Grace, wherever she was, was safe. But he couldn't. The sun was setting, and once complete darkness fell it would be impossible to track.

So he didn't answer Olivia, but galloped off in the direction she had said Grace and Hartley had taken, following the distinct tracks of two horses in the dirt.

Grace opened her eyes slowly. Her head was upside down, and it ached horribly. She felt as if she were bruised all over—her stomach and her legs, her sides and most assuredly her head.

As she tried to lift her head a moan escaped her throat, and a hand slapped smartly against her spine.

"I was beginning to think you wasn't going to wake up, darlin'."

At the sound of his voice, Grace remembered everything, and realized where she was. How could she have fallen asleep draped across Hartley's lap?

She hadn't fallen asleep, she was certain. She had fainted. How disgusting. She had never fainted in her life, though she had pretended to on several occasions.

It was dark. Not just gray but black as pitch. How could Hartley see to keep going? His horse was moving slowly but certainly across the flat ground.

Grace lifted her head and tried to look around,

and to listen. There was nothing. She could see nothing, and all she could hear was the horse's hooves in the packed dirt and labored breathing, the horse's and Hartley's. There was one other sound. The beating of her own heart.

She groaned loudly. The ache in her head wouldn't subside, no matter how she willed it. But at least she was still alive.

Grace stayed silent after that, and endured the sharp aches and pains. Maybe Hartley would change his mind about killing her. Much as she wanted to believe that, she couldn't. He was too calm about the whole plan.

She couldn't rely on the hope that Hartley would change his mind. She could only hope that she could stay alive long enough for Dillon to find her.

If he looked at all. Would he come for her? In her groggy state of mind she couldn't help but think of her father. He had never come for her. Not even when she'd cut off that whining Clarissa's pigtail. Not when she'd climbed from her bedroom window and stayed out till morning. No one had ever known that she'd simply slept in the gardener's shed, cold and shivering. They'd only known that she was out all night.

Not in her last year at school, when she'd made a spectacle of herself in that red dress. The headmistress would write, and her father would send money. But he never came for her. Maybe Dillon wouldn't either.

By the time Hartley stopped, Grace was convinced that she was on her own, that Dillon wouldn't bother to look for her. She had disobeyed his very clear instruction, and, after all, he didn't love her. He would have told her if he had. She'd been living in a fantasy world, believing that he loved her as she loved him.

Hartley slid from the saddle and dragged her roughly with him. She felt as though her head might separate from her shoulders, it was pounding so much, and she swayed on her feet. She would have fallen, but Hartley caught her, pinning her arms to her sides and shoving her toward a rough wall of rock. He pushed her to her knees and tied her wrists and ankles before she knew what he was doing. The rope flew in his hands.

When her hands were tied in front of her, and her ankles were secured, he shoved her to the ground so that her back rested against the rock. Grace watched silently as he built a fire and hobbled his horse. The usually talkative Hartley didn't say a single word as he went about the job of setting up camp.

Grace closed her eyes. If she was going to get out of this, she was going to have to clear her head. She needed all her wits about her.

She took several deep breaths and filled her mind with a pleasing picture. Dillon's field of bluebonnets swaying in the breeze. With every breath the throbbing in her head subsided a little.

Grace opened her eyes slowly. The glow of the fire was faint, but it cast a revealing light around the campsite. Hartley was sipping coffee and munching on a hard biscuit. He hadn't offered her anything, but why waste food on a woman who was going to be dead by morning?

"Why don't you just get it over with, Hartley?" she asked coldly. There was a faint tremble in her voice, the only hint that she was not calm and assured. She knew, was absolutely certain, that he didn't intend for her to die quickly. He was going to take his revenge on Dillon through her. Would he rape her? She wouldn't put it past him, but neither was she certain that he would try. If he did, she wouldn't make it easy for him. The thought of any man but Dillon touching her made her sick.

Hartley grinned at her across the fire. He had that leering look in his eyes that she had come to recognize. She'd seen that look in the eyes of gentlemen, and it was just the same in the eyes of a filthy cowhand.

"What's the rush, darlin'?" With a flick of his wrist he tossed what was left of his coffee onto the fire, which sizzled, but flamed back up again. Hartley never took his eyes from her. He was thin, but Grace knew there was strength in those rope-thin arms and legs. His hat had been discarded, and he had pushed his long hair straight back. Surely the devil looked like that, all weathered and tough, with wings of white at his temples.

He stood slowly, unfolding himself an inch at a time. Then he turned his back on her and went to the saddlebags he had deposited on the ground near his bedroll. He knelt down, took something from the bag, and then opened his canteen.

Hartley walked to her with the tin cup in his hand. Every step brought him closer, and by the time he stood directly in front of her she could hardly take a breath. He dropped down before her and held the cup to her lips. She was so dry, her throat scratchy and her mouth full of dust, that she took three deep swallows before she realized that the water tasted strange. Grace jerked her head away, and a few drops of tainted water landed on her chest. She was effectively immobilized, with her hands and her feet bound, the rock behind her, and Hartley kneeling before her.

"What is that?" she croaked.

"Water," he said as he took her chin in his hand and poured more water down her throat. "Water and a good touch of laudanum."

Grace tried to spit out what was in her mouth, and succeeded in dribbling a bit of it down her chin. But Hartley forced most of what was left down her throat.

"There now," he said smugly. "In a few minutes you'll be manageable enough."

He reached out and unfastened the first three buttons of Grace's calico dress, calico that had been dampened by her efforts to expel the laudanum-laced water. With a fierceness Grace didn't know she possessed, she brought her bound hands up and smacked Hartley's chin.

She did surprise him. His head snapped back and his hands left her. Grace steadied herself for the blow that was surely to come, but Hartley just smiled and backed away from her. He knew, just as she knew, that in a few minutes, half an hour at the most, she would be unable to lift a hand against him. It appeared that Hartley was a patient man, as he had claimed, and was willing to wait.

The effects of the laudanum took her, even as she fought. At first she was simply dizzy and light-headed, and her aches and pains vanished. Even the horrid headache. The fire seemed to swim before her eyes. No matter how hard she tried to concentrate it only got worse, until at last she squeezed her eyes shut.

She tried to bring back that picture of Dillon's wildflowers in her mind, but this time it didn't work. And when she opened her eyes she saw Hartley grinning at her with that insipid grin on his face.

She was so sleepy . . . so tired she couldn't keep her eyes open. They closed even as she willed them to stay open, but she didn't sleep. Her legs and arms were heavy, fluid, and when Hartley finally cut the bonds her hands simply fell away. She forced her eyes open and watched as he cut the bonds at her ankles. She wanted to kick him, but she couldn't move. Her efforts brought about a slight movement that was not even noticeable to the man who had drugged her.

He dragged her closer to the fire, and she felt the warmth as if it were the sun he pulled her toward. The man above her, the man whose face swam before her, unbuttoned her dress to the waist to reveal her lacy chemise. With a shove, he pushed her to the ground and straddled her, toying lazily with the lace and the ribbons.

When he squeezed her breast, Grace found the strength to push against him, to shove his hands away. No man would touch her but Dillon. She had promised him that.

"Get . . . your . . . hands . . . off me . . . you bastard." Her words were thick, not even sounding like her own.

He continued to grin, undaunted by her weak efforts. With his knees he forced her legs apart, and Grace felt his hands on her thighs as he lifted her skirts. She tried to fight him, but couldn't. She couldn't move. Tears of frustration rolled down her cheeks, but they didn't seem to affect Hartley. He was fumbling with his pants. She could hear him groping impatiently at his belt.

And then he stopped. Hartley didn't move for a long moment. Grace tried to focus her eyes, but they wouldn't cooperate. Still, she could tell that someone stood behind Hartley, over him.

"Stand up, you son of a bitch."

Dillon had Hartley's shirt collar in his left hand, and his Colt in the right. He pulled the hammer back with his thumb, and the man beneath him twitched. The muzzle was pressed against the back of Hartley's head, and almost without thought Dillon increased the pressure on the trigger.

Hartley stood slowly, his hands held out to his sides, his arms and legs trembling.

"You wouldn't shoot an unarmed man, would you?" Hartley asked, as Dillon dragged him away from Grace. He couldn't look down at her and retain his control, and he couldn't afford to lose control. So he kept his eyes on the back of Hartley's head.

"No one would blame me," Dillon muttered, and he pressed the barrel of the Colt deeper. Hartley twitched again.

"I didn't touch her, I swear," Hartley said desperately.

"Only because I got here when I did."

Dillon kept his hold on Hartley's collar, but lowered the hammer and holstered his Colt. Shooting was too good and too quick for Hartley.

He spun the man around and swung his fist into Hartley's jaw. The coward dropped to the ground with his hands over his head, and Dillon delivered a swift kick to the man's midsection. Hartley screamed and dropped to the ground, curling up into a ball and whimpering like a whipped puppy.

Dillon turned his head and looked down at Grace. She was just lying there, her eyes half closed, her skirt tossed up around her thighs. She looked like a rag doll, loose limbed and oddly disjointed.

"What did you do to her, you son of a bitch?" He turned back to Hartley to see the man crawling across the dirt, reaching for the holstered six-shooter that lay on the ground near his saddle.

Hartley found the pistol's grip with his thin, trembling fingers, and in a surprisingly fluid motion slid the weapon from the holster. He rolled onto his back and fired all but blind. Dillon didn't hesitate, didn't even think as he drew his Colt and fired. Hartley's shot went wide. Dillon's didn't.

The bullet hit Hartley midchest, and the man dropped his weapon.

"What did you do to her?" Dillon shouted, leaning over the dying man with his Colt still in his hand.

Hartley smiled as he died, an odd half-smile with a bite of victory in it.

Dillon turned away and reholstered his Colt, and he knelt beside Grace. He lifted her head, gently, easily, onto his lap.

"Grace," he whispered, unable to raise his voice.

Her eyes fluttered and opened slightly, and she raised a frail hand. She trailed her fingers along his face, and only then did he realize that his cheeks were wet with tears.

"You came for me," she whispered, and then her hand dropped and her eyes closed.

Chapter Thirteen

Dillon watched her slip away from him, in spite of his command. *You came for me,* whispered as if she didn't believe it was true.

"Wake up, Grace. Come on, honey." With mounting dread he placed his fingers on the pulse at her throat, and then he laid his head against her chest. Christ, her heartbeat was so fast and so faint. It seemed to flutter, delicately and much too uncertainly. What had that bastard done to her?

She started to shiver, and Dillon left her just long enough to grab Hartley's bedroll. Maybe if she were warm and comfortable she would quit shaking and open her eyes. He almost didn't notice the bottle lying on its side, but when he did he picked it up and sniffed at the open neck. Laudanum.

He hurried back to Grace, only to find her motionless and exactly as he had left her. How much had the bastard given her? Too much. He could see that. Unfortunately Hartley wouldn't be answering any questions. That had been the reason for that odd smile as he'd died. If Grace died, Hartley won.

Dillon sat in the dirt and lifted Grace onto his lap. Her head lolled against his chest as he wrapped the blanket around her shoulders, and her hands fell, open and lifeless, at her sides. He placed those hands in her lap, and pulled the blanket snugly around her, cocooning her against the night air.

What if she never woke up? What if she died right there in his arms? He'd never felt so helpless in his entire life. Never.

When he'd first seen the two of them—Grace in the dirt with her legs spread and Hartley on top of her—he'd wondered why she wasn't fighting him, why she was just lying there. And then, dear God, he'd seen her face, and for a moment he'd thought she was dead. She was so white and still.

"Come on, Grace," he ordered. He held her so that she was sitting up in his lap, and the dying fire lit her pale face and tangled hair. He didn't know anything about laudanum, except that too much of the stuff could kill a person. Grace had to wake up. He had to keep her awake and with him until the effects of the drug wore off.

"Talk to me, Grace." He took her face in one hand and held it close to his. "Come on. Talk to me." Dillon was nearly shouting, and all Grace did was wrinkle her nose and frown a little.

Better than nothing.

It took several long minutes of steady talking, but finally she opened one eye.

"Let me sleep, Dillon," she whispered. "Just a little while longer."

"No. Talk to me. Stay with me." He shook her slightly when she started to drift away again. "Tell me about . . . about England. I've never been to England. What's it like, honey?"

Grace's eyes opened, narrow slits in a colorless face. "I just want to sleep."

He begged, and maybe there was something in his voice that reached her. She began to talk. Her words were nonsense at times, and she had a tendency to ramble, but she was talking to him about the girls' school she'd attended in England. Girls' names, muttered nonsense, something about a piano . . .

"I liked it, most of the time . . . when I wasn't getting into trouble."

Finally, a sentence that made sense. As soon as she said the words she tried to close her eyes again. Dillon shook her awake. "What kind of trouble?"

"Whatever I could think of," Grace said dreamily. "At first just . . . temper tantrums, and not doing my studies . . . but that didn't work. So I . . . did some other things . . . but it didn't make any difference. He didn't come. He didn't send for me until it was too late."

Grace made an effort to tilt her head and lift her face to his, and she smiled wanly. "But you came for me," she whispered. "I love you, Dillon Becket."

He gathered her into his arms, just for a moment, holding her head against his shoulder. He couldn't allow her to get too comfortable, to drift away from him again, but he needed to hold her close.

"I love you, too," he said, knowing that she

wouldn't remember any of this. He smoothed a wayward strand of black hair away from her face as he loosened his hold and looked into her clouded eyes. "I love you."

"That's good," she whispered, and then she fell asleep in his arms, and nothing he could do would rouse her. Her heartbeat seemed a bit stronger, though it was still faint and far too fast, and she snuggled against him rather than lying lifelessly in his arms, as she had before.

Dillon kept her warm, and told her again and again that he loved her, and by the time the sun came up he was almost certain that she would live. Her heartbeat continued to grow stronger, though at times she seemed to have trouble breathing. When that happened he felt as if his own heart were going to stop beating, and he tried to breathe deeply. For both of them.

It was late morning when he heard the approaching hoofbeats. His pistol was at his side, and then in his hand, but he couldn't bring himself to deposit Grace on the ground and leave her there.

He recognized the rider in the lead, and reholstered his six-shooter. Billy hadn't wasted his time bothering to collect the sheriff from Plummerton. He had formed his own posse, better than half a dozen Double B hands who rode behind him. When Billy looked down at Grace he jumped from his horse with an agility rare for a man of his years.

Billy looked around the campsite, at Hartley's body and at Grace, still sleeping in Dillon's arms.

"Is she . . ." He couldn't finish the question, but Dillon shook his head.

"She's alive. Barely," Dillon said gruffly. "Son of a bitch doped her up with laudanum."

Billy dropped down so that he was face-to-face with Dillon. He reached out to touch Grace's shoulder, a tentative touch as if to reassure himself that she was still warm.

Grace reacted to his touch, sighing and rolling against Dillon, burying her face against his chest.

Dillon held her tight, and didn't even try to hide his feelings from the older man and the hands who sat their horses, solemn and silent, beyond him. It wouldn't have done any good, he told himself.

"I'd kill him again, if I could," Dillon swore harshly. He barely recognized the sound of his own voice.

Billy just shook his head. "Let's take her on home, boss."

Billy offered to carry Grace back to the ranch on his horse, insisting that Dillon was too exhausted after holding her and staying up with her all night. But Dillon would have none of that. When he was seated on his stallion, Billy handed Grace into Dillon's arms.

Grace opened one eye in response to the prodding she was being subjected to. There was an unfamiliar head, shiny bald in the center with steel-gray fringe all around, bent over her. He had his hand on her chest, and Grace tried to push him away. The balding man lifted his head, and she caught a glimpse of the wooden tube in his hands. A doctor. She relaxed and took a deep breath. He'd been listening to her heartbeat.

Dillon stood at the foot of the bed—her own bed at the Double B—trying to give her a reassuring smile through the dark stubble on his face and his obvious exhaustion. It was a poor effort, but that smile meant more to her than every jewel in her precious carved box.

"She'll be just fine," the doctor said, looking down at her with a concerned frown. "She needs to rest for a few days." The balding man gave her a fatherly smile. "You're a very lucky girl."

Grace's memory returned in a rush, and she bolted upright. That was a mistake. Her head swam, and she felt dangerously close to passing out.

"Hartley," she croaked.

Dillon came to her and lowered her gently onto the pillows. "It's all right. He won't bother you anymore," he said gruffly.

Grace found that she still had a hard time keeping her eyes open, even though she wanted to talk to Dillon, wanted to tell him everything that had happened. Poor Dillon, he looked so tired, so worried.

"He . . . he was going to kill me," she said softly, "but I guess he didn't." She finally gave in and closed her eyes. It was impossible to keep them open, but she could hear everything that was going on around her. Dillon was here. He had found her and brought her home.

"I tried to stop him, Dillon, really I did," she whispered. She frowned, remembering Hartley's hands on her, her inability to move, the darkness that had swallowed her.

And Dillon had told her that he loved her. She remembered that much. But was it really a memory, or was it a piece of a dream? She wanted to believe that it was a memory. It chased away all the rest.

"You're sure she'll be all right?" She heard Dillon asking the question, and knew that he had returned to his post at the end of the bed. He was looking out for her, and she didn't wait to hear the doctor's reply, but allowed herself to slip into a deep sleep.

It was fully dark before Grace opened her eyes again. She'd been so deeply asleep it took her a moment to realize exactly where she was. It was a bit like coming back from the dead.

A warm breeze filled the room, making the curtains at her window dance. She was alive, and she was home.

The quilt had been kicked to her feet, and Grace looked down at the nightgown she wore before she pulled the cover over her legs. Who had stripped off the calico and placed the nightgown on her sleeping body? Dillon? He had been so cautious, never hinting to Olivia or Billy that there was anything between them. Olivia perhaps. She would have been the one to send Dillon into the hall to wait while she prepared Grace for bed.

She covered her face with her hands. It came back to her in a rush, just as it had when she'd awakened earlier. Hartley, pressing her against the ground, his hands all over her. Thank God she could remember nothing more than that. Her hands dropped slowly, and she took a deep breath, driving that memory from her mind. She couldn't face it. Not now.

From her throbbing head to her feet, she ached all over. It was a good ache, because it reminded her she was alive. She sat up and stretched her arms over her head, thankful that she could move freely again.

She wasn't even surprised when she looked down and saw Dillon's head resting there on the side of the bed. It looked as if he'd sat on the floor at her bedside, leaned his head against the mattress, and fallen asleep. With the moonlight on his face she could see the dark stubble on his cheeks, and the stern set to his jaw. Did he never relax? Not even in sleep?

She laid a hand over his head, ruffling his soft chestnut hair with her fingers. He was her guardian, her love, the constant that had been missing from her life.

He stirred under her fingers, and lifted his face to hers. "You're awake?"

Grace nodded. "I can't believe I slept all day."

Dillon rolled up and turned to face her, on his knees beside the bed. "All day, hell. You've been out for two days, Grace. You've worried the devil out of me," he accused.

"I doubt that."

Dillon took the hand that had been resting in his hair, and he held it possessively. "The doctor said you'd be fine, but I wasn't sure. You were so damn still."

Grace lifted the quilt and scooted over, inviting him in.

Dillon shook his head. "You're sick."

Grace smiled at him. She couldn't help it. "Just to sleep, Becket. The floor doesn't look too comfortable."

Dillon slid under the quilt and wrapped his arms around her to squeeze so tightly she couldn't take a deep breath. Gradually his grip loosened, though he continued to hold her close.

Grace buried her face against his chest. All the comfort she would ever need was here in his arms. Only Dillon could fill her once-empty heart, could make her put aside her fears.

He sighed deeply, and nuzzled his face against the top of her head. "One of us had better wake up early in the morning, before Olivia shows up and tries to feed you again." He already sounded drowsy, and almost as if he didn't care if they were caught in bed together or not.

It went against everything she'd ever known, but she didn't care either. She was going to marry him, anyway, so what did it matter?

Of course, he hadn't asked her yet. That nagging thought was with her as she fell asleep, snuggled in Dillon's arms.

When she opened her eyes again, Olivia was bending over the bed, her lined face concerned, a cup of steaming hot liquid in her hands.

A smile broke out on her face, deepening the lines and making her hazel eyes dance. "So you are awake! Dillon said you'd stirred a bit last night."

"Dillon?" Grace lifted her head slightly and looked around the room. He wasn't there. So he had managed to slip out before Olivia's arrival after all.

"He sat up with you last night, you know. You've given us all quite a scare, young lady," she said kindly. "Dillon said you might be able to keep down a bit of tea this morning."

Grace sat up slowly and took the warm mug from Olivia's hands. She sipped cautiously, cradling the heavy mug. Her stomach wanted to revolt, so she took just a portion of the sweet tea. Not even half.

Olivia busied herself around the bed, straightening the quilt over Grace's legs, fluffing the pillows.

"Where is Becket, anyway?" Grace tried to keep her voice casual.

"Working, of course. He stayed with you all day yesterday, and the day before, so he was a bit anxious to get back out there. You know Dillon. If he's not got a hand in it he can't be sure that it's being done properly."

Grace set her mug of tea on her bedside table. "Do you know what happened?"

Olivia stopped her bustling and clasped her hands as she looked down at Grace. She pinched her lips together and furrowed her brow.

"It's just that . . . I don't remember much after Hartley gave me the laudanum. What . . . where is he?" Grace felt a moment of rising panic. Dillon was away from the house. What if Hartley decided to come back? What if Dillon didn't find her this time?

"The man who carried you off is dead," Olivia said sternly, refusing to speak Hartley's name. "Dillon shot him."

"Are you certain that he's really . . ."

A soft, reassuring look passed over Olivia's face. "The boys buried him where he fell. Don't you worry none. That man was right dead."

Grace felt a rush of relief . . . and then a hint of guilt. A man was dead. She shouldn't feel so relieved that any person had died a violent death.

But she did. She remembered too well the way he had looked at her. The gleam in his eyes as he'd poured the laudanum-laced water down her throat. The way his hands had pushed her against the ground.

"Lord, Grace," Olivia said as she forced her back against the pillows. "You're white as a ghost. Maybe I should send Billy for the doctor. . . ."

"No." Grace stopped Olivia with a reassuring hand on the woman's arm. "I'm fine. Just a little weak, that's all. The tea helped. It really did."

Olivia visibly relaxed. "It's too bad that you're

going to miss the festivities tomorrow. The Fourth of July is always a merry day in Plummerton. There's a big picnic, and fireworks. Seth Plummer brings them in every year. Oh, and there's a band. They're not very good, but they're very enthusiastic." She smiled at Grace, a motherly smile that told Grace everything would be all right. "There's always next year."

Next year. Yes. She would be here next year, and the next, and the next. Forever.

"We'll just stay here and have a quiet celebration all our own," Olivia said.

"Don't you dare miss on my account," Grace admonished. "Imagine. Fireworks *and* an enthusiastic band. And a picnic. You'd better not stay here. I'd feel just terrible if you missed all the fun."

"We'll see," Olivia said as she patted Grace's hand. "We'll see."

Grace slipped to the stairs quietly, her bare feet silent. She wrapped the dressing gown around her body and tied the too-long sash. It was Dillon's favorite color, a blue the color of his wildflowers. Bluebonnets.

The house was so quiet she began to think that everyone had gone to Plummerton for the Fourth of July celebration, leaving her completely alone. But she knew Dillon wouldn't leave her.

She hadn't seen him since she'd awakened to find him sleeping at her bedside. She'd waited for him to come to her again that night, but he hadn't, and she'd finally fallen asleep without him. She'd thought perhaps to see him at breakfast, but Olivia had brought her a tray and said that Dillon had persuaded her and Billy to go to Plummerton for the day.

Leaving, she assumed, the two of them at home alone.

But he hadn't come to her room, not even to stick his head in the doorway and say good morning.

He was sitting at the dining room table with an unopened bottle of whiskey in front of him, and if he heard her coming down the stairs he gave no notice of the fact.

Grace stood just a few feet away, afraid to take another step forward. She'd never seen Dillon like this. Angry, but without fire. There was a desolate, stony resignation in the eyes that continued to stare at the bottle of whiskey before him.

"Dillon?" She finally found the nerve to speak, even though she was afraid to interrupt him. She was more afraid of the expression on his face.

"Go back to bed, Grace," he said gruffly.

She shook her head and stepped forward. "No. What's wrong?"

It was worse than she had thought. Dillon lifted his head, moving his eyes from the bottle to her. There was no tenderness in his eyes. No life at all.

"It's over, Grace," he said emotionlessly.

She moved without thinking to stand behind him, and rested her hands on his shoulders. "What's over?"

He didn't answer for a few moments, and Grace waited. The tension in his shoulders didn't abate beneath her hands, but he didn't move away, either.

"Us. We can't . . . I can't . . ." Dillon cursed under his breath, and finally he did shrug off her hands. "I'm getting married," he said coldly. "To Abigail Wilkinson. You remember her. You wore a sheet to the party she gave for us." His words were clipped and distant.

This was a nightmare. Some horrid delusion. An aftereffect of the drug Hartley had given her. Any moment she would wake up and Dillon would be there, and she would tell him what a terrible dream she'd had.

But it wasn't a dream. It was real.

"You can't marry her," Grace whispered. "You love me."

She could see the tension in his neck and his back as he reached out and took the bottle in his hands. "No, I don't."

Grace stepped away from him and leaned against the wall. The strength had gone from her legs, and she felt as if she might collapse. "You told me . . . I remember . . . when you found me. . . ."

"That was a dream, Grace. A hallucination." He sounded so certain, she began to doubt her own foggy memory.

"Then . . . why? Why did you . . ." Her words faded away into nothing.

"Why did I take to sleeping in your bed?" He gave voice to the question she couldn't ask. "Because it had been a long time for me, and you were . . . you are a very beautiful woman. It was just too tempting, having you under the same roof and not being able to touch you."

His voice was so cold Grace shivered. There was not a hint of affection in his words, no love or warmth. Dillon Becket was just like all the rest, only he had succeeded where they had failed.

"But . . . you said you were going to keep me."

He opened the bottle and wrapped his fingers around it, and still he didn't lift the bottle to his lips. "I did keep you, Grace. For a while."

Grace took a deep breath and steadied her legs. How could he have fooled her so completely?

He couldn't have.

"Stand up and look at me," she ordered in a suddenly strong voice. "Tell me to my face that you don't love me."

Dillon hesitated, but he finally pushed his chair away from the table and turned to face her. He'd always had a hard look about him—in the way he stood and in the strength in his face—but he had never looked so stonelike to her. Cold as marble. Hard as granite.

"I don't love you, Grace," he said coldly. His arms were hanging at his sides, and his fists were clenched. "I never meant for you to believe that I did."

She searched for a hint of tenderness in his eyes, but there was none. "Do you . . . do you love Abigail?"

"No. Only a fool marries for love," he said gruffly.

He dropped his eyes first. "Don't worry. I'll still take care of you."

"Like hell you will," Grace snapped. She'd finally let her control slip, and look where it had gotten her. "If you think I'll stay here while you . . . with . . . with Abigail . . . you're even denser and more ignorant than I thought you were!"

"We'll find you a husband."

Grace took a step forward, trying to make herself forget that she had fallen so completely in love with this man. "You'll do *what*?"

"Find you a husband. You're of a marriageable age, Grace; we'll introduce you around—"

She slapped him with all the strength she could muster. It didn't faze him at all. "You're finished with me, and now you're going to palm me off on some poor unsuspecting dupe. Do you plan to tell him that he's getting secondhand goods? Or should we save that as a surprise for the wedding night?"

At least he paled a little, though his eyes remained distant.

"What if there's a baby?" she asked, her voice little more than a whisper. "Did you ever think of that?"

It was clear by the expression on his face that he had not.

"Here you go, sir. And a bonus! She's already breeding!" Grace felt ill. Her stomach churned and her head swam. Her memories were so vague, so distant, and she had tried so hard not to remember. "I don't suppose we have to tell him about Hartley, either, or the possibility that the bastard child might be the spawn of a—"

"No." Dillon reached out and almost took her arm, but his hand fell away. "I . . . He didn't touch you. Not that way. I thought you would remember."

Grace felt a wave of uneasy solace wash over her. "I don't remember much." As she spoke, Dillon's face softened just a little. "Images and . . . hallucinations. Dreams that make no sense." *Like the one where you told me you love me.* She couldn't say that aloud.

"Grace, do you think . . . A baby?"

"I don't have the slightest idea what to think, Becket."

"If you are . . . if there's a baby . . . I'll take care of you." He sounded as if he were about to choke on the words.

"I don't want you to take care of me." She gathered every bit of self-control she had and faced him defiantly. "Find me a husband. I'll let you choose. But he has to have money, and he'd best not be too ugly. I'd prefer an educated man, but I seriously doubt that you know any. At the very least, please choose one of your less moronic acquaintances." She felt the heat rise in her face, and her legs wobbled. She was still weak, and had no business fighting with Dillon at the moment. But she couldn't stop. Not now.

"We'd better make it a hasty wedding, Becket, just in case I am with child. If we're lucky I can pass it off as his, and you'll never have to be bothered with either of us." Her eyes filled with tears, and she hated herself for it. She didn't want Dillon Becket to see any weakness in her. She would be as strong as he was. And as cold.

She took a step away from him, and her legs quivered, just a little. He reached out and grabbed her arm, but she jerked away from him and leaned against the wall for support.

"Don't touch me, Becket. Never again. I'd rather crawl up the stairs than have your hands on me."

Suitably cold, she decided, when Dillon stepped away from her and allowed her to walk away under her own questionable power.

Chapter Fourteen

Dillon watched Grace leave the room, her head held high, her shoulders trembling slightly beneath the thin blue wrapper she wore. He was such a bastard, but there was no other way.

This was for the best, a clean break that left her with no tender feelings. She had to hate him with all her heart. He had no doubt that Grace hated the same way she loved—with everything she had inside her.

It served no purpose to think of what might have been. Only a fool wasted time and energy on such recriminations. And he had been a fool to allow his heart to make plans he couldn't possibly carry out.

The cattle drive had brought in about half of what he needed to pay off old man Plummer. Half. Hell, if the money had even come close, he could have found a way to raise the rest. But the herd had been cut south of Abilene, and there had been a glut at the market, so prices were low.

The only way to save the Double B was to marry Abigail Wilkinson, and that was exactly what he would do come hell or high water. At least one thing he'd said to Grace had been true. Only a fool marries for love.

But that was where the truth ended. He did love Grace. He hadn't known it was possible to love another person so much that you hurt when they hurt. When he'd lifted her into his arms, after he'd shot Hartley, he'd known what it was like to be truly helpless. He couldn't remember the last time he'd cried.

If he'd been able, he would have gladly taken the pain from her, would have gladly suffered for her. He'd killed without a second thought, something he'd sworn seven years ago, coming home after an awful, bloody war, that he would never do again.

But if he could kill Hartley again, he would.

Perhaps he would always love her, deep inside. Even when he was married to Abigail and Grace was another man's wife. It would be comforting to believe that he might stop loving her one day, but he knew that was just another lie.

He should have regretted taking her virginity and going to bed with her night after night, making her love him, but he couldn't. It was all he would ever have of her, memories of a few short weeks.

With a disgusted sigh, Dillon lifted the whiskey, bringing the bottle to his mouth. Perhaps he was just like his father, after all. The old man had gotten lost in the bottle on more than one occasion. More and more, toward the end. It had never been a pretty sight, the old man drunk and wasting away, in the end choosing whiskey over food, his son, his friends.

Dillon threw the bottle across the room and watched with a grain of satisfaction as it crashed against the wall, shattering and staining the wall and the floor with the last of his father's personal stock.

Without the Double B he had nothing to offer Grace . . . literally nothing. Every dime he had was tied up in the place. If he were to lose it to Plummer, he'd leave the ranch with nothing more than a few personal items and his horse. Grace deserved more than that.

"I don't believe you." She spoke so softly, and still he jumped in his chair.

"Go away, Grace."

She shook her head and walked toward him. Her hair was loose and falling over one shoulder, over that silky blue wrapper she wore. This time she didn't hide behind him, but faced him defiantly.

"I'm not going to make this easy for you, Becket. I want the truth. Is it Hartley? Were you lying when you said that he didn't . . . that he didn't touch me?" Her face was white, her eyes red and swollen. He could see the fear there, in her eyes, and he wanted to take her in his arms and comfort her, assure her, tell her that he would never allow another man to touch her.

But he was going to hand her over to another man, a husband who could provide and care for her the way she deserved.

"No." He remained in his seat. "I would have told you sooner if I'd known you didn't remember." He could have asked her how she could think so little of him, could have told her that he would never turn from her for such a reason . . .

but of course it was best if she thought him a bastard.

"Then what?" she demanded. "Have I done something wrong? I can't believe that your feelings can change so quickly. Almost overnight. You can say you don't love me all you want, but I don't believe you." Her eyes flashed at him, cold, blue fire.

"It's nothing you've done," he said tiredly. "It's just . . . I have no other choice."

"There's always a choice, Becket."

He leaned back in his chair and looked up at her. "The trail boss I hired to take the herd to market arrived last night." The truth. Nothing but the cold, hard truth.

"Good. You can pay off the banker who's holding the deed. What does that have to do—"

"You know?"

"Billy told me," she said impatiently.

Grace laid her palms on the table and leaned forward, staring at him with anger and hate and even love in her bluebonnet eyes.

"Rustlers cut the herd south of Abilene, and what my men brought back isn't enough to pay off the loan. And there's less than two months before it's due."

"So? Sell something."

"Like what?"

Grace waved an impatient hand in front of his face. "A parcel of land, some horses . . ."

"The only parcel of land worth having has the water source on it. Without it the rest of the ranch is worthless. The horses, even what's left of the herd, wouldn't bring in enough to pay this loan off." He raked a hand through his hair, impatient, frustrated. "The past couple of years haven't been so great around here. Plummer and

Wilkinson are the only ones who have any money to speak of, and it's definitely not in their best interest to help me out by buying a worthless plot of land for more than it's worth."

She straightened, and a light came over her face. A very unpleasant light. "So what you're saying is that you're going to marry Abigail . . . for her dowry? So you can pay off the loan? That's positively medieval, Becket. You're choosing this ranch over me." It was clear she found that easier to believe than the lie that he didn't love her.

Dillon stood and slapped his hand on the table. "Dammit, I don't want to marry Abigail. I should have been on that trail drive myself! Maybe if I'd been there—"

"Well, why weren't you?" she shouted. "God only knows that no one else can get anything properly done! If you'd been there you could have taken on those rustlers single-handedly and saved the blasted herd. So why weren't you there? What made you decide to trust such an important task to a mere mortal?"

He opened his mouth to tell her, and then shut it again. It wouldn't help matters at all. But he saw the knowledge when it dawned on her face, and she paled.

"It's because you were in New Orleans . . . to meet me," she said softly, her anger dissolving.

"It doesn't matter now."

Grace nodded her head slightly. "I think it does matter. I think it matters very much, to you. You blame me."

"I don't. Even if I had been there, it wouldn't have made any difference." She must have heard the hesitation in his voice, because she clearly didn't believe him.

Shakily, she sat in the chair across the table from him. "So you're going to marry Abigail, and I'm supposed to marry someone else."

"I won't force you to marry."

Grace lifted her face to look at him, and he wished she hadn't. He could see the pain in her eyes, the disbelief. She found the truth harder to take than the lie he'd tried to hurt her with. "I meant what I said. I won't live in this house after you marry her. I won't sit across the table from the two of you and make small talk with your wife while I pretend that I don't love you. I'll marry . . . or I'll leave here on my own."

And she would. Her face was every bit as determined as he'd tried to make his. And as cold.

"I'm sorry."

"Don't," she said as she stood. "Don't apologize, Becket. It was . . . educational."

She turned her back on him and left again, and this time he knew she wasn't coming back.

Dillon was the only gift her father had ever given her, and she wasn't going to be able to keep him.

Grace had dressed, the first day in more than a week that she'd felt she could leave her room. What if she couldn't face Dillon?

No matter how hard she tried, she couldn't imagine herself married to anyone but Dillon. She could teach, maybe, or take a position as governess with a wealthy family. Neither option seemed likely.

She drew back the lacy curtain at the single window in her room and looked across the ranch. She would miss this place, but there was no way she could stay once Dillon had married Abigail.

He stepped from the barn, leading his bay stallion. Dillon had taken to staying away from the house all day, sleeping in the line shack or in the open, or occasionally in the bunkhouse. Olivia had told her that much, mystified that even a young man could work so hard.

But Grace already knew that Dillon had not been sleeping in his room. She knew because she listened for his footsteps every night, waiting in her bed breathlessly to hear his booted step outside her door. But the hallway outside her room was quiet, deserted and silent long after dark.

Dillon mounted his stallion and turned his head to look toward the house. She couldn't tell, with his hat pulled down over his eyes, but he seemed to be staring right at her. She wondered if he could see her there, or if all he saw was the curtain and darkness beyond. She was tempted to stick her head out the window and shout at him. To call him every name she had ever heard, and then some.

He did love her; she was certain of that. And she loved him. Even if he was stubborn and couldn't seem to get his priorities straight.

She watched him ride away, and the beginnings of an idea tickled her brain. He did love her, but maybe he didn't know it. Maybe he didn't know that he needed her more than he needed this ranch. It was up to her to show him, somehow, that neither of them would be happy married to anyone else.

It was a risky plan, and could easily backfire, but it was certainly preferable to sitting around and waiting for Dillon to choose a husband for her.

After a loveless childhood, she'd found she had a heart. Dillon had awakened her heart as surely as he'd awakened her body. She'd come close to death, and had survived. For what? To give up everything she wanted? When she was so close?

For the first time since Dillon had told her of his plan to marry Abigail Wilkinson, Grace felt light-hearted. It was as if those dense Texas storm clouds had parted and allowed the sun to peek through.

She had nothing to lose—and everything to gain.

It was three more days before she caught another glimpse of him, and she was ready. It was just after sunup, and he was leading his bay from the barn. Grace stepped right in front of him. He would have to stop, or run her down.

For a moment she thought he was going to run her down.

"Good morning, Becket," she said sweetly. She had dressed for the occasion, choosing a simple yellow calico that she had fitted herself, nipping in the waist and taking in the shoulders. This was no baggy hand-me-down.

"Grace," he said by way of a greeting, and then he tried to step around her. But Grace was prepared, and quicker than he was as she had no horse to guide. She quickly blocked his path again, and he lifted his eyes from the ground to her face.

"What do you want?" he asked gruffly.

"Well." Grace lowered her voice and spoke in confident tones. It wouldn't do for him to hear any hesitation in her words. "I thought you might want to know that I'm not going to have a baby."

There was a brief pause before he answered, "Good."

"So I suppose it's time we started looking for a

husband for me." She glanced up and stared at the twitching muscle in his jaw. "When do we start? Or have you already begun the search?"

"I've been busy," Dillon said, a gruff attempt at an explanation.

"I know. We've missed you at dinner." She made no mention of missing him in her bed, or listening for him every night. It was difficult not to reach out and grab him and shake some sense into his muddled mind. But Grace kept her hands to herself. Dillon did the same.

"I haven't given it much thought," he said almost sullenly.

"I have," Grace said, and she smiled brightly. "Someone from Plummerton, do you think? I really don't know anyone, except the people I met at the Wilkinsons' party. What about Wade Wilkinson? We'd be related, Becket. Our children would be cousins. You and Abigail could visit us for Sunday dinner, and every holiday."

"You wouldn't like Wade," Dillon said shortly.

Grace nodded her head thoughtfully. "He has a brother, doesn't he? Kirby? He wasn't at the party, so I don't know if he's—"

"You wouldn't like Kirby either," Dillon snapped. He narrowed his eyes at her. "You're taking this awfully well."

Grace smiled. Suspicious, was he? "I'm a practical woman. I might as well make the best of the situation, don't you agree?"

He had to agree. It was his blasted idea.

"I have to get to work." He maneuvered his way around Grace, and she allowed him to go. That was enough for one day.

"Think about it, would you?" she called after him. "I'd like my husband to be someone you approve of, since you are my guardian."

Dillon mounted his horse, keeping his back to her, and he rode away without another word. But Grace was satisfied.

"Yes, give it some thought, Dillon Becket," she said to herself, and she smiled at his retreat.

She was entering the barn, still contemplating Dillon's reaction and smiling brightly, when an arm snaked out of the darkness and grabbed her. Grace didn't have time to scream before a hand clamped over her mouth.

But this time she recognized the method of greeting, and relaxed even before the hand slid away from her mouth.

"Good morning, Renzo," she said sweetly, before she glanced over her shoulder.

He released her slowly, and she turned to face him. He was dressed all in black, as usual, with polished silver conchos on his flat-brimmed hat and his boots. The wide silk sleeves of his black shirt flared dramatically, and as always his thin mustache was perfectly shaped, giving him a rather dashing flair. But there was something different about Renzo this morning. It was the absence of his customary bright smile.

"*Buenos días*, my beautiful Grace," he said in a low voice.

"What are you doing here?" she asked curiously. "I thought you'd be far away by now."

He shook his head. "Ah, I should be. My men have moved on without me, and I have come to ask for your help."

"What could I possibly do for you?"

"I am in love," Renzo said, his voice dark and foreboding. "For the first time in my life, I am truly in love."

Grace raised an eyebrow and took a step back. Surely he was not in love with her? And then she knew he wasn't. There was such a far-off look in his eyes.

"You certainly don't need my help. . . ."

"But I do," he said desperately. "She is a lady, like you. Refined and genteel. Sweet and innocent. I don't know what to do, what to say to a woman like that." He grabbed her hands and held them tight. "Teach me, Grace. You're the only true lady I have ever known. Tell me what to do."

"Who is she?"

Renzo gave her a crooked grin, the grin of a naughty boy. "I don't know her name. I am afraid to approach her, afraid I will scare her away."

"You haven't even spoken to her?"

Renzo shook his head. "Not yet. I don't know what to say to my little jewel."

"Your little jewel?"

"She shines like a diamond in the sunlight," he said dramatically.

He was looking at her so strangely, like a puppy who wanted to jump into her lap but, like a well-trained pet, waited anxiously for permission.

What if she insisted that he stay at the Double B while she instructed him in the proper way to woo a lady? Dillon would be absolutely furious.

Grace stepped back and looked Renzo up and down critically. She placed her hands on her hips and paced in front of him for several minutes before she spoke. "First of all, while I find your outfit dashing, it really isn't suitable for a gentleman, and you must be a gentleman to win a lady's heart."

Renzo nodded his head. "*Sí.*"

"You need something . . . understated. Simple. And I'm afraid the mustache will have to go."

He raised his eyebrows in skeptical distress.

"It's much too rakish," she explained.

Renzo reluctantly agreed.

"She must be very beautiful."

The bandit nodded and smiled. "She is. Not as beautiful as you, of course," he added gallantly, "but she has a beauty that shines into my heart."

"She's a lucky girl," Grace said softly.

"You will help me?"

Grace nodded. She'd never thought of herself as a matchmaker or a reformer of men, but it was such an interesting challenge. And it would infuriate Dillon. That was a side effect not to be quickly dismissed.

"What's your name? Your real name," she clarified.

"Renzo," he said, obviously confused by her question.

"Your full name."

Renzo threw back his shoulders and lifted his chin. "Lorenzo Porfirio Morales," he said proudly.

"Are you wanted anywhere under that name?"

Renzo shook his head. "No. Even my men knew me only as Renzo, and of course we were never apprehended."

"Of course," Grace repeated.

Renzo watched her pace, his patience clearly wearing thin with every step she took. In moments the normally composed man was fidgeting. It really was rather sweet, Grace decided, that love would turn even a man like Renzo into a nervous wreck.

She stopped in front of him and stared into his black eyes. "Lorenzo Morales. That's how we'll introduce you. But first you must shave off the mustache, and we'll get you some new clothes."

"I can stop a stagecoach and—"

"No!" she shouted. "That's the most important change. No more stealing."

He frowned. "None at all?"

"None."

"Not even—"

"None!" Grace insisted loudly. "If you won't do as I say, you can find someone else to help you."

Renzo raised his finely arched eyebrows and looked down at her with wonder in his black eyes. Grace wondered if any woman had ever shouted at the man, or defied him in any way. He was accustomed to being in charge, the leader of his own band of thieves.

And then he gave her a small, crooked smile, combined with a courtly bow. "I place myself in your hands, *señorita*."

Renzo charmed Olivia with the ease of a man who is accustomed to having no difficulty with women, young or old. Even without the mustache, and dressed in clothes Grace had found in the big empty bedroom upstairs, he looked dashing. And nothing like the gentleman he wanted to be.

But he was a changed man, and she was hoping the change would be dramatic enough to keep Billy and Dillon from recognizing him right away. That was a brief and fleeting thought. She knew they would recognize Renzo the minute they saw him.

Olivia, fortunately, had no idea that he was a bandit. Grace had introduced him as a fellow traveler she had met on her journey through Texas. That was the truth, after all.

They had a pleasant meal, just the three of them, before Billy came dragging in. Renzo was just finishing his dessert, a slice of Olivia's raisin pie, when Billy plodded into the room. He gave Renzo a startled glance, as he would have any stranger at the table, and then recognition dawned on his face.

Grace stood and stilled whatever words Billy had been about to speak. "Do you remember Lorenzo Morales, Billy? We met him on the road."

Billy glanced at her, and then he looked at the smiling bandit. Grace could almost see his mind at work, and she held her breath until Billy evidently decided to play along.

"Why, yes. I do remember."

Grace resumed her seat. "He's going to be staying with us for a while."

"He is?" Billy sat down and Olivia brought him a heaping plate of beef and potatoes. "Does the boss know about this?"

Grace shook her head and turned to Billy her most innocent face. "Not yet. Perhaps you could round Becket up after supper and inform him that he has a guest. I would tell him myself, but I have no idea where the man is keeping himself these days."

Billy wolfed down his supper, a suspicious eye on their guest. All in all, Grace was pleased with events so far. Renzo had been well behaved, and Billy was properly cautious. When Billy excused himself, rather brusquely, from the table, Grace knew it wouldn't be long before Dillon made a rare appearance in the house.

He must have been bedding down in the bunkhouse, because it was just a few minutes before Grace heard Dillon storm through the kitchen door.

It occurred to her—belatedly—that she should have warned Renzo about the situation, but it was too late now. Even so, Renzo was smart enough to realize the danger of being confronted by Dillon Becket. Grace gave her bandit a reassuring smile just as Dillon appeared in the doorway.

"What the hell are you doing here?"

Olivia almost jumped out of her chair, startled by the rude and gruff tone of Dillon's voice.

"I'll fix you a plate," Olivia said as she rose, but Dillon placed a hand on her shoulder and forced her back into her seat.

"I've already eaten," he snapped, his eyes on the thief who was dining at his table.

"You do remember Mr. Morales," Grace said calmly. "Lorenzo Morales?"

Dillon looked at her as if she'd gone mad. "I remember Mr. Morales quite well, Grace."

"Good. He's going to be staying with us for a while." She pulled her eyes away from Dillon and smiled warmly at Renzo.

"Like hell—" He stopped suddenly and stared at the shirt and vest Renzo was wearing. "Those are my father's clothes."

"I found them in the large empty bedroom upstairs, where Mr. Morales will be staying."

"You put him in my father's room?" Dillon turned to her, ignoring the subject of their conversation.

Grace sighed tiredly. "Really, Becket. What choice did I have? The smaller bedroom that's unoccupied is such a mess. Olivia's sewing supplies, a couple of chairs that need to be repaired, a chest of winter clothing . . ."

"I could stay elsewhere, if there's a problem," Renzo said gallantly. "We just thought it would be more convenient for me to stay here."

"Convenient," Dillon repeated dully.

Grace rose, glad that she had taken the time to change into one of her nicer dresses. The strawberry silk made her skin glow, and she wanted Dillon's eyes on her, not on Renzo.

With deliberately slow steps, Grace moved to stand behind Renzo's chair and place a hand on his shoulder. "It's really very romantic. Mr. Morales has decided to change his life. To leave behind all that he knows for the woman he loves. I am going to instruct him in the ways of a gentleman."

Renzo lifted his hand to cover hers and, ignoring Dillon, moved her hand to his lips. "I have never known a woman like Grace," he said in a low voice. "She is remarkable."

Renzo looked up at Grace and grinned wickedly.

Dillon's face turned red, and the muscles at his throat were working as he controlled his outrage. "If you think I'm going to allow—"

"Allow what, Becket?" Grace tried to capture his eyes, but they were intent on the hand that was still clasped in Renzo's. "You've always said that this is my home now. Certainly I'm allowed to have guests."

A subtle change came over Dillon. His color returned almost to normal, and some of the tension left his face. There was a look of sad surrender in his eyes.

"Of course, Grace," he said without looking at her. "If that's what you want." Dillon turned on his heel and stalked into the kitchen and out the back door.

Olivia was pale, and apparently confused, as she rose to clear the table. "Sometimes that boy acts so strange. He's just been working too hard," she explained, her tone apologetic.

When they were alone, Renzo laughed lightly. "You could have warned me, *amiga*," he said as he kissed Grace's hand once again, and then released it.

"Warned you of what?" Grace asked innocently.

Renzo stood and turned to face her, and he took both of her hands in his. "You could have warned me of the little game with your Becket. I shall have to sleep with a knife under my pillow and a gun at my side."

"I don't think he'll hurt you," she said, but evidently Renzo wasn't reassured.

He looked down at her skeptically. "I will endure many dangers to become the man my little jewel deserves."

"She's very lucky, Renzo," Grace whispered.

He gave her a devilish smile that told her he agreed with her.

Out of the corner of her eye, Grace saw a hint of movement at the window. She wanted to move her head, but she remained very still, keeping her eyes on Renzo. Were they being watched? By Dillon?

She moved her face forward just slightly, closer to the handsome man who still held her hands, and she smiled slightly. "Kiss me, Renzo," she whispered.

He lifted his eyebrows in surprise.

"I believe we have an audience," she explained softly. "Don't look, but I believe Dillon is watching through the window."

Renzo enjoyed the game, and perhaps even the danger, because he gave her one of his dazzling smiles and bent to touch his lips to hers. He gave her a short but searingly passionate kiss. A kiss that would have melted another woman's heart and left her swooning. A tender hand moved over her back, and he leaned Grace back, just slightly, over his arm.

But Grace was thinking only of Dillon as Renzo released her and she heard the kitchen door slam.

Dillon was back.

Chapter Fifteen

Grace and Renzo managed to step apart before Dillon burst into the room. He was clenching his hands and watching her and her guest through narrowed eyes, but what could he say? He certainly wouldn't admit that he'd been watching them through the window.

Again, Grace thought how fortuitous it was that Renzo had arrived when he did. Dillon already knew that the bandit had asked her—twice—to run away with him. Now he believed that Renzo was willing to change his life for her. Surely if Dillon was to be convinced that he couldn't marry Abigail, Renzo would do it.

Grace and Renzo retired to the parlor, and Dillon was right behind them. He refused to speak, but lit a cigar and kept a close eye on the two of them. Grace and Renzo sat on the sofa, a respectable distance between them, and Dillon placed a high-backed chair so that it faced the sofa before he sat, stretched out his legs, and took a long draw on that disgusting cigar.

There was a most uncomfortable stretch of silence before Renzo rose and excused himself for the evening. A wise move, in Grace's opinion.

Grace half expected Dillon to rise and leave the room on Renzo's heels, rather than continue to be subjected to her company, but he stayed in his chair and watched her silently, an expression nearing puzzlement on his face. There was a little less control there, a bit of uncertainty that wasn't normally a part of Dillon Becket's personality.

Grace placed her hands in her lap and forced herself to remain calm. She would not allow Dillon to confuse or rattle her. All her plans hinged on convincing him that she could and would marry another man.

"So, what do you plan to do with him?" Dillon finally barked harshly.

"With Lorenzo?" she asked innocently.

"Yes, with Lorenzo," he said, seething.

"I'm not sure." Grace leaned forward and faced Dillon as calmly as she could. "He has a charming personality, so I suppose he would make a fair merchant. I must remember to suggest that to him."

Dillon scoffed in disbelief. "The man's a thief. He'll always be a thief."

Grace lifted her hand slowly and pushed back a loose strand of hair that brushed her cheek. "Perhaps you could give him a job."

Dillon didn't refuse hastily, as she had expected, but raised a disbelieving eyebrow.

"It makes perfect sense, Becket. I like it here. Since you don't care for me at all, it shouldn't bother you to have us here." She kept her eyes wide and innocent. Not an easy task.

"I can't believe that he would make a decent cowhand."

"You'll never know unless you give him a chance. And wouldn't it be cozy? You and Abigail, and me and Lorenzo, all snug and friendly under the same roof."

For a moment she thought Dillon was going to explode and come flying out of his chair. His face reddened, his eyes glittered harshly, but when he spoke his voice was calm.

"You said you wouldn't stay."

"But you said I could, if I wanted. Perhaps I've reconsidered your offer. If you can do it, Becket, so can I. I can forget . . . well, we'd best not speak about it." She rose and clasped her hands demurely at her breast. "It's been a hectic day. I should get to bed."

She turned in the doorway and looked back at him. He was in control once more, that shield over his eyes and that tight rein on his emotions. Just a moment ago she'd believed that he was going to leap from his chair and take her in his arms and forbid her to marry another man . . . but not now.

"I'll think about it, Grace," he said in a low voice. "But I want you to think about it, too. He's a bandit. Perhaps he's convinced you that he can change, but I don't think it's possible. I only want what's best for you."

She couldn't take it anymore. What was best for her! Blast him, *he* was what was best for her. He was just too blind to see it. "Good night, Becket," she snapped, turning her back on him while he was in midsentence.

* * *

Dillon climbed the steps with slowly mounting dread. He tried to tell himself that he was only going to sleep in his bedroom because he was already in the house and it was more convenient than going back to the bunkhouse. His own bed was certainly more comfortable than what waited for him out there.

But the truth was, he refused to leave Grace upstairs alone with that damned bandit, sleeping across the hallway from a man who looked at her as if he wanted to toss her over his shoulder and make off with her . . . which was, no doubt, exactly what Renzo wanted to do. Dillon had been sitting in the parlor for better than an hour fuming over that fact.

Grace had smiled at Renzo so easily . . . kissed him so easily.

Dillon knew it would be hard to walk past Grace's door and not walk in. It was killing him, a little every day, to know that she was so close, and still he couldn't touch her.

He shouldn't be so angry. She was only doing what he wanted her to do; she was getting on with her life. But Lorenzo Morales? He could change his clothes, and shave off his mustache, and become a merchant . . . and he would still be a low-down, thieving, Mexican bandit.

His intention to pass by her room without a sideways glance had been hopeless from the beginning. His step slowed as he neared her door, and he finally came to a reluctant stop. All he had to do was reach out his hand and touch the doorknob. He pulled his eyes away from the door and took three steps forward before he stopped again. The house was completely quiet. He couldn't hear a sound from Grace's room or from the room she'd put her *guest* in. What if they weren't asleep, but together in one of these rooms? He could almost see Grace, snuggled in Renzo's arms and holding her breath as she waited for him to pass by.

The very idea made him long to feel Renzo's throat in his hands. It had been bad enough to watch them kissing, Grace's face upturned to welcome the bandit's lips on hers. He hadn't been fast enough to catch them, and he sure as hell couldn't admit that he'd been spying on them through the window.

He laid his hand on the doorknob. If Grace was sleeping soundly she'd never have to know that he'd checked on her. If she wasn't alone . . . then Renzo was a dead man.

He turned the knob slowly, noiselessly. The light from a bright moon spilled over Grace's bed, illuminating a lumpy pile of covers. He breathed a sigh of relief before it occurred to him that he ought to step forward to see if it was really Grace there, and not just a pillow or two positioned beneath the quilt to fool anyone who might think to look for her. She had fooled Billy once with that little trick, the night of Abigail's party. At least there wasn't enough bulk there for more than one person to be nestled in the bed.

He took a step forward, and his shadow fell across the bed. She stirred then, just a little, and he knew that it was Grace. She made that sound in her sleep. A little satisfied sigh. It was one of the things he missed about sleeping with Grace. Those little sighs, and the way she wiggled around, always ending up snuggled against him, like she couldn't get enough of touching him. Sometimes her hair came loose from her nighttime braid as she moved about, and fell across her face—strands of black silk across a pale and perfect cheek. He'd never told her that he'd often awakened early in the morning and just watched her. He could never tell her now. He could never tell anyone.

Without intending to, he moved to stand beside her bed so he could see her face. How was he going to stand it when she truly belonged to another man? Renzo or any other? He reached out to brush back the strand of hair that had come loose and fallen across her face, but his hand stopped inches short. He couldn't touch her. He had to let her go. For her own good, and for his.

He left the room as silently as he had entered it, closing the door gently behind him.

Renzo sat in Dillon's high-backed chair, and Grace placed herself on the edge of the sofa. The role of teacher was a new one for her, and she was most certain Renzo had never been much of a student.

But he gave her all of his attention, and worked very hard. It had been less than a week, and they'd spent most of that time working on his speech and his physical appearance. There was just a trace of an accent now, and though nothing could make Renzo appear ordinary, he at least looked respectably dashing.

The grin he flashed frequently was nothing less than wicked. Grace had tried, for a day or two, to subdue that smile, but she finally gave up. It was so much a part of Renzo, she'd decided it would be a crime to take it away.

"Good afternoon, Miss Jewel," Grace said primly.

Renzo repeated her sentence, and Grace decided that his speech was near perfect. A slight, mysterious accent . . . that formal use of words. He would sweep his poor unsuspecting jewel right off of her feet.

Renzo leaned forward and laid his hands on Grace's knees. "Come away with me, *querida,*" he said in a low voice. "Let me carry you away from this vile, dusty place, and build you a castle where the fields are green and the winds are cool." There was that incorrigible smile again, and Grace returned his smile as she took his hands from her knees and placed them on his own. She was just about to tell Renzo that that was much too bold for the initial meeting, when a voice behind her interrupted their lesson.

"Jumpin' the gun a bit, aren't you, Mex?" Dillon asked calmly.

Grace jerked her hands back to her own lap. Blast him, she hadn't even heard Dillon enter the room!

Renzo just continued to smile, and shrugged his shoulders casually.

"How do you intend to pay for this castle? That's an awful lot of stagecoaches."

"Do you not believe that God provides for the few true lovers who walk the earth?" Renzo's smile faded slightly as he studied Dillon over Grace's shoulder. She still couldn't make herself turn around.

"I believe a man provides for himself, Mex." There was a harshness in Dillon's voice that made the back of Grace's neck tingle. He was so angry . . . but that was the plan. Wasn't it?

"I have provided for myself for many years, *señor,*" Renzo said defensively.

"Thieving . . ."

"However I could," Renzo said almost angrily. "I am doing my best to leave that part of my life behind me. I *will* leave that part of my life behind."

There was a short span of absolute silence before Dillon responded. "For Grace?"

"For the woman I love," Renzo said in a low voice. "Because Grace insists it is the only way."

Dillon said nothing, but Grace knew he was still there, behind her. Of course, as far as Dillon knew, she was the woman Renzo was changing his life for. Still, he said nothing. It wasn't working. Not at all.

Tears stung her eyes, and she prayed that Dillon wouldn't come into the room and face her. She didn't want Dillon Becket to see her crying over him again. But she heard him step closer, until he was right behind her. Another step and he would be able to see her face, and the tears would fall.

"Ah, *querida,*" Renzo said in a velvet voice, and he slid from his chair, seating himself beside her and placing her head against his shoulder protectively. Grace bent her head, presenting to Dillon nothing but a tight knot of black hair.

She heard Renzo whisper to Dillon, "Women can be so emotional, even a woman as strong as Grace. Each time I tell her how I long to change my life for love, tears of joy fill her eyes."

She felt Renzo's fingers touch her hair, and still she kept her head down. If she looked at Dillon at that moment she would probably grab him by the collar and try to shake some sense into him as the tears she had held back spilled down her face.

Dillon's only response to Renzo's statement was to make a low and rather disgusted noise just before he stalked from the room. When he was gone, Grace lifted her head and Renzo moved away from her, returning to his chair.

He sat in that high-backed chair and studied her with a supremely satisfied expression on his handsome face.

"Very well done, I think," he said with more than a trace of pride.

Grace's tears were gone, and she stared at the satisfied man with a frown on her face. "It's not working."

Renzo grinned. "It *is* working."

Grace shook her head, and Renzo leaned forward. "He is furious with love for you."

"Furious with love? That makes no sense."

"He loves you."

Grace shook her head, denying her deepest hope. "I thought he did. I was certain he did. But if he loves me why hasn't he—"

"Tried to kill me?" Renzo finished with a smile.

"I don't want him to kill you, Renzo. But he just doesn't seem to care at all. I guess I was wrong to think that I could make him change his mind."

Renzo took her hand and ran his thumb over her skin. Not so long ago she would have jerked away from his touch, from any touch.

"Mi amiga," he whispered. "Trust me. I know love."

Renzo's lessons were a stunning success. The former highwayman was an apt pupil, and absorbed everything Grace taught him. When his accent was almost nonexistent—he had a remarkable ear for the English language—Grace began to instruct him in the finer things. He learned a phrase or two in several different languages. There was no time to teach him to speak and understand French, Italian, or Latin, but a few phrases, well placed, could be very impressive.

They discussed politics, literature, and music until Renzo knew enough tidbits to carry himself in an intelligent conversation. He was by no means an expert in any field, but Grace felt certain he could carry on adequately.

They worked for hours on his manners, which were already courtly. Still, she found his table manners lacking, and concentrated her efforts there.

Best of all, Dillon was rarely far from the house. Since that day he'd burst in on them, he found work that kept him in his study, or near the corral. He managed to interrupt their lessons at least three times a day, and Renzo had developed an uncanny sense about when these appearances might occur. He usually managed to be leaning over Grace in some almost but not quite intimate way, or clasping her hand in his very casually.

But Dillon never protested, nor did he show any sign that he cared one way or another. He was just there, watching her. Watching over her.

On this particular morning she was alone in the parlor, bent over a novel she had found in Dillon's study. It wasn't very entertaining, but it did allow her mind to escape from the constant worry that had been plaguing her.

"Where's your student?" he asked as he stood in the doorway and surveyed the room, almost as if he expected Renzo to pop out of a corner or from behind a chair.

"He had a few errands to run," Grace said, closing the book and resting it on her lap. She certainly couldn't tell him that Renzo had finally felt confident enough to approach his *little jewel*.

"Banks or stagecoaches?" Dillon asked, tossing his dusty hat onto a very nice wing chair.

The Becket parlor was rather plain, and occasionally a tad dusty if Olivia had been too busy in the kitchen to bother with much housework. The parlor had been a rarely used room, before Grace had begun giving Renzo his lessons there. She managed to give Dillon a stern look as he deposited his dirty hat so carelessly.

"Really, Becket. Shouldn't you have left a little of that dirt outside?" she asked haughtily. She was furious with him. If her plan was working—if he was regretting his decision—he was hiding it well. She should have known that he wouldn't give even an inch. He really did love the Double B more than he loved her.

"There's enough to go around."

Grace placed her novel on the sofa and stood slowly. She had waited for days for Dillon to approach her, and now she was terrified. She certainly couldn't carry on a normal conversation with him.

She had walked past him, and felt herself safe, when his hand flew out and grabbed her arm. It was so unexpected that she cried out as she spun on him.

"Get your hands off of me, Becket!"

He didn't release her. He kept a grip on her arm and pulled her closer to him. "This is the first time in days that I've seen you without your highwayman."

"I told you, Renzo has changed," Grace said sharply. "Please do not call him a highwayman, or a thief, or Mex, or any of those other disgusting names you have for him."

"Do you love him, Grace?" Dillon asked softly, and she could see the pain mirrored in his eyes.

She wanted to shout *yes.* She wanted to hurt him the way he had hurt her. But she couldn't. She couldn't look into his eyes and lie.

"No," she whispered. "You know I don't."

Dillon pulled her close to him and bent his head down to kiss her. "I'm glad," he whispered onto her lips. "I shouldn't be, but I'm so damn glad."

Grace felt herself melting as he placed his lips over hers. Dillon's hands were against her back, in her hair, and she was falling. Falling past that point where she could stop herself. She did want him, and he wanted her. But he didn't love her. The truth hit her like a lightning bolt out of the blue. He didn't love her. She'd been fooling herself to think that she could bring him to his senses. He didn't love her. If he did he wouldn't even think of marrying Abigail or allowing her to become another man's wife.

Willing herself to be strong, Grace pulled away from Dillon. "You've made your decision, Becket," she said coldly. "You can't have everything you want, and you chose Abigail and your ranch over me. You're the one who told me that it was over."

"I know," Dillon rasped.

She had to get away from him and out of this house. He wasn't going to change his mind. He wasn't going to love her the way she loved him.

Grace ran from the room and through the front door. She heard it slam behind her, and she kept running . . . around the house and past the garden. She didn't stop until she was in the barn. Maybe she was like Dillon. Maybe the cool shade and the animal smells were becoming a comfort to her, just as they had been to Dillon when he'd been away from home.

She leaned against the empty stall and took a deep breath. A trickle of sweat ran down her back, and her heart was beating fast and hard. And she was crying. The tears she'd sworn she would not shed were pouring down her cheeks—silent, salty tears that had been locked inside her since Dillon had told her it was over. She placed her hands over her face, shielding her eyes and covering the tears that fell.

And then he was there, taking her in his arms and holding her close. She didn't have the strength to fight him anymore. And she didn't want to. She wanted to hold him, as hard and as long as she could until it was too late. Until he was another woman's husband, and she was another man's wife.

"Don't cry, honey," he murmured into her ear.

"I'm not," she insisted weakly.

Dillon kissed away the tears she claimed not to have shed, holding her face in his hands and raining soft, tender kisses over her cheeks and then her lips.

Grace clasped her hands behind his back, holding him to her, her gift she couldn't keep. It was too late to turn back now, too late to pretend that she didn't need him.

He took her strength with his lips on hers, and with his hands he promised to take her away, to make her forget that she couldn't keep him.

Dillon cupped his hand beneath her breast, and brushed his thumb over a taut nipple, deepening his kiss when Grace moaned low in her throat.

"I want you, Grace," he whispered huskily, pain in his voice as he drew slightly away from her.

Grace pressed her body against his. She could

feel his heart beating as hard and as fast as hers, drank in his heat and his desire.

"You know I'm yours," she whispered. Then she took his hands in hers, laying one against her heart, and the other against her belly.

"I'm hollow without you," she whispered, holding his hands firmly in her own. "There's no one else but you."

She laid her lips over his, and felt the almost imperceptible tremor that passed through those lips and the hands she still controlled. Nothing could make her run away from him now. Nothing.

Grace released Dillon's hands and wrapped her arms around him, holding him close. His hands and his lips were demanding, hungry. Hungry for her. He lowered her into the straw, towered over her and slipped a hand beneath her skirt to caress her thigh and then rest between her legs.

His mouth never left her, but trailed over her cheek, her throat, her chest, lips that were tender and then harsh pushing her, demanding everything. Her legs instinctively spread apart as his fingers danced and delved where she grew moist and ached for him.

She took Dillon's head in her hands and drew him against her, claiming his lips and then touching her mouth against the throbbing beat of his heart there at his throat. She tasted the salt of his sweat, savoring him.

His hands danced over her skin, and with every touch her frantic desire grew. There was nothing but this—the warm feel of his hands and his lips, the passion, the almost desperate wanting that drove away everything else.

A piece of straw pierced the back of her dress, stabbing her with a sharp, dry point. She said not a word, but Dillon must have known, because he rolled over onto the straw himself, and set her down on top of him.

It was quick, the initial thrust, and Grace sucked in her breath and held it. She'd never had him so deeply inside her before, filling her so completely. With his hands on her waist he led her, slowly, rhythmically, until she was certain she couldn't stand it anymore.

Grace licked her lips and stared down at Dillon. Her skirt was hiked up and pooled around them both, and Dillon was still half dressed. She leaned forward to kiss his lips, to take the very breath from his mouth, and still she rocked until her mind ceased to function and instinct took over, driving her toward completion, driving her toward the end. But she didn't want it to end.

When fulfillment came, building and finally shattering her senses, it shook her to her bones, rushed over her and swept away all her pain and heartache. *I love you.* She didn't know if she whispered the words or shouted them or simply heard them in her mind, but they were there.

Dillon thrust into her farther than she'd ever imagined, and she threw her head back as he reached up to her, and with a tortured and husky voice whispered her name just once.

He gathered her to him, drawing her head against his shoulder and smoothing her hair. His hands were gentle, but he said not a word. And his earlier words came back to her. *I want you, Grace.* Not *I love you*, not even *I need you* . . . but *I want you*.

She could feel the chill growing around her heart. Dillon Becket had learned how to turn her own body against her, and he didn't even love her. It had been too long since he'd had a woman, and there she was—practically offering herself to him on a silver platter.

I want you, Grace.

He held her, caressing her hair and her back, and they were still locked together, joined and yet suddenly separate. This had nothing to do with love. It was sex, raw and desperate. What had been hot was now cold.

They heard the carriage approaching at the same time, the crunching of the wheels against the drive that led to the house.

Dillon carefully set Grace away from him and stood to fasten his trousers as he made his way to the barn door. She heard the curse, and saw him speed the efforts to repair his appearance, tucking in his shirt and combing his hair with his fingers.

"Who is it?" Grace asked coldly, picking straw from her hair and brushing her skirt. It was as if they were suddenly strangers.

He turned back to her, but with the sun behind him all she could see was a shadow.

"It's Abigail," he said in a low voice. "Stay here."

He was gone before she could respond.

Grace paced, a few short, frantic steps before she turned, whipping her hair and her skirt around her. The more she thought about Dillon Becket, the more furious she became.

How could he stand there and so calmly order her—*order her*—to stay in the barn while he went to meet his sweet fiancée? Just minutes earlier he had whispered her name, had shown her how much he *wanted* her. And now he expected her to hide in the barn?

"Stay here? Like hell I will, Dillon Becket."

She strode from the barn with her skirt in her hands and cold revenge in her heart.

Chapter Sixteen

Abigail was just rounding the corner of the house on foot when Dillon met her. She greeted him with an innocent smile, and he felt like an even bigger ass than he had two minutes ago.

"Good afternoon, Dillon," Abigail said sweetly. "I hope you don't mind me stopping by, but we really must make plans for the wedding." She blushed, flooding her normally pale face with color.

He hadn't seen her since he'd delivered his unromantic and businesslike proposal. "I guess we do," he said unenthusiastically. Moments earlier he'd been set to cancel the wedding and take off with Grace, if she'd have him. Foolish idea.

He took Abigail's arm and steered her toward the house. The last thing he wanted was for Abigail and Grace to come face-to-face. Especially now.

Abigail didn't take a seat in the parlor, but

stood by the window where soft light fell across her face. She wasn't a bad-looking woman. In fact, some would call her beautiful. She had deep brown eyes and pale blond hair, and skin that—even though she'd been born and raised in Texas—had rarely seen the sun.

He suddenly felt that he was hurting Abigail as surely as he was hurting Grace. She deserved better than a husband who would always love someone else.

Before they'd had a chance to begin their discussion, Grace came through the front door like a tornado, and she stopped just outside the parlor entrance.

"Miss Wilkinson," she said silkily, and just a little breathlessly. "What a pleasure to see you again."

Grace slipped into the room and ignored Dillon, crossing the parlor to stand in front of Abigail.

"Miss Cavanaugh," Abigail said coldly. Her dislike of Grace was undisguised, as she pursed her lips and clenched her hands together. "You're looking . . ." She paused and looked Grace up and down, taking in the plain dress and disheveled hair. Abigail herself was fashionably dressed in a peach suit that looked entirely too warm. ". . . well," she finally finished.

Grace lifted a hand to her mussed hair. "Oh, I know I look a mess. Becket has been teaching me to ride astride." She turned and looked at him for the first time since she'd entered the room, and Dillon felt as if he were going to choke on the knot in his throat.

Abigail raised a hand to her neck. "I always ride sidesaddle, myself."

Grace smiled wickedly. "Don't worry. I'm sure

Becket will teach you everything he's taught me."

Abigail apparently didn't hear anything strange or suggestive in Grace's comments, but listened politely.

"He's a marvelous teacher," Grace continued brightly. "But sometimes he tries to push me too hard. Well, right now I'm so sore." Grace leaned close to Abigail and lowered her voice, but it was loud enough for Dillon to hear her plainly. "I would kill for a hot bath."

Grace looked right at him, and she met his warning stare with hard, glittering eyes.

"I suppose Dillon has told you all about our plans?" Abigail asked timidly.

"Of course." Grace laid a hand on Abigail's arm. "We're all very excited. Why, we were just talking about the wedding just a few minutes before you arrived, weren't we, Becket?"

Dillon couldn't speak. He was waiting. Waiting for Grace to tell Abigail everything that had happened. Would it make a difference? He had never told Abigail that he loved her, had never pretended that their marriage was anything other than a business arrangement.

Abigail faced them both and straightened her back. "There's another matter we should discuss." She looked at Dillon. "Your ward is old enough to marry. I could introduce her to the eligible bachelors in and around Plummerton. It would be best if she were married before . . . before I come here to live."

"Grace has a gentleman friend—" Dillon began, but Grace interrupted, her voice too bright.

"For goodness' sake, Becket. Are you speaking of Lorenzo? He's just a pupil." She cocked her head so that it was closer to Abigail's. "Lorenzo is a lovely man, and I have been helping him.

That's true. But he's definitely spoken for."

Abigail glanced from an almost smirking Grace to Dillon. Hell, if he looked half as confused as he felt, he must look like a complete idiot.

"Then you wouldn't mind if I introduced you to a few eligible men?"

She knew. Or at the very least, she suspected. Dillon didn't expect that Abigail would ever voice her beliefs, and *how* she knew was beyond him. But Abigail didn't want Grace at the ranch after the wedding.

Grace smiled, but the glitter was gone from her eyes. "That's a marvelous idea, Miss Wilkinson," she said hollowly. "I'm sure there are any number of fine prospects in the Plummerton area."

Dillon finally stepped toward the women and found his voice. "I don't see any reason to rush into anything. There's plenty of time to see that Grace is taken care of. She can stay here as long as she wants."

Abigail was not the sort of woman to argue with him, and she met his statement with silence and diverted eyes. She'd told him what her feelings were, and that was where it ended.

But he was worried about Grace. Her face was flushed, and her eyes glinted, hard and hurt. He had hurt her, and he hated himself for that.

There were several moments of awkward silence in the hot, still room. It was Grace who finally moved, stepping backward and away from him and Abigail. Her bravado was gone.

"It was so nice to see you again, Miss Wilkinson," she said numbly. "It's rather warm in here. I think I'll take a walk."

She turned and ran from the room, and Dillon wanted nothing more than to go after her.

But he didn't. He faced Abigail and began to discuss plans for a wedding he dreaded.

Grace ran toward the barn, seeking solace in the cool and quiet shelter. It took her only a few minutes to discover that she could find no peace there. Perhaps she never would again.

She needed to ride. To fly across the ground and forget everything that had happened. Her mare was in the barn, that gentle creature Dillon had chosen for her.

And Dillon's bay stallion was in the corral.

That was a powerful animal, one that would carry her across the ranch and away from Dillon Becket with all the speed she desired.

One of the hands was leading his own horse into the barn. It was fortunate that he had not arrived ten minutes earlier . . . but she wished he had walked into the barn in time to stop her from giving in so foolishly to Dillon. If only he'd come in and interrupted that first kiss, she and Dillon would have come apart, and she wouldn't be filled with so much bitter regret.

Grace all but assaulted the hand, drawing forth her most commanding voice. "Would you saddle Becket's horse for me, Lucas, isn't it?"

He was covered with dirt, and sweat ran down his face. His shirt was soaked with perspiration, staining the cotton shirt from his armpits and down the sides and across the back.

"How 'bout I saddle up Butter for you, Miss Cavanaugh?" he suggested with an easy smile. "The boss don't allow anyone to ride that stallion of his."

"Saddle it," Grace commanded haughtily, "or I'll saddle it myself and then I'll have your job." She knew how to use her voice to her own advantage, how to get a man to do what she wanted. One way or another. And this boy was no challenge at all.

Lucas warily did as she demanded, and then he helped her into the saddle of the prancing animal.

Dillon's stallion was much taller than her own mare, and Grace was surprised to find herself so high off the ground. She could feel the animal's power beneath her, between her legs, and when the horse left the corral she clutched the reins desperately, leaning over its neck and allowing it to run.

Her skirt whipped in the wind, and her hair came loose from its already haphazard knot. She had realized the moment she flew from the corral that she had very little control over the stallion, but she didn't care. She had the wind in her face, and the landscape that rushed by reminded her that she could be far, far away from Dillon Becket in a short time, if she dared.

Where had she gone wrong? How had he managed to trick her into believing that he loved her? If she couldn't love him, she would have to hate him. She would have to forget everything beautiful about him and remember only the bad. The way he had used her.

She passed Billy, barely seeing him, aware only that he called her name and turned his own horse to follow her. She didn't attempt to slow the stallion, not even when she heard her name again, faint, muffled by the wind in her ears and the thud of the stallion's hooves.

Grace glanced over her shoulder and saw Billy bearing down on her, his white hair silver in the sunlight, and he raised a hand to her.

It happened so fast. One minute Billy was waving at her, trying to catch up, and the next he was flying through the air and his horse was on the ground.

Grace pulled on the reins, attempting to stop the stallion. Whatever had made her think she could control an animal as strong as this one? It was a well-trained horse, and finally stopped, but the stallion continued to prance nervously. There was a stranger on his back, and he was excited from the hard and free ride.

Grace dismounted as quickly as possible, and ran to Billy. He was lying in the dirt. Still. Lifeless. His horse was screaming, and one leg was folded up under the animal at an unnatural angle.

"Billy?" Grace laid a hand on his silver hair, and felt the warm blood seeping onto her fingers. There was blood on the rock that protruded from the ground beneath his head, bright red, much brighter than she had imagined it would be.

He couldn't be dead. She wouldn't allow it. "Come on, Billy," she said, trying to make her voice strong. She lifted his head into her lap, and hesitantly, afraid of what she might find, Grace placed her fingers against his throat. There was a faint pulse there. At least he was still alive.

She couldn't leave him, and she couldn't possibly move him by herself.

So she lifted her head and screamed. Surely her screams, and the screams of Billy's horse, together would bring someone running to help. It was a big ranch, but there had been other hands with Billy. Hadn't there?

It wasn't long before she heard the approaching horse, and Grace breathed a sigh of relief. She stroked Billy's head gently, keeping her hand away from the wound. Her skirt was soaked with

Billy's blood, and she tried to ignore it.

The last person she expected to see was Dillon, but she looked up and there he was.

"What the hell . . ."

"He was chasing me . . . and something happened to his horse . . . and he flew off, just flew off . . . and he hit his head. . . ." Grace didn't realize until she started to speak that she'd been crying.

Dillon bent over Billy and did just what Grace had done. He checked for a pulse and inspected the gash on the old man's head.

Grace didn't watch as Dillon rose and went to the suffering horse. But she jumped when she heard the gunshot, and the whimpering animal was silenced.

Dillon whistled for his stallion, and the bay came trotting to him obediently.

"I'm going for the buckboard and a few hands to help," Dillon said coldly. "Stay here until I get back."

Grace lifted her head and squinted against the bright sun. She couldn't see Dillon's face. It was a shadow with the sun behind it. "I didn't mean—" she began.

"If you hadn't run off like a spoiled child . . ." Dillon began. She could hear the ice and the hate in his voice. "I don't have time to discuss this with you right now."

He turned away from her and jumped easily into the saddle, and the stallion galloped toward the house.

Dillon was right. She had run like a spoiled brat, and if Billy died . . . if Billy died it would surely be her fault.

* * *

Dillon pushed his way through the kitchen door. Damn doctor. What good was he? Billy might wake up and he might not. He might live, and he might not. Seemed the good doctor didn't know much about head wounds.

Olivia was standing over the stove, busying herself making a pot of coffee and a pan of broth. She sniffled loudly, and wiped away tears with the back of her hand.

"I thought you were with Billy," Dillon snapped.

Olivia looked up, red-rimmed eyes bright in an unusually pale face. "Grace is sittin' with him."

"That's just great," Dillon muttered as he headed for the hallway that led to Olivia's room. That was where they'd put Billy, so he'd be in the house and easily accessible. None of them had wanted to risk carrying the big man upstairs.

"She'll probably try to smother him with a pillow," he murmured.

"Dillon Becket," Olivia chastised sharply. "Don't you dare say that. That girl's heart is broken. She blames herself."

Dillon turned and faced Olivia, a woman who had been like a second mother to him. He couldn't remember a time when Olivia hadn't been there. He did care what she thought, but he didn't dare let her know that.

"That's because it is her fault," he said in a low voice.

"She didn't put that prairie dog hole there, and she didn't intend—" Olivia stopped short and pursed her thin lips together. "Don't think I don't know the real reason you're angry with her. I'm not blind. I've known you all your life. Bathed you, and rocked you when you had that fever and your mama was so give out. I cried when you went off to fight, and I cried when you came home. I love you like you was my own son, and I've always been proud of you.

"Until now. You're not doing that girl right, Dillon. She's young and confused and she looks at you like you're the only man in the world."

"Olivia," Dillon began, warning in his voice.

"And I never thought to see you smile again," Olivia continued, ignoring his warning. "But since Grace came here things have been different."

"This is none of your—"

"None of my business?" Olivia said as she turned back to the stove. "Well, I reckon you're right. I'm just an employee, after all. Just a cook and a housekeeper. You're exactly right, Mr. Becket. It's none of my business."

Dillon turned his back on her. Damned if he would defend himself to anybody. Even Olivia.

How could he explain to her how angry he was? Not just because Billy was hurt, though that was bad enough. What made it worse was the unwanted ghost of a thought that whispered deep in his mind.

It could have been Grace. She wouldn't have had a chance. The stallion would have thrown her so hard. . . . It could have been Grace lying in that bed, dead or dying. If Lucas hadn't come to him to tell what Grace had done, it might have been hours before she and Billy had been found. He couldn't tell her that. He couldn't tell her that he'd been racing after her when he'd heard her screams and his heart had stopped beating.

He stalked down the hall, intending to confront her. The door was ajar, and he could see Grace sitting by the bed. Her hands were clasped in her lap, and her eyes were on Billy's face. She was speaking, softly but earnestly, and Dillon sidled close to the door to hear what she was saying.

"You might think I'm being terribly silly," Grace said to the motionless man on the bed. Billy's head had been swathed in white bandages, and just a tuft of silver hair peeked out.

"The doctor said you can't hear me, but I don't believe that. I think you can hear me, Billy. Are you listening?" Grace leaned forward just a little. "Don't you die," she insisted. "You don't know what you mean to me, because I never told you. It was just too embarrassing. Too . . . absurd, but . . ."

Grace laid her hand over Billy's chest, over his heart. "You've been more like a father to me than my own father ever was. Sometimes I wonder what it would have been like to grow up here, with you watching over me." There was wonder in her voice, wistful and sad. "You're the only man I've ever known who cared for me and asked nothing in return."

Dillon shrank away from the door, but he couldn't leave. He leaned against the wall beside the door and closed his eyes, and he listened.

"My own father didn't even tolerate me," she said without rancor. "And . . . other men have always been attentive, but they had a price. Even Dillon." She sighed. "I thought he was different, but he's not. I'm just more gullible than I believed I was."

There was a long pause, and Dillon was tempted to return to the open door, to peek inside and see that she was all right. When she did begin to speak again, it was with tears in her voice.

"I promise, if you'll just wake up and be well,

I'll do things differently. I'll . . . I'll get married, and I'll leave here. I'll stay out of trouble. I promise I will. And I'll stay away from Dillon. I won't let him touch me, I swear." Her tearful voice had taken on a touch of desperation, and Dillon wanted to go to her. To tell her that he was not like all the others.

"And when I do get married, I want you to give me away, Billy. And even if I can't have everything I want, I can make a family for myself. I can have children and love them. . . ." Her voice broke, and, still safely hidden in the hallway, Dillon clenched his hands and closed his eyes. "So you have to get better," Grace continued shakily. "You have to wake up."

Dillon retreated quietly down the hallway, toward the kitchen where Olivia busied herself. When he turned and approached the bedroom where Billy lay again, it was with a heavy step, and he was calling Grace's name.

She was waiting for him when he appeared in the doorway.

"Is there any change?" he asked gruffly, trying not to betray what he had heard.

Grace was so pale she looked like a ghost sitting at Billy's side. He had heard the tears in her voice, but her eyes were dry. She shook her head.

"I, um, I should apologize," Dillon said sheepishly. "I was upset. It's not your fault."

"Yes, it is, Becket," she answered him harshly, standing as he moved to the end of the bed. "I acted foolishly and impulsively and this is what happened. I apologize for interfering with your plans. It won't happen again." Her voice was cold and distant.

She brushed past him, looking away as she passed close by. "If you're going to be here for a while, I'll go clean up. But I think someone should be with Billy at all times, so if you—"

"I'll stay," Dillon said, watching her stiff back. When she turned in the doorway he could see that she still wore the blood-soaked skirt he had found her in. The blood had dried, brown and stiff, there where Billy's head had rested in her lap.

"You go ahead and clean up, and sleep for a while, if you want."

Grace seemed to study him with distant eyes, looking over him much the same as she had the first time he'd seen her. Regal and cold. Distant. Alone. Always alone.

"I'll come down in a couple of hours," she said briskly, "but please let me know if . . . if there's any change."

She spun away and left him alone with Billy, in a room that retained her scent and her energy.

And Dillon knew that for the rest of his life he would have that whispering thought in his brain.

It could have been Grace.

When Grace appeared in the doorway, no more than two hours later, Dillon felt his heart sink at the sight of her. It was dark outside, and the room was lit with a single lamp, burning low. But it illuminated Grace well enough.

She'd discarded her usual calico for one of her own gowns, gray silk with a high neck and long, form-fitting sleeves. Her hair, hair that had earlier been windblown, was brushed severely back from her face and secured at the nape. Her spine was rigid, her face impassive, and she stood in the doorway with that regal air that kept others at a distance.

"Why don't you get some rest, Becket," she suggested. "I'll sit with Billy."

Dillon rose from his chair by the bed, unable to take his eyes from her as she stepped into the room. "I want to stay."

Grace turned away from him, ready to escape.

"Wait," Dillon whispered as he reached out and caught Grace's arm. He felt it immediately, the sudden tension in her arm and in her stance.

"Release me, Becket," she said in a low voice, and he did as she asked.

She wouldn't remain in the same room with him. He knew that now. And he knew just as well that she needed to be with Billy.

"Maybe I will try to sleep for a couple of hours, and get a bite to eat," he said casually. "If you don't mind staying."

Grace brushed past him, her eyes on the floor as she made her way to the chair by the bed. There was a pained expression on her face as she glanced down at Billy, but Dillon knew there was nothing he could say to make her feel better.

She was going to ignore the events that had sent her riding away from the ranch at breakneck speed. Perhaps that was for the best, since nothing could be changed.

Dillon made his way to the kitchen through the dimly lit hallway. He poured himself a cup of cold coffee and picked at a hard biscuit.

There was no way he could get any sleep, but he would stay away from the room for a while so Grace could watch over Billy as she wished. Olivia was settled for the night in Billy's cabin. She'd told him that much as she'd inquired after the patient and gathered a few personal belongings from her room. She'd refused the offer of Dillon's bedroom for the night, preferring, angrily, to escape him completely.

So he couldn't even talk to her. Or rather, apologize to her. She'd been right that afternoon, as she usually was. He hadn't been fair to Grace. He expected her to be as practical as he was about the Double B. To love it as he did. To be willing to sacrifice anything for it. That was what he was doing. Sacrificing Grace for the Double B.

But at the same time he was doing what was best for her. It was his responsibility to see that she was cared for. That she marry a man who could give her everything a lady needs.

That man wasn't him. Without the Double B he would be nothing better than a drifter. Ranching was all he knew.

He didn't even hear Renzo enter the kitchen and pour his own cup of coffee. It wasn't until the bandit took a loud sip of the cold, strong coffee and made a grunting noise of disgust that Dillon was made aware of his presence.

The Mexican bandit—ex-bandit—stood casually propped against the stove, his long legs crossed at the ankles, his mouth set in a thoughtful grimace.

"You have ruined a perfectly good woman, *Señor* Becket," Renzo said in a low voice. It wasn't exactly a challenge, but there was a hint of threat in that voice.

"Grace will be fine," Dillon said halfheartedly. He couldn't even muster the energy to hate the thief, especially now that he knew there was nothing between Grace and Renzo.

"I hope you are correct. Perhaps in time, and with some distance from this place, Grace's heart will heal."

Dillon looked up then. Renzo was right. Neither of them would be able to lead a normal life living where they would be reminded every day.

Even if Grace married a local man and lived within a day's ride of the Double B, it would be too close. Could he forget that she lived so close? Could she forget him?

He drummed his fingers lightly on the table as he thought, almost forgetting that he was not alone until Renzo loomed over him.

"I have made many mistakes in my life," Renzo said in a low voice. "I came from a good family. My mother didn't raise her youngest son to be a thief. But when she was killed, along with my little sister and the woman who was to be my wife, I thought I would never care for another living thing. No human or animal. It was simply too painful.

"I hunted down and killed the men who murdered those I loved. Thieves, all of them. That was twelve years ago. I was barely twenty at the time, but in my eyes my life was over. I became like the men who were responsible for ripping my heart away."

"Why are you telling me this?"

"I didn't think I would ever care again. I thought my heart had turned to stone. That my soul had turned dark and shrunk to nothing.

"But I was wrong."

Dillon swirled the dregs of his coffee in the bottom of his tin cup. He didn't want to look up at the man who was emptying his heart to a near stranger who had done nothing but insult him. "What does that have to do with Grace?"

"Nothing, really. I do care for her, my fragile *amiga* who tries so hard to be strong. And I wonder if you will ever again care enough to stand over a sleeping woman and watch, weeping in your soul for want of her." The bandit ignored the warning stare Dillon turned to him. Renzo had been watching his first night in this house, standing behind Dillon as he watched Grace sleep. It was such an invasion. "Forcing yourself to stay away from her because . . . Well, Grace tells me you have your reasons for marrying another. I just hope you don't lose your soul in the process. It makes one's life very lonely."

"This is none of your business."

Renzo gave him a half smile, sad and resigned. "True. I just wanted to have my say before I leave. I'll be gone in the morning, long before sunup."

Dillon didn't know whether to wish Renzo luck or help him pack his belongings. He wouldn't be sorry to see the man leave.

"Tell Grace," the bandit continued, "that I had no luck finding my little jewel today, but I have not given up."

"Your . . . what?"

Dillon didn't get an answer. Grace stepped into the kitchen, a bit of color in her cheeks at last. There was a sparkle in her eyes as she clasped her hands together.

"Billy's awake." That was all she said before she turned and hurried back to the injured man's room. Dillon was right behind her, and went to the opposite side of the bed. The two of them leaned over Billy, as the man studied them with a scowl on his face.

"What the heck's the matter with you two? I never seen two longer faces in all my days."

"How do you feel?" Grace asked tenderly, ignoring Billy's foul mood.

"My head hurts like the dickens, and I'm hungry."

That statement elicited a smile from Grace, and she squeezed Billy's hand. "You really are going to be fine, aren't you?"

"Of course I'm going to be fine. What are you babbling about, girl?"

It became clear that Billy remembered nothing of what had happened. He told them that he remembered seeing Grace fly past him on Dillon's stallion, and that was it. He didn't even remember turning his horse to chase her.

Grace would only allow him to have broth and water, even though he protested heartily that he needed meat to fill his stomach. But he drank the broth and fell into a comfortable sleep, and he was snoring minutes after he'd closed his eyes.

Dillon laid his hands on Grace's shoulders, and then removed them when he felt her tense.

"Everything's going to be all right, Grace."

She turned to look up at him, a determined look on her face. "Of course it is, Becket. Since Billy's recovering, I have a favor to ask of you."

"Anything."

"Abigail Wilkinson offered to introduce me to some eligible men, with the prospect of marriage in mind. Please ask her to proceed with her plans as soon as possible."

She was remembering her promise to Billy, he knew, her promise to marry and raise a family. Her promise to stay away from him.

He couldn't, at that moment, manage to respond in any way. To say yes or no or hell no, or even to nod. And Grace rushed past him, her eyes on the door as she fled from the room.

Chapter Seventeen

Grace took a deep breath, enjoying a rare, quiet moment. It had been a trying evening, though she had done her best not to show it. Dinner had been bad enough, but the after-dinner party was a real trial.

She had managed to have a private moment's conversation with each of the three potential suitors Abigail had presented. Grace had been the center of attention before, had gone out of her way, on occasion, to be just that. But tonight she was ill at ease with the attentiveness. She felt as though she were up for auction, or a prize to be claimed.

Of course Wade Wilkinson was there. It was clear that neither Abigail nor Dillon considered him to be a suitable candidate, which gave Grace all the more reason to smile brilliantly at him whenever the opportunity arose.

Wade had not mentioned his earlier, rejected

offer to court her. He had not attempted to press her, as he had in Dillon's parlor, but had been a perfect gentleman. Wade was not bad-looking. In fact, he was quite handsome, in a rough and rather brawny way. Tall and broad shouldered, with Abigail's brown eyes and pale hair, he was quite genial and unerringly good-natured. Had she overreacted that day in the parlor? Had he really been too bold, or had she panicked? Would allowing Wade to kiss her really be any different from kissing Becket?

Of course it would be. She knew that in her heart. And marrying Wade would mean constant contact with Dillon and Abigail. How could she punish herself like that?

She at first had thought that Nate Johnson was there as a joke. The man was much older than she, a widower with six children. But she soon discovered that his presence was no prank. This was a man who had made his small fortune in cotton and had miraculously held on to a good portion of it. He needed a wife. For his children, he said, and to see to the running of his house.

He was not really an ugly man, Grace tried to tell herself, though his nose was quite broad and had an unfortunate dent in the center, but he had the irritating habit of clearing his throat frequently as he ran stubby fingers through what was left of his hair.

Samuel Plummer, Abigail's third candidate, had watched Grace quietly for most of the evening. The son of the banker Plummerton was named for, he was evidently well educated, and he possessed an air of refinement the other Texans she had met lacked. More handsome even than Wade, Samuel had dark hair and blue eyes and a nicely shaped wide mouth that smiled often, though not as ridiculously often as Wade. Their few private words had shown her that Samuel was a bit shy. He was a lawyer, and had just recently opened his practice in Plummerton. Thankfully he had missed Abigail's welcome-home party, and the spectacle she had made of herself.

The three potential husbands had only one thing in common: they were all in the market for a wife. There were no moony-eyed glances, no whispered words of love, for this would not be a love match but a partnership. A business proposition.

Dillon had managed to be his usual unsociable self, growling and giving one-word answers to questions that were put to him, and averting his eyes whenever Grace happened to look his way. Abigail acted as though this were perfectly normal, and Grace wondered if perhaps it wasn't.

Kirby Wilkinson had made a brief appearance. He was an energetic young man not much older than Grace. It was clear, even though he looked at her appreciatively, that he was far from being ready to settle down.

Old man Wilkinson had eaten dinner with them, but had retired early, insisting on leaving the evening to the young people. He reminded Grace more of Abigail than Wade or Kirby, as he looked Grace over as a man purchasing a horse might study an animal. He'd actually smiled at Wade when his perusal was over, nodding his head in approval.

"My Russian princess," Wade said with a smile as he sat beside Grace on the settee. It seemed her moment of respite was over.

"I feel so foolish," Grace said in a low voice, leaning closer to the rancher in a confiding way.

"And you seem to be forever reminding me of that escapade. Whatever could have possessed me to pull such a prank? I will never know. I do hope you won't think I'm such an impulsively foolish girl all the time."

"I told you before, I thought it was right funny, myself. The look on Dillon's face was priceless. I never saw him turn so many shades of red before. Besides, it served him right." Wade leaned closer to her, until she could feel his breath on her neck. It took all her control not to pull away from the man.

A quick look around the room confirmed her suspicions. No one was coming to her rescue. No one would even know that she wanted to be rescued. Abigail was in deep conversation with Nate Johnson, and Dillon was speaking with Samuel Plummer. But his eyes were on her. Blast him, they had been all evening. Only this time he didn't look away, but continued to stare. How did he expect her to choose a husband with him looking at her like that?

She smiled at Wade. "It's quite difficult to shock a Texan, isn't it? No one seemed particularly scandalized at the party, or even when the truth came out."

Wade chuckled. "Only Abigail. But then, she spends half her life scandalized by one thing or another."

Grace was relieved when someone suggested that Abigail play the piano. At least, for a few precious minutes, she would be relieved of her obligation to carry on fascinating conversation with the man of the moment.

Abigail played well, sitting primly at the piano and pounding out a fair rendition of "Barbara Allen," and then, upon request, "Jeanie With the

Light Brown Hair." She was, Grace conceded, an adequate pianist.

She almost didn't hear Dillon, even as he repeated his question. "You do play, don't you? I thought you said you did."

"Oh, well." She smiled at him coldly. "It's true we did have lessons at school, but it's been a long time, Becket."

Abigail appeared in front of Grace, both hands offered insistently. "Please do indulge us."

Grace knew, could see on Abigail's face, that she was expected to play. And badly. This was one area where Abigail was confident she had the advantage. Grace rose slowly to her feet, ignoring Abigail's offered hands.

"How could I possibly refuse?"

Grace sat on the piano bench and took a moment, smoothing the silk of her garnet dress, caressing the ruby that hung between her breasts. How appropriate that she had chosen this particular piece of jewelry for the evening.

She laid her fingers over the keys and ran them stiffly over ivory and ebony. It had been a while. What if she did fumble? What difference did it make? She played a simple little piece. Mozart. It had been the first piece she'd played at a school recital, when she'd been twelve. It rolled off her fingers effortlessly, smoothly, as it came back to her with ease.

There was a burst of applause when she finished, but Grace didn't even look up. She began to play again, tuning out the others, playing only for herself. The piece began slowly, almost tentatively, then built to a fever pitch. One of Liszt's Hungarian rhapsodies. Gypsy music. Music that set her blood on fire and made her heart soar.

She did, for a short while, forget that she was

not alone, as she pounded her fingers against the keyboard. This was a talent she had inherited from her mother, or so her father had said. That was why he never listened when she practiced. That was why he had always been too busy to listen to a new piece she had learned. But at school her talent made her shine. Even the teachers who seemed to despair of ever getting through to her forgave her when she played.

It had been so long, she'd forgotten how wonderfully lost she was when she played, how the rest of the world went away.

When the music ended and the ring of the keys still reverberated in the air, there was complete silence. Grace placed her hands in her lap and stared at the keys. When the applause started she looked back at the others. Abigail was pale, lips pursed and eyes hard. Nate Johnson, bless the poor man, looked terrified. Samuel Plummer nodded to her, suitably impressed, while Wade looked at Grace and then at his sister with a wide grin on his face. It was Dillon who stood and came to her, laying a hand on her shoulder.

"Is there anything you can't do?" he asked softly.

He was blocking the rest of the room and its occupants from her view, hiding her face from the rest of the party. "I can't keep you," she whispered, her voice so low that no one else could possibly hear her.

Abigail did her best to try to convince Dillon and Grace to spend the night. But Dillon insisted on getting back to the ranch, even though it meant traveling in the dark and arriving late. For that, Grace was grateful. She was tired of smiling at Abigail and putting her best face on for the gentlemen.

"Well?" Dillon snapped before they were even out of sight of the house.

"Well what?" Grace looked away from him, out over the moonwashed landscape.

"Did you . . . did you get a marriage proposal tonight?"

"Oh, that," Grace said tiredly. "Yes, I did."

Dillon didn't say anything for a few minutes, and then he exploded. "From who?"

"From all three, actually," Grace said matter-of-factly. "Wade asked almost the moment we arrived. Such an impatient man. Mr. Johnson, Nate, asked after dinner. And Samuel Plummer made his offer about five minutes before we left. He seems rather sweet. A little shy, perhaps."

Dillon cursed under his breath, giving all of his attention for a moment to the horses that were pulling the buckboard. "Damn it, don't make me keep asking. What did you say?"

"I said that I would consider the proposal."

"To which one?"

Grace turned and looked at Dillon then. He sounded so angry. What had he expected? "To all three, Becket."

Dillon pulled the horses to a halt in the middle of the road. "To all three?"

Grace nodded. He was looking at her as if she'd done something wrong. "I haven't made up my mind yet. Wade is coming for supper on Monday, and Nate will be there Tuesday."

"And Sam on Wednesday?"

"Thursday," Grace supplied the information in a monotone. "Are we going to spend the night in the middle of the road?"

Dillon flicked the reins and got the buckboard

moving again. A muscle in his jaw twitched.

Grace had nothing to say to him. He knew how she felt, and still he'd chosen Abigail. That left her with no choice but to marry another man, and preferably soon. Besides, she had to remember the promise she'd made to Billy while he was unconscious.

"Why didn't you tell me you could play?" Dillon asked, his voice more relaxed than it had been just moments earlier.

"I did."

"You didn't tell me you could play like that," he said, and Grace could hear the appreciation in his voice.

Grace closed her fist around the ruby and watched Dillon. He was watching the road, so she felt free to study his profile. The sharp nose, the hard jaw. She would have to memorize it all.

"Do you remember the red dress I wore at the roadside stop in Clanton?" she asked, a touch of trepidation creeping into her voice.

Dillon snorted, but he didn't look at her. "I'll never forget it."

She almost smiled, but couldn't quite carry it off. "We were having a concert at the school. It was my last year there, and the teachers had planned, as usual, a very sedate and refined evening. Bach. Mozart. Matching white dresses with wide skirts and puffy sleeves." She sighed, remembering. "I don't even recall what I was so angry about. I think it was something the music teacher had said or done, but it was probably just another attempt to get my father's attention. You see, I was to play last. . . ."

"Because you were the best?"

"Yes, because I was the best. And I had that red dress, made with my own hands over a period of weeks. I had worked on it late at night, sewing by candlelight until I couldn't see to sew anymore.

"When it was my turn to perform, I came out in that red dress, and instead of playing the sonata my music teacher had chosen for me, I played the Liszt I played tonight."

"It was wonderful."

"I love it. But it's very improper for a young lady to play Gypsy music that makes the blood boil and the heart beat fast."

Grace was quiet for several minutes, and Dillon didn't ask her any more questions. She was lost in remembering, clutching the ruby.

"After the concert there was a reception, and we were all allowed to attend. Even me, after I was made to change into my proper white dress, of course. A classmate's father, Sir Richard, had disappeared shortly after the reception began. I remember because Nancy was looking for him, and she was afraid he had left without saying good-bye. But he returned a short time later. I saw him watching me, and it made me nervous. He was a much older man, of course, and I was only seventeen. But he watched me so closely, and then he cornered me." Rather like Wade had that day in the parlor, though she didn't remind Dillon of that. "And he presented me with this." Grace held the ruby aloft. "He said he'd thought of it when he heard me play, and he wanted me to have it. Goodness, it was so beautiful, and no one had ever given me anything before. I'll never forget the way it sparkled in the light when he placed it over my head.

"When I was invited to spend the holiday with Nancy and her family, I was so excited," she said cynically. "As it turned out, it was Sir Richard's suggestion that I stay with them."

"Dirty, lecherous old man," Dillon muttered angrily.

"Exactly," Grace said clearly. "You figured it out much more quickly than I did. I guess you could say I was a slow learner. Sir Richard made several subtle attempts at seducing me, but I was so naive. Finally he grew bolder. I actually thought that he . . . that he cared for me the way a father cares for his daughter, before I realized what he really wanted. I was so foolish."

"No. It was his fault. Not yours," Dillon said defensively.

"Well, I made him pay," she said darkly. "I led him to believe that he would get what he wanted. I hinted broadly that a few more gems would make me more . . . willing. And then, when I saw that he was nearing the end of his store of patience, I left. Early one morning while the household was still abed."

"Did you ever see him again?"

Grace smiled. "Only once, at a social function years later. He was very . . . coldly polite. Of course, he had no choice. His wife was on his arm."

Grace let the ruby fall. "After that I traveled all over England, and to France as well. I stayed with old schoolmates, and when that wasn't possible I wrote to my father asking for money. The money always came, and he never asked me to come home. He was willing to part with everything he owned to keep me away. I guess that's exactly what he did."

Everything was so beautiful, silver in the moonlight. The rolling hills, the stars in the sky. A fairy-tale land.

"Is that where you got all those geegaws?"

Grace nodded. "I started collecting jewelry, and men's hearts, though to be honest there weren't many of them offering me their hearts. It wasn't love they wanted to buy. It was . . . well, you know what it was."

"Dammit, Grace," Dillon said in a low voice. "Do you have any idea how dangerous that was? You can't . . ." He almost choked on his protests.

"The trick is to choose a man who loves the chase more than the victory. A man who can be manipulated. He has to be . . . weak, in a way."

She looked away from Dillon and to the moon-washed landscape. "I never would have played the game with you, Becket," she said softly.

Wade ate as if he were starved, and given his size, Grace could imagine that he ate this way all the time. She began to imagine herself in the kitchen, all day long, never quite able to cook enough food to keep him satisfied. He smiled at her often, grinning almost constantly. Did he have to smile all the time? No one could possibly be this happy.

She wondered if he smiled like that when he . . . Well, she couldn't quite picture it, just as she couldn't picture taking any man other than Dillon to her bed. It was inevitable, she knew, if she was to have the family she wanted, but it was impossible to imagine with any sense of ease.

There were just the three of them at the dining room table: Dillon, Wade, and herself. Olivia had refused to eat with them, had refused with an almost venomous glare at Dillon that was very out of character for the warm woman. Billy was still confined to the bed, and had become quite a cantankerous patient.

After dinner they retired to the parlor, a room

that Grace had practically claimed as her own. Already this room was full of memories for her.

Dillon was as surly as he'd been at the Wilkinsons' house, and Wade ignored him, turning all of his attention to Grace.

"I can't tell you enough what a pretty little filly you are." He winked at her as he said this, and Grace bristled. *Filly?*

"You're very kind, Wade," she said demurely.

"So how about it?" he asked, leaning back in the wing chair and watching Grace intently. She was seated in the center of the sofa, and Dillon had chosen his usual hard-backed chair.

"How about what?" Grace asked, and then she knew. He wanted his answer. Now.

"Let's get hitched," he said energetically. "I know there's other fellas out there who'd like to scoop you up, but none of them will take care of you the way Wade Wilkinson will, princess."

Grace had already made her decision. She couldn't marry Wade. Even if she wasn't terrified at the thought of him touching her, it would mean too much contact with Dillon and Abigail.

"I'm terribly sorry, Wade," Grace said demurely. "I can't."

"Wait a minute, here," Wade said, standing as his grin faded slightly. "Think on it a while."

"You're truly a wonderful man," Grace said, trying to spare his feelings. "And you'll make some woman a perfect husband, but I don't think you and I are well suited."

"Oh, I think we'd be right well suited, princess."

Wade stood directly in front of her, just a little too close. Out of the corner of her eye, Grace saw Dillon rise and move to stand behind the sofa. He was at her right shoulder.

Wade looked from her to Dillon and back again with an ever widening grin. "If I hadn't already figured it out, I'd sure as hell have figured it out now. Tell me, Dillon, does Abigail know what's goin' on here?"

Wade appeared to be remarkably calm.

"There's nothing going on here, Wade," Dillon said indifferently. "You've just been turned down, that's all."

Wade was shaking his head. "I shoulda known when you wouldn't let me court her, but I wasn't sure until the other night at Abby's little get-together." He gazed over her head at Dillon. "You really ought not to stare at a woman like that in public when you're engaged to another one."

"I was not—"

Wade stopped Dillon's defense with a raised hand, a sign of surrender. Then he looked down at Grace and gave her one of those tremendous smiles. "If you change your mind, let me know. I wouldn't mind bein' married to the prettiest gal in Texas, and family get-togethers would always be interestin'."

Abigail's brother lifted his hand in resignation as he turned on his heel and stalked from the room with an almost cheerful good night.

Dillon followed Wade, but stopped at the front door. Grace took that opportunity to slip up the stairs. This was all Dillon's fault. He was giving her away, procuring her a husband the way he'd purchase a horse, leaving no room for the workings of her heart.

The man had a butt for a nose. That was all Dillon could think of as he watched Nate Johnson across the table. Some terrible demon deep inside him wanted Grace to choose Nate, an old man who appeared to be passionless. His quest for a wife was completely businesslike, just as Dillon's own plans with Abigail were. A man with six kids and a big house needed a wife.

That was all Nate had talked about over dinner. His kids and his ranch. He was one of a few in the area who continued to raise cotton and cattle, and had done all right for himself. Grace would never want for the necessities of life, for a roof over her head and food on the table.

Nate's oldest son was just a couple of years younger than Grace, a hell-raiser if ever there was one. The oldest of six boys, all terrors.

As Nate talked about his children he called them *full of life*, and *curious*. Dillon knew exactly what that meant, and he began to wonder if Grace would even be safe in the Johnson household.

"It takes every hand available to run a place like yours, Nate," Dillon said thoughtfully. "Six boys." He shook his head and broke a biscuit in half. "I suppose you'd like to have six more."

Nate actually blushed, and his butt-shaped nose turned red. "At least. That's one reason I'd like a young wife. One who could give me strong sons. One a year, I reckon."

That was what had killed the first Mrs. Johnson, Dillon recalled. A baby a year, and a number of them hadn't survived. Eventually it had become too much for the increasingly frail Mrs. Johnson. Damned if he'd allow Grace to be used like a brood mare.

"And what about daughters?" Dillon asked. "Little girls?"

Nate almost beamed. "No sirree. Hasn't been a girl born in my branch of the Johnson family for three generations."

Dillon wondered if Grace was paying attention to what was said. She'd been unusually quiet all evening, and it was hard to tell. Apparently she was listening, because her face went ghostly white.

Dillon placed his elbows on the table and leaned forward. "You're aware that I'm Grace's guardian," he said gravely.

Nate nodded slowly.

"And as her guardian I can refuse any request for her hand."

Nate saw what was coming. "I'll treat her right, Dillon. You know I will. I may be a few years older than she is, and I might not have Plummer's or Wilkinson's money, but I'm stable, solvent, and faithful." He bristled. "You'll find no better man for Grace, Dillon Becket."

Dillon wanted to laugh. Grace deserved much better than Nate Johnson. Why on earth had Abigail invited this man to court Grace?

He stood and looked to the end of the table where Grace sat in what was normally Billy's seat. She was staring at her plate, her supper all but untouched. There was no way Nate would make her happy. He would probably kill her forcing her to have babies every damn year . . . and when she was buried he'd simply search for another young wife.

"I'm sorry, Nate," Dillon said solemnly. "I can't allow Grace to marry you."

He saw Grace's shoulders slump forward slightly as she released the breath she had been holding. Not once had Nate appealed to her. It was as if she didn't exist.

Nate left in a huff, muttering about wasting time he couldn't afford to waste. Dillon saw the man to the door, and when he returned to the dining room, Grace was gone.

Grace assumed Dillon would be away from the house by the time she came downstairs. She'd taken to leaving her room late in the morning for just that reason.

But he was in the kitchen, teasing Olivia about her biscuits. It was the first time in quite a while that she'd seen Dillon in such a mood. Even Olivia was smiling at him, and she'd been so cross with him lately.

Grace turned to walk away, but it was too late. She'd been seen, and Olivia waved her into the room.

"How's Billy this morning?" Grace asked as she stepped into the overly warm kitchen.

Olivia scoffed. "Mean as a snake. Still threatening to leave that bed even though all his clothes are hid." She smiled smugly. "And he ain't gettin' 'em until he's been in bed for at least another week."

Grace tried to ignore Dillon, but he was watching her every move with a satisfied half smile on his face. He munched on a biscuit, standing there by the stove as relaxed as she'd ever seen him.

She kept waiting for him to leave, but he stayed as though planted to the spot, watching her and waiting . . . until he finally turned to Olivia.

"Could you get along without Grace this morning?"

Grace started to protest, but Olivia conceded easily. "She could use a break, poor girl." She took Grace's hand and patted it maternally. "You've not been the same since Billy was hurt. He's healing nicely, and you need to forget what happened."

"I can't."

Olivia turned away from her. "She's all yours, Dillon," she declared, and the argument was over before it had begun.

Chapter Eighteen

They rode at a leisurely pace, silent for the most part. The sun beat down on them, summer heat that drained every living thing of its energy and color.

Dillon felt pleasantly warm from the inside out. The solution had come to him as he'd reclined on his bed, staring up at the black ceiling and unable to sleep. How could he give Grace up? How could he give up the Double B? Why couldn't he have both?

He could.

When they topped a hill he could see the cabin. Sturdy, if somewhat neglected, it was the cabin where the Becket family had lived before the main house had been built on a better plot of land. In the years since, it had been occupied occasionally. Billy had lived there for years, before his own cabin had been built nearer the big house. And Nolan, his oldest brother, had lived there before the war.

Grace was still confused. She had that suspiciously puzzled expression on her face as he lifted his arms to help her to the ground. He released her quickly only because she seemed so anxious to put some distance between them.

He was afraid to move too fast, so he walked Grace around the cabin, treading through tall weeds and yellow wildflowers. First he told her about growing up in the cabin. He didn't remember much, but he had his memories and the stories his mother had told him later on. But Grace fidgeted nervously. It was clear she had no desire to be alone with him, and he remembered her promise at Billy's bedside.

When they were back at the front of the cabin, Dillon took Grace's shoulders and turned her to face him. This time he didn't release her. He wanted so badly to kiss her that he leaned toward her almost without conscious thought, laying his lips over hers. She didn't move away, but stood very still, her mouth soft and accepting. When he pulled away he saw the tears in her eyes, and on her face, and he reached out to wipe her cheeks with his fingers.

"You can stay here," he offered tentatively. "We can fix the place up. Bring in some new furniture and slap a little paint on her. You can have a garden, if you like, and . . ."

The pained flash in her eyes silenced him. She looked as if he'd reached out and slapped her.

"What are you saying, Becket?" she whispered.

He held her face in his hands. "I don't want to lose you."

Grace turned white as she backed away from him, away from his hands. Her bluebonnet eyes were wide, huge in a pale face, and she stared at him as if he had turned into some sort of beast.

"Are you asking me to live here . . . after you marry Abigail Wilkinson?" she asked in obvious horror.

Dillon nodded his head, just beginning to realize that she was appalled by the idea. "I'll take care of you."

"And visit me late at night while your wife is asleep? Sneak past the bunkhouse and over a couple of hills and into my bed when it's convenient for you?" Her tears and the troubled look in her eyes were replaced by pure, hot anger. "Damn you, Dillon Becket. Do you think I have no pride? Do you think I'd live here and watch while Abigail has your children? And what happens when you're tired of me? Would you send me away?"

"Never."

Grace continued as if she hadn't heard him. "I saw enough of faithless husbands in England, but I never thought that you . . ." She almost choked on her words, and he watched as she regained her composure. "Do you really think so little of me?"

"I want you here," he insisted.

Grace stared at him with all the fortitude he knew her to possess. She looked formidable, with that fire in her eyes, as she clenched her fists as if she wanted to strike him.

"You made your choice, Becket," she said coldly.

"I had no choice."

Grace shook her head slightly as she stared at him, an almost incredulous expression on her beautiful face. "If I'd wanted to be a married man's lover, I could have had a much nicer harlot's nest than this one. An apartment in Paris, my own villa. I've had better offers, Becket." There was an almost imperceptible softening of her eyes. "That's not what I want. I can't. . . ." The words died on her lips.

Dillon dropped down and scooped up a handful of dirt. "My blood and my soul run through this ground," he said in a low voice. "My father gave everything he had to make this place work. He's buried on this land, along with my mother and one of my brothers, and the two little girls who didn't live even six months. Without this place, I'm nothing."

"That's not true," she whispered.

"It is true. If marrying Abigail is the only way to save the Double B, I'll do it. But that doesn't mean I don't want you."

Grace backed away from him, and toward her mare. "I love you, Dillon, but you're wrong. It's just dirt. I'll be no man's mistress. Not even yours."

She turned away from him and mounted her mare quickly, turning toward the house. She didn't turn back to look at him as he let the dirt fall between his fingers.

He stayed at the cabin for a while, sitting on the porch, walking through the wildflowers. Dammit, she was right. He'd had no right to ask her, especially knowing the way men had treated her in the past. Sir whatshisname and that damn ruby. The Russian, Mikhail. No wonder she had run.

I love you, Dillon. He could probably count on one hand the number of times she'd called him Dillon in the past month. It was always *Becket*, spit out or delivered with more than a hint of sarcasm. Another way she had of keeping her distance from him?

Did he love her? He knew he did, if love meant wanting her all the time, and feeling nauseous at the thought of another man touching her. When Hartley had drugged her, and he'd thought she might die, he'd wanted to die himself. He dreamed about her, and she was in his thoughts all the time. But would that burn out? If he were to leave the Double B behind and take to the trail with her, what would happen?

He knew what would happen. Eventually she would resent the life they led. She knew as well as he did that she deserved a better life than that of a wanderer.

Would he eventually resent her for causing him to lose the Double B? He couldn't be certain, but he had to say yes. He loved the place, and he wanted to see it go to his children, and then to their children.

He thought about it as he rode slowly toward the house. He would forget her. He had to. Once he was married to Abigail, everything would be different. He had to leave Grace and the memory of what they'd had behind. By the time he reached the house he was determined to tell her as much. To apologize for his inappropriate offer. To write it off to exhaustion and frustration.

But he never got the chance. He entered the house through the kitchen, and there was Olivia crying silently, sniffling loudly every few seconds.

His first thought was that Billy had taken a turn for the worse. But when she looked at him he knew that wasn't the reason for her tears.

"What did you do?" she asked coldly.

There was no use pretending. Obviously Grace

had come in upset, and now Olivia was upset as well. How did a man survive in a houseful of women?

"Nothing. I came to apologize to Grace."

"Well, you're too late."

Dillon felt a cold grip at his heart. "What do you mean I'm too late?"

"I hope you're satisfied with yourself," Olivia chastised sharply, wiping away her tears. "She's gone."

"What do you mean, she's gone?" Dillon asked, stomping through the house searching for Grace. He looked into every room, waking Billy and ignoring Olivia as the woman followed him closely.

He finally ended up on the front porch. Everything inside him said *Go after her*, but he stopped on the steps.

"Where did she go?" he asked softly.

"Plummerton," Olivia answered with a loud sniffle. "She was gonna take that mare, but I had Lucas take her in the buckboard. I just couldn't allow her to go off all by herself."

Dillon nodded his head. "You did right, Olivia." And, maybe, so had Grace. The attraction between them was too strong. Maybe apart they would be able to forget. To get on with their lives.

"She just stuffed a couple of dresses into a little bag and said she'd send for the rest." Olivia began to cry again. "I'm gonna miss that little girl."

Dillon turned and went back into the house, leaving Olivia standing alone on the front porch. The house seemed cold in spite of the heat, and empty. More empty than it had been in years. He remembered that hollow feeling. It had taken over the house after his mother had died, for a time.

Grace was gone, and even though he knew it

was for the best, he still felt as if she had kicked him in the gut and left him on the ground to flounder.

Grace checked into the hotel with her single bag, and Lucas promised to see that Olivia packed the rest of her belongings. Then he would deliver the baggage himself. Grace had only been able to manage a halfhearted smile for the young man who'd watched her so warily.

Her room was small but clean, and properly furnished with a small bed, a vanity and a chair, and a wardrobe for her gowns. It was a room often rented to patrons who intended to stay for a while, the clerk had told her with a smile. Some of the jewelry would have to be sold for expenses. Good heavens. She had no idea how long she'd be staying in the tiny room.

She just knew that she could no longer stay at the Double B.

Anger had consumed her for a little while, and then she'd realized the hopelessness of it all. Dillon loved the Double B. It was a love she found hard to understand, because she'd never really had a home. Even as a little girl, her father's house had been cold and lonely, not a place she would cherish in her heart.

Pragmatically, she turned her mind to the future. She'd have to get a message to Samuel Plummer, and tell him not to go to the Double B for supper tomorrow. No telling what sort of reception he'd get. Dillon was bound to be furious with her for refusing his offer and for running away.

But she didn't have any choice. She would have a husband and a family, and she would raise her children with all the love and affection she had missed. Even if she didn't love her husband, she could still care for him. It didn't have to be the white-hot passion she felt for Dillon. Maybe a more sedate and manageable affection was more appropriate for building a future. She didn't need or want a man who made her lose control with his every touch.

Grace stood at the window and looked down at the street. Plummerton was a bustling little town. The bank was just across the street, and there were shops all along the main thoroughfare. The general store, the blacksmith, the sheriff's office . . . and there was more. A dress shop, a café, two saloons. It was a comfortable little town. A good place to settle down. But Grace knew she couldn't stay. Plummerton was too close to the Double B, and Dillon. She needed distance, as much distance between her and Dillon Becket as she could manage. She couldn't conceive of running into Dillon and Abigail at the general store, or the annual Fourth of July celebration.

A familiar figure walked down the boardwalk on the opposite side of the street and paused in front of a vacant building. He peered through the windows and appraised the exterior of the building from the street.

With a satisfied nod of his head, Renzo walked into the bank.

What was Renzo doing in Plummerton? For a moment she was afraid he had gone into the bank to rob it, but she dismissed the idea quickly. He hadn't appeared to be armed, and his stance had been so casual. But she stood anxiously by the window just the same, waiting for Renzo to reappear.

She didn't have a long wait, but the minutes

dragged by. When he stepped onto the boardwalk, as confidently and innocently as any other citizen, Grace breathed a sigh of relief.

She had been so intent on the bank's entrance that she hadn't seen Abigail. Dillon's fiancée was walking delicately toward Renzo, a blue parasol that matched her day dress closed and clasped in one hand, her tiny little nose in the air.

Renzo removed his hat as she walked by, and bowed from the waist, mouthing a greeting to Abigail. Abigail nodded, politely and frostily, letting her eyes rest on Renzo for no more than a second.

But even after she passed, Renzo's eyes stayed on Abigail. He held his hat over his heart and gazed after the woman who had snubbed him, until she climbed into her carriage and her driver took her away.

Grace couldn't believe what she had just seen.

Bloody hell. Abigail Wilkinson was Renzo's little jewel.

Grace decided to visit Samuel Plummer's office and deliver the message herself. The office was located in a small building, and a freshly painted sign hung above the door: SAMUEL PLUMMER, ESQ.

The inside of the office was dark and stuffy, a problem not diminished by the dark furnishings and the heavy drapes that hung over the windows. It was no doubt meant to give the place a professional air, but Grace found it oppressive.

Sam was bent over a stack of papers, and he lifted his head when she entered and closed the door delicately behind her. The smile that crossed his face was one of delight, and he rose immediately to cross the small room and take her hand.

"What a wonderful surprise, Miss Cavanaugh." He bent over her hand and kissed it, his lips barely touching her skin. It was pleasant, but that was all. She didn't tingle in his presence, and her heart easily managed to maintain its steady pace.

But he didn't frighten her either. Not the way Wade did. Not the way men always had in the past.

"You may call me Grace," she said with a smile. "Under the circumstances, I think that would be acceptable."

Here was a man with impeccable manners, a winning smile, and a handsome face. Samuel Plummer was looking for a wife, ready to start a family. He had dark hair and blue eyes a shade or two paler than her own, and Grace could almost imagine what their children would look like. She had to focus on the family she wanted.

Sam was more educated than most of the Texans she had met, and he was cultured. He'd appreciated her talent at the piano, and she would, at least, be able to carry on an intelligent conversation with him.

And he was a little shy, a quiet man. He would be easy to control.

"The reason I'm here," Grace began, gently pulling her hand away from him, "is that I wanted to let you know I'll be staying at the hotel here in Plummerton."

He didn't ask why she had left the Double B, though she could see the curiosity in his eyes. "It will be delightful to have you so close by."

"I didn't want you to ride all the way out to the

Double B tomorrow evening and find that I wasn't there."

He looked down into her eyes, very boldly for such a timid man. "I hope that's not the only reason you came to see me. You've brightened my afternoon immensely."

Grace had a moment's indecision, and she bit her bottom lip. He grinned at her, as though he found her reticence charming.

"Do let me take you to dinner tonight," he insisted. "The café serves a wonderful evening meal. I've never been disappointed."

Grace's indecision was gone, and she gave Sam a brilliant smile. She didn't love him, but she did like him. She would make him a good wife. People married for reasons other than love all the time. She'd seen it countless times in England, and of course Dillon was prepared to do anything to save the Double B.

Dillon. After all he'd done, his choices and his hurtful suggestions, she shouldn't care about him at all. Even now, in the midst of this anger and frustration, she had no command over the workings of her heart.

It came to her as Sam took her hand again. There was no reason for Dillon to marry Abigail, if he didn't want to.

Grace didn't draw her hand away from Sam this time, but let her hand rest in his larger one quite comfortably. His hand was not rough, like Dillon's, but smooth to her touch. There was strength there, too.

"Perhaps you can give me an answer to my proposal?" Sam prodded gently, hopefully. His face reddened a little, and Grace knew what she had to do.

"Tonight, Sam," she said sweetly. "Over dinner. You'll have your answer."

Then she gave him a smile that left little doubt as to what that answer would be.

If only she'd taken the time to pack more of her clothes before she'd left the Double B. Of course, she hadn't been willing to take that extra time, and she would just have to make do.

The striped green muslin would do quite nicely for the occasion. It was just a little austere, and very elegant. She sat outside the banker's office, and not a hint of her nervousness displayed itself in shaking hands or trembling lips. This was too important to ruin with anxiety. If ever she'd been strong, this was the time for it.

Mr. Plummer opened the door to his office and invited her in. He looked like a banker, a pale, overweight man who spent all his time behind a desk and discussing finances over steak dinners. He had a florid look about him, and Grace couldn't even imagine that he was Sam's father. There was no resemblance at all.

"Miss Cavanaugh," he said as she entered, curiosity blazing in his eyes and a bit of humor in his voice. "To what do I owe the honor of this visit?"

He offered her a chair, and she seated herself slowly, regally, and only then did she lift her eyes to him. "Would you please close the door, Mr. Plummer? What I have to discuss with you is a private matter."

He did as she asked, with a superior smirk on his face, and then he seated himself across the massive desk from her.

"Mr. Plummer, your son has asked me to marry him," Grace said chillingly.

He nodded his head once, indicating that he

was well aware of Sam's proposal.

"I am considering accepting his offer, Mr. Plummer, and I'd like to make you a proposition."

He raised his bushy eyebrows and leaned forward on the desk. "Just what the hell are you getting at, little lady?"

Grace gave him a small and distant smile. "First of all, let me tell you what I can do for you."

Plummer leaned back and gave her a look that told her he was certain she could do nothing for him.

"You're a very rich man, Mr. Plummer," she began.

The banker nodded.

"You have a town named after you, and all the property and wealth a man could want."

"Young lady, you're not telling me anything I don't already know. Just exactly what do you think you can do for me?"

"Is this what you want for your son?" Grace waved her hand to indicate the desk, the room, and even the town they were in. "Sam is a very intelligent man, but I don't see that he has much of a future in Plummerton." She took a deep breath. "And he can give you the one thing you can't get for yourself."

Grace smiled and paused. This was where her plan would either work or fall apart. "Power. Not just over a town, but over an entire state. Perhaps even a nation."

He continued to stare at her with no emotion evident in his face.

"Politics, Mr. Plummer. With my support Sam can go as far as he wants."

"If Sam was interested in politics, what would he need you for?"

Grace gave the old man a confident stare. "Mr. Plummer, I've dined with royalty. Several of my school chums have married very well. They're duchesses and princesses, the toasts of London and Paris." She sighed, as if tired of defending herself. "One particular friend will be visiting the United States within the year, and her husband . . . well, I'm not at liberty to reveal his name at this time, but he is very interested in touring the Wild West. There will be lots of press coverage, balls given in their honor all over the country. I can introduce Sam to the cultural and political elite. After that, it's up to him.

"But I have great confidence in Sam. Once he's been introduced to the right people nothing will stop him. Of course, we will have to move to Austin. The legislature will be our first step."

Plummer leaned back in his chair and grinned. He'd taken the bait. "Politics, huh?"

Grace allowed him a few moments to ponder the possibilities. Of course, there was no old friend visiting the States, but she would handle that dilemma later.

"And what do you want in return?" Plummer asked. "Since you mentioned a proposition, I assume there's something you want."

Grace took a deep breath. It wouldn't do for her to ruin it all now. "I want the deed to the Double B," she said coldly.

Plummer raised his eyebrows in surprise. Whatever he'd been expecting her to request, that wasn't it. "Why?"

"I want Dillon Becket to owe me. I want him to lay every last cent he has into my hands to get that deed back. And if he can't pay off the loan . . ." She shrugged her shoulders and smiled wickedly. "I'll take great pleasure in being his boss, before I kick him off the place."

Revenge must not have been a foreign concept to Plummer, because he seemed to be enjoying her tirade. "What did he do to you?"

Grace stood, facing the old man, and she jerked off her gloves. With a flourish she placed her palms before him. "I was made to churn butter until these hands blistered, and to milk cows and pull weeds. This scar here?" She turned her hands over and pointed to a tiny white scar. "A blasted chicken. I was raised and educated to be a lady, not a slave. That man treated me like a servant, and I will not allow him to escape unpunished."

The old man's almost colorless eyes twinkled. "I don't suppose Sam knows anything of your shenanigans."

Grace sighed dramatically. "Of course not. It wouldn't do for Sam to be aware of my . . . *interference* is such an ugly word. Shall we say encouragement and enhancement of his career?"

"He wouldn't even let me finance a decent office for him here in Plummerton. Insisted on doing it all himself."

Grace tried her best to look supremely bored. "Do you doubt, Mr. Plummer, that I have powers of persuasion that you do not?"

Plummer was pursing his lips, thinking hard. "You have a deal, Miss Cavanaugh. You will receive the deed to Dillon Becket's ranch after the wedding."

Grace gave him a confident smile. "Before the wedding, Mr. Plummer, or we will not be able to do business together."

He grinned like a wolf, his face all teeth and eyebrows. It was very unpleasant. "Don't you trust me, Miss Cavanaugh?"

She remained composed, as cool as he was. "No, Mr. Plummer. I do not."

Plummer laughed out loud, throwing his head back and guffawing. Grace didn't know if he was laughing at her bold request, or simply laughing at her. Had she made a complete fool of herself?

But she didn't make a move to leave. In fact, she didn't move at all. Plummer's laughter died away, and he studied her with condescending eyes. "As you wish, Miss Cavanaugh. You will receive the deed at the wedding ceremony."

"The day before," she insisted.

"That morning," he countered.

Grace met the old man's cold eyes. "I find that arrangement agreeable."

Plummer showed her to the door, his eyes sparkling with the possibilities she had presented him. Grace's face didn't change. She maintained her cool exterior, and her voice didn't tremble at all.

But she felt as if she should be shaking all over. She'd just sold her soul to the devil for the Double B.

No, she corrected herself, that wasn't quite true. But she had just made a bargain with the devil for Dillon Becket.

Chapter Nineteen

"Renzo, what a fascinating shop." Grace appreciatively studied the goods that were artfully displayed. It had taken mere days for Renzo to open his business. Evidently he had taken her statement that he had the personality of a merchant quite seriously.

There were several silk dresses in bright colors displayed against one wall. Odd pieces of jewelry were arranged in a glass case, and there was a collection of silver. Candlesticks, platters, and a unique little box. It wasn't until Grace stopped before a collection of fans and gloves that she felt that first hint of warning.

"I have a fan just like that one," she said, pointing to a cream lace fan that was beribboned and very distinctive.

She lifted her face to Renzo. He was proud of his shop, and had a near gloating expression on his radiantly handsome face.

Grace sighed, afraid of what the answer to her question would be, but she had to ask. "Where did you get your merchandise? You opened the shop so quickly."

Renzo shrugged his shoulders. "I stocked the store using several different sources." He wasn't looking at her, but wiped a nonexistent bit of dust from the counter.

"Tell me this isn't all stolen," she said in a low voice.

Renzo gave her a curt bow. "If you wish, *amiga*."

"Blast it all, Renzo," Grace snapped, ignoring the feigned expression of distress on his face. "What if you get caught?"

In a flash the anguish disappeared, and he appeared smugly confident. "I will not get caught. And besides, this was all stolen long ago. Months, weeks ago. No one will know."

Grace lifted the fan and folded it with a snap, smacking Renzo on the forearm smartly. "Is this the only item of mine that you kept? What else might I find in The Jewel that once belonged to me?"

Renzo tried to look repentant, but there was a sparkle in his black eyes. "I kept only two items, *amiga*. That fan and a . . . a certain undergarment that I found quite fascinating."

"Renzo!" Grace smacked him on the arm again. "How could you?"

He narrowed his eyes. "It is best that things did not work out as I had wished between us. I would hate to have to punish you for striking me . . . not once, but twice."

The words could have been menacing, but they weren't. They were delivered with Renzo's own strange sense of humor, with a smile and a twinkle in his eyes.

"It matters not, now that you are promised to another, and I have found my little jewel."

Grace sighed. She couldn't imagine Abigail being anyone's little jewel, and she certainly had never brightened Grace's day like a diamond in the sunlight. What on earth had Renzo seen in Abigail?

"When is the wedding, *amiga*?" The tone of Renzo's voice was almost solemn suddenly. Grace had discovered that Renzo understood her all too well, and he knew that she didn't feel for Sam the way a woman should feel for her husband. He also knew how much she still cared for Dillon, even though the matter was never discussed. Perhaps that was why his question was delivered as a soft caress.

"Five days," Grace said sternly. Her decision was made, and she bloody well wouldn't regret it. "You'll be there, won't you?"

"Of course, if you wish it."

Grace was anxious to change the subject, and she glanced around the fascinating store. "And you will be associating with legitimate suppliers in the future?"

Renzo assured her heartily that he would, but Grace had a feeling that one would always be able to find the odd, fine piece in Renzo's shop, The Jewel.

Behind her, the door opened quietly. Renzo's first real customer, and Grace knew by the tender smile on his face that that customer was Abigail Wilkinson.

When Grace turned to face Abigail, she thought the pale woman was going to turn and run. But she didn't. Abigail lifted her chin and straightened her spine, almost as if readying for battle.

"Good morning, Miss Cavanaugh," Abigail said primly.

"Miss Wilkinson."

They stared at one another until Renzo stepped between them. "Grace, you must introduce me to your friend," he said, his eyes on Abigail.

Grace wanted to roll her eyes and smack him on the arm again, but she introduced them formally, watching as Renzo took Abigail's hand and bent over it with a courtly bow.

Five minutes later Abigail was as charmed by Renzo as every other woman he had ever met. He showed her his merchandise, commented on her own mauve silk dress, and gazed deep into her eyes each time he spoke.

Watching Renzo work was fascinating. He stayed close to Abigail, leaning in a bit closer than would be considered proper. There had been a time, Grace thought as she watched her friend fawn over her enemy, when she would have frozen if a man stood over her so closely. Dillon had changed that, and she supposed she should be grateful. But she couldn't muster any gratitude for Dillon Becket at the moment, no matter how hard she tried.

Renzo maintained eye contact whenever he or Abigail spoke, hypnotizing his little jewel with his attention. It was rather like watching a cobra, Grace surmised. Before Abigail had been in the shop ten minutes she was completely under Renzo's spell.

Abigail studied the pieces of jewelry intently, finally choosing a bracelet she was certain would complement her best gold gown. Grace wondered, with a sinking heart, if Abigail was planning to be married in her best gold gown.

When Renzo went into the back room to find proper packaging for the purchase, Abigail turned to Grace.

"I heard that you were staying in town."

Grace nodded. "It's much more convenient, with the wedding so close. There are plans to be made, meetings with the minister, fittings for my wedding dress. You know how it is." She took a deep breath and summoned all her courage. "When are you and Becket getting married?"

"Two weeks," Abigail said in a small voice. "Will . . . will you be there?"

Grace wanted to tell her that there might not be a wedding, but she couldn't speak for Dillon. Even if he had the deed to the Double B in hand, he still might marry the daughter of the neighboring rancher. It would be good business.

"I don't think so."

Abigail nodded, looking away from Grace with obvious relief. "I suppose that would be best." She snapped her head back up and boldly met Grace's eyes. "You know I love Dillon very much. I've loved him since we were children. I believe I was eleven when I knew that one day we would be married."

Grace almost couldn't speak. "I'm glad to hear that."

"I know that you . . . have feelings for him." Abigail blushed. This was as awkward for her as it was for Grace, and she was terrible at hiding her feelings. "But I can give Dillon what he wants. I can save the Double B."

With a surprised lift of her eyebrows, Grace stepped toward Abigail. "You know?"

"Of course. I know Dillon doesn't love me, but

in time he will. I'll see to that. I can make him love me, if . . . if you'll stay away from us."

"I plan to," Grace said sharply.

Renzo burst from the back room, oblivious to their awkward conversation. He held in his hand a small porcelain box, and he opened it to reveal Abigail's bracelet displayed on a bed of velvet.

"My gift to you, Miss Wilkinson," he said as he handed the porcelain box to Abigail, wrapping her pale fingers around it with his own strong, brown hand. "Something so beautiful should be protected."

This time Grace did roll her eyes, confident that neither Renzo nor Abigail could see her. They were staring at one another with a fascinated daze in their eyes.

"Why, thank you, Mr. Morales," Abigail said breathlessly.

"Please call me Lorenzo," he said in a voice barely above a whisper. "If you speak my name it will be like a ray of sunshine on a cloudy day. It will warm my heart and my soul."

Abigail blushed and glanced to the floor, but she didn't wrest her hand away from Renzo.

Apparently they didn't hear Grace as she made her exit, shaking her head and muttering about charming bandits and gullible ladies.

Dillon had tried to work himself to exhaustion, just to keep from thinking about Grace. But it hadn't worked. Every sign of her had been removed from the house, packed up and carted off to Plummerton. For a while he had been able to sense her, as if her essence lingered in the air, but now even that was gone.

He didn't just miss her; he ached for her. He hurt with missing her. Not that it made him change his mind. The hurt would fade, and eventually he would forget exactly what she looked like. Just as he could not quite picture the faces of people he had known as a child, or those long dead. Ghosts, best forgotten.

But right now he could close his eyes and see her as clearly as if she stood before him. Sometimes, at night, he actually reached out for her, half expecting her to be sleeping at his side. For that split second he was content. And then he realized that the bed was empty, that he had sent Grace away.

Naturally he had heard the news of her engagement to Samuel Plummer. Seth Plummer, that weasel, was paying her expenses until the wedding, relieving Dillon of all responsibility . . . and any excuse to see her.

Plans for his own wedding were under way. Abigail was making all the arrangements, and Dillon didn't want to have anything to do with them. He knew the date, the time, and the place, and all he had to do was show up. He'd even balked at the requested meetings with the minister. The man might have refused to marry them in the church, if Wilkinson wasn't such a big contributor.

All he had to do was show up.

Grace smiled across the table at her intended until she thought her face would break. She didn't feel like smiling, but Sam was making such an attempt at being charming that she didn't dare let him know how she felt. Empty. Hurting. Coldly hollow.

Every night since her arrival in Plummerton, he'd taken her to dinner. The café, the hotel dining room, and one horrid evening at his father's house. Seth Plummer had looked at Grace with a weak smile and a knowing gleam in his eyes that Sam evidently missed. Maybe the old man always looked like that.

Sam had always been a perfect gentleman. He'd kissed her once, when she'd accepted his proposal, and that had been a chaste, passionless brush of his lips. He always treated her like a lady, and Grace felt like such a deceiver.

He reached across the table and covered her hand with his. "What's the matter? You're not yourself tonight."

"I don't know if I should mention it. . . ." Grace's voice faded away, and she stared down at her untouched plate.

"You can tell me anything," Sam said earnestly.

Grace lifted her eyes to look at him. He was handsome and attentive and intelligent . . . and she would never love him. But she would make him a good wife. She would be faithful and she would care for him the best she could.

"Have you ever given any thought to leaving Plummerton?"

He raised his eyebrows. "Whatever for?"

"It's a small town, and I just know you could go far in a big city."

Sam smiled at her and squeezed her hand. "I have wondered, on occasion, whether or not I would succeed in, oh, Houston or Austin."

Grace nodded her head. "I'm sure you would do well anywhere. But have you ever considered an even bigger city? New York? Boston?"

Sam studied her intently, with just a hint of a smile on his lips. "Do you miss the finer things, Grace? I know you were raised to have the best of everything. To be a social butterfly and the belle of the ball. But I don't know if I'm cut out to live in the East. I was educated there, but all I thought of was coming home. I belong in Texas."

"Will you think about it?" Grace asked almost desperately. She needed to get as far away from Dillon as possible, in order to forget him. If not Boston or New York, then Austin or Houston.

"For you, sweetheart, anything," Sam said as he studied her with pale eyes that could hide nothing from her. And she knew that if she wanted it enough she could get this man to go. To leave his home. She felt like the lowest creature on the earth, because leaving Plummerton would make Sam miserable.

No. She wouldn't allow Sam to be miserable. She would make him happy, no matter where they lived. He would never regret leaving Plummerton.

He walked her from the café to the lobby of the hotel. The manager was nowhere in sight, and Sam glanced from side to side before he leaned close to Grace and whispered in her ear.

"Two more days, sweetheart, and you'll be my wife." He kissed her lightly on the cheek, and Grace wondered if he could tell that she had suddenly gone cold. She felt as though the blood had drained from her body and left her nothing but an empty shell.

She walked up the stairs alone, knowing that Sam watched from the lobby. He had never taken her any farther than the bottom of the staircase that led to her room. Ever the gentleman, Sam had always shown her respect. That was one thing she had never gotten from Dillon Becket. It was at moments like this that she tried to hate Dillon, but of course she couldn't.

It occurred to her that she could simply disappear. She could sell a few pieces of her jewelry to support herself until she could find some sort of work.

But eventually she would need to marry, if she was to have the family she wanted so badly. There would not likely be any candidate better than Samuel Plummer, and she didn't expect to fall in love again. Not ever.

And by marrying Sam she could give the only man she ever would love the one thing in the world he cared about.

Grace stepped quietly into Renzo's shop. It was the first time in days that she'd found the little store empty. Every lady in town wanted a look at The Jewel.

She really didn't want to socialize, and she had so far managed to avoid the everyday bustle of Plummerton. Just a moment with Renzo, that was all she wanted. He was the only person in town she didn't feel she had to put on a false face for.

Even Renzo was absent, and Grace walked the counter, looking at the merchandise as she waited. There were several pieces gone, a few new ones in their places. She didn't want to know how he had come by his new merchandise so quickly.

Where was he? Surely he hadn't tired of his new vocation so soon that he was leaving the shop open and unattended for just anyone to plunder? If anyone should be cautious where thieves were concerned . . .

Grace stepped past the curtain that separated Renzo's display area from the storeroom and small bedroom where he'd been sleeping. Perhaps he was working or resting and hadn't even heard her.

He was bent over something, and all she could see was his broad back, the black shirt stretched across his straining muscles.

"There you are," she called. "Didn't you hear me come in? I could have . . ."

Renzo jumped up and spun around, and almost dumped a disheveled Abigail on the floor in the process. Grace had never seen Renzo look like this—his careful control gone, the mischievous sparkle in his eyes replaced by fire.

"Oh my," Abigail said breathlessly, glancing past Renzo and blushing, as well she should. Her lips were swollen, a strand of hair fell across one cheek, and the top two buttons of her prim green day dress were undone.

Grace stared at them for a moment, realized her mouth was hanging open, and snapped it shut.

"Oh my," Abigail said again, straightening her hair as she chewed on a red bottom lip.

Grace turned on her heel and swept through the curtains. She wouldn't say a word. She would pretend that she had seen nothing.

How could that woman claim to love Dillon one day, and then fall all over Renzo the next?

She spun back around just as Renzo broke through the curtains. "*Amiga,*" he began warily. "I must apologize."

"No. I should have called out for you instead of barging in. I never dreamed . . . I didn't mean . . ." She couldn't be angry with Renzo. He was only pursuing what he had wanted from the moment he'd seen Abigail. It was Abigail, that little traitor, whom Grace wanted to confront.

Abigail stepped into the room and hid for a

moment behind Renzo. When she stepped into the open, Grace saw that she had repaired her appearance. Her hair was neat once more, and her dress was properly fastened at the neck. But there was nothing she could do about the high color on her face.

Grace was trying to think of something damning enough to say, something sufficiently full of venom, when Abigail ran past her, poise gone, restraint forgotten. Dillon's fiancée didn't stop until she was standing in the open doorway.

Grace stared at Abigail's back for a time, watched it stiffen and straighten, watched the neck grow a bit taller. And then Abigail turned slowly to face her.

She looked directly at Grace, ignoring an obviously miserable Renzo. "Miss Cavanaugh," Abigail said, her voice shaking slightly. "Would you care to join me at the café for a cup of tea?"

The café was quiet, and Abigail and Grace had a corner to themselves. A china pot of steaming tea sat in the center of the small round table, and two matching cups had been placed before the silent women. It seemed so absurdly normal, Grace thought as she waited for Abigail to speak. So . . . un-Texan.

Finally Abigail lifted her head and took a deep breath, apparently gathering the nerve to speak. She looked so forlorn, so lost, that Grace almost felt sorry for her. Almost.

"There's really no one I can talk to," Abigail said defensively, and in a conspiratorially low voice. "My mother died when I was ten, and . . . I don't really have any close friends."

Blast it, Grace thought as she spooned too

much sugar into her tea. The woman was going to beg.

"I won't tell," Grace said harshly. "It's none of my concern how you conduct yourself. Just because you're a woman about to be married . . ." Grace stopped speaking when Abigail's eyes shone with unshed tears. It was going to be bloody difficult to chastise the woman Dillon was to marry.

"I'm so confused." Abigail leaned forward, closing the space between them. "Could you tell me . . . I mean, have you ever . . ." She chewed on her bottom lip, first one side and then the other, and she tapped her pale fingers against the teacup. "Have you ever been kissed?"

Grace didn't have a chance to answer that question before Abigail rushed forward. "I don't mean a normal little kiss, I mean a . . . a—" Abigail turned an almost alarming shade of red—"a real kiss that makes your knees wobble and your stomach drop."

Abigail's brown eyes were wide, and she waited expectantly for an answer.

"Yes," Grace said simply and softly.

Abigail leaned back and sighed with relief. "Then it's normal. Thank goodness. I thought there was something wrong with me."

"Renzo?"

Abigail nodded shyly. She looked so much younger than at any other time Grace had seen her. Her lips were not pursed tightly; her forehead wasn't furrowed. She looked fresh and . . . beautiful. Grace had never thought Abigail beautiful before.

And she wasn't finished. There was still a question in her brown eyes. Abigail stirred her cup of tea unnecessarily, and the clink of the silver spoon against china was the only sound in the room.

"Have you ever kissed Dillon?" Abigail asked so softly that Grace could barely hear her.

"Yes," she answered just as softly.

Abigail lifted her head and met Grace's eyes. "Did it make your knees wobble and your stomach drop?"

"For heaven's sake, Abigail," Grace said harshly, leaning forward and sloshing a bit of still-hot tea onto the table.

Somehow Abigail continued to look innocent. And she waited for an answer.

"You see," she said, ignoring Grace's outburst, "Dillon has kissed me a couple of times, and . . . and . . ." She shook her head slowly. "It was all right, but . . ."

"It wasn't like Renzo's kiss?" Grace finished for her.

Abigail shook her head slowly. "Not at all. And now I'm so confused."

Grace laid her hands on the table, palms pressed against the tablecloth. She was shaking, but it was so deep she didn't think Abigail would notice. Actually, she could have been in convulsions, and Abigail wouldn't have noticed.

"I've kissed Renzo, too, once," Grace confided. The light in Abigail's eyes told her all she needed to know. The flash of jealousy hadn't assaulted Abigail when Grace had confessed that she'd kissed Dillon. "It was . . . pleasant, but that was all."

Abigail looked more confused than ever. "But . . ."

"It was Dillon who made my knees weak," Grace confessed softly.

"Oh dear," Abigail said softly. "How can I

marry Dillon when I know . . . when I've fallen in love with Lorenzo?"

Renzo had been right all along. Abigail was his little jewel, and he had known it the first time he'd seen her.

A spark of hope was lit within Grace, and she tried to contain it. "Do you think," she began hesitantly, "that your father would make Dillon a loan? A loan large enough to save the ranch? If he had just a little more time . . ." She stopped suddenly. Abigail was shaking her head.

"Pa wants that ranch one way or another. Either I marry it, or he buys it from Seth Plummer after Dillon defaults on the loan. I've . . . I've heard him discussing it with Wade several times."

Grace's heart sank. For a moment she had thought she could save the Double B, and Abigail and Renzo, but she couldn't have Dillon and the home she really wanted.

No, she couldn't have Dillon. Even if he wasn't married to Abigail, she would still be Sam's wife. She might have found honor late in life, but it was important to her now.

Abigail was in a panic. Her once red face was stark white, and her brown eyes were huge. Her hands and her lips started to tremble.

"What am I going to do?" she asked desperately, looking to Grace for an answer.

Grace closed her eyes. She never would have thought that she'd be comforting Abigail Wilkinson, soon to be Abigail Morales, if her instincts were correct.

"I have a feeling," Grace said with a calmness that she did not feel, "that after tomorrow things will be different. Just don't . . . don't say anything to Dillon until after tomorrow. Preferably not until Sam and I have left town."

Abigail didn't question Grace, but nodded her head.

"You love him, don't you?" Abigail asked softly after a short and uncomfortable silence.

Grace steeled herself. The question made her want to cry, but she couldn't. "It makes no difference," she said sharply.

"It's not right," Abigail argued naively.

Grace stood slowly. She'd had all of this conversation that she could stand. "Take good care of Renzo. He needs someone to keep him out of trouble."

If this request confused Abigail, she didn't show it. She just nodded her head slightly until Grace turned her back on the woman and walked away.

Dillon paced in the study. Today was the day. Everyone else—Olivia and Billy, Lonnie and Lucas—was preparing to attend Grace's wedding to Sam Plummer.

If you could call it preparation. Olivia had spent half the morning crying, and the other half glaring at him. As if there was anything he could do. Billy had worn the same uncustomary frown that had marred his normally pleasant face for days. They made no secret of the fact that they blamed Dillon for everything.

Billy had that deep scowl on his face as he stalked into the study. "You really ain't goin'?" he snapped.

Dillon shook his head and avoided looking directly at the man. Billy could read him too well.

"Well, if it makes you feel any better, she don't want to see you, neither."

Dillon did look up at the big man then. When

had Billy seen Grace? He hadn't left the ranch since the accident. He was lucky Olivia was allowing him to attend the wedding.

"Is that a fact," he said coolly.

"She was here this mornin', bright and early. Snuck up on the front porch like a thief, makin' sure you weren't in the house 'fore she'd come in."

Trying to appear calm, Dillon sat in the chair at his desk. It was piled high with bills and invoices, and an accounting book was open in the middle of it all. "What did she want?"

"Rode out here on a borrowed horse to make certain I would be there to give her away, and that Olivia would be there, too. Poor Olivia can't quit cryin'."

The tone of Billy's voice told Dillon that he was to blame for Olivia's depression as well as everything else that had gone wrong.

"Give the bride and groom my best wishes," Dillon said brusquely.

Billy placed both hands on the desk and leaned forward to put his face close to Dillon's. Rarely had Dillon seen the man angry, but he was about to burst with it right now. He looked like a big silver bear, ready to attack.

"I'm goin' to town to watch that little girl ruin her life. Don't you dare sit there and ask me to give her your damn best wishes. If I could I'd take 'em and shove 'em down your damn throat."

He had known Billy all of his life, and he'd never heard the easygoing man curse. Not once.

Dillon wanted to defend himself, but he knew it would do no good. Maybe it even helped Billy a little to vent his frustration and his anger. Dillon damn well wished he had some way of doing that.

He listened as they left, Olivia sniffling and Billy stomping. Lonnie and Lucas were curiously quiet, but then, they didn't know the whole story. They didn't know, as Billy and Olivia obviously did, that he had fallen in love with Grace, made her fall in love with him, and then sacrificed her to save his home.

Dillon stalked through the house after they had left. This was exactly what he'd wanted . . . wasn't it? He had no right to be angry because Grace was making a life for herself.

He made a fresh pot of coffee and sat at the dining room table as he sipped the hot brew. From the seat he chose he could look into the kitchen. There where he had watched Grace lounging in the water, where he had touched her as she made that first, tough batch of biscuits. He wished almost desperately that he had made love to her there on the floor that first time, rather than carrying her up the stairs. He wished he had made love to her on the sofa in the parlor, on the dining room table, in every room in the house, so that everywhere he went he would have a memory of her in his arms.

He returned to the study. There was a clock there, and he kept turning to it as the morning passed. He was counting the hours and the minutes until it would all be over, and Grace would be married to Sam Plummer.

He needed to remind himself of the reason he had turned away from Grace, the reason he had to marry Abigail. He thumbed through the invoices on his desk, and ran his fingers over the columns of damning figures in the book. But the longer he sat there the less certain he became. If he had made a mistake it was the biggest one of his life, one he would never recover from. With a violent sweep of his hands Dillon brushed the desktop clean. Papers went flying, and the books landed with a thud on the floor, closing on the page he'd been studying.

And a single document that shouldn't have been there caught his eye as it fluttered to the floor.

He reached over and lifted the document between his fingers. The deed. The deed that Seth Plummer had held for nearly a year.

She had been in this room, and left the deed for him to find . . . only later. After it was too late. After she had married Plummer's son.

He held in his hands the answer to his dreams. His ranch. The legacy of his father. And he realized, too late, that Grace had been right all along.

It was only dirt.

He flew from the house with the deed clutched in his hand. What if he was too late? Billy was right. Grace was ruining her life. For him. So he could have a piece of land that meant nothing to her and everything to him. At least, it had once meant everything.

But not anymore. He hadn't realized it until he'd held the deed in his hand.

He'd traded Grace for a piece of paper and a handful of dirt.

Chapter Twenty

She felt cold. Even though it was August and sweltering hot, Grace felt chilled to her bones.

And terrified.

Somehow she was proceeding down the aisle of the church, clutching a fresh bouquet of yellow flowers and walking toward Sam Plummer. He looked so happy, so peaceful, so assured. Grace knew if Billy wasn't holding her arm she wouldn't be able to stand.

Let alone walk.

There were faces all around, but she didn't see them. Most of them were Sam's friends and his father's acquaintances, in any case. Olivia was there, somewhere, and of course she had Billy beside her. Renzo had promised to come, but she couldn't bring herself to search the crowded church for him.

The wedding gown she wore had been finished just that morning, and it fit her so tightly she felt as though she were truly a prisoner trapped in its bonds. That alone was terrifyingly symbolic. A prisoner of white satin.

With a passage of words, Billy passed her into Sam's hands. Why did she feel so heartsick that Billy was giving her away?

Behind her, she could hear someone sobbing quietly. She listened, realizing after only a moment that it was Olivia who cried for her. It was not unusual to see tears of joy at weddings, but Grace knew Olivia was not crying with joy. The woman who had become her friend knew, as few did, that this was a mistake.

It was a mistake. That thought pounded in her brain until she could think of nothing else.

And then she thought of Dillon, squatting in front of that old cabin with a handful of dirt in his hand and his heart in his eyes. This was the only gift she could give him.

Grace stood at the altar, motionless, holding her breath as the minister spoke. What came from his mouth was gibberish, it seemed, but he looked to her for a response.

This was a horrible mistake, but she could go through with it for Dillon's sake, so he could keep the Double B. Abigail would be free to marry Renzo, if she decided to follow her heart. Grace could make three people happy with a few simple words.

The minister was looking at her expectantly, and so was Sam.

"Could you repeat that?" she whispered.

The minister didn't have a chance to repeat himself, as the door to the church burst open and Dillon Becket all but ran down the aisle.

"Am I too late?" he asked breathlessly.

Grace stood at the altar and stared down at

him. How could he do this to her? What was he doing here?Had he come to watch her marry another man?

"Am I too late?" he repeated, louder.

"Yes, dammit, you're too late."

The minister looked disapprovingly at Seth Plummer, as the father of the groom rose from the front pew and faced Dillon.

Dillon's face drained of color, and he looked away from Grace to the man who had answered his question.

With a muttered curse he tossed the deed, crumpled and sweat dampened, at the banker. "I don't want it. Not like this." He turned back to Grace. "You were right all along. It's only dirt."

Grace started to lift her hand to him, but Sam held her firmly in place, his hand possessively over hers. Behind Dillon, over his shoulder, she saw Billy rise.

Dillon didn't take his eyes from her. He didn't move forward, and he didn't retreat, he simply stared at her and waited. Grace's heart was pounding so loudly she was certain Sam could hear it, that everyone in the church could hear it.

"I don't recall," Billy drawled casually, "that the bride has spoken her vows yet, so I don't see as how it's too late for anything."

Color flooded back into Dillon's face, and his gray eyes flashed at her. "Grace Cavanaugh, this is the dumbest stunt you've ever pulled."

Seth Plummer grumbled, and he shook his fist at Dillon, a fist that clutched the deed to the Double B. "We had a deal, and I won't allow you to interfere."

Dillon's face hardened, and he spun slowly to face Plummer.

"You can have the Double B. You can have the land, and the house, and the stock. But you can't have Grace." There was such determination in his soft voice that Grace felt her heart melt. He had come for her. Almost too late, and in a rather unromantic way. Dumb stunt, indeed. But he had come for her.

"Are you sure?" she whispered as Dillon fixed his eyes on her again.

"I wouldn't blame you if you decided to marry Sam anyway. I've made a mess of things, Grace. But he won't love you like I do. No one can."

He took a step toward her, and Grace let the bouquet she held slip from her fingers and fall to the floor. Sam released her, and she turned her face up to him.

"I'm sorry, Sam," she said softly. "But I would have made you miserable."

He had a resigned expression on his face, but there was no shock there, no real pain, and Grace remembered that he had never loved her, had never professed to love her. Their planned marriage had been as much a business deal for him as it had been for her.

She gave him a small smile. "Wait for love, Sam. You'll know when it hits you. It's like a thunderbolt that knocks you off your feet and leaves you winded and aching and glad to be alive."

Sam gave her a cynical smile. "I do like you, Grace," he whispered. "I thought that would be enough. But if this is what you want . . ."

Dillon reached out his hand, and she took it, allowing him to pull her away from the altar.

"It is, Sam," she said with a grin.

Before Dillon and Grace could proceed down the aisle, the passageway was blocked by three large bodies. Plummer, in the front, and toward the middle of the aisle Abigail's father and her brother Wade. Fortunately they didn't wear weapons, but their stances made it clear that Dillon was going to have to fight his way out.

And then Billy stood, drawing a six-shooter that had been concealed under his coat. Almost simultaneously Renzo stood. With a flick of his wrist a derringer appeared in his hand.

The minister was sputtering, terrified at the very idea of bloodshed in his church.

But when Billy spoke, his voice was calm and authoritative. "You'd best let the boss and Miss Grace leave peaceful-like." He had his gun trained on Plummer, and Renzo was aiming at the Wilkinsons. Abigail was seated at his side, tugging at his coattails.

"Lorenzo, please!" she hissed.

"Quiet, *querida*," he ordered softly. "We will discuss this later."

Abigail obediently released his coat and folded her hands in her lap. Now it was she who had the Wilkinsons' attention, as they turned away from Dillon and Grace.

"Abigail Wilkinson," her father said, seething. "What is the meaning of this?" He looked at the armed bandit turned merchant, and then back to his daughter.

That left Plummer, and Sam brushed past Grace to confront his father. "Let them go," he said quietly, but with an authority in his voice that obviously shocked his father.

"Don't you dare talk to me like that!"

Sam took his father's arm and forcibly moved him aside so Dillon and Grace could pass. Dillon held her hand and pulled her along the aisle, as if he were anxious to escape into the sunlight.

Grace paused beside Abigail and Renzo as they faced the Wilkinson family. Renzo gave her a shrug and a crooked smile before Dillon tired of waiting for her and lifted her into his arms to carry her the rest of the way down the aisle.

Outside, with the sun beating down on their heads and a hot breeze against their faces, Dillon set Grace on her feet and placed one hand against her cheek.

"I'm so sorry," he whispered. "Will you ever forgive me?"

"That depends," Grace said evenly, laying her hand over his. "Did you mean what you said in there?"

"Every word."

"You love me?" she whispered.

"Yes." He lifted her feet off the ground and crushed her against his chest. "So much I can't bear the thought of losing you. Even if I don't have anything to offer you but that love. That's selfish of me, I know. I can't—"

Grace laid a finger over his lips. "I love you, Becket. No matter what happens, we'll find a way."

Dillon kissed her tenderly, his lips pressed almost hesitantly against hers, and then he set her on her feet before he spun around and stalked back to the church door.

"Plummer, you son of a bitch! I've got two weeks left!" he shouted through the open door. "If I see your hide near the Double B before then I'll skin it, tan it, and use it as a saddle blanket!"

When he turned back to Grace he had a wide smile on his face.

"Let's go home."

* * *

The moonwashed room was twice as big as her old room, this master chamber where Renzo had stayed when he'd been Dillon's *guest*. This was where Dillon had carried her, upon arriving back at the Double B. He'd held her in front of him all the way home, and had said barely two words. But he'd lowered his lips to her neck frequently.

He was sleeping beside her as if he didn't have a care in the world. Once he had made up his mind, it seemed he really didn't mind losing the Double B, after all.

But she minded for him. She wanted him to have everything he wanted.

She reached out and touched his hair, trailing her fingers through the chestnut strands. She wanted to touch him all the time, to feel his hands on her, and his lips on hers, and to feel him deep inside her.

With a low moan Dillon rolled to his side and pulled her against his chest. Her breasts were crushed against the hardness of his muscled torso, and she buried her nose against his throat. She loved the smell of him, the taste of his skin, and she ever so lightly touched the tip of her tongue to the skin at the base of his throat.

"Are you asleep?" she whispered.

"Not anymore," he growled, dragging her body across his until her mouth was against anxious lips. His tongue flicked across hers, and then delved deeper into her mouth, loving her, driving her wild with wanting him. The pulsations deep within her pounded to an ever increasing primal beat. Growing with every breath she took, every caress of his lips and his hands, they made her forget that a world existed beyond the bed they lay in, that time continued to move on.

He rolled her onto her back and continued his

tender assault, caressing her breasts with gentle hands, moving his mouth to those nipples and suckling until she thought she would scream.

When he placed his fingers between her legs and teased her with a promise of what was to come as he locked his lips to her breast, she arched her back and pleaded with him.

"Please, Becket," she whispered harshly.

Dillon lifted his head from her breast and moved his lips to kiss her tenderly as his fingers continued to play.

"Please, Dillon," he whispered into her mouth. "Please, Dillon," he repeated. "Say it, Grace." Between each word he kissed her lightly.

"Please, Dillon," she whispered.

He rolled on top of her, keeping his weight on his forearms. She cried out softly when he entered her, sheathing himself in one powerful thrust.

He filled her, loved her, whispered low words into her ear. Grace couldn't help but whisper his name as the powerful pulsations increased until she erupted under Dillon's tender assault.

Dillon's own completion came with hers, with a whisper of her name and a final thrust. His pleasure and his seed, his love and his sacrifice.

"I love you, Dillon," she breathed against his neck, so softly she didn't think he would hear her.

But he did.

"I love you, too, Grace." He gathered her into his arms with a tenderness that surprised her. He could be so unyielding one minute, so gentle the next.

Dillon rolled onto his back, keeping Grace in his arms so that she rested against his chest. Smiling, she gazed into his eyes. "Don't you like it when I call you Becket?"

He scowled at her playfully. "Before too much longer I'll be able to call you Becket, myself. Might get too confusing."

As far as marriage proposals went, it was rather odd, but she smiled and kissed him in response.

"What do you think about that?" he asked. "Becket." He spat the name out harshly, as she often had, and pressed her head against his broad chest.

"I had no idea you were so sensitive," Grace said softly, her lips against his skin.

"From now on, whenever you call me Becket . . . you know exactly what's going to happen."

Grace lifted her head and gazed into his eyes. "The kind of punishment I just received?"

Dillon nodded solemnly.

"Well," she drawled wickedly, giving him her best attempt at a Texas accent. "I'll be sure to remember that."

Once his decision had been made, Dillon seemed to have no reservations about leaving the Double B behind. They discussed their options. Where to go: north, east, or west. His only demand was that they be married in the house before Plummer took over.

Grace found him in the study, poring over the books and the invoices on his desk. When he saw her he pushed them aside and smiled. She loved that smile, so rare and so perfect.

But she knew, as she'd just seen him bending over the papers on his desk with a frown on his face, that he still dreaded the thought of leaving it all behind.

"Are you sure?" she asked without preamble,

sitting in his lap as he scooted his chair away from the desk.

She didn't need to be more specific. Dillon snaked his arm around her waist and pulled her to him, burying his head against her neck.

"Sit in my lap and ask me if I'm sure," he mumbled, his breath warm against her skin. "What kind of answer do you expect?"

Grace trailed her fingers through his hair. His voice was almost lighthearted, with a touch of humor as rare as his smile. "Is there no other way?"

Dillon grunted and kissed her neck, trying to change the subject. "I've paid off everyone else. All the debts are clear but the one to Plummer. Hell, five thousand or five million . . . ain't got it, honey. Have you decided where you want to go?"

"Five thousand dollars?" Grace asked. "Is that all?"

Dillon pulled away from her. "Is that all?" he repeated. "Isn't that enough?" His fingers played up and down her side. "Actually, with what I've got left, I need five thousand one hundred and twenty-one dollars."

"I could sell my jewelry."

Dillon quieted her with a kiss. "Those geegaws of yours can't be worth that much, honey. Don't worry about it. I'll take care of you."

"I know that, but—"

Dillon hushed her as he had before, with his lips on hers. He didn't even want to discuss it with her.

Grace relaxed and melted in his arms, but she didn't forget. Dillon had no idea how much some of her *geegaws* were worth . . . but it might be difficult to get that much for them on such short notice. And she didn't want to get his hopes up only to have her plan fail. Even as he kissed her and his fingers danced against her neck, Grace formulated a plan—until he made her forget everything.

They were in the back room of Renzo's store, The Jewel, and Grace held up the serpent pin Mikhail had given her. She pointed out to Renzo the quality of the gems, the handiwork, and the originality of the piece. She did the same with every piece in the box . . . including the silver bracelet he had given her.

He was skeptical and made no bones about it. "There is not much time."

"They're worth a lot more than five thousand dollars," Grace snapped. "A *lot* more."

"I could take them to San Antonio," Renzo muttered uncertainly. "Perhaps there—"

"Fine. Just remember, I need five thousand one hundred and twenty-one dollars, not a penny less. And I must have it by the end of the week."

Renzo raised his eyebrows. "I hate to leave my little jewel, even for a few days."

"Her father has forbidden her to see you."

Renzo's smile was wicked and assured. "*Sí*. But no words can keep us apart. At night I climb into her window," he revealed, "and make love to her until—"

"Renzo!" Grace interrupted sharply, but she couldn't be angry with him. "You shouldn't be telling me such things."

He shrugged his shoulders. "One night I will convince her to run away with me. So when you hear that my little jewel has disappeared, don't be alarmed."

Grace had a hard time picturing Abigail Wilkinson running off in the night with Renzo, or anyone else, for that matter. But then again, she also had a devil of a time picturing Abigail admitting Renzo into her bedroom late at night.

Renzo sighed deeply. "I cannot refuse you anything, *amiga*. You have made it possible for my dreams to come true." He took her hand and bent to kiss it. "If not for you, Abigail never would have looked at me twice, and she would certainly never have admitted me into her heart."

"Thank you, Renzo," Grace said, smiling down at his black head that was still bent over her hand. He remained there for a few seconds, and when he lifted his head he was grinning devilishly.

"I told your Becket on the day we met that you were his greatest treasure. I was speaking of your beauty, which is unrivaled in all the world. But today I know that what I said was a certain truth, and it has nothing to do with your face or your graceful body or your silken hair. You are the treasure of his heart and soul, and he is a most fortunate man."

"Renzo," Grace said as she placed the box of jewels in his hands. "That tongue of yours is going to get you into trouble one day."

Renzo winked at her, his black eyes flashing merrily. "Perhaps, but not on a day when I speak the truth."

Chapter Twenty-one

"Well?" Dillon snapped at Olivia as the wide-hipped woman hurried down the stairs.

"She says she needs a little more time with her hair," Olivia explained as if she understood perfectly.

Dillon groaned. "The minister has been waiting for over an hour," he said as Olivia planted her feet at the bottom of the staircase, a formidable guard. "I don't care what her hair looks like. I don't care what she wears." His voice rose gradually until he lifted his head and shouted at the top of his lungs. "She could wear a flour sack, and she'd still be perfect!"

Olivia patted his arm and tried to pull him away from the stairs. "I'm sure she heard you, and half the county probably heard you as well. Be patient. Don't worry, she's not going to change her mind."

Dillon looked down at the woman, trying his

best to appear calm. "I'm not worried. I just want to get this over with."

This was to be his last day in the home he'd been raised in. His last day on the Double B. The deadline on the loan was close of business today, and Grace had decided to have the wedding at the last minute. He'd tried to hurry the wedding along, but she had been stubborn, insisting that they wait. And she'd refused to give him a reason for the delay.

Of course he wasn't worried. She wouldn't change her mind at the last minute. Would she?

He slipped past Olivia and ran up the stairs, taking them two at a time and placing himself at the master bedroom door. Their bedroom for the past two weeks, though Grace had insisted that he sleep in his own room last night. Some superstitious nonsense.

"Grace!" he called as he pounded on the door. "Come on, everyone's waiting."

"Don't come in," she said nervously, the strain of the day in her voice.

"I won't. There's no lock on this door. I could have come right in, but I didn't." Dillon tried his best to reason with her. "It's just that Billy's getting a little anxious, and so is the minister."

There was a pause before she spoke. "Is Renzo here yet?"

Dammit, she'd asked about that low-down thieving Mexican bandit a thousand times since that morning. "No! What difference does it make? We don't need that bandit here to get married."

"But . . . but he has your wedding present."

Damned if he didn't hear a little hesitation in her voice. He wanted so badly to open that door. . . .

"I don't care about any wedding present. I don't want a wedding present. I want to get married . . . now!"

He knew he'd been too harsh when Grace didn't answer at all.

"I'm sorry, honey." Dillon laid his hand against the door. "You haven't changed your mind, have you?"

Grace went to the door and dropped her forehead softly against the hard wood. "Of course I haven't changed my mind," she said softly. "I love you, Dillon. Can't we give Renzo another half hour?"

On the opposite side of the door, Dillon groaned. "All right," he finally agreed. "A half hour. But I swear, Grace, if you don't come down in half an hour, I'm coming in to get you."

"No!" Grace raised her head away from the door. "You can't see me until I come down the stairs. It would be bad luck."

He didn't say anything, but she knew he was still there. "All right," he finally muttered. "Half an hour, Grace."

Grace looked out of the window again. It faced the front of the house, so she would certainly be able to see Renzo approaching. Where the devil was he? Had it been completely stupid of her to give those jewels to a former thief? She had been so certain Renzo had changed, for good, but maybe it had been too much of a temptation for him. At least she hadn't told Dillon what she'd done, so he wouldn't be disappointed. But he would find out, sooner or later, that her jewels were gone, and then she would have to tell him the truth. Blast it all, he had never liked Renzo.

She wanted so much to be able to do this for Dillon. She wanted so badly to be able to save the ranch for him. But if her plans failed, if they were truly left with nothing, they would still be married. They would still be together, and that was all that really mattered.

Grace ran to the window at the sound of thundering hooves. The dark figure approaching the house had to be Renzo. It had to be! A moment later she was certain it was true. There was no mistaking that confident bearing, even from a distance. When he stopped in front of the house Grace ran to the door, opened it a crack, and shouted for Olivia to show Renzo up.

"I'll be damned. . . ." She heard Dillon's voice rising above the rest as Olivia attempted to show Renzo to Grace's room. She could hear footsteps on the stairs, muffled and many, and she placed her face in the narrowly opened door.

"Dillon," she called his name, hoping to be heard above the raised voices. He heard her, because moments later he was on the other side of the door she quietly closed.

"Please let him in, Dillon," she pleaded.

"The devil I will," he shouted. "You won't let me in, but you want me to let some damn bandit walk into that room with you? Like hell I will."

He was frustrated. There was an edge to his voice, a tightness that crept in when things didn't go his way.

"I love you, Dillon," she said tenderly.

There was silence on the other side of the door, and then a loud sigh. "You sure do know how to take the wind out of a man's sails, honey." His voice was much calmer, if still a little strained. "You know I love you, too, don't you?"

"Yes."

"I guess I can let the son of a bitch in, but he better not be in there too long, or I'll drag the minister up here and he can marry us where you stand."

Grace smiled. "Ten minutes. No more."

Dillon allowed Renzo to enter the room, and the former highwayman opened and closed the door quickly.

Grace couldn't ask. What if he hadn't been able to get enough?

But Renzo wore his usual unconcerned grin. "You look fabulous, *amiga*."

"Well? Were you able to . . ." She couldn't finish.

Renzo held aloft a bulging saddlebag. "Exactly five thousand one hundred and twenty-one dollars. I thought I would not get quite enough, and then a man offered me twenty dollars for the carved box the jewels had been stored in. I held out for forty-one, and the fool paid it." He grinned mischievously.

"You cut it too close, Renzo. I was afraid. . . ." She couldn't finish her thought, couldn't let him know that for a moment she hadn't trusted him.

His grin widened. "Once a thief, always a thief?"

"I only doubted you a little, when it got so late."

"I would have been here sooner, but I had to see my little jewel."

"You stopped to see Abigail before you came here?" Grace asked. She could only smile.

"*Sí*. I missed her." He seemed mystified by the very notion.

Dillon stood as still as he could in front of the minister. But his thumb tapped against his thigh, and he unconsciously twisted against his tight collar. Olivia had insisted that he wear a dark suit and a white linen shirt, and she'd polished his boots until they shone. The toe of one of those boots was tapping nervously.

Renzo had appeared moments earlier, a good five minutes before his time was up, and told them that Grace was ready. Billy waited at the bottom of the stairs, and Olivia sat in the single chair. A few of the hands stood to the side and Renzo stood, grinning widely, on the opposite side of the room.

Dillon had wanted music for her, but the moment he saw her he knew he wouldn't have heard it had there been an orchestra. She walked down the stairs with that same regal air she'd conveyed when he'd first seen her, but now there was a smile on her face.

She'd worn blue, for him. It was the ice blue gown he'd seen her in that night at Abigail's house, when he'd decided she looked too damn good to share. Grace's eyes never left him, even as Billy took her arm at the bottom of the staircase and led her to him. He couldn't stop the grin that spread across his face.

What a vision she was, his Grace, dressed in blue and smiling at him as though there weren't another person in the room, in the world, and carrying in her hands, rather than a bouquet of flowers, the carpetbag she had carried on their trip from New Orleans.

When she stood beside him she set the carpetbag at her feet and placed her hands in his.

The minister began to speak, his deep and sonorous voice echoing through the house. This was a moment Dillon would remember forever. Married in this house, to this woman.

Olivia had begun to cry loudly, a maddeningly frequent occurrence, and Grace turned to the minister. "Could we speed this up?"

The man looked as shocked as Dillon felt. After stalling for hours, she wanted the man to hurry up?

"I beg your pardon?" the minister asked with frown.

"As fast as possible." Grace lifted her face to him. "Please."

Dillon nodded his assent.

"Do you, Grace Cavanaugh, take this man as your wedded husband, to—"

"I do," Grace interrupted.

"Do you, Dillon Becket, take this woman as your wedded wife—"

"I do," he said with a grin. Short, but memorable.

"I now pronounce you man and wife," the minister said, barely hiding his dismay. "You may kiss the bride."

But when he leaned over to kiss her, Grace bent and retrieved the bag.

"Here," she said, thrusting it at him. "Your wedding present."

Dillon took the bag from her. It was heavier than he had expected. He needed to kiss her, but she made it a brief caress, drawing away from him. "Hurry, Dillon. We don't have much time."

He opened the bag and peered inside. Money. Gold and silver coins and greenbacks, a jumble of it inside the bag. He raised his eyes to Grace. "What is this?"

"Five thousand one hundred and twenty-one dollars," she said, unable to hide her excitement. "If we hurry we can get to the bank before it closes."

"How . . ." Dillon began, but Grace had

grabbed his hand and pulled him toward the study.

"I'll explain while you get the rest."

It was ten minutes till closing time when they burst into the bank. Plummer's office was at the far end of the room, and the door was open. Grace was dragging Dillon along, the bag that contained the money Renzo had gotten for her jewels and the rest of Dillon's cash clasped in her hands. A teller tried to stop them, but they stormed into Seth Plummer's office.

"Here," Grace said triumphantly, dropping the bag onto his desk. "Here's your blasted money."

Plummer barely raised an eyebrow, and Grace opened the bag, dumping the contents onto the desk.

"Count it," she ordered.

"I will." His eyes traveled over her shoulder, and she looked behind her to see a dozen pairs of eyes on the scene in Plummer's office—tellers and customers, openly curious. She smiled at them all and took Dillon's hand.

Plummer counted the money, and Grace tried to pace nervously and hold Dillon's hand at the same time. Her husband was surprisingly calm, as he watched the banker count out the bills and the coins. Once he looked at her and gave her a reassuring smile, and she squeezed his fingers tightly. There was a surprising calmness in those eyes, gray and warm and peaceful. This was a look she had rarely seen in his eyes, and she was glad that she had been the one to put it there.

"You're short," Plummer said, snapping at them. "Twenty dollars."

"That can't be!" Grace cried. "It's all there. . . ."

Plummer shrugged his shoulders. "I'm terribly sorry, Miss Cavanaugh."

"Mrs. Becket," Dillon said coldly, and with slow assurance.

"Mrs. Becket," Plummer repeated.

Dillon began calmly to gather the bills and lay them in the bag.

"But . . . can't you give us a little more time? This is practically all. . . ."

Plummer was shaking his head, and Dillon was picking up stacks of coins and dropping them into the bag, as if he didn't have a care in the world.

"Don't worry about it, Grace. Plummer wants the ranch, and he can have it." He smiled at her. "I have you."

"But it's your home."

Dillon lifted the heavy bag. "This will give us a start somewhere else. It doesn't matter where we are, Grace."

"Excuse me." Renzo breezed into the room with his usual flair, and Dillon rolled his eyes. "I understand there is a problem here?"

"No problem," Dillon snapped.

Renzo reached into his pocket and withdrew a handful of coins. "I was just making a withdrawal, and I heard that you were twenty dollars short. You may have forgotten, but when we first met you were kind enough to make me a loan of . . . eighty dollars, was it?"

"Ninety," Dillon corrected him coldly.

Renzo casually flipped a twenty-dollar gold piece onto Plummer's desk, and ignored the fact that the banker was turning crimson. Then he placed seventy dollars in Dillon's hands.

Dillon dropped the bag on Plummer's desk, and as he watched Plummer rifle through his desk drawer for the deed, his smile slowly grew. Grace took his hand and squeezed it, and he twined his fingers through hers.

They left the bank with deed in hand, and ran into Renzo on the sidewalk. He was leaning against a post with a nonchalant air, lighting a cigar.

Dillon faced the man he had insulted and openly hated, and said the words that didn't ever come easily to him. "Thank you."

Renzo shrugged casually. "I heard the tellers talking as I closed my account. Plummer palmed a gold piece while you weren't watching. That's why you were short."

"That son of a—"

"You were closing your account?" Grace asked at the same moment Dillon spoke.

"*Sí.*" Renzo lifted his eyebrows rakishly. "My little jewel has agreed to elope with me. Tonight. I have sold my business for a pittance to the man who owns the general store, as I don't expect to be back for quite some time."

"Your little jewel?" Dillon asked.

"Abigail," Grace whispered, leaning close to her husband.

Renzo left them, flashing a grin and waving dramatically. Grace still thought he and Abigail the most unlikely couple.

She faced Dillon and grabbed the front of his shirt. When she tilted her face up she smiled and stared into his eyes. He was her husband. The Double B was her home. What more could she ask for?

"I don't know what to say to you, Grace," Dillon muttered. "Thank you? Not enough. I love you? You know that. What can I say? A man's not supposed to have everything he wants."

There was a kind of wonder in his voice that warmed Grace's heart.

"I don't see why not."

Dillon bent his head to kiss her gently, to brush his lips against hers. Abigail's description had been pretty accurate, she decided. Her knees were wobbly, and her stomach dropped to her toes.

Grace pulled away from Dillon, took his hand, and pulled him toward the stallion that had carried them both to Plummerton. "Take me home, Becket."

Epilogue

The Double B, 1878

Dillon stood in the doorway, content to watch for a moment as Grace held the jewels he had given her on her lap.

Pearl, five years old and the picture of her mother, sat on one knee, listening solemnly to the story her mother was reading. She was already a beauty, with Grace's fine features and black hair, and his own gray eyes. Pearl could be as solemn as her father at times, but when she laughed she laughed with all her heart and soul.

Ruby sat on Grace's other knee, fidgeting as usual, winding one finger through the reddest, unruliest hair Dillon had ever seen. Olivia was almost certain that there was a Becket in his past with hair like Ruby's. A grandmother of his, though she couldn't remember much more than that. Ruby had none of Pearl's serenity, but was possessed of a liveliness that sometimes made Dillon dread the years to come. She had her mother's bluebonnet eyes, and there were times they shone brighter than Grace's ever had.

He let his eyes linger on Grace for a moment. He still loved to look at her when she didn't know she was being watched. He still loved to watch her sleep. They'd been married six years to the day, and she hadn't changed a bit. Even when he searched for a flaw, he couldn't find one.

Ruby saw him first, of course, and burst from her mother's lap like a ball of fire.

"Daddy!" she screamed, throwing herself at him, trusting, knowing that he would catch her. Dillon lifted Ruby, and in another moment Pearl was there, arms raised, and he lifted her as well.

Grace sat serenely, still perched in the wing chair. "How do you expect the girls to learn to read when you constantly interrupt their lessons?" They were the words of a harsh schoolmistress, delivered with a smile and a warm voice.

"I missed you," Dillon said simply.

"In the middle of the day?"

Pearl rested her head against Dillon's shoulder, and Ruby tried to jump up and down in his arms.

"Where's Cav?"

Grace sighed, and finally stood to come to him. "Cavanaugh is asleep, and don't you dare wake him. He kept me up half the night."

"I know."

"The Becket men don't require much sleep, as a rule, do they?"

Dillon shook his head slowly.

"Daddy! Daddy! Daddy!" Ruby called in conjunction with energetic bursts of her little body. "What does Double B stand for?"

"Becket's Beauties," Dillon answered, playing the familiar game.

"That's us!" Ruby squealed. "What else?"

"Becket's Bride."

"That's Mama," Pearl said seriously.

"What else?" Ruby asked insistently.

"Becket's Brood."

"And that's all of us," Grace said, leaning in to give Dillon a quick kiss.

"I have a present for you." He kissed her briefly once again. "Close your eyes."

Grace obediently closed her eyes, and so did Pearl, but Ruby was already searching the parlor for her mother's gift, her eyes probing into every corner.

Dillon whistled loudly, and the sound made Grace cover her ears for a moment, but she didn't open her eyes.

Billy appeared first, and Lonnie and Lucas were right behind him. They grunted and sweated under the strain of their burden.

Dillon deposited the girls at their mother's feet and lent a hand.

When everything was ready he went to Grace, taking her hand and leading her to her gift.

"Can I open my eyes now?" she asked patiently.

"No," Dillon said softly. He sat down and pulled her into his lap. "Not just yet."

Billy and the hands waited anxiously. Pearl and Ruby clasped their hands and stared at the contraption behind their father with wide eyes.

"I wish I had been able to give this to you six years ago as a wedding present, rather than as an anniversary present today."

It had taken a few years, but the Double B was back on its feet and better than ever. Now he could give Grace anything . . . and she asked for nothing.

"Open your eyes."

Grace did just that, and her eyes widened when she found that Dillon was seated on a piano bench, and a fine piano had been placed against the wall.

"Oh, Dillon."

She took his face in her hands and kissed him thoroughly. "However did you keep this a secret from me?"

"It wasn't easy," he confessed. "I almost told you twice. But I wanted to see your face . . . like this."

She was positively glowing, and her eyes danced as she looked the piano over.

"Do you think you remember how to play?"

"Of course I remember," she said, just slightly insulted.

"Will you play for me every night?"

Grace smiled and nodded.

"Will you teach the girls to play?"

Grace nodded again. "And Cavanaugh, too."

Dillon made a face, even as he tightened his arms around her. "He's six months old, honey."

She assured him that she would wait until he was older—a little older—and Dillon deposited his wife on the padded bench.

There, in the center of the body of the piano, was an intricate carving. The Double B brand, two Bs, back to back.

Becket's Beauties.

Becket's Bride.

Becket's Brood.

Linda Winstead

Annabelle St. Clair has the voice of an angel and the devil at her heels. On the run for a murder she didn't commit, the world-renowned opera diva is reduced to singing in saloons until she finds a handsome gunslinger willing to take her to safety in San Francisco.

A restless bounty hunter, Shelley is more at home on the range than in Annabelle's polite society. Yet on the rugged trail, he can't resist sharing with her a passion as vast and limitless as the Western sky.

But despite the ecstasy they find, Annabelle can trust no one, especially not a man with dangerous secrets—secrets that threaten to ruin their lives and destroy their love.

_3796-3 $4.99 US/$5.99 CAN

Dorchester Publishing Co., Inc.
65 Commerce Road
Stamford, CT 06902

Please add $1.75 for shipping and handling for the first book and $.50 for each book thereafter. NY, NYC, PA and CT residents, please add appropriate sales tax. No cash, stamps, or C.O.D.s. All orders shipped within 6 weeks via postal service book rate. Canadian orders require $2.00 extra postage and must be paid in U.S. dollars through a U.S. banking facility.

Name ____________________
Address ____________________
City ____________________ State ______ Zip ______
I have enclosed $______ in payment for the checked book(s).
Payment must accompany all orders. ☐ Please send a free catalog.

"A captivating tale not to be missed!"
—Raine Cantrell

Renata Parkhurst can't believe her luck. The proper daughter of a Philadelphia doctor has run away to her cousin's Colorado spread hunting for love, and the day she arrives, a wounded rancher falls right into her arms.

Although everyone in Silver Valley believes that Jake Wolf is a cold-blooded murderer, no one would accuse him of being a lady-killer. Yet even as he grudgingly allows Renata to tend to his healing, he begins to lose himself in her tender caresses.

The townsfolk say that Renata has a better chance of being hit by lightning than of finding happiness with Jake. But to win the heart of the man of her dreams, the stunning beauty will gladly give up all she possesses and chase the lightning.

__52002-8 $4.99 US/$5.99 CAN

Dorchester Publishing Co., Inc.
65 Commerce Road
Stamford, CT 06902

Please add $1.75 for shipping and handling for the first book and $.50 for each book thereafter. NY, NYC, PA and CT residents, please add appropriate sales tax. No cash, stamps, or C.O.D.s. All orders shipped within 6 weeks via postal service book rate. Canadian orders require $2.00 extra postage and must be paid in U.S. dollars through a U.S. banking facility.

Name ____
Address ____
City ______________________________ State ______ Zip ______
I have enclosed $______ in payment for the checked book(s).
Payment must accompany all orders. ☐ Please send a free catalog.